JEWEL OF PROMISE

JEWEL OF PROMISE

MARIAN WELLS

BETHANY HOUSE PUBLISHERS
MINNEAPOLIS, MINNESOTA 55438
A Ministry of Bethany Fellowship, Inc.

Manuscript edited by Penelope J. Stokes.

Cover illustration by Brett Longley,
Bethany House Publishers staff artist.

Published by Bethany House Publishers
A Ministry of Bethany Fellowship, Inc.
6820 Auto Club Road, Minneapolis, Minnesota 55438

Printed in the United States of America

Library of Congress Cataloging-in-Publication Data

Wells, Marian, 1931–
    Jewel of promise / Marian Wells.
       p. cm. — (Treasure quest books)

    1. United States—History—Civil War, 1861–1865—Fiction.
I. Title. II. Series: Wells, Marian, 1931–   Treasure quest books.
PS3573.E4927J4 1990
813'.54—dc20   90–471
ISBN 1–55661–127–7   CIP

BOOKS BY MARIAN WELLS

The Wedding Dress
With This Ring

Karen

The STARLIGHT TRILOGY Series
    The Wishing Star
    Star Light, Star Bright
    Morning Star

The TREASURE QUEST Series
    Colorado Gold
    Out of the Crucible
    The Silver Highway
    Jewel of Promise

MARIAN WELLS and her husband live in Boulder, Colorado, which gives her immediate access to the research and documentation of the historical surroundings of this book and the books to follow in this series. A well-known author, her research and background on Mormonism provided the thrust for her bestselling STARLIGHT TRILOGY, the *Wedding Dress* and *With This Ring*.

To my special people:
David, Carol, and Alisha Wells,
with thanks to David
for his help on the manuscript.

CHAPTER 1

Mike Clancy steered the *Golden Awl* into the shade of the giant oak tree. Looking up at the long branches hanging low over the Mississippi, he grinned with satisfaction. They created a tunnel of cool shadows, but it was more than cool comfort Mike sought. Thinking of the cargo in the main cabin, Mike felt the familiar thrill of apprehension.

With the last thrust of the paddles, he sent the little sternwheeler in against the bank. He nodded to the Negro roustabout watching him from the main deck. The fellow jumped to the bank, tugged the boat close and wrapped the rope around the tree. By the time the man came aboard, Mike had clattered down the metal stairway and was waiting at the railing.

He nodded to the roustabout and lowered his voice. "This is a nice quiet place to spend the night, Jake."

"The old river's mighty low," Jake murmured. "Them frogs going to have mud up to their knees."

"Shall we drop a fishing line over while we're waiting on sunset?" The man nodded and went after the tackle. Mike poked at the can of worms nestled in the coil of a rope. Silently they baited their hooks and dropped them into the water swirling past the hull. Jake pulled in his first fish, nodded toward the river, and said, "Might be that boat 'longside of us this afternoon was river patrol."

"I wondered too." Mike muttered. "He cut his speed every time we did." A yellowing leaf dropped into the water, and Mike looked up at the tree. "Riverboating is about finished for the fall—for the likes of us, at least. Don't feel safe taking it down without a full crew."

Jake pulled in a big catfish. "Reckon the darkies will make a good stew out of this one. Want I should take it upstairs?"

"Might as well. Clean them both. I'll keep my hook in the water until dark. Tell them to keep the place dark. They can open the door to the cabin, but not a sound. We're sure missing Olivia this trip; the little ones need someone to give them attention."

With a nod Jake carried the fish upstairs. Mike coiled his line and leaned against the railing, whistling tunelessly as he watched the river. The darkness deepened until his arms, folded across the railing, seemed an extension of its whiteness.

A fish jumped midstream. Mike was watching the phosphorescent arc when he heard a whisper of sound. Leaning back against the white bulkhead, he strained to hear over the thumping of his heart. When he heard a rustle of dry leaves, he relaxed. "Deer or cow," he muttered.

But as he peered into the shadows, a shadow moved away from the trunk of an oak, paused, came swiftly down the bank, and leaped over the railing. Even in the darkness he could see the creature as it landed on the deck, nearly at his feet. He grasped the object and felt warmth and motion. A voice squealed. "Oh, another one," he muttered.

The warm softness pulled away from Mike. "You startled me. I didn't know anyone was here. Take me to your master."

The voice was feminine and very Southern, confirming his suspicion. "I *am* the master," he said. "What is your business?"

There was a gasp. "Business? I guess—I need a ride. I have money; I'll buy my trip north. You must be going that way—at least, you're pointed upstream. Send someone to fetch my valise—it's over in the bushes."

He hesitated, annoyed by the demanding Southern voice. *This one's no doubt been beaten for being arrogant.* He heard Jake's footsteps on the stairs. "Jake, go get that bag." Abruptly he grasped her arm. "Who told you about us?"

"No one. I—I've just been looking for a ride. I'm running away."

"That's obvious. Are you alone? Does your master live close by?"

"Master? No, no, you don't understand. I've walked forever."

Still uneasy, Mike tried to see the face hidden by deep shadows. Slowly he admitted, "Well, we've made it a point to not turn anyone away. But there's always a possibility—for the sake of the others I don't want to be caught. Come on. We'll get some food into you. I suppose you haven't eaten for a couple of days. Oh, Lord, I wish Alex were here," Mike muttered, leading the way up the stairs.

The first gleam of moonlight filtered through the branches of the tree as he walked into the cabin. The glow from the cookstove fire outlined the dark heads of the people lining the table. He closed the door and said, "We'll need some light. We have another passenger for the Underground Railroad."

Mattie turned from the stove. "There's candles on the table just awaitin' on y'all. Tessie, get us another trencher for this stew. Goin' to be crowded in here, Mike."

"Let's get the trenchers filled, and then some of you can move out to sit under the stairs."

The candle flared, and the line of dark, shining faces was illuminated. Mike turned toward the girl. He caught his breath. Stunned, he could only stare from her flaming red hair to her wide blue eyes set in white, white skin. He fought the dismay in his voice as he said, "With that accent I figured you to be a slave. Couldn't see in the dark. Well," he turned back to the silent group, "it's obvious I've taken on a passenger I shouldn't have. Miss, we'll haul you up to Paducah, and then you can look for accomodations more comfortable."

She narrowed her eyes and looked at Mike. "Slaves, huh? This is one of those boats that haul stolen property up to Canada? Well, I sure didn't guess that. I—" Slowly she stopped, aware that she was making her own situation more difficult. "Please, can't you give me a ride? I can't risk being caught. I did run away. I must go as far north as possible."

Jake stepped close to Mike. "Suh." By candlelight Mike could see his eyes were uneasy. "Suh, wasting time in Paducah, we could get caught right off. Maybe that boat was river patrol."

Mike looked into the young woman's wide eyes, saw her clasped hands, and turned to pace the cabin. He recalled Alex's story about Olivia joining the group in much the same way. For a moment Mike brightened. *She's just a little snip of a thing.* Her eyes were dark, wide circles in the gloom of the cabin—lovely eyes. He softened.

"Guess we don't have a choice," he said gruffly.

———

The following day, with the morning sun nearly overhead, Mike heard the girl's heels clicking rapidly up the stairs to the pilot house. She swirled through the door, settled her billowing skirts and ran her hands over her hair. "This wind is tearing me apart!"

"Rough water ahead," he muttered after a quick glance at her.

"Mind bringing up a fresh pot of coffee?"

"Me? I'm no slave. I'll tell that girl Tessie to bring it to you—after I've had my say. I told you last night I'd pay my way, but I didn't agree to share my cabin with slaves. Them—the children fussed all night." She lifted her chin. "Please get them out of there before tonight."

Mike studied the current, watching the upcoming snag. Working to keep the impatience out of his voice, he said, "I can't shove all those slaves into the same cabin. Those women feel just as you do; they want a little privacy, away from the men. You'll have to be content with matters as they stand."

"I shall not!" She stomped her foot. "I'll sleep on the deck before I spend another such night."

Mike sighed. "I've been sleeping in here. You can have the pilot house. But mind you, the wind blows through here at night."

"Well, I suppose it would be better for *you* to sleep on deck than *me*."

As she went through the door he said, "Please don't forget the coffee. And *you* bring it, I want to talk to you."

An hour later he heard hesitant steps on the stairs. Visualizing her struggle with the pot of hot coffee, he grinned. *Little lady, it just may not hurt you a mite to be on this trip with the likes of us common folk.*

She carried the coffee pot and mugs in the familiar wooden box. There was bread and meat also. "Pour the coffee and bring it here. It's a nice smooth stretch of river; I can handle the bread and meat, too."

She came with the coffee and bread. Curiosity filled her eyes as she held out the sandwich and said, "I'll hold the coffee."

He studied the hand holding the sandwich. Her fingernails were ragged, as if they had been chewed. As he accepted the sandwich, he felt her rough hand against his.

She watched him take a bite, then asked, "You're Irish, aren't you? I guessed. You sound like a fella I knew—" she gulped. "Your brogue, it is."

He nodded, swallowed the bite and said, "Name's Mike Clancy. Folks came from Ireland." He gave her a quick look. "That makes me on about the same level as the slaves, doesn't it?"

She blinked. "You mean—I'm not looking down on you 'cause of that."

"You haven't introduced yourself, Miss—or Missus."

She hesitated. "I'm Elizabeth Peamble. My friends call me Beth."

"And I'm to call you Missus?" He saw the dimple in the cheek turned toward him.

"No, just call me Beth."

"So, Beth Peamble, what is your destination?"

"North." She straightened her shoulders, suddenly turning a bright smile on him. "I know the next question. Most young Southern women don't run around the country without kin—without escorts." She fell silent.

"Well?" Mike waited.

She turned away, sighing. "My mother died last spring, and Father sent me to live with my mother's sister in Memphis. I hated it. I was just a nanny for the wildest young'uns on the earth. Daddy wouldn't listen to me, and so I just took off. They'll have to learn I can't be treated that way."

He watched her eyes, thinking, *She's whistling in the dark. One minute she's a woman, then she looks as if she's frightened of her own shadow. I wonder what's going on?* Finally he asked, "So after they find out, what are you going to do about it?" The silence stretched long enough for Mike to pass a long line of barges. He glanced at her.

"I haven't planned that far." Her voice was faint. She moved restlessly around the cabin. He had time to notice the grace of her movement, the well-formed slenderness of her body.

He looked at the delicate cotton frock she wore, but he was thinking of the coarse touch of her hand when she had given him the sandwich. *Last night, when she spoke, I guessed she was a slave. Why? She doesn't sound like Olivia. Even in the dark I would know Olivia is—a lady.*

Watching the swirling water, he turned the wheel. She came back to him. "I suppose, unless Daddy does something about it, I'll need to get a job. What do women do up North?"

He chuckled. "Get married and have babies."

For a moment she looked startled. He saw the dimple again. "Suh, are you proposing?"

"Well, you might give me time to think about it. Right now I would like more coffee." She poured his coffee and came back to the wheel.

"Do you live on this boat all the time?"

"No. When I'm not on the boat I live with a Quaker family in Pennsylvania."

"I suppose they have something to do with the slaves."

"Yes."

"Why do you do this?" Beth asked.

"I suppose I have a moral responsibility to these people."

"*People!*" she gasped. "How can you call them that? They're slaves."

"The same God created us both. Matter of fact," he teased, grinning down at her, "in the dark I guess I don't notice the difference."

She frowned, and he added, "Before God, I feel responsible."

"You sound like He's watching." Her voice was frosty.

"I'm very aware He is."

He glanced at her as she whirled away, asking, "Do they—the Quakers—take other boarders, at least for a short time?"

"Boarders?" Mike faced her, liking the way the sunshine set her hair on fire and accented her creamy skin. He gazed at her. "Your eyes are nearly the bluest I've seen."

"Nearly?"

"Yes. But Beth, you may not like that place."

"Then I'll find another. Surely someone will take in a motherless girl until she can make her own way."

He cleared his voice. "How would a motherless Southern girl like living in a home where they care for runaway slaves?"

She kept her head down as she answered, "I'll have to think about that situation. But it does seem they could find a better occupation."

CHAPTER 2

Back home in Mississippi, summer would barely be over, and the first cool tinges of fall would begin to blow in on an autumn wind. But here in Canada, winter was already on its way. Olivia gazed out the hotel room window at the bright cold morning, tears streaming down her cheeks.

"Go home?" she gasped between sobs. "Alex Duncan, we've scarcely arrived! A fine honeymoon this has turned out to be. Please—" Olivia turned in time to see the hotel room door close abruptly. Her shoulders slumped. "Actually," she admitted ruefully, "I know he doesn't like this either." Her hands relaxed and she shook her head. "You are acting like a baby, Olivia. No wonder he escaped on the run! Poor man."

She turned back to the window and shivered as she looked down the street. "Winter is coming early to Canada; since I don't like snow, that should make me glad we're leaving."

The morning sun highlighted the frost outlining each needle on the evergreens. "Lace crystals," she murmured. "October trees decorated for Christmas. And I don't feel like Christmas." Her tears threatened to return as she looked around the room she had called *the honeymoon cottage*. This regal room, with its rose silk damask, crystal mirrors, and deep carpets was far from being a cottage. Admiring again the carved and polished dark walnut furniture, the corners of her mouth began to turn up. "Admit it," she murmured, "you're just sick with disappointment. For the first time since you've met Alexander Duncan, he's been yours exclusively. Now it's time to face life, with all that it holds."

———

The door behind her opened, then closed softly. For a moment she stiffened, trying to recover the emotion that had fueled her hasty words. She turned to see Alex, his blue eyes pleading. With a gasp she rushed to him. "Alex, it doesn't matter; nothing matters except us—even a honeymoon finished before it is properly started. Just don't leave me like that."

"Olivia, I wasn't leaving you. I simply couldn't make myself heard. I decided action was best."

"So you ran! Just like a man under fire!"

"Fire? It was those tears. That's something most men can't handle." He pulled her against his frosty coat and she shivered.

"Hear me out." He took her hands. "I didn't intend to make you think I was angry or trying to force my will. I just made an important decision to purchase something, and I knew I must get it quickly."

"Get what?"

He thrust the small velvet box into her hands. "I've been wanting to buy a gift for you. Something very special. I felt we needed it."

"We?"

"Yes, I as much as you. Several days ago I saw this, but at the time I couldn't decide. At first it seemed beautiful, and then I ended up feeling nearly depressed; and I didn't want you to feel that way. Now it seems right. I'll explain. Open it."

Holding the tiny jeweler's box, she went to sit in one of the blue velvet chairs in front of the windows. "Look, Alex, the sun has turned the ice crystals into shining jewels." Her voice trailed away in a whisper as Alex took the box and opened it.

"My dear husband, it's beautiful!" Olivia gasped. "How could it be depressing?"

She lifted the brooch out of the box. "Black onyx, covered with a filigree of gold. Alex, the design is as delicate as lace against the onyx. It shines like life itself!" She touched the row of diamonds edging the oval.

"It does seem so," Alex murmured. His face was close to hers as she pinned the brooch to the neckline of her frock. His big finger touched the golden design. "It caught my attention when I realized how the black stone made the gold come to life. The tiny blossoms seem nearly ready to drop into your hand."

Olivia looked up. "Alex, I noticed this in the shop when we went to have your watch repaired. I must admit that I shivered when I saw it. It attracted me, yet it nearly made me cry. Why?"

He shook his head, cleared his husky voice, and said, "I'd just been reading a passage in Isaiah. It seemed fitting. Me with my earring, you with your jewel." He fixed his intense blue eyes on her. She saw the swift uncertainty in them before he smiled. "I'll read it to you."

He brought his Bible and knelt with the book in Olivia's lap. Thumbing quickly through the worn pages, he glanced at her. "This is from Isaiah 61. 'I will greatly rejoice in the Lord . . . as a bride adorneth herself with her jewels. For as the earth bringeth forth her bud, and as the garden causeth the things that are sown in it to spring forth; so the Lord God will cause righteousness and praise to spring forth before all the nations.' "

"It's beautiful Alex. But there is still a troubled shadow in your eyes, and it has something to do with home. You've been reading those newspapers and talking for weeks."

"The United States is approaching a crisis," he admitted, "and I've been dumping it all on you."

She looked up at him. "Lincoln is running for president, and you think there's not a possibility of his succeeding."

"Livie, for us it's one step deeper. I'm just seeing the full import of my decision long ago. But right now I don't want to risk pulling you into all the trouble."

"Alex, I don't like the thought of war, or the trouble we could get into by helping the slaves. But remember, I'm in this with you because I chose to be. We took this path without knowing the outcome of our decision, but we can't jump out when there are difficulties."

"Half an hour ago, I thought you'd forgotten!" he grinned at her.

Sheepishly she said, "I started fussing when you mentioned going home. Well, I'm sorry. But do you really think there's going to be deep trouble?"

"It's impossible to believe otherwise. Caleb's been talking to the slaves pouring into Canada. They're angry and frightened, but they're also strangely excited. Livie, the slaves seem to have a spiritual sensitivity we lack. They see hard times ahead, and they're coming out of the South in masses." He took a deep breath. "I have two major things to do."

"Now, before the election and before winter?"

He nodded. "I have to make one more trip south, and then visit my parents."

"Why?"

Shaking his head slowly he said, "I'll be happy to snatch another few slaves and run them north. About my parents, I'm not so certain. It's arrogant to think I can sway the thinking of the South, even the thinking of my own family. But I can't live with myself unless I've given it another try."

"I'm very much ashamed of myself," she admitted. "When you began talking about leaving, I wanted so badly just to hold you close and push away other people. Alex, when I watched you leave, I felt as if my words had ripped apart something precious."

"Olivia, you know I'd rather hear your disappointment and anger than to have you hide your feelings. I'm disappointed too."

"We've been here less than a month. It will be at least another month before Bertie and Caleb's baby is born."

He winced. "I know we should stay. I can't give you any reason for going, except for a bunch of newspaper articles and a vague feeling."

"Like black storm clouds on the horizon?" She fingered the brooch and watched him take a deep breath. "Alex, I have seen you like this often enough in the past two years to realize your hunches come from the Lord."

"The war is moving closer." He slid to the edge of his chair and took her hands. "Olivia—"

"Now will you tell me why you bought that expensive brooch?"

"It's not enough to say I love you?"

"No. You were reading Isaiah 61. Verse one is an important verse for you. 'He hath sent me to bind up the brokenhearted, to proclaim liberty to the captives and the opening of the prison to them that are bound.' Did those words have anything to do with it?"

"Olivia, I honestly acted without facing all the deep implications. Maybe I felt you needed something to remind you—"

"Of the promises I had made. Perhaps," she said slowly. "And now you're thinking about war." Getting up, she walked to the window. "War," she murmured. "Perhaps what we've done makes us responsible for this frightening possibility."

"Helping the slaves escape, you mean?"

"That, and other things as well. I keep thinking about Matthew and Crystal. Their hurt is still mine. How my heart aches for them! Oh, Alex, for us love is the most wonderful thing that could have happened. But for my dear foolish brother and his precious wife, it turned out to be devastating."

"Only because of their choices," Alex said.

"Alex, you make it seem as casual as ordering dinner from a menu! Yes, Crystal made a terrible choice; she loved Matthew too much to risk admitting her father was a slave."

"And when the truth came out," Alex added heavily, "your brother acted just as any Southern gentlemen would act. He walked out of the whole situation. Olivia, my dear, I'm still convinced that love is more durable than those two people believe."

"But it's too late now. We don't know where they are. I wish she would write! And I've been wondering if Matthew will fight for the South."

There was a tap on the door and Alex turned. "Must be our breakfast," he said as he went to the door. It was Caleb, and just behind him was the waiter with his loaded cart.

Caleb studied their faces as the waiter set the table in front of the windows. The door closed behind the man, and Olivia said, "Caleb, come have breakfast with us. Even if you have eaten, I know your appetite is hardly satisfied."

Caleb grinned as he waited for Olivia to move to the table. "Alex ordered like he expected me." There was a hint of curiosity in his eyes as Olivia handed him the plate of sausage.

"I wish you had brought Bertie with you."

"She's feeling poorly these days. That baby's going to be a big one," he chuckled. He gave Olivia another quick glance. "We're disappointed you won't be here when he comes."

"Girls can be big, too," Olivia said with a grin.

Caleb's eyes twinkled. "Not that big. 'Sides, I figured out Alex had serious talk in mind when he told me you two were going back right away, and maybe you wanted to say something to me."

As she poured the coffee, Olivia watched Alex's sober expression. "We were still discussing it when you came. We will be returning as quickly as possible. Naturally we're both disappointed with having to leave now, before the baby."

Caleb drank his coffee and looked at Alex. "You thinking there's going to be a fight?"

Alex winced. "I try to not let myself think that way. But I must admit there's a strong possibility. In the past several weeks, the newspapers coming out of the South have produced a constant stream of rhetoric denouncing Lincoln and stressing states' rights."

Alex tapped the newspaper lying on the table. "Offhand, I'd say the rumbles coming out of the South indicate a crisis. Some are saying Lincoln's election will be the final straw. I don't like to think that. But clearly it's a political struggle, North against South, Republican against Democrat."

Caleb had forgotten his breakfast. Finally he looked at Alex. "If it gets down to a fight," he said softly, "it won't seem right if us slaves don't do our part."

"Remember the Fugitive Slave Law," Alex muttered, picking up his coffee. "I figured you'd feel this way—you and all the others. But sit tight, or you'll all end up back down the river."

Caleb shook his head as Alex spoke. "You do us a wrong to refuse to let us fight. You know how we want to be accepted as—"

"Citizens, honorable and responsible," Alex finished. "You'll get your chance later, when the fuss is over. In addition to the risk to you all, there's the added factor of it being unnecessary. At most it will be a military skirmish, a show of strength, and then a settlement." He shook his head. "Both sides will compromise. The abolitionists will protest and the Southern Democrats will make Congress very uncomfortable for a time. And then we'll be back to where we were before."

Caleb finished his muffin, no longer conscious of what he ate. Slowly he wiped his fingers on the napkin. "Seems like a mule pulling a plow around in circles. Doesn't get the field plowed, and he's right back in the same spot. Maybe it'd be better to get the job over with."

"You're talking about war," Alex said, astonished. "Are you saying you think it will develop into something more than a skirmish?"

Caleb looked down at his plate. Finally he lifted his head and looked Alex in the eye. "You thinking a man like Lincoln won't push freedom for the slaves? Might be he won't, but the slaves don't feel that way. There's this feeling Mistuh Lincoln won't let us down. You think the South would let their slaves go without a big fight?"

CHAPTER 3

Alex lowered his newspaper and looked at his wife. "How would you like to take the long way back to Pennsylvania?"

"What do you mean?"

"By way of Washington. I want to know just how life is shaping up in the capital. Perhaps we'll hear some speeches, see a little campaigning."

"You think Lincoln will be there?"

"No. Nor do I expect significant campaigning in Washington right now. It will be a fortunate day for us when it's no longer considered inappropriate for the candidate to do his own campaigning for the presidency."

"Just before we left Pennsylvania, Stephen A. Douglas had begun campaigning for himself."

"He's the exception. He's also been in the public eye long enough to do just as he desires." Alex paused, adding thoughtfully, "I've read he's in the South now, doing his best to talk secession out of people's minds. They say he's not well, barely able to talk above a whisper."

"But why would he go south?"

"Seems to be concerned for the future of the Union—in an increasing measure. The debates between him and Lincoln changed him—nearly sounds Republican sometimes."

Thoughtfully, Olivia studied Alex's face before jabbing her needle into the linen she was embroidering. Finally she said, "Yes, I believe I would like to go to Washington."

Two weeks later Olivia pressed close to the train window to catch her first glimpse of Washington. "What a lovely, peaceful place Washington is!"

"There's not much you can see from a train window," Alex said, "but we'll have our man take the carriage past the Capitol and the White House before we go to our hotel. We're approaching the railroad station."

"I'm glad the sun is shining today," Olivia said as she followed the porter to the hack stand. "Aren't the maple leaves brilliant? But it surprises me to find all the rolling, grassy hills. I expected houses and tall buildings cozying up against each other."

"There's the Capitol, and in the distance, the White House," Alex pointed them out as the cabbie snapped his whip over the heads of his team.

They were just entering their hotel when Olivia heard someone call, "Alexander Duncan!" The stocky, white-haired man approaching held out his hand and stared at Alex. "I thought you had left for Cuba."

"Cuba?" Alex slowly put out his hand, holding Olivia close at his side. "My dear, this is Mr. Mallory. Sir, this is indeed a total surprise. We've just arrived. I would like to present my wife, Olivia. Mr. Mallory is a very dear friend of my father."

"Mrs. Duncan, I am delighted." Quickly shifting his gold-handled cane, he bent over her hand.

Frowning at Alex he said, "Your father told me you had married and were living in Pennsylvania. He was rather uncommunicative about you. What are you doing in Pennsylvania?" He pulled out his watch and looked at it. "Late. Well, no matter. I would like to see you later; however, I have appointments every evening this week. If I can possibly procure an invitation to a presidential reception later this week, will you be available?"

"Available? Most certainly," Alex murmured as Mallory nodded and hurried out the door.

"Who is he?" Olivia whispered wide-eyed.

"Mallory," Alex groaned. "The last person on earth I wanted to see this week."

"Why?"

"Remember when I told you about my last drunk in Boston? I think I mentioned Mallory."

"So this is Mallory! What does he want?"

"Well," he grinned, "after the way I failed him back in Boston, and skipped out without contacting him again, I can't believe he's still interested in priming me for Washington. Probably just curious about my life over the past three years."

"And what are you going to say?"

"That has me worried. I don't feel free to discuss my activities with a man who would quickly turn from being a friend to a foe. I've had enough of jail."

"And we have the slaves to think of," she said thoughtfully. "I'm certain any information could end up being used to trace the *Golden Awl*. Perhaps even to cut off this line to Canada."

"I think we need to pray for protection from Mallory, and a very careful, nimble tongue."

He patted her arm. "Tomorrow, while I roam the Capitol, you'll need to look for a new frock. And please, dear wife, make it so spectacular that Mallory will forget his questions."

"Alex, we can't afford a dress like that!"

"Since Sadie's barrel isn't around, we can't afford not to buy one. I'm teasing my dear. Of course we can afford it. Shall I come with you?"

"Men and shopping! By mid-morning you will have forgotten your brave statement and will want me to buy just anything."

———

When Olivia returned from shopping the following afternoon, Alex was pacing the floor in their room. She saw his pleased grin as soon as she walked in.

"Was the morning that interesting?" she asked.

"Interesting, yes. But I'm grinning because of Mallory's note. He had to leave town, but he enclosed invitations to the Presidential reception to be held Friday evening. Did you find a frock?"

"Yes, and it's nearly like the one from Sadie's barrel. Deep rose, with a charming neckline and smaller hoops. Oh, and a tiny lift in the back, held in place with silk rose buds."

"A bustle?" he feigned anger, but there was a twinkle in his eye.

Olivia poked him in the ribs. "I'm starved."

"I've made reservations for us at one of those places where the important people are said to go. I've had my suit pressed."

As she watched him button a fresh white shirt, she spoke slowly, "Alex, I think it's a good idea for you to be seen in Washington. You have what they refer to as a commanding figure. Already I've seen and heard enough to know that's important here."

He paused and turned toward her with a troubled frown. "Yes, I know. Appearance is important, especially in the South. I wonder if that will that be another strike against Lincoln?"

"You are starting to sound as if it is terribly important for Lincoln to win the presidency."

"I still don't have much hope," Alex said. "But I care enough to be in Pennsylvania in two weeks in order to cast my vote."

———

Before noon the next day, Alex and Olivia joined the throng of visitors moving through the doors of the Capitol. A young man standing in the doorway handed Alex a pamphlet. "What is this?" Alex asked, turning the booklet over.

"If you aren't a Republican, we'd like to make one out of you. You know the House investigating committee has compiled a large volume reporting the corruption of the Buchanan administration. This is an abridged version, prepared by the Republican convention for the purpose of informing the public."

"Is that so? Well, this should make interesting reading. Thank you!"

The fellow nodded. "You sound Southern, but I'm guessing you have an open mind."

"Isn't all of Washington Southern?" asked Olivia. "It seems I've heard only Southerners."

"Mostly politicians from the deep South. But a number have made Washington their home." He touched Alex's arm to direct his attention and nodded toward a man coming from the door marked *SENATE*. "Do you know Jefferson Davis?"

Alex shook his head. "Not personally. I know he's a senator from Mississippi."

"Back in February of this year, Jefferson Davis pulled the veil off the Southern heart. He presented their demands to the Senate with resolutions clearly stating that neither Congress nor territorial legislature could—mind you, here was a strong word for those fellows to swallow—*impair* the constitutional right of a citizen of the United States to take his slaves into United States territories. He went on to say that it was the duty of the Federal government to protect these slaves as property, just as they would any other property."

"What happened then?" Alex asked.

"Well, you know the Democratic caucus is dominated by South-erners. Of course they endorsed the resolutions."

"And that was the resolution responsible for the split in the Democratic Convention in Charleston," Alex murmured. "I hadn't heard it spelled out this clearly. I recall that turn of events was responsible for getting Breckinridge's name on the ballot in the South." As he spoke, he glanced at the gentleman who had joined them. The man nodded at Alex, but didn't speak.

The young man continued, "Well it's no secret Lincoln's name isn't even on the ballot in the deep South. Down there it's a contest between Bell and Breckinridge, while up here it's Lincoln and Douglas running against each other."

"Alex," Olivia said, handing the pamphlet to him, "you'll need to read this before tonight. It says Buchanan is guilty of graft and bribery in issuing government contracts. The book names firms receiving contracts who made contributions to the Democratic Party. And there's much more; I haven't read it all."

"Then let's get through this place and head for the hotel," he replied.

Later, as they left the Capitol, Alex turned to look up at the unfinished dome. "Incomplete. That's the way I'm feeling about this whole situation. It is starting to seem there's a job to be done, beginning with the government. Our nation will be incomplete until that happens. That flag up there promises much more freedom than we have now." He squeezed her arm as she blinked at tears in her eyes. He tried to lighten his voice. "Looks like a tricky situation we're getting into—if Lincoln wins the election."

––––––––––

The October dusk brought coolness to the air. When Olivia stepped out of the carriage, she shivered and pulled her cloak tight. She slipped her hand through Alex's arm as he said, "Your gown is lovely, my dear. Earlier," he added, "I was so stunned by the silk flowers I forgot to tell you so. Do I understand you'll be standing all evening?"

They moved quickly through the reception line. Olivia had a brief glimpse of President Buchanan, felt his limp hand, and was then propelled swiftly through the stately rooms.

There were more names and handshakes; information bombarded them. Alex murmured in her ear, "Ever heard so many Southern accents?"

"Not since I left Mississippi. Alex, look!" Olivia grasped his arm, and Alex turned.

The slight man dressed in white looked startled, then his eyes narrowed. With a quick word to his partner, he strode forward. "Alexander Duncan, Olivia, what a delightful surprise! The lure of home reaches across the miles, doesn't it?"

"Lucas Tristram," Alex said slowly as he met the extended hand. "This is indeed a surprise."

"It is encouraging to see my talks netted one prodigal." He bowed toward Olivia, "I trust the other one will return before this affair is resolved. We need every man we can get."

"Why, Mr. Tristram—" Olivia looked the man directly in the eye. "Surely you aren't reading more import in this election than is warranted."

"My dear Mrs. Duncan, this election can draw the line sharply between North and South. Of course we are watching this with bated breath. But on the other hand, many of us still find it impossible to believe the conservative citizens of the North will deliberately vote a black-Republican into office."

"Black?" Olivia turned as a woman whirled out of the crowd. Her hoops tipped dangerously as she swung about and stood near Lucas, waving her fan while listening. "My good man, I am a solid citizen of the North, no matter that I was raised in the deep South, I still believe the gentleman when he says he will not tamper with slavery."

Olivia watched with interest as the woman's escort appeared just beyond the edge of her skirt. Bobbing his mane of snowy curls he added, "We have kin in Louisiana, and they sift all the rumors and ship them our direction. I feel we have a good handle on the boiling kettle right now. My sister tells me the secessionist crowd is working this election to the hilt. Lincoln is an excuse, just like the tariffs were an excuse back when nullification was the talk. She also says there's strong Union feeling in Dixie."

Another gentleman slipped into the circle of people. "Call it excuse if you will," he gestured widely, with his cup of wine punch swinging dangerously close to Lucas' white linen elbow. Olivia winced as the bright liquid sloshed against the crystal. "The South will never be happy until they are free to live as they please. What's wrong with two countries? Look at Europe, there's a bunch of little countries pushed up against each other. It can happen on this continent. And the South will be expanding soon."

Lucas spoke as he looked around, "It isn't a matter of *if.* Sooner or later Cuba, Mexico, and Central American nations will join our ranks."

A newcomer added, "And it's a matter of rights. When has the South ever tampered with Northern rights? It's obvious we are two completely different peoples."

"The Northerners are only a cut above the slave—uneducated, unrefined. Mechanics and laborers. It is a trial to visit the Northern cities with their smoke and noise," the woman clinging to his arm added.

Olivia noted that his nods of approval punctuated her statements as she continued. "Unfortunately, the gulf is so wide we can't communicate with our Northern neighbors. What do they know of the finer things of life?" Her fan snapped shut like an exclamation mark.

Olivia and Alex continued to push their way through the crowd toward the door. She turned to take his arm as she heard the final remark. "Don't you forget this. Buchanan has pledged himself to secession, and we're certain to hold him to it. South Carolina will shatter the Union. Like Samson in the Good Book, she'll embrace the pillars of the country and pull them in upon herself."

Back in their hotel room, Alex removed the cufflinks from his shirt while Olivia watched his image in the mirror. Turning, she asked, "Alex, there are real differences, aren't there?"

"Between North and South? Yes. Some of the differences aren't good; the South would be at a decided advantage if there were to be a war."

He faced her. "There's the proclivity of Southern men to settle their arguments with their fists or dueling pistols. You don't see this in the North. Neither do you see the stress placed on a military education such as we have in the South. I was surprised to discover the small size of the Northern Army and the lack of military academies."

As Olivia brushed her hair, Alex added thoughtfully, "Another thing. You talk to the Northerners about war and they can't believe it's a serious subject. But Southerners respond with excitement, as if it's a lark."

He paused. "Differences? Yes. And our differences may just plunge us into a conflict we cannot avoid."

CHAPTER 4

Oh, it's good to be home! I didn't dream I would miss this place so much." Olivia turned slowly in the middle of the keeping room of the farmhouse in Pennsylvania. From the stone fireplace at one end of the room to the stove in the kitchen at the far side of the house, there was warmth and comfort. She looked at the heavy beams overhead, admired the flicker of fire warming the plastered walls, and touched the shawl across the back of the settle.

"Sadie, you've finished knitting this shawl since we've been gone."

"Aye. Just one load of slaves came through. There was little to occupy the time." Going to the rocking chair beside the fire, she picked up the skein of blue wool and said, "Besides, I didn't have a body around to keep me hopping from one end of the kitchen to the other. I missed thy chatter."

"What are you making now?"

"A shawl for Beth, that new child Mike brought home. Doesn't have a wrap to ward of the chill."

Alex came down the stairs. "I've taken the bags upstairs. Sadie, since you've moved us out of the little room we'll have to be upstairs with the rest of the guests."

"Guests!" Sadie chuckled, "Now Alex, thou can't go pulling that on me. I needed the nursing room, and thee two needed more room than thee had down here. Besides, thou knowest thou art family, and

I'll not have it otherwise. I suppose family can be shuffled around without complaining."

"This new girl," Olivia said, helping herself to an apple from the wooden bowl on the long table, "I believe you called her Beth Peamble. Is she really *Mike's* girl?"

Sadie chuckled, shook her head and then frowned. Slowly she said, "She keeps us all guessing. Right now I think she's anybody's girl, if they can keep up with her. She's nice; can't help but like the little one, but—"

Olivia searched through the nut bowl on the buffet. "I don't suppose you've heard from any of the others."

"Crystal, Amelia, Matthew? No, my dear." Sadie sighed and tugged at the skein of yarn. "Come here and hold out thy hands, I need to get this wool into a ball."

Alex came out of the pantry, cookies in his hand. "Is Amos in the barn?" Sadie eyed the cookies and smiled at him. "I'm taking him one," he said.

"Yes. I don't suppose they fed thee in Canada or Washington. Better take more; Mike should be out there too. He's been doing something to the *Golden Awl*. He's also been muttering something about another trip before winter sets in."

Olivia turned at a whisper of sound behind her. A girl blinked sleepy eyes and said, "I fell asleep, Sadie. These must be your friends, Alex and Olivia." She looked at Olivia, "*Friends* is putting it mildly. You should have heard her, it's been—" Her Southern accent slipped into mimicking Sadie's gentle voice. "Alex says this, and Olivia does that. I can't even wash dishes without being told how you do it so well. I'm glad to have you here—to show me how to wash dishes." Her grin was mischievous, and Olivia laughed.

The outside door opened and Mike came in, his eyes searching out the girl across the room. He smiled and then said, "Olivia, and Alex, it's good to have you safely home!"

Alex gestured with the cookies. "I was just ready to come looking for you. Want a cookie? Is Amos coming in?"

Mike took the cookie and nodded. "I'm mighty glad to have you here. I've been thinking about another trip. We had a full house last time."

"He had me sleeping in the pilot house," Beth murmured. "And trying to cook. Ugh! That was laughable! Me cooking for the darkies, when all my life—" She paused, gazing curiously at Olivia. "You're Southern. How can you work against us?"

"What do you mean?" Olivia asked slowly.

"Mike told me what you've been doing, helping the slaves escape. You know it's causing all kinds of problems. I heard tell—she stopped suddenly. "But then, you wouldn't be interested."

"Yes we are," Alex said, going to sit on the stool beside Sadie. "I'd really like to hear what they are saying in the South."

"Well for one thing, there's stories of slaves being stirred up by the Northerners telling them they are as good as anybody, no matter what their color. I hear in Texas a body can't sleep for fear. There are constant rumors of slaves banding together, intent on no good. A fellow in Alabama told us the slaves are putting poison in the wells in Texas, and in his home state they're burning houses. It's all 'cause of the abolitionists. I know for a fact the slaves were happy before." She paused, glanced quickly around the circle and added, "They're saying all these problems make the risk of separating from the Union seem very attractive."

"And do you think so?" Alex asked.

Beth's eyes sparkled. "It sounds exciting. But they're saying it would never amount to much. Like nullification—a few threats and the North will start making concessions."

"Have these stories been circulating for a long time?"

She shrugged. "I don't know much about it, except what I hear. It's only been this past year."

"Have you seen any of the stories in the newspapers?" Alex pressed again.

"No. I've just been told about them."

"Beth, is it possible these statements are all lies, meant to discredit the North? I think all of us, both North and South, deserve the truth. It's necessary if we're to make a good judgment, and that holds for every part of life—not just politics."

She took a bite of apple, and when Olivia finally decided Beth would say no more, she turned to Mike. "We've been talking about another trip this autumn."

"It'll have to be soon," Alex warned as he reached for an apple. "What is the status of the *Awl*?"

"Just needs work on the engine, fresh oil. We'd better take on a barrel of oil. It costs dearly on the other side of the Ohio." He eyed Alex, "You've been to Washington. What do you think?"

"I didn't like what I heard." He turned to Sadie. "Remember Lucas Tristram? We met him at a reception in the White House. Seemed happy to see me there—called me a prodigal son returned home."

Sadie peered at Alex. "Did thee say—"

"Not a word about anything," Alex said as he and Mike moved for the door. "When he gets home, he'll realize he did all the talking." Sadie chuckled, but Olivia saw the shadows in her eyes and heard her sigh. Beth followed the men as they went out to the barn.

"I keep thinking and praying about them," Sadie said. "Matthew and Crystal, and Amelia too. Prayin' is about all I can do. That Tristram caused more trouble than a whole hive of fussed-up bees," she added sadly.

Sadie finished winding the ball of yarn. "Might as well do another one while thee sits here. Our supper is in the oven, and I don't get a chance to visit much."

"What is the story about Beth? Is she going to stay here?"

"Doesn't seem in a hurry to move on. She pays her way, seems to have plenty of money. Aye, and her story seems to vary once in a while." Slowly she added, "Seems spunky. I'm sparing with my sympathy. Poor Mike! Thou hast seen nothing until thou seest the way she leads him around by the nose like a pet pig.

"Aye, and here I am gossipin'! But Olivia, 'tis hard to be sympathetic when thou art listening to her story and seeing her dimples flashing while there's mischief in her eye. Poor Mike."

That night Olivia sat on the bed beside Alex, saying, "Beth makes me uneasy. According to Sadie, she's from one of the wealthy cotton families. But Alex, didn't she talk *too* much about her family's wealth?"

Alex nodded. "For having been as well educated as she claims, she seems to lack the polish I would have expected."

"Didn't know a thing about Sir Walter Scott." Olivia grinned. "For a Southern lass, that's nearly unforgivable!"

———

By the middle of the following week, the *Golden Awl* was back on the river. During the second week, while the shallow draft boat plowed through the low water of the Ohio, the weather soured, turning to icy rain and sleet.

Thinking of the red-haired girl they had left behind, Olivia chuckled as she watched Mike braced behind the wheel of the *Golden Awl*. The storm slung icy water through the window; Mike was drenched, but he whistled as if it were mid-June with soft breezes blowing. Olivia shook her head as she poured hot coffee for him. *Sadie, my dear friend*, she thought, *Mike can take care of himself!*

"Where's Alex?" he yelled over the storm.

"In the cabin. He said to tell you he'll be up to take the wheel in about ten minutes." Mike shook his head and pulled his cap down on his head. "But you've been up here for hours now," she insisted.

"Just let me get around the bend. The Mississippi is coming up, and I like to be the one to hit the water." He glanced at Olivia. "There's activity on the river. Since we made the last trip together, I've been seeing more patrol boats and commotion in the ports." He pointed. "Looks like there's a new ship on the river. Pretty good sized." He pointed to the paddle wheeler coming around the bend.

"Very grand," Olivia said. "Must be all passengers. I don't see a bale of cotton anywhere. What kind of activity did you see?" She tugged her slicker close.

"In port, mostly trimming things up. Building new wharfs, buildings. Saw some stockpiles that surprised me. Looked like barrels of oil. Machinery of some kind."

"Hear any rumbles or war talk?"

He gave her a curious glance. "You getting jittery over the situation? Alex and I voted for Lincoln to be President of the United States only two weeks ago and now you're acting like the Lord isn't in charge of all this."

"Isn't it amazing that we knew by the next day that Lincoln won the election?"

"Trust the Republicans to get things organized. I just wish it wouldn't take so long to get him in the White House. Five months from election to inauguration seems a long time."

"Mike, do you think the South will cause trouble—maybe secede?" His face settled into a thoughtful frown, but he shook his head. Olivia continued, "Did Alex tell you about our trip to Washington? Did he mention hearing that Buchanan was committed to secession?"

"Yes. But talk is one thing, Olivia; action is another. I'm inclined to think the South is big at talk, but I think the prevailing notion floating around the North right now is to treat her like a spoiled child and let her fuss. She'll come around sooner or later."

As the days passed, the chilly northern winds fell behind them and the air sweetened with lingering autumn as the *Golden Awl* moved swiftly southward down the Mississippi.

They were nearly to Vicksburg before problems began. Day after frustrating day they limped along the Mississippi, with barely enough power to move them. Finally, they discovered a widening crack in the boiler.

Jake, the roustabout, summed it up. "It ain't doing us no good to burn all that wood and get steam leaking out all the cracks."

Alex and Mike stared at each other across the table in the cabin. Alex hadn't touched his breakfast. Now he gave a frustrated sigh. "To top it off," he said, "it's going to be nearly impossible to get a new boiler this time of year. It'll have to come down from Ohio or Illinois.

And if we have to wait on a boiler, we're pushing against time. Before we can get our people and head up the Ohio, ice will have closed the river. I guess I should have allowed more time."

"We had to stick around for the election," Mike reminded him. "We all knew it was cutting it close, but it was a gamble we had to take."

"But that's the end of the gamble," Alex said shortly. "From here on out we have to play it very safe. We can't risk problems; the lives of the slaves depend on our caution and good judgment."

Alex sloshed the coffee around in his cup while Olivia controlled her urge to remind him of the cooling porridge.

Finally Mike spoke up. "Alex, you and Olivia have been talking about visiting your folks in South Carolina. How would it be if you go now?"

"What would you do?"

"Spend the winter here. Get the repairs made, and be ready to take the *Awl* home around the first of April."

"We could meet you back here. The Lord willing, we could continue on with our plans. Jake, what do you and Tim want to do? You're both freedmen."

"I want to stick close to Mike here. The South's kinda upset right now, and I don't wanna be sent down the river." He paused. "Maybe we all could find jobs for the spell we'll be here."

Alex looked at Olivia. "How about it? Ready to go meet my parents?"

She nodded. "We're close to Natchez. Perhaps when we come back we can visit my mother and father."

Alex got to his feet. "Come on, crew. We're going to have to get this boat into port as soon as possible."

———

The next morning Olivia began to pack while Mike and Alex headed for the nearest shipping office.

The old gray-haired seaman confirmed Alex's guess. He listened as Alex described the problem; shaking his head, he said, "I can get you a boiler, but it'll take a month or so."

When Mike and Alex returned to the boat, Olivia was standing on deck, waiting beside her packed trunk. Alex looked from the trunk to his wife's face. "Olivia, you must have guessed correctly. I have the train tickets in my pocket."

At the train station in Vicksburg, Alex pulled out their tickets and said, "It's unfortunate we didn't discover our problem in Memphis. We're going to have to backtrack to Corinth, Mississippi and then turn east. We'll cross Alabama and Georgia before we reach the coast and Charleston."

The shriek of the train whistle pierced the morning air. The platform where they stood began to tremble. They turned to watch the dark cloud of smoke above the trees. Alex pulled Olivia's arm through his and smiled down at her. "I trust you know about trains in the southeast. Before this trip is over, you will have grown very weary of changing trains and mopping soot from your face."

As she wrinkled her nose, he added, "But you'll have the desire of your heart—my constant and undivided attention."

As the train shuddered and steamed into silence, she watched the men back wagons of wood and coal toward the locomotive. Turning to Alex, she murmured, "Well, I do appreciate your total attention, but I'm beginning to wish that I had learned to knit. Will it take forever to get to Charleston?"

"At least. When the trip becomes too monotonous, we'll stop and do some sightseeing."

———

When they reached Atlanta, Alex decided they needed a sightseeing break. That first morning they awakened refreshed by a gentle, rose-perfumed breeze lifting lace curtains to invade their hotel room. Olivia sat up and breathed deeply. "Oh, this is wonderful! I'd forgotten such air existed."

"Coal and wood smoke does that," Alex murmured. "But don't you want to sleep longer? We can smell the roses later. I promise you, if there's anything worth seeing in Atlanta you will have seen it before we get back on the train."

She turned from the window. "You can sleep; I intend to enjoy every minute of this. Shall I bring you a rose and a croissant when I return?"

"You win." His grin disappeared as he sat up.

"What is it, Alex?"

"I've been awake for an hour, thinking about the talk we've been hearing on the train. I had the distinct impression every statement began with 'They say in Charleston. . . .' Most certainly they didn't seem too concerned about having Lincoln as President, neither did they seem to think Buchanan was doing such a poor job."

"What about the old gentleman who said the South will never allow the humiliation and degradation of having Lincoln inaugurated as president? The people around him scarcely looked his direction."

"I had the feeling they've heard that statement before."

"But not one of them seemed to have considered the implications of war. The gentleman was shocked when I suggested war carries a terrible price." She paused.

"Think about this pleasant place being fired upon," he mused.

"Fired upon? Oh, Alex, how horrible!"

Olivia went to the window, pulled aside the lace and leaned against the window frame. Deep crimson roses covered the trellis just below their window. Beyond the garden hedge she could see the street lined with stately houses, shielded by their secluded gardens. Brick, gleaming white paint, or old stone stamped them with character. Olivia reacted with a familiar pang of homesickness. It could have been a street borrowed from Natchez.

"It is beautiful," she murmured, "but a beauty existing within bounds. I cannot imagine a calf eating petunias like they do in Pennsylvania, nor can I imagine a crinoline in a corn patch." She turned to look at Alex. "At home in Mississippi, there is this same lovely order. Alex, what would happen to these people if there were war? It would be shattering. Given their gentle life, could they survive?"

Alex came to stand beside her. His eyes were troubled as he looked at the scene. "I hope and pray it doesn't happen. If it does, I pray the people—all of us—survive to be stronger than ever before." He turned, put his arms around her, and pulled her close. "Have we changed this much—enough to make comparisons and worry about the differences?"

She leaned back and ran her hands across his bare shoulders. "I don't know," she whispered. "But I am certain of one thing—the longer we are married, the more I realize how impossible it would be to live without you."

CHAPTER 5

When the train finally reached Charleston, Olivia and Alex stepped off to find that the last hint of sunshine and roses had disappeared. Olivia looked at the sodden gardens, the gray skies and drizzle. "Finished," she whispered as she looked around. "All the glory of autumn has ended."

Alex looked down at her. "My dear, I've just changed our plans."

"Why is that?" She looked up into his troubled frown.

"I've been thinking about all the months that lie ahead. As I've told you, Father and I didn't leave each other with good feelings." Alex spoke hesitantly. "He knows we're coming if he has received my letter, but I have no idea how he will receive us." He clasped her hand.

"It's less than a week until Christmas," he continued. "We could hire a hack to take us out to the plantation immediately if necessary, but I'd rather have this time with you before we go. Do you mind if we just stay here for several days? We'll rest and shop for Christmas gifts."

"Are you thinking Lincoln's election will complicate matters between you and your father?"

"I anticipate it will."

"Then let's stay. I am tired, and this storm is miserable."

Alex beckoned to the hack waiting just beyond the garden. Olivia drew her cloak tighter. "It is fortunate that Pennsylvania's weather forced us to come with heavy clothing."

As the cabbie loaded their baggage, he listened to their conversation regarding things back in Pennsylvania. Looking at Olivia, he said, "You from the North? Y'all, with your Southern accent! Surprising they didn't run y'all out of black Republican country. Aye, and I think it must be very good to be at home again. Now, will y'all be staying at the Wayfarer Inn? I'll carry you and the missus right there.

"Y'all gotta good view of the bay and the forts, not that there's any action right now. They say Major Anderson will be dining Christmas Day with some of Charleston's best. Good of them to befriend the chap. But, you know, he's Southern. I suppose they're hoping he'll choose the right side."

He hesitated and eyed Alex, who replied, "I haven't heard any South Carolina news for the past month. Since we have been traveling I haven't had opportunity to scout out good newspapers."

The cabbie leaned forward. In a whisper, his eyes sparkling in delight, he advised, "Y'all just sit tight. We may have some very good news for you in a day or so. Now, let's get you settled at the Inn."

As the cabbie deposited them at the front door of the Inn, he whispered to Alex, "I'll give y'all a hint of things to come. On December 8th a guard was placed over the United States Arsenal right here in Charleston. They were preventing the transfer of ammunition to Fort Moultrie."

"They?"

"I supposed you'd seen the soldiers marching around Charleston. Been here since the eleventh of the month. South Carolinian, of course. 'Nough said for now. Hey, buddy, if ya need a ride, call on old Mac."

As they followed the bellhop into the Inn, Olivia whispered, "Alex, tell me, what are those blue things everyone is wearing? It appears to be a feather emblem."

Alex looked and his jaw tightened. "I'm not certain. But let's discuss it later. I wish I could find some newspapers!"

After the door closed behind the bellhop, Olivia turned to Alex. "I feel completely in the dark! Alex, we've no idea what has been going on here. And I want to know why, even on the train, every question you asked was answered with blank looks and yawns. Is it possible the people are unaware too?"

"Did you notice the absence of national newspapers as we traveled? The small town tabloids carried only local gossip. And the blue feathers are called *cockades*. I understand they were the symbol of nullification in the thirties. Back then the North gave in to South Carolina's demands."

"Is it possible South Carolina is having these ideas again?" Olivia sighed and moved around the room. "Well if nothing else is accomplished, we'll go back to Pennsylvania knowing much more about the feelings of the people in the South."

———————

In the morning, a key turning in the lock awakened Olivia. Blinking in the pallid light of another rainy day, she watched Alex come into the room, drop his coat in the corner and spread several damp newspapers to dry. She sat up, pulled both pillows behind her back and snuggled the comforter beneath her chin.

"Newspapers! I didn't even know you had gone."

"You were asleep," he murmured, not looking up from the newspapers.

"What did you find out?"

"Senator Wigfall of Texas made a speech in the Senate, announcing that the Union would be dissolved; the eight cotton states would secede followed by Virginia, Tennessee, Kentucky, and Maryland; and that Washington would become the capital of this Southern confederacy. In addition he proclaimed he owed allegiance not to the United States, but to his own state."

"That is unbelievable!" Olivia gasped. "Oh, Alex, how could a United States senator say such things?" She stopped laughing when she saw his face. "Alex, are you thinking the South is seriously considering secession? Do you suppose that cabbie last night was right?"

"Possibly. Olivia, I think it would be a good idea to have breakfast downstairs. Perhaps we can find interesting table companions and get a better idea of what's going on."

"I'll hurry."

The dining room was empty. The waiter took them to a table close to the windows. With a smile, he said, "You will have an interesting scene to watch. May you enjoy your breakfast. I appreciate the opportunity to serve honeymooners."

After eating, Olivia smiled at Alex and said, "We may get our honeymoon yet. At least the waiter thinks we are newlyweds."

Alex lifted her hand and kissed the tips of her fingers. "Does that help the image?"

"Alex, the rain has stopped; look at the people on the streets. . . . Do you hear church bells?"

"Church bells midweek? We have to see what the excitement is all about."

When Olivia and Alex left the Inn, the church bells were still tolling at intervals. The rush of people past the dining room window had slowed, but the sound of excited voices continued. They joined the crowd moving toward the center of the city.

A group of young men passed, calling back. "If you're going to the convention hall, you'd better hurry, or you'll miss it!"

A white-haired gentleman drew even with them and Alex turned. "Sir, we are visitors to the city. What is the excitement?"

The man stopped and looked at them. Olivia could see the flash of fire in his eyes as he spoke to Alex. "The South Carolina Convention has this day settled the affair once and for all, the durn fools. They signed secession papers. South Carolina is no longer a part of the United States of America. They stand on their own—proud and cocky." He shook his head.

"Why the bunch in control of the state offices couldn't back down and give a bit, I don't know. Won't be celebrating when the cold facts hit them. It's one thing to be a spoiled young'un, but it's quite another to be a cocky punk trying to whip the biggest kid on the block."

"You don't support the cause?"

"I own slaves whom I intend to free when I die. Don't support the cause when it's apt to rip the Union apart." His piercing eyes were calm now, nearly thoughtful as he said, "Don't claim to have all the answers to life, even to knowing the Lord's will. Seems we'd come closer to pleasing Him if we'd have a little give and take."

They watched him swing his cane and hurry down the street. Alex said, "It's possible Father is in town. I'll send a note around to his club." He pulled Olivia's hand through his arm and they quickened their steps as someone handed Alex a leaflet. The people ahead of them were turning toward the city park.

"I hear a band playing," Olivia murmured. "And look at the crowd. All of Charleston must be here."

Alex glanced at her. "According to this circular, the speaker is an editor from New Orleans." They moved closer to a man in a frock coat who was waving his arms.

"That black Republican Lincoln didn't win fairly and honestly, he was a pawn of the abolitionists. And I tell you, my brother Southerners, one vote cast for Lincoln is a deliberate, cold-blooded insult and outrage. In this election, we have been slapped in the face over and over. We shall not stand for it. I assure you that my state, as well as all the other cotton states, will join you in withdrawal from a Union which has shackled our necks."

It was afternoon by the time Olivia and Alex left the park. Olivia's mind was reeling with the statements she had been hearing: "*We South*

Carolinians relish the life before us. We are free forever of the black Republicans, the dominion of suppression. We are free people at last!"

Alex spoke softly. "Olivia, this building just ahead is the club to which Father belongs. I want to leave a note; maybe he will be here sometime during the week—if he isn't here now."

As they continued down the street, Olivia asked, "Is your father a member of the state convention?"

"Only if it's happened since I've been away from South Carolina. But that wouldn't surprise me. Father owns a great deal of land hereabout. Further south he owns rice plantations, in addition to the home acres just out of Charleston. He calls Shadylane home." He gave her a quick grin. "In the summer it isn't shady enough. But the rice plantation is fever country. The whites stay out of the area during the summer."

He read the question in her eyes. "Yes, he loses several slaves every summer, and that doesn't include the slaves nearly ruined by the heat and fever."

"It makes my father's cotton plantation seem like a toy." She glanced at him. "But bad things happen there, too." She took a deep breath, smiled, and added, "Let's walk along the shore road. I need to clear my mind."

The late afternoon mists were moving inland with the gentle wind. "How about going out to this point?" Alex nodded his head toward the embankment. Beyond the railing, the land sloped sharply. Tucking Olivia's hand under his arm, he pulled her close. "That distant spot must be Fort Sumter. And this little fort with the island behind it is Fort Moultrie. Sounds as if there's a chance of confrontation. According to the newspaper, South Carolina has made it clear that she thinks the Union will be happy to turn these forts over to her. There's also a fortification off Florida. But if South Carolina has much influence, I suppose she'll pull Florida out of the Union."

"The speaker this afternoon indicated that all of the South has been waiting only to see the direction the election would go. We've heard some very strong statements against Lincoln, but surely he can't be as bad as Buchanan."

"Buchanan is very pro-South; that doesn't make him bad in the eyes of the Southerners."

Olivia tucked her hand in Alex's and they walked back to the Inn. There was a note from Alex's father. "He will escort us to dinner at the club. He'll be here at seven. Come along, sweetheart; you'll want to rest before meeting my father."

CHAPTER 6

I'm glad I included this dress at the last minute," Olivia chattered as she turned in front of the mirror. "Though why I had the impulse, I'll never know. Probably because it was too pretty to leave home. Certainly one doesn't wear a dress like this when one is cooking for the—" Olivia hesitated and added, "People." She turned to Alex with a swift bow, spreading the dark green velvet skirt.

"It makes your skin even more beautiful," Alex murmured as he bent to kiss her cheek. "And it makes me regret not having you all to myself this evening." He watched her pin the brooch to the low neckline of her dress.

"You know I'm very nervous about meeting your parents."

"Fortunately Father roars only at me. He'll be a perfect gentleman. In addition, he's a pushover for a beautiful woman." He touched the brooch and she watched his smile fade.

"Alex, what is it?"

"The gold against the onyx. The dark onyx makes the gold seem even more delicate. Will the gold endure?"

As they walked slowly down the stairs, Olivia was deeply conscious of Alex's hand, the strength and warmth of it. She smiled at him, touched the brooch, and then went forward to meet his father, who was getting to his feet.

"I needn't be told who you are," she murmured as she smiled at the older counterpart of Alex. "Now I know how he will look when he has gray hair."

"My dear Olivia!" He bent over her hand. "I hope only that you are not disappointed enough to run away!" He turned to Alex. "The selection of your wife is one thing in which you have earned my total approval. Welcome home, Son; I hope it is to stay."

Without waiting for a reply, he strode toward the door. "The carriage is waiting for us, and we shall have a delightful dinner together. We are going to the Congress House."

They were seated away from the stringed ensemble, shielded by an ancient screen of rosewood, breathing air perfumed by the cluster of roses adrift in a crystal bowl. The elder Duncan nodded at the white-clad man in the shadows and addressed Alex. "It was fortunate you thought to leave a message at the club."

"Have you a role in the convention?" Alex asked.

"Only as an interested landowner, hanging on every word our men have to say. I suppose you're aware of the decision."

"Yes, we were greeted by church bells and people rushing toward the city park early this morning," Alex said as the waiter brought out a platter of shrimp surrounding a bowl of spicy sauce. "Ah, I see you remembered I like the shrimp with piccalilli. But then the House is famous for it, and you like it too."

Alex turned to Olivia. "Does Mississippi serve shrimp in this manner?"

She nodded. "We've had it at home and I like it. But I think Mother's cook uses more pepper."

After the chocolate mousse and rich French coffee had been served, Alex's father pushed aside the roses and leaned forward. The sparkle of excitement in his eyes was unmistakable, and Olivia's heart sank. She glanced at Alex. Noting the white line of his lips, she dipped her spoon in the mousse and prayed, *Father, please help him! Neither of us want to offend this man who means so much to Alex.*

With his spoon poised over his coffee, the elder Duncan asked, "Well, what you do think of all that has happened?"

Alex's shoulders sagged. "It's a disaster. The worst possible decision South Carolina could have made."

Slowly the white-haired man stirred his coffee. "Why do you say that?"

"For starters, the convention didn't put the secession ordinance to a vote by the people."

"They were totally confident it was the will of the people," Mr. Duncan said softly. "Son, you are too young to remember the significant events we've seen through over the years, but we've labored under this burden of suppression and the threat of ruin for many years."

"Since the thirties there's been talk," Alex said. "I've heard about it all my life. In addition, we were exposed to a thorough discussion of the legal ramifications at Harvard."

Shrugging off the implications of the statement, the elder Duncan said, "The North and the South are more foreign to each other than the worst Hottentots and the gentry of England. In addition to not understanding each others' needs and rights, our values do not awaken the slightest response in the wooden breasts of the North."

"Are you referring to the slavery issue?"

"Certainly. Son, you know as well as I that we can't get along without slave power."

"Not without making the fortunes you have been making. Father, I can't agree with slavery," Alex protested, "but that isn't the factor involved. Lincoln has said from the beginning that while he doesn't approve of slavery, he will not rule against it. He believes slavery will eventually phase itself out of existence."

"There's not a one of us who sees Lincoln as anything other than a warmonger, a black Republican. In the past we listened to him insist that abolition was not his intent, but now he is strangely quiet on the issue."

"Father," Alex protested, "when this last outcry came from the South, Lincoln's supporters tried to get him once again to issue a statement declaring his intention to refrain from tampering with slavery. We were in Washington at the time. Although he wasn't in the city, his reply was in the newspapers. He asked what he should say to the South, since it had all been said before. He seemed to think saying the same things again would be a mockery, a goad to those waiting for something they could interpret as a retreat from his original position. A symbol of weakness."

Alex took a deep breath and continued, "The South's fair-haired son, Stephen A. Douglas, was quoted as saying he felt so strongly against secession that he'd like to hang every man higher than Haman who would work to break up the Union by resisting its laws."

Olivia watched a red tide move over Mr. Duncan's face. He leaned forward, grasping the edge of the table with both hands. "Alex, I will not allow you to address this issue when you've removed yourself so completely from our troubles. What can you know about our problem except Northern lies? It's black—" He stopped, put his hand to his throat, and struggled to rise.

"Father!" Alex jumped to his feet and caught him before he fell.

The hospital room was lighted only by the flickering flame of one small lamp. During the hours that passed, Olivia's eyes focused first on the lamp and then Alex's troubled face.

The clock began striking midnight as the white-coated doctor dropped the stethoscope, smiled, and straightened up. He beckoned them to follow as he left the room. "Your father will be fine by morning. Just a touch of apoplexy, no doubt brought on by excitement and rich food. I suggest you let him rest here in the hospital for a week, and then you can safely take him home. He's asleep now; you can see him in the morning."

When Alex and Olivia were back in their own room, Olivia put her hands on Alex's shoulders.

"I can see in your face that you've taken the responsibility for all of this."

"I made him angry."

"I thought you were gentle. The words were hard, but isn't it possible he was angry because you spoke the truth and he knew it?"

Alex yanked off his tie. "Perhaps, but I shouldn't have pressed the issue." He looked down at her and suddenly smiled. "Sorry, sweetheart. This has been an ongoing thing between Father and me. It seems I do nothing right around him."

He wrapped his arms around her. "I'd forgotten how bad it was. Livie, this is going to be a difficult time for us, and I'm afraid our unpleasantness is going to spill out on you."

"What about your mother? Hadn't we ought to send a message?"

His grin twisted. "It isn't a life or death situation. Knowing Father, I'll save myself some problems if I consult him before sending a message. Since he mentioned meeting our train, I doubt she will expect him home this soon."

Early the next morning, when Olivia and Alex arrived at the hospital, they found Mr. Duncan eating breakfast and growling over the restrictions placed on him. He shoved his breakfast toast at Alex and said, "I feel as well as I've ever felt. Talk some sense into that doctor; I want to be out of here by noon."

Alex shook his head. "Father, the doctor is taking every precaution to make certain you'll be around long enough to be a grandfather. I think you'd better cooperate. Now—"

Startled, Alex's father beamed at Olivia. Hastily she corrected his assumption. "Not now. But we do so badly want your grandchild.

Please rest. We've brought every newspaper we could find. And we'll stay in Charleston until you are ready to go home."

"We need to know whether you want us to send a message to Mother today," Alex added.

"Absolutely not. I'll not have you worrying her. She doesn't expect me until the end of the week. Thank heavens you asked before contacting her," he snorted, looking at Alex.

He turned to Olivia and the frown on his face disappeared. A sheepish grin crossed his face. "Actually, you can do me a big favor. Bertha gave me a shopping list a yard long. Would you mind?"

Olivia sighed with relief. "Oh, Father Duncan, I love to shop! I'll be happy to do it. Perhaps Alex can carry parcels."

He leaned back against the pillows and picked up his toast. "That would be a fine idea, Alex; just bring me some more reading material. Oh, and stop by the club, will you? I've written some notes and left them there. Being in the hospital will save me a lot of running around."

It was Christmas morning. For a moment, before Olivia remembered where she was, her thoughts were filled with sleigh bells and snow, the warm cinnamon smells of Sadie's kitchen.

But a gentle, "Merry Christmas, my darling!" brought her to reality.

Olivia rolled over and looked up into Alex's face. "Oh, Alex!" He handed her a tiny package topped with a silver bell. She jingled the bell softly. "And here we are, in Charleston, stuck in this hotel, while your mother celebrates Christmas by herself and your father—"

"Growls at the nurses. I had expected the doctor to relent and send Father home yesterday. He did look grave, and I certainly can't fault him for his concern. However, Father isn't an easy person to be around."

Alex bent down and kissed her. "I don't have any mistletoe, do you mind?"

"Not if you'll forgive me for not cooking a Christmas goose." She caught her breath as she opened the box and lifted out a pair of booties and silver spoon.

"I saw the look on your face after my silly remark to Father, and I want to apologize. I wasn't thinking. But neither was I considering a baby something to joke about."

She wiped the tears from her face and slipped her arms around his neck. "Alex, don't say more. I understand, and you didn't hurt me. I want your child desperately. But more than a baby, I want you. Please don't ever think I'd put a child before you."

He held her close and kissed her. "Olivia, I've seen your disappointment and talked to the Lord about it. I've asked for a baby, but it must be in His good time."

She nodded and blotted the last tear with the sheet. "Besides visiting your father, how shall we spend this Christmas day?"

"I have another surprise for you. When I took Father's last message into the club yesterday, I met a lovely lady—the most charming hostess in the city of Charleston, they tell me.

"Naturally, she was curious about the messages and the circumstances we are in. She wouldn't let me out the door until I'd promised to bring you to dine at her home today. There will be quite a crowd, and she insisted another couple wouldn't inconvenience her."

That evening in the stately Charleston home, surrounded by roses, mistletoe, candles, and towering Christmas trees, Alex and Olivia met Major Robert Anderson as their host introduced him to the other guests.

"Major Anderson is the officer in command of Fort Moultrie." Olivia looked from the United States Army uniform to the grave face.

He shook hands with Alex, and kissed Olivia's hand as she said, "Sir, the commanding officer at Ft. Moultrie! It is indeed a pleasure to meet you." For a moment his eyes flashed with interest and curiosity, but their host had his hand under Major Anderson's arm, leading him on.

During the evening, Olivia watched Alex meet the major's eyes on several occasions. Each time she saw the curious flash before his attention was claimed. The evening ended, and while they were at the door, Major Anderson also came and shook hands with Alex. "I'm deeply sorry we haven't had opportunity to get acquainted," Alex murmured. "May I say we'll be praying for you?"

The drawn features lifted in a smile. "Alexander Duncan, I appreciate that more than you'll ever know. Perhaps someday—" he paused and glanced down at the woman slipping her hand through his arm. With a brief nod, he left the house.

The day after Christmas, when they arrived at the hospital, they found Alex's father out of bed. Impatiently he pushed aside the newspapers and said, "Dr. Myers has released me to return home tomorrow. Now, Olivia, here's another list of items to be purchased. If you two will be here around noon with the carriage, I shall be ready to go." He took a deep breath and grinned. "There's nothing that makes a person appreciate good health more than being confined in such a place for nearly a week."

After breakfast the following day, Alex said, "We have all morning to ourselves. What would you like to do?"

"Not any more shopping!" Olivia moaned. "I've had enough to last me for the next year. But it's lovely outside. I would like to walk along the waterfront again before we leave."

The early morning wind had cleared the last wisp of mist, and the sun was warm on their faces. Olivia looked across the bay and remarked, "Look how the water sparkles."

"There seems to be a touch of excitement in the air today." Alex nodded in the direction of the people hurrying along the street. They crossed the street and started along the avenue bordering the waterfront.

Olivia glanced up. "Alex, look at the people standing on the balcony of the tall building just ahead of us."

"It appears they're using glasses to look at the harbor," Alex said. "I'd like to walk that way."

"Is that Fort Moultrie?"

"Yes, you can see it right off shore. The fortification to the south is Fort Sumter." He pointed out the line of shadows. "Too far away to see anything."

"That looks like smoke," Olivia murmured, but Alex had turned away to greet a young man hurrying past.

Tipping his hat the fellow said in a distinct British accent, "Jolly bit of excitement. Didn't expect a holiday to serve this kind of interest." He pointed toward the fort.

"The foxy Major Anderson has pulled out of Fort Moultrie during the night. If you look closely, you'll see smoke coming up. Abandoned the fort. It appears he's burned all he can't move and has taken refuge in Fort Sumter. See the folks up there?" He pointed.

"It was with a great deal of outrage that the citizens of Charleston apprehended his move. Some are saying it violates the agreement made with the government—with the Union. Pardon. For a moment I'd forgotten that Washington is now a foreign power."

"But just what has he done that's wrong?"

Olivia exclaimed, "Oh, look, there's a boat heading for the island!"

"Come, let's go up to the place where the others have gathered," the young man urged, lifting a leather case. "I've got my field glasses and shall be glad to share them with you."

When they reached the balcony a heated discussion was taking place. They heard, "Three cheers for the Union; it was rotten to make all those passes at the poor fellow."

"I say he has violated the agreement stipulated. This is an overt step toward starting war with us."

"Not so. Everyone knows Buchanan told the fellow to occupy either Fort Moultrie or Fort Sumter. If the deal was in his hands, we can't complain if he moved south for the winter."

There was a hoot of laughter, and the gentlemen beside him said, "It's the State of South Carolina who has made a bad move. If this leads to battle, she'll be blamed."

"Ridiculous! South Carolina's totally peaceable."

With a snort the man beside Olivia dropped his binoculars. "Peaceable! The city is crawling with troops, worse'n a flea-bit dog." He pointed at the harbor. "Now look, there's a ship moving toward Fort Sumter as fast as it can go."

"That fort is right in the entrance of the port. They can block the harbor if they receive reinforcements from Washington."

A sober face turned toward Alex. "Makes us look like a bunch of ninnies, sitting here with our hands folded. There's not a thing we can do. We daren't fire a shot, and they don't need to. They're sitting up there nice and cozy."

CHAPTER 7

Beth Peamble turned from the window with a sigh. "I've lived all my life in the South. This snow and cold is nearly more than I can endure. What do you people do during the winters?"

"Winter?" Sadie said thoughtfully as she put down the newspaper. "Why, all the things we don't have time for in the summer. The menfolk suffer most; we women stay inside. The river traffic comes to a stop."

Sadie roused herself and added, "Makes me think of Mike. Do wish we could hear from him. 'Twas was good to have the letter from Olivia, telling us all about the trip on the train and about Alex's family. His father sounds like a—" She pursed her mouth and wrinkled her brow, and eyeing Beth she weakly added, "strong-minded man. But his mother sounds like a very lovely person."

"A father like my father," Beth said with a touch of bitterness in her voice. Sadie folded her hands in her lap and waited. "A Southern father knows more about running a plantation than—"

Sadie waited again. The words burst out of Beth. "I don't suppose you want to hear about my home."

"Thou needn't justify thyself," she said. "We don't judge the past. Thou art welcome until thee chooses to leave."

For a moment Beth hesitated, and Sadie watched the changing shadows in her eyes. Abruptly she moved and said, "Since my mother died—"

"Oh, I'm sorry to hear that."

"Two years ago. Since then Father hasn't been easy to get along with. Y'all—" She paused and suddenly grinned. "All this business with the Quakers. It drives me wild to hear the language in church."

Sadie chuckled, "Thee dost not have Quakers in the South?"

"Not where I live." She eyed Sadie. "I know how you've been helping the slaves escape, but people like me—why do you take us all in? I know you took in Olivia and Alex as well as Mike Clancy."

Sadie studied the unhappy face of the girl and felt a squeeze of pity in her heart. She recognized the symptom as nearly a daily occurrence. "The Lord's laid it on us to do so. He's blessed us bountifully, and we feel the need to bless others."

Beth was silent as she watched the leaping flames of the open fire. Fingering the edge of the afghan on her chair, Sadie watched the glow of the fire intensify the brilliance of Beth's unruly curls. At the same time the light pointed out the petulant, unhappy twist on Beth's mouth. The low-cut cotton dress revealed too much of Beth's chilled flesh. "I believe we ought to find something warmer for thee to wear, a good woolen."

Beth's smile flashed. "Me? Coming from a cotton plantation and wearing wool?" The smile disappeared. "Besides, I hate sewing! I'd rather wear rags than stitch another terrible frock."

Sadie peered at her. "I didn't think Southern girls stitched anything but fancy work."

Beth's face flushed. "I—Mother thought it was needful." She jumped to her feet and started for the door. "I should be doing something."

"The dishes are clean and dinner is simmering on the stove."

"No, I mean something . . . to earn my way. I can't impose myself on you any longer."

"Well, if the problems continue to grow, thee wilt find a job most likely. Perhaps we'll all be put to work."

"Problems? What do you mean Sadie?"

"Nearly the end of January, it is, and look at this newspaper." She lifted the paper and pointed to the lines of bold print as she read. " 'Since the first of the year, in concert with the attempt to reinforce Fort Sumter, the Southern states have been tumbling out of the Union. To date this is the list of those who have joined South Carolina.' " She flipped the page. "Mississippi, Florida, Alabama, and now Georgia and Louisiana have gone out of the Union. They're expecting Texas to be added in February, and that's most of the cotton states.

"Poor foolish ones they are, taking action that can't be undone." Sadie sighed and folded the paper.

"Oh, don't take it so," Beth said. "Everyone in the South knows it's all just a push to get the North to give in."

"I'm a fearing it won't work this time; it's gone too far," Sadie said darkly, reaching for the paper again. "Horace Greeley's quoted right here, saying to Mr. Lincoln that he's fearing more than anything else that the North will back down and make a shameful compromise just to keep the Union together. He goes on to say such action would disgrace the Union to the place we'd never be able to lift our heads again."

Beth studied Sadie's face. "You sound as if you like Mr. Lincoln, but I know Amos didn't vote for him."

"I like him, but he's a disappointment to us Quakers. They called him a black Republican, but I don't see him as caring that much for the slaves. I'm of the opinion he will straddle the fence. He's said over and over he'll not set the Negroes free. The work done to get the Republican Party started in the first place was for the purpose of winning freedom for the slaves."

Beth was silent for a long time. Sadie watched her, noting that she appeared ready to speak and then seemed to change her mind. Finally she said, "The fellows in town were talking about getting up a state militia, just in case there's a battle. Sadie, do you think there's going to be a war?"

Sadie picked up her knitting and took three stitches before answering. "I don't know, but I get a shivery feeling down inside when I think about it." She looked at Beth. "If there is, wilt thou go back to the South?"

"Father wouldn't welcome me," she whispered. "He told me if I left, I couldn't return."

"Seems a sad way to treat a young lady," she glanced at Beth, saw her uneasy, quick glance. Sadie knitted in silence.

Finally Beth said, "It seems there's just nothing to do except get married." Sadie dropped a stitch.

As she concentrated on recovering it, Beth walked restlessly around the room.

When the stitch was safely on the needle, Beth stopped beside Sadie and said, "The problem is I wouldn't want a Northern fellow; I can't cook or anything."

"You could learn." Sadie's voice was muffled as she bent over her knitting. "Olivia did."

"A Southern girl would have to love a man terribly to go that far.

I don't think I could. But then the best thing would be to find a rich man."

She sat on the stool at Sadie's feet. "Sadie, are there any rich, single men in Pennsylvania?"

"There's a farmer over in the next county. I hear he owns most of the land in that end of the state. Has livestock. He's a widower. They said his wife didn't lack for anything." She glanced up and saw Beth's face brighten, then added, "Heard his wife died from pneumonia last winter. Got it milking cows in January."

Beth shuddered. "I can't milk cows," she said as she left the room.

Sadie watched her go. *Pretty as a picture,* she thought, *but I don't want our Mike Clancy tangled up with the likes of her. At least, not unless she comes around to getting close to the Lord like Olivia did. From the way she talks, there's little indication she's tender-hearted. At least it seems unlikely unless I do a lot of praying.* She paused, pursed her mouth, and grinned. *Might be a good idea to ask the Lord to be finding Mike a good girl, so I can pray for Beth without the added worry of Mike falling for her.*

Thinking of the way Mike had behaved just before the last trip south, Sadie sighed, "Might be too late, Lord."

On the sixth of March, Amos came into the kitchen expecting to find his dinner. He found Sadie hunched over the newspaper spread on the surface of the table. "Do we eat inauguration news today?"

With a sigh she looked up. "Thou art early. There's soup from last night heating on the back of the cookstove. I'll slice some bread for thee. But Amos, listen to this. 'From the lack of long hair in the crowd packed elbow to elbow for the inauguration of President Lincoln yesterday, it appears only Southerners absented themselves from the glorious affair. From New York to California, as well as Vermont and down the Ohio, people flocked to the nation's capital to see the inauguration of the President. Some visitors still carried carpetbags, for there were more visitors to the capital than hotel rooms available. . . . Mr. Lincoln rose at five o'clock this morning. He partook of a light breakfast while his inaugural speech was read to him. . . .'"

Sadie looked up. "Makes thee think thou art right there. They said the day before, visitors packed the Senate chambers to listen to debates. Must have been interesting."

She sighed and moved the newspapers as Amos carried the soup to the table. "I think we'll all end up liking Lincoln, no matter what he does about the slaves." She looked at him and added, "It also mentioned Quakers from Pennsylvania being there at the inauguration. Here's a comment on Mr. Lincoln's speech. It says the President of the United States took an oath to 'preserve, protect, and defend the government.' Mr. Lincoln added he intended to do just that." Sadie folded the paper and said, "I'll look forward to getting a complete copy of his speech."

In late March, Amos came into the kitchen while Sadie and Beth were preparing dinner. "Heard in town that the ice has broken on the Ohio. Might be that Mike'll be coming back pretty soon. His last letter sounded uneasy about the squabbling in Tennessee. Said folks were mighty touchy, and the possibility of bringing more slaves out was unlikely. So I'll not be looking for a crowd with him."

Sadie nodded over the pan as she stirred. She had seen the way Beth's eyes brightened when Amos mentioned Mike. Staring into the soup, she chided herself for being full of suspicion.

As they sat down at the table, Amos looked at Sadie with a troubled frown. "The newspaper hints at a continued rumble coming from the South. I'm wondering about Alex and Olivia. Haven't heard from them for over a month now. It'll feel mighty good to have them home again."

Sadie left the table and went to the parlor, saying, "I think I'm hearing voices. A few minutes ago I thought I heard splashes in the river. I dismissed it, thinking it was the young'uns. Now—"

They all heard the sharp rap at the door and Beth flew past Sadie. It was Mike, his roustabouts, and three passengers. Sadie pulled them into the house. As she headed for the kitchen, she saw Mike and Beth in the hallway, smiling at each other.

The next morning when Mike carried his coffee to the table, he addressed Sadie with a troubled frown. "I wrote to Olivia and Alex, but didn't hear from them. I have a feeling they didn't receive my letter. Could cause problems for them, since we'd agreed I'd stay there until they returned this spring. When they left last fall, their intention was to spend the winter with his kin and return to Vicksburg in time to make a trip further south. Of course, that's out of the question now. The South has the Mississippi heavily guarded right now."

"Guarded?" Sadie asked.

He nodded. "It isn't supposed to look like war, but they're keeping their eyes on every vessel on the Mississippi. If—maybe I should say *when*—there's trouble, they intend to keep the Mississippi under control." He sipped his coffee and added, "I'm inclined to think, from listening to the people, that there's not just slaves running; some of the pro-Union whites are also leaving." He glanced at Beth. "It appears there's a major final push to get out of the South."

He waited a moment and then said, "If you have any desire to go home, Beth, this may be the last opportunity."

"How would I get there?"

"I believe you could make it by railroad. I could take you down the Tennessee River and let you take a train from there."

She shook her head. When she lifted her face, there was a small smile visible. "I closed the doors behind me when I left. Father told me I wouldn't be allowed to come home. I guess I'm an orphan now." The words were jaunty, but her smile seemed bitter.

Mike touched her clenched fist. "You know Sadie and Amos will always have a place for you."

"I can't impose forever." She got to her feet and carried dishes to the dishpan. Turning she looked at Mike. "I may find a place up here where I can earn my keep." She made a wry face. "What do ex-Southern belles do to earn a living?"

CHAPTER 8

Alex and Olivia reached the hospital to find Alex's father holding court from his bed. A cluster of dark suited figures surrounded him.

The group stepped back as they approached. "Father, has something happened?" Alex asked.

"No," he said impatiently. "I was just taking a nap when these gentlemen stopped by to tell me the latest piece of news. I suppose you've heard Anderson moved his troops to Fort Sumter during the night."

He waved his hand abruptly. "I haven't had time to get up and dress. However, I must finish my meeting. Gentlemen, I would like to present my son and his wife, Olivia. Now let's get along with the meeting."

The men moved uneasily. One detached himself from the circle and approached Alex and Olivia. "I'm Thorton Hudson." Gravely he said, "This is a very uncomfortable situation. I say this to you because I know you've been living in the North and possibly have some Northern sympathy.

"Unfortunately, the situation has deteriorated drastically. Major Anderson chose to move his men."

Olivia glanced at Alex, saw the white line of his lips as his father said, "Jefferson Davis has headed for the White House to see President Buchanan and make known our displeasure with the situation."

Thoughtfully, Mr. Hudson added, "Moultrie was clearly non-threatening, but Sumter is another matter. In addition to blocking the harbor, they're completely fortified."

"We saw the incident," Alex said, "including the boat moving in on the fort just as Old Glory was raised and the cannon discharged." Seeing the discomfort on the circle of faces, Olivia carefully nudged Alex with her toe. Alex turned toward the bed. "Father, shall we come back later?"

"No," he sighed regretfully. "I'll dress and join you quickly. It is starting to look as if there's nothing more to be accomplished." He turned, "Gentlemen, will you do me the favor of keeping me informed of all that transpires, and dispatching the information to me, including the enemy's newspapers?"

As the carriage left Charleston, Olivia felt her tension begin to ease. She relaxed against the cushions and watched the winter landscape.

Alex and his father were deep in conversation when the carriage turned down the avenue shaded by spreading live oaks. Grateful for their quiet conversation, Olivia leaned against the doorpost and eagerly studied the plantation Alex had described to her.

As they reached the house at the end of the lane, she saw it was comfortable rather than pretentious. There were mellow gray shingles, deep windows, wide stone chimneys, and shady verandas with sturdy balconies supporting fragrant bittersweet. The scene spread feelings of home around her.

When the carriage stopped, Olivia found it easy to smile as she stepped down to greet the little round woman who stood on the veranda. Olivia had one glimpse of a snowy pile of curls topping a serene face before Bertha Duncan hugged her. "Oh my dear, what a lovely wife my Alex has!"

Olivia watched Alex sweep the woman up in his arms before he turned to her. "Olivia, come get acquainted; I can guarantee you'll love each other."

After his father had been settled in bed, Alex took Olivia down to the library. Looking around the familiar room, he said, "Father hasn't changed a thing since I've left. His complete set of Shakespeare is still in the same place. And so is Aristotle, still looking as if the pages have never been touched."

He grinned at Olivia. "If we were to stay in the South, I might have time to do more reading."

"Oh, Alex! It is a lovely home, of course, but—"

"I was teasing. But since we're going to be here for the winter, you might as well get acquainted with the rest of the place. Father has some wonderful horses." He smiled down at her as he took her hand. "While we have all this free time, let's enjoy his stables."

In the isolation of the inland plantation, January quickly slipped past. Except for the newspapers, Olivia could have forgotten the troubles pushing at their door. With dismay they read of the escalating secession. One after another the cotton states were marching out of the Union to join South Carolina in the newly formed Confederacy.

Late in the month, on a cold, rainy day, Alex returned from Charleston with more newspapers and a portfolio of papers for his father. Olivia was in the library gleaning bits of information from the discarded pile of papers on the table.

She looked up as he came into the room. "Father is in his bedroom. Alex, I have the impression he isn't as well as he would like to believe." She kissed him, warming his ears with her hands.

Alex nodded. "I agree. I'll take these things up to him and talk to you later."

When he returned to the room he said, "Today looks like a good day to start on Aristotle."

Her dismayed face appeared over the top of the newspaper. "Alex, when the world is falling apart, how can you think of Aristotle?"

"Actually, I wanted to know whether or not you had gone to sleep behind that newspaper."

"They're very informative," she murmured. "I wanted to read them quickly before your Father discovers their content and burns them."

"He hasn't seen them?" He sat down beside her and peered over her shoulder.

"For some reason, they didn't make it upstairs. I found them in the trash basket."

"Tim must have thought he'd read them. Maybe it's just as well. Father isn't lacking for reading material."

"Alex," Olivia said slowly, "this paper from Washington says Scott sent two hundred soldiers and supplies to Anderson on a private vessel called *Star of the West*. Word of his action leaked, and the ship was fired upon by South Carolina artillery. This happened January 9th." She dropped the paper. "Fired upon! Alex, how terrible."

"Father knows about that. We've had quite a discussion. But there's something else to consider, Olivia. If *Star of the West* had been armed, they also could have fired. That's how close we came to starting a war."

"Events are happening at an alarming rate. Alex, what shall we do?"

Alex shook his head and sighed. "We came to mend fences with Father, but it isn't happening. He's more stubborn, more insistent on the states' rights issue than he's ever been. Olivia, I can't convince my parents to feel the way we do."

"What about slavery? Alex, if your Father would only seek the Lord Jesus Christ with all his heart, then I'd feel we had accomplished all that's necessary. Surely the Lord would change his mind."

"Olivia, my parents consider themselves to be true followers of Christ; they also claim to care deeply about their slaves and to be concerned about their welfare. What if Father never changes his opinion about slavery? Can we say they aren't Christian? I've heard Lincoln quoted as saying he recognizes the fact that Southerners read the same Bible, serve the same Lord. He added we will all be judged by the same God, both the Southerners and the Northerners. Lincoln says the will of God prevails, even while each side claims to know the will of God. I agree with him, even in the unstated idea behind it: we are responsible for our own beliefs and actions." Alex stared at the floor.

Olivia touched the brooch at her neckline as she heard him say, "Life calls for decisions. Sometimes we make them without giving a moment's thought. There are decisions we can't back out of. Sometimes we'd like to forget them. But the more deeply involved we are, the more impossible it is to retreat. I guess a good decision carries moral responsibility."

She saw the shadow in his eyes and thought, *We helped the slaves. Now there will be a war, and Alex knows he must fight.*

South Carolina was beginning to come alive. Soft green surrounded the burst of blossoms. The newly budded trees were visible from the balcony door opening off Olivia's bedroom, and the breeze coming through the door bore a gentle, rain-cleansed air filled with the scent of spring.

Walking back and forth, Olivia paused to breathe deeply of the perfumed air. She closed her eyes, shutting out all except the scent of spring, and felt the tension in her body momentarily ease.

The door opened and Alex came in. "The newspaper. Does it have a good story about Lincoln's inauguration?"

"No. Total silence," she answered. "How sad to see President Lincoln being treated this way. I would have loved being there. I closed my eyes and put myself there in front of the Capitol, listening to his speech."

Alex nodded. "The South's attitude toward the inauguration is sending out frightening signals. I've been talking to Mother," he continued. "She's trying to coax Father into seeing a doctor."

Slowly shaking her head, Olivia said, "I can't understand him."

"I think I do. First, he doesn't want to face the facts. He's having heart problems, and he is convinced that if he ignores the symptoms, they'll disappear. It hasn't helped to have us talk about returning to Pennsylvania this month. I feel he's determined to keep us here."

"Perhaps it would be best to delay our going," Olivia said slowly. "I've noticed, after his initial curiosity about your earring, he's shown only scorn when you mention God. I would feel terribly disappointed if we were to leave and something were to happen to him. Alex, you two have done little except argue the right and wrong of the situation at Fort Sumter."

"I know," Alex said. "I should be able to find a better way to communicate with him."

"Alex, we need to pray for patience, and we need to ask God for the opportunity to talk about why we are living as we do."

"I've tried to bring up the subject, but there are other things on his mind. Olivia, I'm his only son. You know what that means?"

With a smile and a sigh of exasperation she nodded, "You are his heir. I've heard him. He wants to see you remain here, take over the plantation, and carry on the tradition, just as he did for his father. Oh, Alex, it's as if we are going around in circles with him! I didn't dream things would turn out this way."

With a rueful grin, Alex dropped into the chair. "I was afraid it would be this way, but I expected him to at least hear me out. I still haven't told him how we've spent the past two years. I think he has some vague idea that we've been enjoying life on his money, and now it's time to get to work."

She paused and glanced down at the brooch. "When you gave me this," she said, fingering the gold filigree, "you showed me that verse in Isaiah, 'The Lord God will cause righteousness and praise to spring forth before all the nations.' It's humbling. The Lord causes the changes; there's nothing I—we can do. It's His place to act, not ours."

Alex wrapped his arms around her. "Yes, he's in control of all this. We know so little of His plan."

"Nearly every Sunday since we've been here, we've heard the rightness of the Southern cause preached from the pulpit. Perhaps in God's eyes we are all wrong, all arrogant, and all in need of repentance."

"But when will repentance come? Will it be too late?"

"To save the Union? Can we expect God to rescue us from our folly when folly is hatched from our stubborn right to choose our own way?"

Slowly Olivia sat down and examined her hands. "I don't understand, Alex. We know slavery is wrong; why can we see this so clearly, and at the same time they see their situation with the same clear vision? We are at an impasse. Is God obligated to solve the problems we have created? Will he keep us from—"

"From killing each other before there's repentance and humility?"

"Repentance? How can you repent of something that is right?"

Slowly Alex shook his head. "The only real _right_ I know in this whole situation is that these people deserve freedom and a chance to live just as we live."

"Your father has over a hundred slaves," Olivia said slowly. "It will ruin him if he must free them."

"Olivia, remember that God loves us all very much, and He loves the South just as much as He loves the North. Psalms says, 'The earth is full of his unfailing love.' " Alex walked to the door and turned. "We must remember that God loves the Negro slave. Somehow, I have the feeling this love for the slave will have a great influence on who wins the war!"

"I hope you are successful in convincing your father of this."

"Right now I have another problem to fight," he said, his voice muffled. "How does a Christian point a gun at a man and pull the trigger? How does he deliberately kill another human over a situation which should be handled with words, not war?"

The door closed behind Alex. Olivia bent double in her chair and hugged her trembling legs against her chest. "Dear God, the Union is torn apart right down the middle. It seems every day one more state moves into their camp, and the possibility of war is beginning to seem horribly real. And my husband—will this tear him apart, physically and emotionally?" She paused. In the silence there was only the painful beating of her heart.

That evening at dinner, Alex said, "Father, Mother, we need to be returning to Pennsylvania."

Olivia watched disappointment crumple the face of the white-haired woman as she looked at Alex. "Olivia, please talk sense into your husband," she said. "At least he will listen to you. We need you both desperately. You can see Father isn't well."

Olivia put her fork on the plate and leaned forward. Softly she said, "We know. But Father needs to see a doctor more than he needs Alex here. You know we have the boat and pilot waiting in Vicksburg."

"We'll plan to leave the fifteenth of this month. April is a good time to travel across Georgia and Alabama," Alex continued. Turning to his mother he added, "Pennsylvania is a lovely place; you'd like it. I wish you two would sell the plantation and find a home away from the fever belt."

"Sell?" Mr. Duncan straightened in his chair. "I'd rather turn the place over to your sister's lazy husband than to sell."

Bertha Duncan's voice was drawn with tension as she said, "You know that Mr. Mallory has been at you to sell out to him, why—"

"The scoundrel is offering just half what it's worth," he snarled. "Now that the South has made the move she should have made thirty years ago, he thinks to get rich at my expense!"

"Father, I must say this—" Alex paused to push away from the table. "You are gambling that the North will continue to allow secession. I say it won't."

"I suppose you are going to quote Lincoln again," his father's voice was heavy.

"No, Father, this time it's Douglas. Just before the election he went South to the people. He warned them against entertaining any thought of secession. Over and over he said the whole of the North will rise up to prevent the Union being torn apart.

"Father, we haven't heard the last of this. I'm becoming more afraid for this nation. Yesterday I spent the day reading the Constitutional documents. I agree with every voice coming out of the North. The Constitution doesn't support the action the South has taken. It is treason. Also, if Washington doesn't take action soon, the North will cry out against the new administration."

Mr. Duncan leaned his hands against the table. "For most of my adult life, the South has been pushing her cause against the North. Just you watch; they'll give us everything we ask for. I predict that before the year is out, we will be in control of Washington, either by default or by design!"

"And if you are wrong," Alex added, "you will be ruined." He got to his feet. "Father, I don't like opposing you. I wish you would take your pattern for living from the Lord Jesus Christ rather than the men around you."

For a moment Mr. Duncan looked astonished, and then he laughed. "It is hilarious to think of the impact I would have! Don't you see, Son? We are moving forward with confidence and trust in God . . . in the rightness of our cause, simply because we've long understood what is right."

"Father, today's newspaper says Lincoln has informed South Carolina of his intentions to resupply Fort Sumter with provisions. Another article from Alabama called for action from South Carolina. It sounds as if Alabama agrees war is necessary."

Mr. Duncan laughed. "War? I'll agree that the hot-heads have been *saying* this, but it *won't* happen."

————

The following morning, a sealed dispatch lay on top of the newspaper beside Mr. Duncan's plate. Olivia watched her father-in-law slit the envelope, blanch, and slowly sit down.

Alex came into the room. "Father, is it bad news?"

"No, but it is surprising news. I never expected this." He touched the envelope and looked up at Alex. "Jefferson Davis has ordered Beauregard to take Fort Sumter before the relief fleet arrives. Lincoln threw down the gauntlet—war or peace. President Jefferson Davis has decreed war."

Alex's mother had been standing in the doorway. Now she dropped her hand from her throat and came into the room. Stretching her hands toward Alex and Olivia, she said, "My dears, now you must stay. Only here will you be safe."

The steam rose from the silver coffee urn, and sunlight flicked prisms of lavender and pink from the crystal. Olivia watched a slender black hand reach out with its offering of hot muffins. Alex spoke. "We will stay, but you must know the reason. Newspaper articles from North and South have left one remarkable fact stamped on my mind. Union feeling is strong in the South. I am Southern. It is in my blood, and strangely it stirs my loyalties, no matter how much I abhor slavery. I'll stay as long as I can find a listening ear."

"What do you intend to do, Son?"

"Take my plea to every head of state I can find. Before there is war between the states, there must be war in the states. We must shake down every wrong idea and decide whether or not we want to accept the consequences of war. I'm convinced this is one question the South hasn't considered."

"Son, knowing the Southerners as you do, are you expecting success?"

Slowly Alex said, "You are reminding me that they'd rather fight than compromise? That war is inevitable? That the North will be intimidated by the strong military background of the South, and yield without bloodshed? Father, there is Union feeling in the South, but in the North the Union principle is stronger than life. Remember the stories of the Revolutionary War? That same feeling is still alive."

"But it is also here! We'll die before we capitulate." Abruptly he sank back in his chair. "You know you'll be fighting against everything I believe in. Do you expect me to harbor an enemy in my home?"

"Father, I'm not fighting just for the Union; I'm also trying to gain another opportunity for you and your neighbors to win this conflict in the only honorable, and profitable way. True, it will cost you."

"And what is the cost?" the senior Duncan asked heavily.

"The handwriting on the wall says that before this is over, all of you will be required to free your slaves, unless you do it now. I believe war can still be averted. It frightens me to think of the alternative."

"Free my slaves? That is financial suicide. You're asking me to gamble on the North winning! Never would I be so foolish."

The sun shifted from the table to the carpet before Mr. Duncan spoke again. "I will risk the loss of all before I'll bow to your suggestion."

CHAPTER 9

At noon Mike came into the kitchen. Sadie glanced up, saw his grin, and commented, "Thee hast been up to something."

"I have a job. Henry Peterson needs a pilot for a tug. We'll be floating barges down the Ohio. Barrels of oil, steel, and some coal."

"Seems a comedown after helping people to freedom."

"I know. But I can't sit around all spring waiting for Alex and Olivia to return." Just as Beth came into the kitchen he added, "I'll clear out my room. No sense cluttering up the place with my junk when I'll be gone most of the time."

Beth walked around the table to face him. "Where are you going?"

Mike shoved his hands into his pockets, teetering on his heels. Looking down at Beth, he said, "I'll be escorting barges down the Ohio to Cairo."

She went to take the plates from Sadie. "We'll miss you; it could get lonesome around here. Too bad they don't hire women." She slanted a glance at him and brushed past with the dishes. "With the fussing in the South," Beth continued, "it's hard to decide what to do. Maybe I'll consider going into Philadelphia to look for a position."

"Hadn't ought to do that," he said slowly. "With the unrest and the state militia forming, doesn't seem right for a single lady to be there without a—brother or some such to look out for her."

Beth's eyes flared. "I can take care of myself."

"Missus Thatcher told me they're looking for a girl to work in the hardware store in the village," Sadie interjected. "Won't pay as much as the city, but thee won't have the expense of renting a room. Terribly lonesome it would be if all of thee be gone."

Mike's grin widened. "Sadie can shoo off all the fellas she doesn't approve of." He continued to smile down at Beth. When Sadie saw the blush starting on Beth's cheeks, she pursed her mouth and bustled to the stove.

"Mike, thee could tell Amos dinner is ready. Beth, will thee carry the cornbread to the table?" Sadie added, "Beth, child, thou art more than welcome here. I hope it will not be too lonely with Mike gone."

Sadie paused. "The tide of feeling is rising. There is talk of war growing stronger each day. I do not know how Lincoln will respond, but my heart aches for the young. They will be the ones to suffer."

Beth's eyes were troubled. "But will I be welcome here in the North? Everyone knows I'm from the South."

"Thy mouth will make or break thy welcome." Beth looked puzzled, and Sadie explained. "If thee takes sides and speaks badly against all the North holds dear, thou wilt gain enemies."

Amos and Mike came into the kitchen. Amos looked from Beth to Sadie. "Had to carry some wood into the village. There's news. Jefferson Davis has made his decision. He ordered General Beauregard to fire upon Fort Sumter. 'Twas over thirty hours of shelling, with the fort nearly destroyed before Major Anderson surrendered. Sadie, my dear, I fear war has begun."

"Did Lincoln say this?"

"No, but I did."

"And everyone else in the North is saying it, too," Mike added as he pulled out the chair for Beth.

They bowed their heads to pray for the meal. For once, Sadie noticed Beth was quiet and thoughtful when Amos said, "Amen."

"That newspaper said President Lincoln has called for seventy-five thousand militiamen," Sadie said. "But he wants them for only ninety days. Does he expect the war to be over then?"

Mike looked up. "It sounds like it."

"According to the newspapers," Sadie said slowly, "feeling in the South has been harsh. I cannot believe even Lincoln will make the people change their mind in just three months. Too bad, he said such nice things about not being enemies with the South when he was inaugurated."

"I don't think changing their mind has much to do with it," Mike said thoughtfully. "Most people hang on to their feelings longer than that." He looked at Beth. "If he doesn't convince the South that war is a bad idea, then he'll need to convince the whole world that the North is stronger than the South."

"Do you believe that is so?" Amos asked.

"No!" Mike and Beth spoke together.

Beth said, "Southerners are proud people. They will fight rather than yield."

Mike nodded. "I've spent enough time in the South to know that Southerners are fighting men. They settle their quarrels with fists and pistols."

"Many of our young men attend military academies," Beth said, "even when they've no intention of having a career in the military."

————

The following week Mike left on his first trip as the pilot of a smart little tug escorting a line of barges down the Ohio.

Beth took the job at the hardware store. Each evening she returned home full of the sights and sounds of the village.

Mike had been gone for nearly a month when Sadie started to see a change in Beth, an independent spirit growing in her. Amos noticed too; he said, "Beth, you are better than a newspaper. So the young ones are beginning to seriously consider the war talk?"

Beth nodded as she carried the bowl of green beans to the table. "At first," she said, "they were treating the whole thing like a lark. But lately there's more serious talk.

"Pennsylvania's filled their quota for militia," she reported, "such is the enthusiasm for war. The Quakers are against war—" She threw a glance at Sadie. "So are some of the coal miners. Young men from the whole county have taken up soldiering in Mr. Cassaway's meadow."

Sadie listened to her chatter and noted the excitement in her eyes. "Where do all these young men stay?"

"Those who live close by return home at night, but those from the far end of the state have set up a regular city of tents around the meadow. They cook their dinners there and string their washing all over the meadow."

Amos lifted his face from reading the newspaper. "No doubt they'll be put to the test. Says here that Missouri, Tennessee, and Kentucky won't send their men to fight for the Union. Sounds like they'll be seceding. This article also lists more states seceding—Virginia, North Carolina, and Arkansas."

"A fellow from Virginia claims the dividing line between Union and Confederacy must be slavery, not North and South," Sadie commented. "I thought all in the South were for slavery; now I understand there's some talk of even Delaware being soft on slavery."

Beth shook her head. "Some people in the South own slaves and live in big houses, but not very many. It is only—" she slanted a look at Sadie, hesitated, and slowly said, "the people who are refined."

"Refined?" Sadie said blankly.

"Cultured; those who want the finer things in life and come from good families. Those with money."

"Oh." Sadie went to the stove after the hot rhubarb pie.

Amos watched her and then turned to Beth. "What do you call the other people?"

Beth shrugged, bit her lip, and finally said, "They are farmers. Poor people, I suppose."

"What about the factory workers, those who live in towns?"

"Factory workers?" Beth echoed. "Why, I've never met any of them. I would suppose they are poor too."

"Are they in favor of slavery? Do they believe in it so badly that they'll fight for it?"

"Sir," Beth said slowly, "I honestly don't know. I don't know any except my own kind of people."

Amos returned to the newspaper. "Seems someone ought to be considering how the others feel about slavery and war. These others just might be the ones who have to do the fighting when they really get into it."

Sadie watched the frown lift from Beth's face. "Amos, that could be so. Maybe the war won't last long with poor people fighting. They have other matters to tend to, like planting."

———

When Mike came home for the first time, he carried news. Sitting at the table with Sadie and Amos he sipped coffee. "Your coffee is reason enough for a body to not leave home." Then sobering he added, "Looks like we'll all be leaving home, badly as we want to stay."

He faced the questions in Sadie's eyes. "I've been down to Cairo this last trip and seen the changes. Wouldn't surprise me if some strong fighting takes place down the Mississippi pretty soon. Guess I did right to come on home with the *Awl* when I did."

The back door opened and Beth came into the kitchen. As she pulled the scarf from her head, she saw Mike. "You're back," she said softly, pushing her long hair away from her face. Sadie saw Mike's face and turned to watch the girl, wondering how she could fail to see the expression in Mike's eyes.

When Mike didn't answer, Beth looked up, blushed, and brushed at her hair. "I've been riding the little filly into town to my job. I took the clerking job at the hardware store. I'll be back in a minute." She dashed toward the stairs.

Sadie bit her tongue, but the words came anyway. "Mike, don't go to setting thine heart on such as her. She's flighty; I know the kind. She'll break thy heart and then look for another to break."

"I know," he muttered, moving his cup around in circles. "I know the kind, too. Besides, I could never afford to keep one such as she is— a lady." Sadie listened to his words, thinking that the expression in his eyes seemed to speak differently.

Beth whirled into the kitchen. She had changed her dress. With a swish of her full skirts, she went to help Sadie. "There's frolicking in town tonight," she informed Sadie. "A fair with games and music and food to eat. It's meant to show a good time to the fellows."

"What fellows?"

"The lads who've been learning how to be soldiers. The townspeople got this up. A thank you and a sendoff. They're raising money, too, selling pies and such. Even handiwork to raise money for uniforms and arms for the men." She paused, examining Sadie's expression. "I know you believe it's wrong to fight. Do you believe in helping them?"

Sadie shuddered. "Buy bullets and guns? No, my child. I couldn't live with myself. I'll be ready when the lads need cookies and new socks."

"Beth, do you want to go?" Mike got to his feet. "I'll take you into town. After all, a young lady can't go alone." He grinned down at her.

Sadie saw the frown start on Beth's face, but abruptly she smiled. "That would be nice. I know a girl who is very anxious to meet you."

After dinner, Mike harnessed Amos's old mare to the light buggy and brought it around to the door. Beth dashed out the door and was in the buggy before Mike could get out. She was breathless as she said, "Thanks so much, Mike. I wanted to go badly, but without you asking, I couldn't have gone. It's terrible to have these people frown at me all the time."

"All the time?"

"Oh, Mike. They just don't understand young people having a good time. All of us girls are earnest about giving these fellows a good send-off. Might be some of them won't come back if there's a real battle—" She caught her breath.

"Beth," he said carefully, "it isn't that Amos and Sadie don't want you to have a good time, it's just that—" He paused, suddenly realizing the gap that existed between Beth and himself. "We believe these kinds of frolics are not—healthy."

"Mike!" she turned to stare at him, "I didn't think you believed like they do."

"We think that the Christians should not participate in some of what will pass as entertainment tonight. It might be that Amos and Sadie are wiser than you give them credit for being. Anyway," he grinned at her, "I'm here to keep you safe, so we might as well enjoy it."

By the time Mike had found a place to leave the horse and buggy, Beth had blended into the crowd. He found her at the horseshoe pitching booth. He also saw the young man beside her. Mike noticed the uniform first, and he saw Beth's flaming hair and pale face nearly touching the shoulder of the smiling soldier.

Mike hesitated, shrugged and walked toward the couple. Beth turned with a smile. "Oh, Mike, I want you to meet Lieutenant Roald Fairmont." She nodded at the lieutenant. "This is Michael Clancy. He's the fellow who's been piloting cargo downriver." Linking her arms through theirs she smiled, saying, "We're going to have a wonderful time! There's dancing and games. Mike, did you see all the booths? I should think they'll raise money galore."

Mike acknowledged Fairmont's stiff greeting and asked, "How long is this fair to be going on?"

"Until the end of the week." She turned to Roald. "Do you want to go down to the square? There's dancing."

He nodded and they were about to excuse themselves when they were interrupted. "Mike—oh, Mike Clancy!" Mike turned toward the voice. It was the butcher's daughter, calling and waving as she came toward him.

She was still gasping for breath as he said, "Tessie Coiles, is the market on fire?"

"No, but I need your help desperately," she pleaded as Mike blinked in surprise. "Please don't turn me down. Several of the fellows were to help set up tables and cook sausages, and they haven't come. Will you—"

"Certainly I'll help." He followed as she turned to dash back the way she had come.

Mike set up tables while Tessie covered them with checked oilcloth and set pots of mustard in the middle. Later he went to the makeshift firepit and turned sausages while she stuffed buns with the savory, sizzling meat.

The crowd had thinned and the embers were turning to ash when Tessie turned to him. "Mike, you'll have to eat this last one."

Following him to the table, she put down the tankard of lemonade and sat down on the other side of the table. She shoved the mustard pot toward him. " 'Twas nervy of me to take advantage of your kindness, especially since I scarcely know you. Have seen you around town, and at church sometimes."

"I enjoyed myself," Mike admitted. "I was starting to feel like a third wheel when you rescued me."

She nodded. "I know Beth's wanting to snatch as much time as she can with Roald. She's smitten, and it's no wonder. Wouldn't any girl go for such as he?"

Uneasily Mike studied the sausage. "Has she been seeing him for some time?"

"Oh, yes. Since he first came to help around here they've been stepping out together. He hasn't had any competition. Everyone knows Beth is his girl." She paused, studied him curiously, and added, "I thought you knew, since you've both been living at the Coopers. Hope I'm not causing any problems."

Mike took another bite of the sausage, drank some lemonade, and answered, "No, I haven't kept in touch with Beth since I've been off hauling barges."

"It's starting to look like we can't keep out of war with the South," she said slowly. "Are you going to join up to fight?"

"I don't know. I'm still struggling with it. I guess I have a Quaker conscience. Right now I see myself contributing by piloting the tug. Maybe that's all I'll get around to doing if the war's a ninety-day affair."

"Do you really think it will be?"

"No." He gave her a quick glance. "I've been pretty far south in the past year, and I don't like what I've been seeing and hearing."

"Such as?"

"The rumblings of discontent against the North, and there's no bones made about the feelings. They're making the most of it." He glanced at her, realized she didn't understand, and tried to explain. "The feeling's been drummed up by the nice-looking fellows standing on soapboxes and giving it out to all who'll listen. Speeches heard over and over begin to have an effect. It isn't a message of brotherly love and kindness that many people in the South are hearing."

He drank the last of the lemonade and stood up. "I see Beth heading this way. The moon's settled just beyond the trees; it's time to collect my passenger and head homeward. Thank you, Miss Tessie, for an enjoyable evening."

"Oh, there you are," Beth said coolly. "I hope you two had a good evening. I'm exhausted; Roald and I danced until our feet nearly fell off."

"Oh," Tessie said, "I haven't heard the music for nearly an hour." She gathered up Mike's dishes and ducked her head shyly. "Thank you, and good evening to you both."

CHAPTER 10

The oppressive heat and humidity drew Olivia from her chair to the library window. As soon as she pushed aside the heavy draperies to allow a breeze, she saw Alex. For a moment she could only watch, aware of the scene pressing against her heart. The horse walked slowly and Alex slumped in the saddle—a strong message of defeat and discouragement.

After watching a moment longer, she crossed the room to where Alex's parents rocked their chairs in unison. Young slave girls wielding palm leaf fans tried to stir the heavy air. She looked from the perspiration on the girls' faces to the flushed, weary couple in the chairs. "Alex is home. He's just coming down the lane. I'm going to the stable to meet him."

"Let Claude take care of the horse," Mr. Duncan said impatiently, moving his face to catch the breeze.

"You know Alex. He won't be content with turning his horse over after this long ride," Olivia answered as she passed their chairs and walked down the hall to the kitchen entrance.

Alex pulled the saddle from his mount just as she entered the stable. "Hello, my dear," he murmured with a wan smile.

"You're exhausted. Let me take your saddlebag." She lifted her face for his kiss.

He shook his head, "I don't want to touch you until I've been up to my neck in cool water. It seems I'd forgotten how beastly the heat is in South Carolina." A black youth appeared at Alex's elbow. "Tim, take this mare to the pasture. She's had all the water she needs." He turned to follow Olivia.

"Alex, go to the bath house; I'll bring clean clothes for you. Would you like something to eat?"

He shook his head. "Lemonade would be fine." She watched him turn into the bath house beside the kitchen door.

When Olivia came back with the tall glass of lemonade and a change of clothing for Alex, she found him submerged in the big tin bathtub. He looked at her with a twinkle in his eye. "And now you're huffing and puffing with the heat. Why didn't you ask Lucy to help?"

She stopped beside the tub, touched his wet hair, and said, "Alex, it honestly hadn't occurred to me."

"Pennsylvania taught us a number of things, didn't it?"

"I suppose so." Olivia sat down with her face toward the open north window. "But why the past tense? Don't you anticipate seeing it again?"

"It's just seems to have happened an age ago."

"Tell me about your trip."

He shrugged, sat up, and reached for the soap. "Discouraging. I'll give you a run-down on it later. Right now I'd rather enjoy cool lemonade and my wife."

"It seems months instead of weeks since you left. Alex, is there any real value in these trips?"

"Right now I wonder. I did run into an old classmate when I came through Ashton. He's asked us to dinner tomorrow night."

"From Harvard?"

"No, prep school. We've known each other since boyhood. He is married to a girl we both knew." Alex glanced up. "How is Father?"

"Seems to be well, except for suffering from the heat."

"Olivia, I'd like to be out of here before the end of July. I'll explain later. But I feel it's important to leave Father well."

She glanced quickly at him. "I should have guessed. It's war news, isn't it?"

He nodded. "The farther north I go, the more the rumble increases. It's the border states—Arkansas, Missouri, Tennessee, Kentucky. Ever since most of Virginia seceded, she's been fighting the other half. The western part of Virginia wants nothing to do with being cut out of the Union. Of all that's happened since April, this has encouraged me more than anything else."

"Your parents are in the library."

"Let's go. I'll have to give them some report."

When Alex stepped into the library, he looked from one face to the other. "Mother and Father, you are nearly ill from the heat. Isn't it about time you treat yourselves better than this?" He bent to kiss his mother and clasp his father's shoulder.

Mr. Duncan roused himself and turned to the little slave. "Here, girl! Why aren't you stirring up a breeze with that fan?"

"There's just not a sign of cool air," Bertha Duncan said fretfully. "Alex, my lad, how good to have you safely home. You don't look bedraggled from the heat!"

"I've been up to my ears in cold water for the past half hour. Now tell me why you and Father won't go to the mountains to get away from the heat."

"Because your father—"

"Can't leave this place in the hands of an incompetent overseer." Mr. Duncan sat straight in his chair and waved away the child with the fan. "It appears the longer I live, the less I can trust people to do their jobs right."

He turned stiffly in his chair and addressed Alex. "Tell me, what did you find and where have you been?"

"I've been as far as Richmond and, Father, I've found it in much the same frame of mind as Charleston is."

"By that you mean—"

"Determined to press on with the same course. No one would give me an honest ear, but they were willing to give me a thousand reasons why the South should pursue her efforts to be completely separated from the Union." He paused. "It's interesting; I haven't heard slavery mentioned all month. The Federal government is determined to hold the Union together, and the Confederacy is shouting 'freedom.' "

Mr. Duncan snorted. "Don't forget that freedom includes the reason for the freedom we've always had."

"Freedom to maintain slaves for economic reasons?" Alex paused. "One thing hasn't changed, and that's the harsh language used to describe the North and every member of the present administration."

Alex leaned back in his chair and studied the carpet at his feet. Finally he said, "I wasn't going to mention this, but I've heard it so often in the past month it's starting to make me very uneasy. The avowed goal of the Confederacy right now is to capture Washington. When I expressed my skepticism initially, I was shown several newspaper articles dating back to April mentioning this goal. Considering the language being used, it is no wonder the idea seems to be exciting men nearly to a frenzy. Troops were gathering and drilling in every village and city I passed through."

When Alex awakened the next morning, he found Olivia, propped up on the pillows, soberly watching him. Rubbing his eyes, he touched her shoulder and asked, "What is it, dearest? Why that expression?"

She tousled his hair and accepted his kiss before saying, "I've come to a decision related to what you said last night just before we went to sleep."

"I said lots of things. What are you referring to?"

"The trains being crowded with troops, the ugly reception you had in Richmond, the pressure put upon you to join the army. Alex, I'm convinced half of the difficulties you encountered would have been avoided if you had been escorting a woman."

"And you want to volunteer for the job?" He chuckled, tweaked her nose, and said, "No thanks, dear bodyguard; you're going to stay safely at home."

She wrapped her arms around him and snuggled close. "Just think of what a good team we would be. Sometimes men listen to women when they won't listen to men."

"I'm not listening," he murmured as his lips traveled down her cheek.

She shoved him away and sat up. "Alex, I'm bored, terrified, and lonesome. I want to go with you. Furthermore, from your description of events, I'm beginning to wonder whether or not we'll be able to get back into the North." Then she tried her smile on him, "Please!"

"It's starting to sound better all the time," he grinned. "Go ahead, beg me some more." His voice was light, but as she pushed him down and kissed him, she saw the shadows in his eyes.

"Alex," she whispered, "we're in this together; please don't say no. We must be together every chance we have."

He shoved the pillow behind his shoulders and admitted, "Olivia, I honestly didn't believe I should take you, but I must admit it sounds worth considering. I've been so lonesome for you I could scarcely stand it. I need someone to talk to, and I prefer it to be you."

"Settled. When do we leave?"

"As soon as I can get Mother and Father into the mountains. There's a resort in the Allegheny Mountains in Virginia. It isn't very far from Roanoke. Mother and Father were there years ago and have often talked of returning. We'll take them, spend several days with them, and then our work begins."

As Alex and Olivia sat down to breakfast, Mike Clancy's letters were delivered. Alex held them in his hands and turned them over. The first letter was crumpled and spotted with moisture. The second bore a recent postmark. He opened the crumpled one while Olivia leaned over his shoulder to read. "This was written months ago!" he declared.

"Mike's taken the boat back to Pennsylvania. Sounds as if he's done quite a bit of observing and listening. Mike's a smart lad, and I trust his decision. Seems the rumbles had him running for Pennsylvania just before all the April events. That's good.

"From the sound of things, I've a feeling if he'd waited another month we wouldn't have a boat. Well, we won't need to worry about going to Vicksburg for the *Golden Awl*. Most certainly he made a good decision, and it's out of the question to consider taking more people out."

Olivia was scanning the second letter. "Alex, you need to read this. It sounds as if we could use a trip to Tennessee and Kentucky."

Alex took the letter, and she watched his eyebrows lift. "So, there's strong Union feeling in the two states. For the sake of North Carolina and Tennessee, it's too bad I didn't go up there this spring."

"And any secession that's been done can be undone! Too bad we didn't come up with this brilliant idea last April," Olivia said.

Alex grinned. "We? I guess I should have listened to my wife."

The senior Duncans came into the breakfast room. "And what grand plans are you two making now?" Alex studied his father's face before answering.

"Father," Olivia said, "you look as if you didn't sleep last night."

"It was too hot, and mosquitoes buzzed around my head all night."

"Too hot even now," Bertha breathed, waving her handkerchief. "How I would love to escape this place!" She threw a quick glance toward her husband.

"Olivia and I have an idea," Alex said. "Father, remember the Misty Mountain Inn? For years you and Mother have talked about returning there. How about all of us going now? Olivia and I will need to be returning to Pennsylvania shortly, but we'll spend at least a week with you in the mountains."

Olivia saw both of their faces brighten, and she beamed back at them. "Let's go now before another hot week passes!"

That evening as they dressed for dinner with Alex's schoolmate, Olivia asked, "Is this evening simply social?"

Alex turned to look at her. "I honestly don't know. But if I've a friend in the area who'll be candid with me, it's Henri Classone."

She pinned the brooch to the low neckline of her pink silk organdy. "I'm ready."

"You look as cool as a peppermint." He kissed her cheek. Taking her arm, they started down the stairs. "I have some hard questions to ask Henri tonight, but let's also plan to enjoy the evening."

He helped her into the buggy. "I hoped to stir up a little cool air with this rig. Do you have something to cover your hair?" Olivia nodded and shook out the folds in the pink lace scarf.

She turned with a smile. "If it's only to Ashton, I haven't much time to learn about Henri and his wife."

Alex nodded and flipped the reins along the horse's back. "To begin with, Henri is managing his father's South Carolina property now. During our growing up years, the family lived here. Now his people are in Louisiana. They have a little scrap of land there—just enough, Henri said, to make his father feel useful. I'd like Father to consider something on the same order—" quickly he glanced at Olivia "—except that I wouldn't want to be the one running his place."

"How would it be possible without slaves?"

"It's not out of the question. We'd be paying wages to people motivated to work. I'm convinced freedom and the security of a home and family would help give these men a sense of pride and accomplishment. I'd need to build decent cabins for the families." He grinned down at her.

"But, frankly, I can't see myself content with being a gentleman farmer. I'll have to admit, after being away from Boston, I'm getting a desire to get back into law again . . . maybe politics." He glanced at her, then rambled on. "Seems when I complained to the Lord about how things were going in Washington, He indicated that if I saw the problem, I needed to do something about it."

They rode in silence. Olivia smiled and touched his arm. "Alex, talking about the future is exciting. I do believe the Lord has a place for us, and also interesting things to do the rest of our lives."

"But there's the present to get through first."

"I was also thinking that, I just didn't know how to say it. Is it significant that we're able to look ahead with excitement?"

"I don't know, my dear. Right now there are enough difficulties to make me prefer postponing my thinking for the time being."

Henri met them at the door. He bent over Olivia's hand and said, "My wife, Clarissa, will be with us in a moment. We have a month-old baby boy and she wants to show him off."

He led them into the drawing room. Olivia was still admiring the pastel beauty of the room when a round, dark-haired woman came into the room carrying a fussing baby.

With one glance at Olivia's face, she deposited the infant in her arms. "Oh," Olivia sighed, "he's so little and soft. What adorable hands. He'll be blonde like your husband."

"Now Andrew, don't fuss." Clarissa patted the baby and explained, "He's hungry, but I did want you to see him awake. I'll be back shortly." With the baby snuggled against her shoulder, she smiled at Olivia and left the room.

"Come have some fruit punch while we wait for Clarissa." Henri led Olivia to a chair and a slave placed a tall, cool glass beside her.

As she sipped the punch, Henri turned to Alex. "I was surprised to hear you'd left the area. Didn't think a true son of South Carolina would do such a thing. Have you returned to take over the family farm?" He chuckled at his joke and sipped punch.

"No. As a matter of fact, Olivia and I will be returning to the North as soon as we've finished here."

"North?" Henri looked startled, his grin faded. "Man, you can't be serious about returning to the North now! They'll eat you alive. What is your business here?"

"We came primarily to visit the folks. Mother and Father hadn't met Olivia. Last December seemed a good time. Certainly we didn't expect events to move as rapidly as they have."

Henri nodded. "The war."

"You asked about my business now," Alex said slowly. "I'm a self-appointed committee of one for the purpose of trying to talk sense into people."

"Specifically what do you mean?" Henri asked cautiously.

"I believe there are strong Union people in the South. My intention is to talk to as many as possible. Henri, it isn't too late. If there's a strong enough voice, the Southern confederation will be forced to listen to us. I intend to unite those opposed to secession, those determined to preserve the Union."

Henri's chuckle started with a mirthless shaking of his shoulders. Olivia watched it erupt into an explosion of sound. She straightened in her chair, carefully placed the glass on the table and said, "I beg your pardon, sir; what do you find so hilarious?"

Henri wiped his eyes. "I would apologize if you weren't both Southerners. I spent weeks at the convention in Richmond as a delegate from South Carolina. Actually I had no legal involvement with it. I was there only to encourage the members of the convention to seriously consider secession. Alex, will you believe this? Of the members of the convention there was a large majority who were dead set against secession. They were entertaining the hope of being a liaison between the North and the South. Of course all of us from the deep South were determined to sway the opinion toward secession. I must say we did our job well. I might add, they were bombarded with reasons to side with us. So you see, I'm not the one to be hearing your cause."

He got to his feet, bowed to Olivia. "I hear Clarissa coming, and my man indicates dinner is served."

During dinner, Henri kept the conversation light. As they finished their compote of fruit, Henri looked at Alex and asked, "Shall we retire to the library and allow the ladies to talk about babies, or shall we invite them to join us? Clarissa hasn't heard the tale I wish to give you."

"Oh, let's stay together!" Olivia exclaimed. "I'd like to hear it too."

Clarissa nodded. "I was here during that time in April. It was just before the baby was born." She wrinkled her nose as she added, "And a tiny baby certainly can occupy time—I've still not heard much of his fascinating story."

As they sat down in the drawing room, Henri waved his hand and said, "In all fairness, I must state your cause of attempting to hold the Union together is admirable. But for the most part, we Southerners are forced to choose between two good things: the Union or the sovereignty of the state. Alex, you know that. Most certainly, state sovereignty must prevail."

Clarissa spoke softly. "Little as I know about financial matters, I do know without our slaves, we would be ruined."

"Well said, my dear." Henri smiled at her and turned to Alex. "It sounds selfish and narrow-minded to outsiders, but you know the complete impossibility of maintaining life to this standard without slaves."

As Henri spoke, Olivia watched the black butler move slowly around the room. His motions of tidying and setting out liquor bottles seemed contrived. Henri turned with a frown. "James, we won't want anything except iced fruit punch. The heat makes liquor unappealing," he added to Alex.

They watched the man leave the room. Alex caught Olivia's eye, and she knew he was thinking of Caleb.

As the door closed, Henri turned to Alex with a grin. "Now I'll tell you why I can't support the Union; indeed, why the idea is laughable.

"When I was convinced the Virginians would endorse secession, I immediately started for home. At Charleston I stopped at the military academy. When they discovered I'd just returned from Virginia, they commandeered my services to lead them against the Union. Of course—" He glanced at his wife with a smile "—I extracted a promise that I'd be home for the birth of my son." Looking at Alex, he added, "It was mostly a token gesture, sending troops into Virginia to join with theirs in our first assault against Federal forces."

"If this was in April," Alex said slowly, "then it must have been the Harper's Ferry incident. I read about it in the newspapers. Needless to say, the newspapers were from South Carolina, and I didn't believe the accounts."

Henri leaned forward. "Alex, I assure you they were true. I was there. When our small detachment moved on Harper's Ferry, it was an arrogant, stupid thing to do. Had we not filled ourselves with all kinds of bravado, we would have seen how preposterous it was.

"Here we are, moving against one of the largest arsenals in the country. In addition, there is also an arms factory there. We knew the arsenal contained the Union's largest store of arms. In the same location was the Baltimore and Ohio Railway, the linkage between the western rivers and the east coast. Close by was a flour mill, one of the largest in the country, and fully operational. I think you get the picture. It was one of the most important military posts in the country."

Henri chuckled again. "Would you believe that a little group of men captured the entire Union holdings? There was only a handful of us from the South Carolina unit. We met at Halltown with the Virginia troops; together we counted two hundred and fifty. Fortunately, a squad from the Fauquier County Cavalry joined us with a piece of artillery. It appeared some residents of Halltown would join us if we needed them.

"About nine o'clock we moved up on the Ferry. Evidently they'd received warning, because we were challenged by sentry after sentry. We'd just realized we were in over our heads and decided to send in a flag of truce when the whole place exploded! We found out later the fellow in charge had concluded we were a multitude. He laid charges throughout the arsenal and the factory; he also lined up the trains, and when the fuse was lit, the whole place went up. We tore out of there, went back to Halltown where they told us all the fellows stationed at the Ferry had been seen crossing the Potomac. Some of the Virginian troops took off after them. Guess they chased them all night."

He paused to laugh. "One additional thing; we put out the fires in the workshops and saved a large number of the rifles, so the South was well paid for their efforts that night."

There was silence in the room. Just beyond the open window, Olivia could hear the peaceful chirping of crickets.

After a moment Henri said softly, "Alex, give up your crusade; we need you here."

They were nearly home when Alex straightened and flicked the reins along the back of the horse. Olivia stirred beside him and he turned to look down at her. "I'm very angry," he murmured. "I've nearly allowed myself to be blinded by wishful thinking. Things are much worse than I'd guessed."

"What are we going to do?"

"Go home. But first I want to stir up every loyal Unionist." In a moment he added, "I'd hoped to influence Henri for the Union, but instead he's made an even more ardent Unionist out of me."

CHAPTER 11

Mike came in the Coopers' back door. Sadie nodded and continued kneading her bread dough without missing a stroke. "Thee's making it home more often these days," she said.

He grinned and patted her shoulder. "And thee has questions in thy eyes," he teased.

"I can guess. Since that soldier boy went to Washington, Beth's lonely, and thy chance has come."

"You make me sound like a very mean fellow. Actually, I'm lonesome for your cooking."

"Might have known an Irishman would be kissing the Blarney Stone." She dropped the dough in the bowl and tucked a towel around it.

"Well, have you heard from Alex and Olivia?"

She nodded. "They received thy letters, both on the same day. They plan to begin their trip home in July . . . which means they've started." She added thoughtfully, "Our young man sounds discouraged by all the happenings. Alex mentioned trying to talk to people about staying true to the Union. Seemed surprised at the attitudes that prevail."

"What kind of happenings did they name?"

"Talked about Harper's Ferry and the taking of the naval base at Gosport. 'Twas an awful shock for them to hear about it all, especially when they're surrounded by the enemy."

"Are those his words or yours?"

"Mine, most certainly."

"I didn't think he'd regard homefolk as enemy." Mike moved restlessly around the keeping room. "Beth is still working at the hardware store? Does she get out with the young people?"

"Thou know'st the answers," Sadie answered shortly as she finished shaping the dough. She washed her hands and said, "Most certainly she's out romping with the young folk every chance she gets. My, the projects the folk can think up as a means of making the soldier boys content!"

The back door closed and they looked up. Beth hung her bonnet on the hook beside the door and came in. "Mike! You're back again so soon. Are there problems?"

"Thanks for the welcome!" He grinned down at her. "No problems. I've been pulling barges as fast as they can load them. Ohio will take anything they can get: steel, coal, oil. There's a new factory going up in Cairo. I think it's for gunpowder; I'm guessing that because of the troops training there."

"I've heard the uniform factory in Pittsburgh is starting to hire women," she said as she sat down and picked up the newspaper. With a quick glance at Mike she added, "In peaceful Pennsylvania that spells war more clearly than anything else."

"Uniforms and fellows drilling?"

She thought for a moment, then smiled teasingly at him.

Sadie put down her knitting. "Mike, as long as thou art here, wilt thou go pick corn for dinner?"

"I'll help." Beth got to her feet, and Sadie saw the quick flush of pleasure on Mike's face.

Mike headed for the far end of the garden. When Beth caught up with him, she asked, "There's corn close to the house, why don't you pick it there?"

"I need the walk." He grinned at her and saw the color come to her cheeks. As they turned down the long row of corn, Mike asked, "So what do you hear from Fairmont?"

"Not a thing." Her voice was low as she bent to examine an ear of corn. She looked up. "But then I didn't really expect to hear from him."

Her voice was defensive and he turned to look her in the eye. "Who are you trying to convince—me, or yourself? Of course you expected to hear from him. I suppose he's busy." She turned her back. Mike took a deep breath and spoke quickly. "If a buggy ride will help, let's go out for a while this evening."

She eyed him until he said, "Do I pass inspection?"

"Oh, Mike! I just didn't expect that. It's rather like going out with your brother. But all right." She pulled an ear of corn and added, "You were cool to me when we came back from the send-off frolic for the boys. I guess that surprised me."

"Well, now that I know where you wear your heart," he said lightly, "I won't expect anything. Next time, at least do the guy a favor by letting him know what the score is in the beginning."

"Yes, Mike; yes to both. I could use a ride in the moonlight."

"I think we have enough corn. Let's take it down to the well and pull the husks."

By the time the supper dishes were washed and dried, the moon had risen above the trees. When Mike made his request, Amos looked from Beth to Mike and said, "Might as well, there's not a full moon every night." His eyes twinkled as he added, "Too bad there isn't an extra seat in the buggy; that way Sadie and I could go sparkin' too."

Mike turned the buggy down the river road and then let the mare pick her pace. He looked at Beth. "You aren't considering work in the factory, are you?"

"I don't know," she sighed. "It's pretty lonesome around here with the fellows gone. This July there hasn't been one hayride, and when the young people get together, their conversation sounds just like the old folks—war."

"Beth, could I give you a little brotherly advice? Don't go to Pittsburgh to the factories. It's not safe for a pretty young girl."

"Brotherly? Mike, some might think different if they see us—" He moved restlessly on the buggy seat and waited.

Finally she resumed the conversation, "I wonder how it is back home? Do you suppose the young people there feel the same about the war?"

"No." He was aware of her turning to him. "Beth, I've been hearing enough to draw a few conclusions. Southerners, young and old, aren't the least unhappy over the war. One of the reasons I got out of there in a hurry was the high feelings against the North." He fell silent, then added, "Seemed to be a mood of celebration. Here it's like a constant wake. We're not partying over this conflict."

"Might be the area. Quakers don't seem prone to party over anything," she commented dryly.

They crested the hill just outside of town. Below them, the road made a wide, gentle swing down toward the river. Mike pulled on the reins, and they stopped on the crest of the hill. In the silence the river's splashing seemed amplified. They heard the gurgle of water over rocks, the splash of fish, the sound of an oar.

A skiff came into sight. They watched the couple move through the path of moonlight. While the fellow pulled at the oars, the young girl trailed her hand in the water. As the boat passed into the shadows, Mike said, "Not too neighborly, are they?" He saw her puzzled glance and hastily added, "I prefer talking to rowing."

The silence was finally broken by Beth. Her voice was heavy as she said, "So what do you want to talk about—me? Mike, nearly every time I look at you there are questions in your eyes. What is it you want to know?"

"Beth—" He spoke reluctantly. "I do have questions, but you've never given me any right to ask them, so—" Quickly she slid across the seat and kissed him on the cheek.

"Does that give you the right?"

"You want me to ask? I'd gotten the feeling you think I'm just a clod."

"Well, from the very beginning I felt you were like a brother, burdened with the responsibility of a pesky sister."

"I suppose I still feel that way."

"It isn't very flattering."

"I was the skipper when you came looking for a ride. You were a bedraggled young'un looking nearly as bewildered as the load of slaves I was carrying. If I'd leered at you, you'd have taken off."

"I suppose so."

"Beth, stop me if I'm wrong, but I have the feeling you've left unfinished business behind. I've no right to pry, but if you want to talk about it, I'll listen."

In silence they waited as the freshening wind moved across the fields, sweeping through the corn, snatching at the branches of trees. The breeze brought the scent of mud and water, the echo of faraway voices.

Below, the skiff moved out of the shadows and drifted downstream. Now the girl leaned against the fellow's shoulder, while with one trailing oar he held the boat steady. The two heads merged for a moment and the boat drifted toward the bank.

"I guess I'm like that," Beth murmured. "Afraid I'll get out of control." She glanced at Mike and hastily added, "I mean the boat, not the girl. I run when I can't see the next step clearly."

"That's what happened at home?"

"I suppose mostly it was Father considering marriage with a woman I didn't like. More than all my old feelings about Mother, I felt buried. Like when you're stacking hay—you put it where you want it, but all of a sudden it comes sliding down around you."

"Are there other things too?" Mike asked. "It takes more than a handful of hay to make a stack."

"Yes, other things." She turned on the buggy seat. "Mike, I don't understand all this Quaker belief about God. You people make me very uneasy. I'm starting to get this desire to run out on it all."

"There's nothing about God that should send you running. Beth, it's the opposite. God untangles the problems we have, if we let Him."

"I've gone to church all my life, but He hasn't untangled anything for me."

"Have you asked Him?" Mike turned to face Beth. "There's just so much God can do for us until we start asking for help."

"Help? Mike is there anything you've ever wanted desperately?"

"Not desperately," he said slowly. "At least so far I haven't felt that way."

"I feel that way," she whispered. "I call it my *if only* feeling. Right now I have the *if only* feeling. What is it that will make me happy?" She moved closer. With her hands on her knees she studied Mike's face intently.

Mike chewed his lip and tried to remember what it was that he had wanted to tell Beth. Her face came closer, "Mike?" Carefully he bent over and kissed her. Her soft lips moved under his, and he pulled her close.

Finally he released her. With a shaky laugh, he said, "Beth, I was going to say something, but I've forgotten what it was."

Beth moved away, smoothed her hair, and whispered, "Mike, you weren't acting like a brother."

"Shall I apologize?"

She hesitated. "We must go. Tomorrow is a work day."

———

When Mike closed the door of his room and leaned against it, he was deeply conscious of Beth just down the hall. He looked at his hands. They seemed full of the memory of her softness.

Clenching them, he groaned, "God, I made a big mess of this evening. I set out tonight to be the big brother she seems to need. Honestly, I am worried about her. She's impetuous, like she's never had a mother to tell her you don't go around kissing just any fellow."

He crossed the room and sat down on the edge of his bed. After thinking of the way Beth's eyes had looked by moonlight, he dropped to his knees beside the bed. "Lord, I'd be a real piker if I stole a soldier's girl. I don't think she understands about being a Christian. I got the feeling she thinks belonging to a church will do it." He hesitated, then quickly added, "I feel this responsibility to talk to her about You, but when I'm close to her I seem to forget about everything else. Please help me to do it in the right way." He gulped, "And help me to forget about kissing her. It isn't right; just thinking about it makes me feel like a silly sixteen-year-old."

————————

The following week, Roald Fairmont returned to Pennsylvania. When Beth returned from work, she brought him to the Coopers' farm.

Mike noticed the sling as soon as he opened the door. In the parlor, with Sadie and Amos speaking sympathetically, Beth explained, "He's out of the war for now. But he'll be able to train the other fellows, that's why he's back."

"I was at Bull Run," Fairmont explained. "It's a broken arm, a simple break, but I can't handle my rifle."

Amos studied him with interest. "Sadie, can thou find another plate? This fellow's been to war and I want to hear all about it."

Mike said, "Those Rebs gave you fellows a rough time."

Fairmont glanced at him. "When you get into the real stuff, it turns out fighting isn't as easy as it looks. Classes didn't prepare me."

"West Point?"

Roald nodded. "We left Washington with thirty-five thousand troops. Seemed like enough to push the whole South into the Atlantic Ocean," he said ruefully. He looked at Amos. "Matter of fact, sir, we were just a bunch of raw soldiers trying to hang together. The ninety-day recruits were even worse off than we were."

Amos said, "I've been following the talk and reading the newspapers. Now it seems to me like the troops were spread out all over the United States. Is that a good idea?"

Mike looked at Amos. "Are you referring to the fighting going on in the West?"

Amos nodded, and Fairmont said, "The Arkansas-Missouri scrapping, as well as the affair between Tennessee and Kentucky? There are also troops down by the Gulf of Mexico, as well as several spots on the Atlantic."

"Kinda spread thin, weren't thee?" Amos asked. "I suppose Lincoln and his men know what they're doing. I just wish they'd get it over with in a hurry."

"Sir, after what we went through," Fairmont said soberly, "most of us are convinced this war's going to be around for a time." He glanced around the room. "The papers were making out that we weren't up to doing our job. Sir, we were all greenhorns, both North and South. But they were getting up reinforcements while we were being pushed back, and all the time tangling with Congressmen and their wives who had followed." His voice was bitter as he added, "Thought they were going to a picnic, a real lark, this first big battle. What most of us want to know is: how come the Rebels knew just what our plans were?"

Roald shivered, and with his voice low, admitted, "The worst part of it all was the Rebel yell."

"What is that?" Mike asked, looking at the young man huddled in the rocking chair.

Roald lifted his head. "An ungodly scream. Most of us thought a bunch of demons were after us. It's more like an unearthly wailing. Pretty near paralyzed the bunch of us, we just stood there and shivered, didn't know what to do next. You know the rest, how we turned tail and ran." His voice was bitter.

Mike leaned forward in his chair. "Roald, I suppose you fellows have been beating yourselves over the head with the defeat every day since the battle. Have you seen any of the newspaper stories?"

"I think every Southern newspaper was dropped on our steps," he admitted. "They all carried the same theme: The North is inferior to the South. A Mobile, Alabama, paper made the prediction we'd never move beyond cannon shot of Washington. Right now, I guess I have to agree with them."

Mike stated, "The story that impresses me most came from the fellow writing for the London *Times*. He called the battle a prick in the North's balloon, but he said that's good. He predicted it would bring the people to an understanding of the nature of the conflict. I'm still chewing over that statement." Mike added, "But I agree with the mood of the country. This conflict isn't going to be settled easily."

"Might be," Amos rumbled slowly. "A genuine purging goes clear down to the roots. A wildfire in the forest takes off the tops of trees, but in a year or so, things are right back where they were."

"And the problems aren't solved."

As Beth came out of the kitchen, Sadie put down her knitting and said, "Might be for the salvation of this country. Most certainly it needs something that goes down to the roots." She patted Roald's hand. "Now you come have supper with us. I think Beth has it on the table." She paused and added, "We'll celebrate your return and wish farewell to Mike again. He's leaving tomorrow."

As they left the parlor, Fairmont asked, "Where are you going, Mike? Intending to join the army?"

"No, I'm skipper of a tug taking barges down the Ohio to Illinois."

Fairmont scrutinized him for a moment. "Can't you let some old man do that? The army needs young men."

Mike hesitated, unwilling to bring out his questions before the piercing eyes of the man. He glanced at Fairmont's bandaged arm and muttered, "Maybe later. Right now they're short of pilots."

———————

Six weeks passed before Mike brought the tug back up the Ohio and was free to return to the Willows, the Coopers' home. The late summer sun was setting when he walked in the Coopers' back door. For a moment he thought the house was deserted, then he heard the rustle of a newspaper and a sniff. It was Beth.

He crossed the room to the rocking chair pulled close to the cold, dark fireplace. The look on her face suppressed the cheerful welcome he had prepared.

"Problems?" he questioned, sitting on the stool beside her chair. "Want a big brother to listen?"

She sighed, rubbed a hand across her eyes and muttered, "This newspaper. Nothing but bad news. Roald has left. His arm is healed, and he's gone to Washington. I suppose I'll hear he's been killed next." Her hands trembled, and she pressed them against her eyes.

"Aw, Beth—" He swallowed, feeling hollow as he admitted the obvious reason for her tears. "You're worrying for nothing. You—"

Abruptly she pushed the newspaper away and straightened in her chair. "It's all Lincoln's fault! Now, Mike, don't go defending him! If he'd just not called for troops back in April, all this could have been settled without people getting killed."

"No, Beth, that isn't so."

"Most certainly it is. When he did that, all the other Southern states started seceding. Right and left they were pulling out of the Union," she cried, jumping to her feet. The tears were rolling down her cheeks and he tried to ignore them as she continued, "Now this paper says Missouri's fixing to go out of the Union too. One after another, and I suppose that's the smartest thing to do."

"Beth, I was in the South in April. I have newspapers I bought at the time. As soon as Ft. Sumter was attacked, and with its surrender, the crowds in the South started celebrating."

"I don't believe that."

"I'll let you read the newspapers. Richmond, Raleigh, and Nashville took to the streets to celebrate their victory over the Yankees. They were waving Confederate flags and cheering on the cause of Southern independence. Furthermore, they insisted that other states join in the cause. Independence for the South means freedom from all that the Union stands for."

He snorted, "It wasn't Lincoln's call for men that started the war. The Southern states had already decided that independence was worth fighting for."

She pondered his statement in silence. Looking up with a shrug she added, "You say that as if you hate me and the whole South."

"Beth, I don't hate you. I hate the cowardly way the Unionists allowed the Confederate sympathizers to control the politics in their states." He paused, staring at her with unseeing eyes as he added, "I guess I'm being too hard on the Unionists; I might have been right there with the others when the Virginia crowd threatened violence against them at the time of the convention for secession. Guess they did right to close their mouths and take themselves out of the vicinity."

Beth walked restlessly around the kitchen. She sat down and twisted her handkerchief into knots. Finally the words burst out. "I suppose I'm not being honest. Guess I should go home."

"What do you mean?"

"This battle at Bull Run—at first I thought the North was at least worthy of respect. Now, after the battle, and hearing how the South is saying the Yankees are afraid to fight, that they are like schoolboys with their toy guns, well, I guess I don't have much respect for the North. Mike, they're going to lose. I can't believe they'll win this war, and I hate to be on the losing side. I'm ashamed of it, but I might as well be honest."

Sadie's mantel clock chimed out the hour, and when it finished, Mike got to his feet. "Guess I'd better go help Amos with the milking." He paused, looked down at her and said, "Yes, Beth, I suppose you'd be happier if you'd go home."

CHAPTER 12

Alex was in the library when the carriage stopped at the door. From his position at the desk, he glanced out the window, saw his father step out and reach to help his mother. Alex watched Clayton Duncan escort his wife to the front door and return to the carriage. Surprised by his father's unusual action, he left the library.

Bertha Duncan turned as he came into the hall. "Here you are!" she remarked as she walked toward him, pulling off her gloves. "I just asked Tanner to find you. Let's go into the library for a moment."

Alex held the door for her. "I saw Father getting into the carriage, is he leaving?"

"Yes. Right now he's at the stables. He'll be returning for his bag. He's going to Charleston and will be there several days. It's a matter of raising financial help for the army. He didn't say much to me. Mentioned something about arrangements to send delegates to Europe. It seems these men will be seeking recognition of the Confederate States as a separate nation." She slanted a glance at him, sat down, and reached for her fan.

"Please order something cool for us to drink," she murmured. "I find myself unusually tired this afternoon."

"Katie just brought some iced fruit juice," he said, going to the tray on the table. "So what is the idea behind a new delegation to Europe?"

"We need help, and the situation will be desperate soon. The ports are blocked, and we can't move cotton to Europe, neither can we get the imports we need to continue to support this war."

"And you want me to say again that I believe Europe will refuse? Mother, it isn't prejudice; I simply believe the leaders in Europe are too cautious to allow themselves to be pulled into a conflict between the states. I honestly believe they expect the situation to be rectified very soon."

"And you don't?"

"I'm beginning to wonder. The North is too stubborn. There's strong sentiment in the South for maintaining the Union, but I also believe South Carolina's past threats have run their course of effectiveness." He paused and smiled. "Right now I'm hoping both sides will come to their senses and make some compromises."

"Son, do you really feel that way, deep down?"

Alex took a deep breath. "I want to, but Mother, I'm fearful. Need I commit myself to saying more?"

"No. And that's the reason I must talk to you. First, I'm certain your father will not go to Virginia to the lodge. We'll simply need to cancel the plans."

Alex sighed with frustration, "Oh, Mother, you both need it! Can't you influence him to take better care of you both?"

"Alex, I must say this quickly before—" The door opened and Alex's father looked into the room.

"Bertha, have you told Alex I must go? Oh, there you are, Son." He came into the room. Alex watched his father's studied smile and quick gait as he crossed the room.

"Father, you're not convincing me that you are well. Surely you'd be better off going to Virginia until the hot weather is over. This business can wait."

"No. I've also heard another fact which will keep us home. In town they've posted a notice asking people to cancel unnecessary travel on the railroads. Because of troop movements, there's a great deal of inconvenience in attempting to travel just now."

"Troop movements? I wonder what's happening?" Thoughtfully Alex added, "I'd been fearing this. Certainly that's a good reason for you to stay at home. I only wish you had gone before hot weather."

Alex went to the door as his father backed into the hall. "I'll probably finish my part of the discussion by tomorrow, certainly on Friday."

Bertha Duncan touched his arm. "Clayton, I've asked Tanner to bring a bag for you. Are you using the surrey?"

"Yes my dear; I'll return before the first of the week."

Alex and his mother returned to the library, and she paced the room restlessly. "Mother, please, sit down and finish your drink. Olivia will be here in a few minutes, I—"

"Alex—" She turned abruptly and clutched his sleeve. "I must tell you this quickly. Also, please, please don't mention this to your father—or anyone else."

"Mother," he took her arm and looked into her face. "Do you feel faint? Your face—"

"No. But I've done something which I know your father will disapprove of. Hopefully, I've covered my tracks."

"Tracks? What—"

She lifted her hand. "Just listen. You know I own property inherited from my father. Well, I've sold it all to your father's friend, Mr. Mallory."

Alex rubbed his chin slowly. "Father will be extremely angry. Did you get a decent price for it?"

"Only fair; certainly not what it's worth, but I'm done with it. Just don't let your father know this has taken place."

"Well, I know he mentioned Mallory trying to buy some of his land. He felt the man was taking advantage of the—problems, since he offered a price that seemed too low. Mother, why did you do it?"

"For several reasons." She stopped, gulped her fruit punch, and leaned forward. "Alex, I've never admitted this to your father. It would make him angry, and he would be forced to quarrel with me."

She got to her feet and walked slowly to the windows overlooking the driveway. She leaned against the window with her hand braced against the frame. "Alex, I've discovered that you and Olivia have been working for the Underground Railroad. I pressured her with questions, and finally her expression gave her away. We've not mentioned the subject again, and I'm not certain she knows I've discovered your secret."

As he opened his mouth, she lifted her hand. "If it weren't for that knowledge, I wouldn't dare say these things. You see, I've felt for a number of years that it is wrong to hold the Negroes in slavery. I can't help it. It's just not right."

"But what does that have to do with selling your property?"

"It's my part. I'm convinced the slaves must be freed, and that this will never take place without a great deal of bloodshed."

"And you expect the South to lose?"

"I *want* the South to lose. Alex, here's the money." She handed him a thick envelope. "There are some in banknotes, but most of it's in Federal security bonds."

He looked at the papers and said, "If you have Federal bonds, then this means you did this some time ago, before we came."

"Why do you think so?" she asked curiously.

"I can't believe it would be possible to purchase Federal bonds now."

She blinked tears from her eyes. "That's correct. And would you believe, I had no idea how I would get money into the right hands. Little did I guess my own son was involved when I prayed so desperately for guidance."

She handed him a leather pouch. "Here's gold for your immediate needs." Her hands trembled. She dabbed at tears on her cheeks. "Oh, Alex, take that precious girl and leave the South while you can! I'm fearful, and I don't know why. Everyone around me seems to believe we've won our case against the Union and soon all of this will be over. But in my heart, I still feel fear."

"Mother," he said slowly, "you frighten me. It makes me even more reluctant to leave you."

"For the sake of the slaves, you must leave. Alex, I'm afraid if you stay you'll be pressed into the army. During your prep school days you had military training; that will be important to the South."

"I don't believe the South will force anyone into battle against his will." Slowly Alex got to his feet. "But with this money, you've made it possible for me to continue doing the work. We were beginning to wonder how much longer we could keep up the fight."

Crossing the room, he bent over her. Suddenly he dropped to his knees beside her chair and wrapped his arms around her. "Mother, I can't leave you here. I know that Father will never change his mind, but since you've admitted your feelings, it makes leaving too difficult to consider."

She hugged him, then pushed him away. "If you stay, there's nothing more you can do for the slaves."

Slowly he got to his feet.

"Why did you say you wanted the South to lose the war?"

"Can you think of any way to make the South *want* to surrender their slaves?"

The door opened. Olivia stepped in. She looked from one face to the other. "Is something terribly wrong?" she whispered.

"No, my dear," her mother-in-law's lips quivered. "On the contrary; it is finally *right*." She stood up. "Alex will tell you all about it. Now, please excuse me; I've had a very busy day and I'm extremely tired."

After the door closed behind her, Olivia followed Alex to the table. She watched him empty the contents of the envelope onto the table. Then he opened the leather pouch and poured the gold coins on top.

"Federal securities," he said. "Mother has sold her inherited property."

He turned to face Olivia. "She has given me this because she doesn't believe slavery is right and she wants us to have the financial resources to carry on the fight."

Olivia gasped. "And we were nearly out of money. But how did she find out?"

He chuckled. "I should have warned you. Years ago I discovered I couldn't hide anything from my mother. She asked you some questions and made some good guesses on the basis of your reactions."

"Oh, dear," Olivia murmured. "I'm afraid I wouldn't make a very good spy."

"She wants us to leave soon. Father has changed his mind about going to Virginia. He had an excuse I can't fault. He's checked the train station and found that the railways are asking people to cancel unnecessary trips because of troop movement."

"Troop movement? Alex, what is happening?"

He shook his head. "I don't know." He walked around the table and faced her. "Olivia, I would like to continue talking to people."

"It seems so fruitless."

"I was thinking the same thing. It's been discouraging to recall the reactions of those I'd most expected to give me an audience. But there's an article from one of the newspapers published in Tennessee. It appears there's a very real confrontation going on in Missouri, as well as in Tennessee and Kentucky. The newspaper was old, but I trust the situation still stands. In all of these states the Unionists have been fighting the secessionists, and it's starting to look as if they have a good chance of winning large numbers to their side. I'd like to go to Tennessee and see what help I can be. Only—" He avoided her eyes. "I want to take you to Pennsylvania first."

"Why?" she cried.

"Because it sounds as if these states are no place for a woman to be."

"Aren't there women living in those states?" she demanded. "Alexander Duncan, you said yourself that having me with you would be an asset. Why have you changed your mind?"

He grinned. "Well, I guess I'll change it again." She flung herself into his arms, and he laughed as he pressed his lips to her forehead. "Oh, my dear, I don't think I could live a minute without you. Of course you may go if you wish. It could be an uncomfortable situation, but I'll be happy to have you there. Let's begin packing."

When Clayton Duncan returned from Charleston, he brought additional news. "Son, I've heard just this weekend that it is now necessary to obtain a pass in order to travel between the North and South."

Alex handed his father's valise to Tanner. "I'd heard something to that effect. I've been wondering how to handle the situation. Guess we'll just have to check it out when we reach Richmond."

"You plan on traveling north through Virginia and into Pennsylvania?"

"Ultimately we'll be going that direction," he said lamely, wondering about the quizzical expression in his father's eyes. "We saw all we wanted to see of Mississippi, and because of the difficulty of travel, it doesn't seem advisable to try to visit Olivia's parents now."

Nodding, Clayton Duncan started after Tanner. "Well, don't be in a hurry to travel anywhere. The heat inland is fierce right now. One of our committee came up from Richmond, said life has nearly come to a standstill there."

"One thing the heat will end is the scrapping that's been going on for the past three months," Alex murmured. "Might even give some of us who believe in negotiation a chance to make ourselves heard."

His father turned to stare at him. "Don't count on that," he said dryly. "Our men are in the mood to fight, regardless of the heat."

"Have you heard news?"

"Just the same old refrain. One side is shouting, 'On to Richmond,' and the other's saying, 'Take Washington.' "

"Olivia and I have decided to leave before August." As soon as the words were out, Alex was caught by the fleeting expression of pain on his father's face.

Clayton Duncan turned away. "It shames me to admit I've raised a son who'll so easily throw over all the values of home with nary a backward glance."

Alex groped for words to say the difficult in a painless way. "Father, you've taught me to stand behind what I believe. You've said a whipping hurt less than a lie. I guess I'm about to prove that. Only there's one thing you didn't tell me—that honest, undecorated truth sometimes hurts everyone concerned."

He gulped, faced his father, and forced out the words. "I didn't realize our visit would make you hope when there's no hope to be had. Father, neither Olivia nor I would be honest if we stayed to tend the family farm to please you and Mother, when deep inside we know we'd be going against God's will for our lives."

"God doesn't approve of the South?"

Alex couldn't look at the hurt behind the words. "Father, you know

God loves the people in the South, just as He does the people in the North—and the slaves." His father turned and strode rapidly into the house without another word.

———

On July twenty-second, Clayton came into the library and dropped the newspaper on the table in front of Alex. "So, it's begun in earnest," Alex said wearily.

"Yes. Your President Lincoln is pushing this. He's been accumulating troops in Washington for weeks now."

"And the South knows all about it?"

"Of course. For several weeks we've been getting all the news we need. You see, Alex, we've all the necessary friends in Washington."

Chewing his lip, Alex picked up the newspaper. The *Richmond Whig* declared, "The breakdown of the Yankee race, their unfitness for empire, forces dominion on the South. We are compelled to take the scepter of power. We must adapt ourselves to our new destiny."

When he looked up, Clayton Duncan dropped another newspaper in front of him. "This one tells about the battle, ending with the totally demoralized Yankees being treated to our famous Rebel yell." He paused, chuckled silently, and added, "I'd give anything to have been there. Half of Washington brought their lunches to watch the battle. When they went home, they went in a hurry. The paper says hoop skirts, picnic baskets, senators, and wagons were all mixed up with the fleeing Union Army." He chuckled again. "Next battle, I'm going to get them to let me know in advance so I can be there. Might be I'll take *my* picnic basket."

He started for the door. "Son, don't be in too much of a hurry to get out of here. The trains will be tied up for some time. Our men captured twelve hundred of your men, and it'll take a little while to get them moved and safely put away in prison. Might be they'll need to start building more prisons, if this is any indication. I have heard, however, that they'll be working out a system of prisoner exchange."

During the night Olivia stirred, sat up in bed and strained to hear the sound that had awakened her. The windows were open to the heavy, hot air. She heard frogs, and a whippoorwill called from a tree outside.

Alex stirred. "What is it?"

"Alex, something is wrong. Footsteps—that's a horse leaving." He pulled on a robe and went to the door.

Olivia pressed close to him when he stepped into the doorway. They saw the elder Duncan returning to the house, and Alex asked, "Father, what is it?"

"Your mother; she's ill. I've sent for the doctor. It seems to be her breathing." Alex dashed to his mother's room.

A slave holding a fan hovered close to the bed. "Tilly, lift me," Mrs. Duncan gasped.

"I will," Alex murmured, bending over his mother.

"Can't breathe."

Alex's voice overlapped hers as he lifted her and placed pillows behind her back. "Is that better, Mother? The doctor will be here soon." Olivia rubbed at the tears on her face. When she saw Alex's expression, she came to the bed and picked up the cold, white hand.

"Olivia, it's—all right." Her hand was still cold, but it tightened on Olivia's.

———

Dawn had brightened the sky before the doctor straightened up and looked at them. "She'll be fine now. It's her heart. I've given her some medication. For the rest of her life she must take it, do you understand?"

They nodded. Alex followed the doctor to the hall. Glancing at Clayton sitting on the edge of the bed, rubbing his wife's hand, Olivia hurried after Alex.

"Not lung problems, heart," the doctor was saying. "Alexander, she won't live long. That heart is simply worn out. I heard you and your wife are leaving, and I thought you should know." He turned away, picked up his bag and said, "I'm sorry."

Olivia concentrated on his tiny smile, the cold, curious expression on his face. "Thank you for telling us, Doctor," she murmured. "Of course we wouldn't think of leaving now."

His smile thawed. "She'll appreciate that. She sets great store by her family. But I don't think she will be with you much longer." ·

CHAPTER 13

Mike stepped out of the house just as Beth came from the barn. "How's the hardware lady?" he grinned down at her.

"Hello," she said slowly. "I didn't expect to see you back so soon."

"Might be around for a while. It's getting pretty tight trying to ship along the Ohio. Missouri's been at it again. Fickle as a flighty female," he muttered, and Beth giggled. "Naw, that's not fair to females," he admitted. "It's not the state's fault either; it's a bunch of cowed people who can't get up their nerve to send the Rebels packing. First they decided to be on the Union's side, then they sit back and let the Rebels take over."

"What happened?"

"It wasn't one thing, it was a whole series of happenings. The governor is just plain pro-slavery. In the Kansas struggle, back in the fifties, he moved into the territory with his gang. He was pushing slavery. That's where he first tangled with General Lyon. Might say they had each other's number before all this started.

"Back in January, Jackson was inaugurated as governor. He made it clear he thought Missouri belonged with the South, even though he had to work with a Union legislature. Long after he had told Lincoln he wouldn't send men to fight, he turned around and asked Jeff Davis for artillery to take over the St. Louis arsenal.

"Well, I could keep going on and on. Needless to say, when General

Lyon came on the scene, the two locked horns. It cost Lyon his life, but it sure set Jackson's men back on their heels. Now I suppose the Confederates are back to courting his favor again because of forts Belmont and Columbus. Belmont is on the western side of the Mississippi, and Columbus on the eastern. Both are important if the Confederates intend to hold the river."

Mike watched Beth move to the woodpile and select a log for a seat. "Am I boring you?"

"No," she said quickly. "But I'm wondering why this is all so important."

"Just the struggle going on for territory. It's like watching wildfire. You think it's out, then it flares up somewhere else. You don't dare turn your back for fear you'll get your tail feathers singed."

Beth laughed and Mike continued. "When General Lyon came, he announced he'd fight to the finish to get the Confederates out of Missouri. He'd already decided they were bound to push as hard as we'd let them. A feisty fighter he was—showed us a good job of it. One time he stood with his men until the Rebels were right under their guns. They fired one volley and then went after the enemy with bayonets. That's when General Lyon was killed."

"The North will miss such a general," Beth said slowly.

Mike nodded. "General Fremont took over for him. Right now there's Confederate troops gathering in the southeast corner of the state. They're threatening Cairo in Illinois. That's why I'm home. In fact, I heard President Lincoln's calling for closing the Mississippi River to anything except essential traffic."

"What's essential?"

"Troops, ammunition. The situation in Missouri's been touchy for a long time; now there are problems with Kentucky and Tennessee."

"It's bringing war close to us. It's scary."

She turned her face. Mike hesitated, then finally asked, "Is Fairmont still around?"

She looked up. "Why do you ask?"

"Looking for information—troop movement, and so forth."

She laughed. "And I thought you were going to lay siege—whatever that means."

With a grin he came toward her. "That word is best illustrated." He backed her up against the apple tree, caught her shoulders, and kissed her. "That's siege."

"Oh," she smiled up at him. "I thought siege had something to do with follow-up fighting."

"It does," he murmured, kissing her again. "There. Did you miss me a little?"

Beth backed away and touched her red cheeks. Wide-eyed, she looked at him. "A little," she admitted. Then she turned away. Mike had time for only one swift mental kick before she turned again. In a rush of words she said, "As long as you'll be here, you might as well come to the frolic next week: a hayride and watermelon feast."

"Sounds wonderful. I'd stop the war for that." He hesitated. "Are they still training soldiers down in the pasture?"

"Yes. Roald is in Washington again, but he expects to be back before the end of September." A question leaped into her eyes.

"What are you thinking?"

"Just wondering if you intend to go to war, too."

"Right now, no." He hesitated. "I prefer shipping. But before this is over, we may all be in battle."

Beth sighed and turned toward the house. "I must go help."

"How's the job going?"

"I suppose it's all I can expect around here." She tossed her hair back and looked up at him. "It keeps me busy when there's nothing else to do."

"Sadie tells me the women are working on packages for the soldiers, getting together socks and sending home-baked cookies."

She nodded. "We all get in on it when there's a rush to pack them up." She slanted a glance at him. "Mike, are there lots of soldiers being killed?"

"And wounded, and taken prisoner. It's not a lark," he said slowly. "And I pray to God that it'll soon be over, even when I'm doubting it will."

"Do you think God favors the North?"

He looked at her. "No, of course not. He loves all people."

"Then there isn't a right side or a wrong side?"

"I'm not certain," he said slowly. "We feel slavery is wrong, and that it's wrong to split the Union. But in the end, it's God's judgment. Only He knows the real right and wrong of the situation. It seems to me the worst wrong is fighting, regardless of the reason behind it. If we're Christians, then we ought not to be fighting."

"Does that make a difference?" She tossed her hair away from her face. Her eyes clouded, "Seems you're lifting up Christianity like a high and holy untouchable. Doesn't sound very attractive. Guess I'd rather just admit I'm not all that good, but I'm happy with what I am." She opened the door and slipped into the kitchen.

The following week when Mike and Beth returned from the hay-ride, Sadie cornered Mike in the kitchen. Picking straw from his hair, she said, "Mike, if thee touches a hot stove, thou wilt be burnt."

He searched for a light touch. "Aw, Sadie, a fellow doesn't get anything without trying."

"Nonetheless, thou art too good for the likes of that lass." Her eyes were heavy with conviction, and he nearly asked the reason for her concern.

Finally, managing a grin, he said, "Seems Fairmont and meself are coming in and out of here like puppets on a string. May the best man win!"

"I fear he will," she said darkly as she passed him on the way to her bedroom.

———

Mike was still thinking of Sadie's brooding statement and her frown the next week when he took the little tug and one barge down the Ohio.

When he docked at Cairo, a man in uniform came aboard. Looking curiously around, he entered the pilot house. Nodding to Mike he said, "Captain Ammit, Skipper."

Mike introduced himself. "I've expected this. My boss in Pennsylvania informed me the tug would probably be commandeered."

"We can use it," Ammit said. "But right now we're in need of men as well. You've been down the Ohio a half dozen times with a full complement of barges since we've been stationed here. That tells us something. Have any thoughts about joining the navy?"

Mike sighed gently. "Haven't given it much thought; this kind of shipping is about all I know. Don't consider myself an expert."

"Would you be interested in a couple of trips downriver? We can use your experience, and you can size us up."

"Sounds like it might work," he admitted slowly.

"I'll make arrangements for you to meet with Flag-Officer Foote and General Grant." The fellow grinned at Mike's expression. "We don't usually try this hard to make a good impression on our recruits. I've mentioned you to the two of them, and they're interested in talking to you." He backed out of the pilot house. "I'll be in contact; meanwhile stay with your vessel."

Late the following afternoon, Ammit made another appearance. "Clancy, if you are available now, I'll take you up to see Commander Foote and General Grant."

"Guess I'd better change my shirt."

Ammit laughed. "Go ahead; I hope you find the interview worth a clean shirt."

When Captain Ammit opened the door to the narrow, box-like room, Mike looked around. He was struck by the room's resemblance to a packing crate. He eyed the rough, unpainted walls, the equally crude table, and the man hunched down in his chair with his feet on the table. "Good luck, Clancy," Ammit muttered, backing out of the room.

The man in the crate hunched himself higher in the chair. "Yes?"

Mike cleared his throat and said, "I have an appointment to see Flag-Officer Foote and General Grant."

"Foote will be along shortly. Please state your name and business."

Uneasily Mike moved his shoulders. "Well, I suppose there's nothing secret about it. Captain Ammit contacted me, and said Commander Foote and General Grant wanted to see me."

"And?"

Mike hesitated. "Oh, I'm Mike Clancy, I've been piloting a tug on the river for the past year."

The man's feet came down; he stood and leaned across the table with his hand outstretched. "Glad to meet you, Mike. I'm Grant. Sit down." Slowly Mike sat. He observed the rumpled uniform and the sad eyes. Grant said, "Ever hear of a gunboat? Well, we're having some put together for us, and we're desperately in need of pilots."

The door opened. "General Grant—" The man in naval uniform nodded, came into the room, and sat down at the table.

"Michael Clancy, sir." Mike sat down and waited.

Grant muttered, "This is Flag-Officer Foote. Andrew, want to tell Mike what a gunboat is?"

Foote studied Mike. "You look young for a pilot, but we'll know soon enough when we get you in an ironclad." He pulled out pencil and paper. "This is what it looks like. Designed by a man named Samuel Pook, they've been dubbed Pook's turtles."

He leaned back and looked at Mike. "The gunboats are paddle wheelers, with a flat bottom. All of the strategic parts are shielded by iron plates. The boat carries thirteen guns, and manpower to handle them. They're shallow-draft, designed with waterways like the Tennessee River in mind." Foote began to grin. "I can see the idea is intriguing."

"Sir, when are you going to build these—turtles?"

"They're in the process of being built right now. So far we have two completed. We'll have all of them in the water before the end of the year. Meanwhile, we have a lot of work to do in order to be ready to use them. Ever train a pilot?"

Grant spoke up. "How about taking us on a little fishing trip on that tug?" A half-grin pulled at his serious face. "I'll provide the fishing poles, and you think of some good fishing hole, like the Tennessee or Cumberland Rivers."

Foote chuckled. "I hope you're kidding. Think we can get past those forts?"

"Not in uniform, and I'm not certain you can act stupid enough to get yourself into such a situation," Grant said with a chuckle.

Mike scratched his ear. "I'm not certain stupid men would be out in a boat like the tug in the first place." He looked at Grant. "Must it be a tug? If you're wanting a sounding, I'd take it with a pole. From looking at the terrain and the nature of the water, I can pretty much tell what we'll get into. Seems best to just go in there in a skiff." Mike paused, eyed Foote's expression, and murmured, "Oh, I get you. You wanna know how I handle a clumsy boat in such water, and you're not serious about going in. I've never taken a boat into the Tennessee."

Commander Foote stood up. "Well, Mike, if you're interested in giving this a try, we might as well go look at those boats." He grinned at him and added, "Guess I'm not too worried about how you handle a boat—or won't be after today. Come along."

CHAPTER 14

It rained the day Bertha Duncan died. It was a cold December drizzle that reduced everyone to shivering misery. In the hours preceding her death, Olivia huddled in the library, close to the smoky fire, thinking of the family upstairs: Alex, his father, and that brittle sister of his.

Near dusk, Alex came into the room. His face was drawn and his lips taut and white. "You needn't have left the room," he said sitting down beside her.

"I thought it was time for you, Father, and your sister to be together with her."

"She's gone now. It was the last time we were a complete family," Alex mused. He looked at Olivia. "To her, you were a very dear part of the family."

"Alex, I'm glad it's over. These past weeks have been difficult for all of you. She was terribly weak and tired of life. I'm glad she was ready to meet God."

"Yet it's difficult to surrender her." He turned to face her. "Olivia, last night you heard Mother beg us to leave as soon as the funeral is over, and you know why. She had anticipated problems with Father over the property she sold to Mallory; naturally the whole situation will come out when her will is read." For a time he stared into the fire. "This weather seems dismal enough; now I must tell Father we'll leave soon. Will you come with me?"

She got up and went to his side. For a moment before he stood, she pressed his head against her bosom and the brooch tangled in his hair. "You need a haircut," she murmured, pulling his curls away from the gold blossoms.

Catching his face in her hands, she lifted it, kissed him, and then whispered, "I remember one day at Sadie's when we were at complete odds with each other. While I poured your coffee, I saw your hair curling against your neck in this way. I wanted so badly to touch you. But then I had no right."

"Olivia, my dear," he murmured, burying his face in her neck. "You are my comfort, my anchor, and my love. How I thank God for you."

"And I for you," she whispered, pressing her lips against his hair. "Oh, Alex, last night, watching your father's face, I was so miserable. It seems life can be utterly perfect, and then this. I wish I dared to beg you to never leave me alone, but—"

He pressed his fingers against her lips and pulled her onto his lap. His voice thick with emotion, he whispered, "Please, dear, say no more. We both know how uncertain life is now. Let's just try to hang on to the precious moments."

He reached for her lips and Olivia snuggled against him. The smoldering fire burst into flame, and the smoke disappeared. To Olivia it became a cheery crackling shield between them and all that lay beyond.

Finally Olivia sat up with a sigh. "I've also been thinking of how painful life has been for you these past months. Wanting to be with your mother when instead you were tramping around Charleston and every little village a day's ride from here. Alex I know how disappointing it's been for you to go seeking people to listen, and how doubly painful it was to have them sneer at your burdens and ideas." She cupped his face in her hands and forced his eyes to meet hers.

"You've said little to me, and I can guess why. I've felt so powerless to force myself past that wall of hurt. I've wanted to carry the burdens you are desperately hiding. The cause has torn at me, too." She paused. "I'll be glad to head north."

"Olivia, you've opened the door for me to disappoint you," he murmured. "There's been just enough good talk with people to encourage me to keep trying. I've been praying the Lord will direct me to those who must be warned, admonished, encouraged. Can you possibly put up with some more of this?"

She stroked his beard and touched the gold ring in his ear. "Alex, certainly—just as long as you keep me with you."

————

A week later, Olivia and Alex stood with Clayton Duncan at the railway station in Charleston. It was still raining.

Olivia huddled in her cloak while Alex and his father engaged in low-pitched, polite conversation. Olivia listened idly, but her heart was responding to the pain on those two faces.

They all turned when they heard the train whistle. Olivia went to slip her hand through Clayton's arm. Carefully she suppressed the words she wanted to say and formed a smile. "Dear Father Duncan," she murmured, "it's difficult to leave you here in this miserable rain. After being away from the South for so long, I do believe Pennsylvania's snow makes a more pleasant winter. I'd love to see you enjoy it." It was the wrong thing to say, and she felt him stiffen.

Quickly she pressed her lips to his cheek. "Don't come out to the train. Soot and rain will make a terrible mess of your coat. Are you planning to go to your club? You should, since you've promised us you'll see your doctor tomorrow. Have a nice dinner, and get a good rest."

The two silent men shook hands and Olivia continued to chatter over their silence as they walked to the door of the station.

The train had left Charleston behind before Olivia dared face her husband.

"I was just wondering—" Alex began.

"If we'll ever see him again," Olivia finished. "I was thinking the same." She huddled in a miserable lump against the slippery horsehair upholstery and braced her cold feet against the foot support in front of her.

"Father gave me a stack of newspapers and a small hamper of sandwiches. Would you like this robe over your feet?"

Olivia nodded and sighed deeply. "I was wondering if the worst part is behind us. Alex, do you suppose he guessed our secret when he discovered the tickets were for Richmond?"

"It's too bad we couldn't discuss the problem," Alex muttered. "But no. He mentioned the Inn we had planned to visit last summer and said that we shouldn't try to go home through Washington. His expression was strange. I wonder if there's something being planned?"

The head in front of Alex swiveled around. "No doubt it's troop movements. Seems they're constantly shuffling them from east to west and west to east. But there's nothing going on now. I'm Harold Thorpe. I was in Washington last month and they're still reeling from the whipping we gave them at Manassas last July. Don't think they'll do much for a time. This weather puts fighting out of the question. Would you care for some newspapers?"

"No thank you, sir." Alex hesitated and asked, "What is your destination?"

"Washington."

"I understand there's a need for passes if one moves between the North and South."

"That's correct. It isn't difficult if you know the proper person to ask. An army officer will usually hand them over promptly enough."

"Do you mind if I ask your business in Washington?"

The man looked at Alex with a sparkle in his eyes. "Do I look like the world's most unlikely spy?"

"I beg your pardon; I shouldn't pry."

"I don't consider it out of line from a brother Southerner." Mr. Thorpe picked up his newspaper and turned to read.

It was ten days before they reached Richmond, Virginia. As the train protested its way to a creaking halt, Olivia took Alex's hand and carefully stepped down from the quivering machine. Turning to look at it distastefully, Olivia said, "I can't believe this trip has taken so long. Alex, this frightful monster is the laziest train in existence."

"Now, Olivia—" He grinned down at her. "You're being unfair. We've changed trains at least every day, we've spent hours on spurs waiting for the track to be cleared, and in addition, we've driven miles to reach trains."

"It will be a happy day when they decide to make all the trains the same gauge and to have them meet at one central station."

"Don't blame it all on the iron monster. And now, my dear, with your sooty nose and frock, I think you rate a long rest before we go farther."

Mr. Thorpe stopped beside them. "So, we meet again! I didn't know we were on the same train. Will you join me later for dinner?"

For a moment Alex's eyes brightened, then he glanced at Olivia. "It would be delightful, sir, but I'm afraid my wife needs a very steady, flat bed under her right now. Perhaps some other time."

The man touched his hat. "Unfortunately I'll be leaving for Washington in the morning. Here's my card. When you are in Washington, look me up. By then perhaps we'll all be celebrating in the streets and it will be good to renew our friendship."

They were settled in their hotel room before Olivia asked her question. "Alex, what did Mr. Thorpe mean when he referred to celebrating in the streets of Washington?"

"The South's plan to take over Washington, of course," he murmured as he studied the street below their window. "Last summer's battle was the Union's attempt to foil the Confederate plans on that score."

"And they are still planning on taking Washington?"

"I expect to see the battle resumed right where it left off; perhaps very soon."

"I'm surprised. That angry article in the Charleston paper last month berated Beauregard for not pushing into Washington. It seemed unfair to the man." She sighed. "But then, I can't quite reconcile the enthusiasm of men for fighting."

"What do you mean?"

"The troops on this last train. They were as excited as boys over a ball game."

"Part of that is the Southern male," he murmured. "At times I think we've lost sight of what it means to be a gentleman. I've become very much aware of this since we've returned to the South."

He gave her a rueful grin. "You are right about being an asset to me. This winter, while you stayed at home with Mother, I've had countless occasions when I barely escaped with my skin intact. Right now it's dangerous to hold an opinion differing from the flow of popular thought—namely, the right to be free from all restraints of the Federal government, and the right to have slaves."

Olivia finished hanging her dresses and turned to study Alex. "But there's the other side. Can you honestly hold to the opinion of President Lincoln?"

"Do you mean the opinion that the seceding states are in a state of rebellion, that they have no Constitutional right to take this action, and secession is therefore treason? Olivia, I've read everything I can get my hands on about the Constitution. I've spent hours pondering the problem—perhaps even trying to justify the situation the South is in. But I can't quarrel with Lincoln's opinion."

"I'm glad to hear you say that; it makes me feel better. There's been so much argument, I was beginning to think the whole world was right and we are wrong."

"I suppose that's bound to happen. *But*, Olivia," he said, his voice brooding, "we must carefully study out a problem and then make up our minds that no matter what, we will uphold the right and reject the wrong."

"Alex," she whispered, "sometimes it is so lonely—like last Sunday in church. That parson was completely confident that the Southern cause is God's."

"Even in things of the church," Alex murmured, touching her

cheek, "we must live close enough to God to understand and take our direction from Him."

"And that's what you're doing," she whispered. "Oh, Alex, I wish I had all the answers, and that I were as sure as you."

A faraway expression filled his eyes. "Olivia, I'm not sure. I still agonize over this situation. There's not a day but what I find myself struggling over the right and wrong of this war."

On Sunday, Olivia woke to the pealing of church bells. With her eyes closed she tried to think her way back to Pennsylvania, listening to the chorus of bells ringing out across the hills. Only the Quaker meeting house, stoic and sparse, didn't rend the air with the music of bells.

She felt Alex stir and opened her eyes. "I'm thinking of Pennsylvania and the church bells," she said as he slid his arm under her head.

"Strange, we humans," he murmured. "Some of us think holiness is found in plainness and simplicity—"

"With whispers instead of joyful shouts, silence instead of music and bells. Presbyterian and Quakers," Olivia added.

"But in conflict, we work together. The Presbyterians send their men to battle, and the Quakers feed, clothe, and nurse them. Perhaps it's just as well. The touch of God on our lives resounds with diversity as attractive as the multitude of bells. Listen, my dear, and rejoice as you see fit." He chuckled and kissed her.

Prim and proper, their Quaker hearts covered with Presbyterian clothing, Alex and Olivia joined the throng going into the building under the belfry.

Shielded behind their hymnal, Alex said, "Thy Quaker heart responds well to these Presbyterian hymns."

"Thou art wrong, dear husband," she whispered back. "This hymn was written by Charles Wesley."

And after the sermon, they were greeted with a hearty, "Good morning; how happy I am to see newcomers! I'm Matilda Armstrong." Olivia looked down at the white-gloved hand stretched toward her, and then upward to the round figure in black taffeta. She smiled at the halo of white curls and sparkling blue eyes.

Someone grabbed Olivia's hand and eased her out of line. Matilda Armstrong tipped her head toward Alex. "Do you live in Richmond, or are you visitors? No matter," she said hastily. "I've come to invite you to my home. Every Sunday after church I gather up all the interesting people I can find and stuff them with sandwiches and pastry so that they are obligated to entertain me with conversation. Do you have a carriage? I'll direct you there." They shook their heads, baffled.

"Oh, then join me in my carriage and we'll all ride together. Come, we'll have to lead the way."

She skillfully maneuvered them around the crowd at the door and down the steps to the carriage.

Through the early hours of the afternoon, Olivia listened to the music of laughter accompanied by the ring of crystal, and decided Matilda Armstrong hadn't a serious thought in her head. But by midafternoon, she began to think differently.

Matilda's eyes gave her away. In an unguarded moment Olivia knew she had been measured and assessed.

As the last guest carriage pulled away from the front steps, Matilda led Alex and Olivia back to the parlor. "Now, my dears, let's get acquainted. Would you care for more tea?" She began pouring.

Handing the cup to Alex, she said, "You impress me as a very shrewd businessman. Am I right?"

"Ma'am, why do you think so?"

She chuckled, "Because every stranger in town who doesn't look frightened nearly to death is a shrewd businessman looking for a way to sell Jefferson Davis everything he doesn't need to carry on a war."

Alex laughed. "In reality I think we fit the first category. We are sojourners, looking to stir up trouble before we leave town."

Her eyes sparkled as she leaned forward. "My, how interesting! What type of trouble are you looking to stir?"

Alex placed his elbows on his knees, dropped his voice, and said, "We're Union sympathizers. I'm trying to talk sense into everyone I can. Mrs. Armstrong, why did you guide us around the parson and his greeting committee this morning?"

"Because I watched you during church and I thought to myself that you were both very disturbed by the sermon. So you two don't believe that the Bible, God's Word, supports slavery as something pleasing to God. I'm very anxious to hear your opinion. But just to set the record straight—" She paused, peered at Alex, and said, "I don't tell all of my guests this, but my Negroes are freedmen. I pay them a good wage just to stay here and take care of me. Furthermore, your frown during the sermon made me very curious. What can I do for you?"

Alex looked startled. He paused before asking, "Shouldn't I be saying this to you? I suppose I should be pointed in the right direction.

You see, Union sympathizers need to be encouraged to stand up for their beliefs. After being in South Carolina, I came to the conclusion there's more Union people in the South than we two have realized. We need to be heard. Mrs. Armstrong, I've the feeling you've never been in a position of allowing others to do your thinking for you. Unfortunately this isn't so for many people, namely those either too timid to express themselves or those who find it easier to bend with the flow around them."

"You are correct. But that's human nature."

"It hadn't ought to be. Christianity makes me very aware of how important our opinions and values are to those around us."

Matilda Armstrong reached for her calling cards and began to write notes on them. She looked at Alex. "Then you realize the seriousness of the situation we're in?"

He studied her with narrowed eyes. "You can't be speaking about the possibility of losing forever our Southern values of states' rights and the right to own slaves?"

"Of course not. I'm talking about freedom. My dear Mr. Duncan, our Constitution supports freedom for all. If one segment of our society isn't free, then not one of us is free."

She got to her feet and handed Alex the cards. "I've written a name and address on each card, also your name. It would be wise to make certain these cards do not get into the wrong hands."

Alex stood looking down at her, and Olivia said softly, "Mrs. Armstrong, your interest in us tells me that you must be in an uncomfortable position in the capital city of the Confederacy. Would you consider traveling North with us?"

Matilda turned to smile at Olivia. "Thank you, my dear, however strange my ideas are here, I enjoy the comfortable position of an old and perhaps slightly strange citizen. Also, I've work to do here. The Lord will keep me intact until He's through with me on this earth. God bless you both now. I'll have Roger take you back to your hotel."

CHAPTER 15

It had been a month since Mike had last seen Cairo, Illinois. As he took his barges into dock, he surveyed the new look of the city. The presence of the military had grown from a trickle to a stream. He studied the large number of uniforms on the street, both army and navy. With a grin he murmured, "No doubt about it; Cairo is going to play a big role here on the edge of the Mississippi."

Later he carried his gear into the crude barracks that would be home for him. Eyeing the fellows who stood around, hands in pockets, he dropped his bag on an empty bunk and said, "I'm Mike Clancy. It's easy to see we're going to be in this together."

The group moved around him. He surveyed the raw, uncertain faces of the men. "You fellas bring me up to date."

A lanky fellow with cornstalk hair and a scarecrow grin spoke up, "Always glad to have a new navy man on board; there's plenty of room. Where you from? Had boat experience? I started out army but they needed more men for boats."

Mike looked around the room crowded with bedrolls and clothing. "Seems things are getting together fast. What'll we be doing?"

"I'm maintenance. Painting, oiling, and anything else a steamboat takes to get it in order. Upstream they're making Pook's turtles. Man, those things will withstand anything—if only they'll float. Ironclads, they call 'em."

With a chuckle, Mike nodded, "I've seen them; can't wait to get one on the water."

"Aren't you scared?" Mike felt the grin fade from his face as the youth added, "This war business is worse than I thought. Old Deaver and I came out here after the Battle of Bull Run." He paused, shook his head, and said softly, "Navy work is bound to be less bloody."

Another fellow joined them, leaning against the wall. "Name's Cecil Dade, come up from Kentucky. Reckon I was taken on because I know the area."

Mike looked around the group. "Know what's planned?"

"Nothin' except we're here to help out the Union in Kentucky," Dade said. "Don't know what that means yet. But it's going to have something to do with boats and soldiers. Meanwhile, we're busy and life in town's just fine for us fellers." Dade paused. "Got a girl back home?"

Mike hesitated. "Well—"

"Oh, one of those kind. Guess she's better'n nothing. Seems they all have to go through that stage, trying to decide which fella they want. I suppose the other man's in the army."

"An officer," Mike admitted.

By November Mike had repaired, polished, and piloted an unwieldy gunboat around the mouth of the Ohio River. The warm autumn weather was holding, and the Ohio promised to remain free of ice for weeks to come. Thinking of past trips, Mike recalled ice jams and freezing weather, and wondered how long it would be before the weather could force them out of Cairo.

At the beginning of the following week, he and two other pilots were called into conference with Commodore Foote and General Grant.

As Foote sketched out their route, he breathed a sigh of relief. "At least we won't need to worry about ice in the rivers," he muttered to Deaver. "Not that our job won't be tricky enough even in good weather."

Foote put down his pencil. "Fellows, we're support for another offensive. You might say our job is to distract the opposition. The major battle will be taking place farther down the Mississippi.

"You men will be taking transports with troops down the Mississippi. Our job will be to get General Grant and his men to this point." His finger wandered down a map, following the Mississippi until he touched a spot in Missouri a dozen miles below Cairo. "Here they will be diverting the attention of personnel at Fort Belmont with an attack.

It shouldn't prove to be an unusual risk, but we'll need to be prepared for the eventuality of Fort Columbus, situated across the Mississippi in Kentucky, getting into the picture."

He paused, held up the map, and pointed. "Belmont is just below the bend of the Mississippi, on the west bank. Columbus lies directly across the Mississippi. We will discharge Grant's troops at this point, under cover of darkness. Here we'll lie to wait for them." He got to his feet. "There's one item I need to mention, although it won't affect you. Fort Columbus is Confederate held, and they've tried to impede traffic down the Mississippi by stretching a heavy chain across the river between these two forts. Since our men will disembark two miles above the forts, that needn't concern us. I warn you about the chain because, if there are problems, you shouldn't try to be a hero by taking your transport into this area in an attempt to rescue our men. You'll create more problems than you would solve. Men, set your watches, and be on hand to begin loading at six this evening."

In the early hours of the morning the ships moved away from shore. The sky was overcast and the air heavy with the promise of rain. Later, before dawn, Mike stood at the rail as the dark forms of troops slipped over the side. Only an occasional grunt and the clank of metal indicated the business of the three transports. When the last boot rustled through the dry marsh grasses and the night sounds returned, Mike settled at the rail and strained to follow the sound of advancing troops.

Dawn had begun to light the landscape when he heard gunfire. First Mate Jones joined Mike at the railing. Silent, lined side by side, they listened to the guns, the shouts of battle. Finally Jones moved uneasily and pointed. "Mike, what's going on over there?"

Mike turned as the first cannon fired. Peering through the mist, he said, "Fort Columbus is getting in on it." Now there was a thunder of sound as cannons fired one after the other. From their side of the river, they heard cheering from the men at Belmont.

"Mike, this is like a rat trap," Jones groaned. "Our men don't stand a chance. Why don't they head for the boats?"

"Retreat?" Mike shook his head. "Let me have those glasses for a minute, Jones," Mike muttered. "I can't believe my eyes. Our men are completely surrounded."

He lifted the field glasses again and let out a groan. Jones took the binoculars and whistled softly. "Those guns! There are three tiers of batteries, at least fifty guns pointing over the river."

"Look up that hill. There are guns for miles along the summit. I hope Commodore Foote knows about them!"

Late in the afternoon, they began to see the men in gray retreating into Fort Belmont.

When Mike was able to pick up the line of blue uniforms straggling toward the boats, he turned to Jones. "There are bound to be men injured. I'll move in closer while you prepare to receive them."

"Not much closer," Jones warned. "Remember what Foote said, and remember those guns."

Mike eased close to the shore where the troops huddled. He saw the crew go over the side and turned away from the sight of the wounded being carried aboard. But try as he might, even while he held the glasses and watched the fort across the river, the presence of the wounded stabbed him. When the boats finally moved into the river current, the moon was overhead.

They were within sight of Cairo when General Grant came up to the pilot house. Mike saw the man's lined face. "There's fresh coffee, help yourself." Grant nodded, took a cup of coffee, and slumped in the corner of the room.

When they docked, Grant turned to Mike and clapped him on the shoulder. "It doesn't get any easier. War is hell. Thanks, Mike; you'll make a good gunboat man."

Mike didn't answer; he was conscious of the hard knot in the pit of his stomach. Grant was nearly out the door when he looked at Mike again. "There'll be more of the same in a couple of months." The slight smile on his face didn't touch his eyes. "Might as well take off a couple of weeks, through Christmas. Go see that girl of yours—I suppose you have a girl back home? Most fellows seem to," he mused as he closed the door behind himself.

Mike was accustomed to the river, so it seemed strange to be taking the train through the countryside. As he neared home, he noticed that the tattered autumn foliage was rimmed with frost. People hurried through village streets bundled in winter wraps, while the long afternoon shadows seemed to have arrived too soon.

A drayman gave him a ride into town. Mike was grateful for the man's heavy silence and curt nod as he dropped him on the street corner in the evening stillness. Still numb from the journey and the weight of his own thoughts, he stood there, pondering spending money for a ride out to the Coopers' farm.

The lights were being extinguished at the hardware store when he saw Beth come out into the street. While she wound the shawl tightly around herself he called, "Beth!"

She turned, looking astonished and then pleased. "Mike, you're home! Didn't the navy like you?" She came to lean on his arm and laugh into his face.

"They seemed to; in fact they've let me have leave until after Christmas." He took a deep breath. "I'm without a way home. Do you suppose I could ride with you?"

She looked startled, then smiled coyly. "Well, it's dark enough; I don't think my name will be ruined forever. Come along to the stable with me."

"Beth, maybe ladies don't do things like this in the South. I wouldn't want to offend you." She laughed, wrinkled her nose at him, and took his hand.

As they left the stable, the wind tore at Beth's shawl. "I hate winter," she murmured. Pressing her shoulders against Mike, she added, "You must be cold too; that jacket doesn't look heavy enough."

"I'd have been colder walking," he murmured into her hair. "This is a pleasant surprise; I feared you'd moved on to Pittsburgh or some such place."

"Well, life isn't any more exciting, but I'll stick to my job until spring at least. Mabel Croan is there—in Pittsburgh. Her sister Abby says Mabel isn't saving any money because it costs so much to live there. Even with paying Sadie, I've managed a new dress and coat this autumn."

Looking beyond her, Mike said, "It's too dark to see the Cassaway's meadow. Are they still drilling there?"

Beth stiffened. "Yes," she said slowly. "Roald has returned. Says he'll probably be here until next summer. He's of the impression they'll have him training soldiers instead of fighting. I hope so." They rode in silence.

In the Coopers' barn he lifted her from the horse and noted she made no effort to move away from him. He tilted her chin and kissed her. She stepped back from his arms. "Brother Mike," she teased, laughing up at him as she whirled away toward the house.

Feeling as if the events of the past month were only a dream, Mike entered the Coopers' kitchen and sniffed the air. "Apple pie? Sadie, how did you know I was coming?"

She pinched his cheek gently. " 'Twas a bird, no doubt. Now don't ask why I've been baking apple pies three times a week for the past two months."

Amos came into the kitchen. "Welcome back, Mike. Have exciting tales to give us?" he asked with a chuckle.

"Sir, I suppose you've been reading about the doings on the Mississippi. We took a transport down to Fort Belmont with Grant's men. They got shot up pretty bad but managed to make it back to the boat. That General Grant seems to know his stuff."

"Wish we could say that of McClellan," Amos said with a sad shake of his head. He patted Mike's shoulder. "Good to have thee home, son."

Sadie said, "Just today we had a letter from Alex and Olivia. They've stayed in South Carolina because of Mother Duncan. The doctors didn't give any hope for her recovery. 'Tis her heart. So I don't know when we'll see them."

She turned to Beth. "Thy lieutenant stopped to remind thee that he shall be unable to take thee to the party tonight. It seems he'll be soldiering." She paused, glanced at Mike, and added heavily, " 'Tis well thee always has a spare." And then as if to make amends, she added, "The bonny ones never lack for attention."

Beth looked up and saw Mike watching her with his sad, questioning expression. She threw him a dimpled smile, but as she went into the kitchen she chewed her lip.

Sadie handed her the platter of meat and vegetables. " 'Tis sometimes a hard row to hoe, being bonny. Beth, thee must be more tender with hearts, or thou wilt find thyself shunned."

Beth sighed, looked at Sadie, and said slowly, "Do you know I don't intend this? I wish Mike didn't act as if I'm the only young woman in the county."

"Thou doesn't care for him."

She stared at Sadie. It was a statement, not a question. "He's—not exciting. I always know what he's thinking, and he's always there. With him, love isn't a game; it's terribly serious and—"

Sadie nodded. "Not a challenge. And thou art too young for anything except games." She placed the neat slices of bread on the plate and handed it to Beth. "Thou would be bored with marriage once thou managed to get acquainted with thy husband."

"Oh, I hope not," she murmured. "Because I've every intention of marrying Roald Fairmont."

"Then why art thou teasing Michael?"

She shrugged. "The rumor gets back to Roald, and he's green with jealousy. I've discovered that helps." She watched Sadie go into the keeping room, shaking her head as she walked.

For a moment Beth paused to listen to the homey sounds: the laughter, the clink of dishes. Somehow the sounds made her feel more lonesome than ever. Beth tried to smile as she went to the table, noting how the whole room seemed to glow from the warmth, laughter, and the aroma of good food.

Mike was watching her, but she carefully avoided his eyes as she took her place at the table. After the apple pie, he said, "I'll take you to your party—"

"Oh, no, Mike, I—" she paused, seeing the hurt on his face. "I'd rather stay home this evening. It's—so cold." Her own impetuous words astonished her. She gulped, trying to ignore the disappointment welling up inside.

There was a perplexed frown on Sadie's face as she began to gather the dishes. "Thou can make popcorn," she murmured, nodding at Mike.

"I think Mike would rather tell Amos about his navy life," Beth said. "I'll help you with dishes."

Later Beth went to sit on the stool beside Sadie. She took up the skein of wool and slowly wound it into a ball as she listened to Mike and Amos. Watching Mike covertly, she noted dark shadows where before there had been only serious Irish eyes. He was describing the sights and sounds of battle, and Beth's attention was caught.

"I'd never given the process of battle much thought," he muttered, staring into the fire. "But it gets to you. It's cold, determined slaughter. Young fellas going out, tight-lipped and white-faced, coming back exhausted, their bodies bloodied and their faces suddenly old."

"Mike, thou art a Christian. How does thou reconcile the loving Savior and His influence in thy life with murdering thy fellow man?"

"I don't know," Mike said miserably. "I keep thinking of those men out there. Alive one minute, and then—"

He turned to Sadie. "Yet, there are reasons for fighting. We've all worked to see the slaves have a chance to survive. That means breaking the law. That's wrong. Sometimes I wonder if it's possible to live without doing somebody an injustice. How do we decide which wrong is more acceptable?"

"Mike," Beth protested, "you know the South is fighting for freedom, not slavery. We fight because the North is forcing us to. Why should we in the South act and live as the North decides we should?"

Mike watched as she talked, his eyes narrowed. "Beth, it depends on who's doing the talking. Here's another interesting point. In the North you can protest against the North and no one even slaps your hands. In the South I dare not voice a complaint against the South. Why is that?"

She tossed her head impatiently. "Mike, I think you are trying to pick a quarrel. I've never had any problem airing my strong opinions."

"Might be that your opinions don't differ from the rest of the South," Mike said slowly. He got to his feet. "Sadie, where is the popcorn?"

When the last of the popcorn had been eaten, Amos reached for his big Bible. "Sadie and I'll be reading this aloud to thee, and then we'll take ourselves off to bed."

With the thick book on his lap and his finger finding the place, he read, " 'For my thoughts are not your thoughts, neither are your ways my ways, saith the Lord. For as the heavens are higher than the earth, so are my ways higher than your ways, and my thoughts than your thoughts. . . . So shall my word be that goeth forth out of my mouth: it shall not return unto me void, but it shall accomplish that which I please, and it shall prosper in the thing hereto I sent it. For ye shall go out with joy, and be led forth with peace: the mountains and the hills shall break forth before you into singing, and all the trees of the field shall clap their hands.' "

Beth watched Amos' gnarled hands close the book, tenderly stroking the worn cover. He got to his feet. "Mike, will you put backlogs on for me? Don't forget the keeping room. Feels cold tonight. Might snow. Come, wife." With a smile he reached for Sadie's hand.

Beth stared into the dying flames. " 'Go out with joy, and be led forth with peace,' " she murmured. "That sounds like a very good thing to have—joy and peace."

"But it's also true," Mike insisted.

She hesitated. "Mike, it's poetry; you can't expect these kinds of things in real life."

Mike looked up and met her eyes. "Joy and peace are two things Jesus promises to His followers."

"Are you a follower?"

"Yes, most certainly. Beth—"

She stood up and yawned. "Mike, I'm a working girl. Goodnight." She wiggled her fingers at him and with a teasing grin headed for the stairs.

Mike watched until she disappeared from sight. With a sigh he got up and reached for a log, murmuring, " 'So shall my word be that goeth forth out of my mouth: it shall not return unto me void.' "

He placed the log, stared at the dying embers, and said, "Lord, that's a promise. Help me give Beth Your words. She's starting to be very important to me."

But as he closed the door to his room, he thought of his ardent kiss and Beth's teasing "Brother Mike." He felt his face grow warm. He sat on the edge of his bed and muttered, "After all my resolve, I've done it again. I'd not want a fellow running after my girl. I can't let her be important to me, except as a sister. Lord, what can I say? I'm ashamed—sorry. I'll never be able to help her at this rate. Guess I'd better learn to act like a brother."

That next week, with the snow falling and the wind blowing, Mike opened the door to Roald Fairmont. Stomping the snow from his boots, he came to the fire. "We were to go to the Jordan's home for a party," he said, hanging his coat on the hall rack, "but I'm fearful for Beth. It's very cold."

He turned as she came down the stairs. "Oh, Roald, what a disappointment. It's terrible outside!"

"I can't believe that anyone will venture out on such an evening," he declared, taking her extended hand and drawing her into the room.

"But stay," she insisted. "We can find games to play, and perhaps Sadie will let us make molasses candy. Certainly it's cold enough!"

Sadie came into the parlor. " 'Tis cold enough for ice cream and snowmen, too. Good evening, Lieutenant Fairmont. Thou art more than welcome. I do believe thou should stay until morning; 'tis dangerous to be out in this weather."

"I heard bells, do you have a sleigh?" Mike asked. Fairmont nodded, and Mike headed for the door. "I'll put the horses in the barn."

When he returned to the house, Roald and Beth had joined Amos in the keeping room. Sadie´ was in the kitchen. Beth nodded toward her. "She's making donuts."

"I'll help." Mike started for the kitchen. "I haven't had donuts since I left here in August."

"No need for help right now," Sadie called. "They must rise before cutting."

Roald turned as Mike came back to the fire. "Beth tells me you've joined the navy."

"Not exactly," he said slowly, sitting down in a rocking chair. "I was commandeered. Seems the navy is seriously deficient in steamboat pilots."

"They keeping you busy?"

He nodded. "Spent some time getting the vessels in running order. Took some transports down the Mississippi. Grant had a supporting skirmish at Belmont."

"Did you take it?"

"No. It would have been nice, but that wasn't our main purpose. Besides—" he paused, grinning, "Fort Columbus across the river started pitching balls at us. Sure have a bunch of big guns." Mike paused. "Beth tells me you'll be training fellows here."

"Looks like it for now. I'd rather be in the thick of it. This war's dragging on too long." Restlessly he crossed his legs and glanced at Mike. "Not that I had a great deal of confidence in the ninety-day plan. How do you see the whole situation?"

Amos leaned forward. " 'Tis a shame we can't find a peaceable way of settling the whole affair. It frightens me to see the young fellows heading out like they're going to a picnic. Matter of fact, I don't believe anything easily won is worth much."

Roald leaned forward. "Did I hear you right? Are you saying you think a victory now is without much value?"

"Certainly. Not that I'm in favor of fighting," he said hastily, as Sadie came to the door. "It's a feeling that when there are two strong forces, there's going to be one hard fight, clear down to the finish."

Amos studied the fire, chuckled, and looked at Roald. "When I was a young'un growing up, we had a tomcat on the place. The neighbors down the way also had a tom. Neither one of us had any trouble with our cats until there was a reason, and then, oh, how they did fight! A pretty little miss cat moved into the territory, and then the action began."

"Sir, I don't think we're behaving like tomcats," Roald protested. "At least the North isn't. We're only bent on preserving the Union."

"And ruining the South." Beth lifted her chin. "Roald, you know we only want to go out of the Union in peace. If you soldiers would simply stop fighting, there'd be no problems." She looked around the circle of serious eyes. "I can't understand y'all. Why does it matter one way or another whether we have slavery, even if we stay in the Union?" She flounced her long red hair impatiently. "I know. The United States is just like Mike."

"Me?" He protested in amazement as she turned to him.

"Yes, you. You're as pigheaded as anyone else in the North, wanting to tell us what is wrong with us. Take slavery for instance. When the South says slavery is God's will, then what right have you to say it isn't?"

Amos' voice rumbled out, "Little lady, there's a standard the Lord wants us to use in deciding. Hast thou heard of the Golden Rule? Do unto others what thou would have them to do unto you? Well, methinks thou can't say slavery is right until thou art willing to be a slave thyself."

"But these people wouldn't have anyone to take care of them if they were freed."

Mike leaned forward to look at her. "They are humans, just as we are. In the first place, they were forced to leave their homeland; in the second place, we've never done anything to make it possible for them to learn a trade, get an education, or have a voice in making decisions."

"But don't blame this all on God," Roald said with a chuckle. "Leave Him out of the deal. We've made our bed, we'll have to handle the whole situation the best we can."

Sadie sat down beside Beth. "Thou means thou hast no understanding of God being interested in the way thee lives?"

Roald shook his head. "I've no understanding of God. It seems foolish to believe that someone is in control of all this mess. Why doesn't He do something about it all?"

"Hast thou asked Him?"

"Thou would have a sense of God," Amos said, "if thou would look for Him."

"An abstract idea," Roald said impatiently.

"But the results aren't abstract," Mike put in.

"Heaven, eternal life?" Roald shook his head. "The whole idea is based on unprovable statements."

"Love, joy, peace—maybe not tangible, but certainly provable. One day you don't have them, and the next you do." Mike glanced at Beth and watched her eyes widen.

He looked back at Roald. "War is bad. I've a feeling it's going to get worse. How does a fella go into battle not knowing whether he'll come back?" He waited while Roald stared into the fire with a half-smile on his face. "I believe I'd want to know whether or not there's a God up there listening when I pray."

CHAPTER 16

As Olivia put her bonnet on, she asked, "Alex, are you certain you want me to go with you to see this man, Lawrence Reingold? You haven't met him, after all. Your only contact with him is this letter you received yesterday."

"Yes, it'll save my having to repeat the whole conversation when I get back." He grinned and kissed her cheek.

"Oh, Alex! I don't want to keep him from being candid."

"Knowing you, I expect you'll keep him answering questions before he can think of what he's saying. Besides, since we know that he is a friend of Mrs. Armstrong, we should have little fear of baring our concerns before him. Come along, my dear."

As they entered the office indicated in Mr. Reingold's letter, Alex grinned at Olivia. He had seen the sparkle of approval in her eyes as she looked at the building, seeing the busy men hurrying in and out, and a line of important-looking stenographers.

As soon as they stepped through the door of the law office, a young man left his desk and came to them. "Mr. and Mrs. Alexander Duncan, I presume. Come this way; Mr. Reingold will see you immediately."

In the office, a gray-haired man turned from the window and came toward them. Alex thought he relaxed slightly as he glanced from Olivia to the card he held. "Mrs. Armstrong has asked me to see you. Come sit down and tell me what I can do for you."

Caught off guard, Alex hesitated, and Olivia said, "Then you must be in sympathy with Mrs. Armstrong. She's such a delightful person. But I think she's of the opinion we're—" She hesitated and looked at Alex.

"You're in an uncomfortable position in Richmond, especially if you intend to announce your loyalties. Mrs. Armstrong can get by with such indiscretions simply because her family has been part of Richmond since before the turn of the century. We tolerate a great deal from old family."

The man moved around his desk and pulled a chair close to them. "If you need a pass for the trains, I can provide that. However, I must urge you to pick your destination with care, and be advised that from here north, it will be difficult to travel."

He paused and settled back in his chair with a slight smile. "It appears the Union is putting nearly as many spies in the South as we are placing in Washington."

"Spies?" Olivia gasped.

Alex leaned forward. "Is that so? I didn't realize this was going on. But, sir, we aren't spies."

"Then what is your purpose?"

Alex hesitated before saying, "We've been hearing about the large number of people in the South who are in reality supporters of the Union. We understand they don't want war or secession." He shrugged. "I've been beating the bushes in South Carolina trying to raise some strong Union sympathy."

"South Carolina!" Reingold looked surprised. "Of all places, that will be the most difficult. I can give you suggestions, but I'm wondering what you hope to accomplish by wasting yourselves this way. Secession is a reality; a few people won't turn the tide now. Why aren't you in the army? Surely that would be more effective."

Alex took a deep breath. "Sir, I'm not certain that's the way the Lord wants me to fight this whole situation. I believe the slaves must be freed, and I believe the Union must be held together for the sake of the people—all of them. But it appears to me that to go out and shoot a man won't solve anything."

The man settled back in his chair and tented his fingers. "I agree. Thank God I'm too old to fight. At least this is a decision I needn't struggle over. Young man, I hope you find the answer within yourself, because it's easy to see you're miserable with it now. And your grand designs to pull the Unionists together and put backbone into them— I'm not so certain it will work."

"There seems to be a trend to allow the loudest voice to make decisions for the people. It happens in the North, too," Alex added hastily. "I think that's wrong. I've a conviction that if enough people are encouraged to organize and stand up for their true feelings, perhaps it will make a difference in several states."

"You're probably right. And who knows, that opinion might make a difference, especially in the western slave states." Reingold straightened and leaned forward. "Unfortunately, when some of us get past fifty, we find it hard to be idealistic to the point that we'll take to the streets to push our cause."

He paused. "You might be interested in this tidbit of news. I've been hearing reports coming out of Louisiana indicating that in the past several months there's developed a dissatisfaction with the Confederacy. Some of the leading people of the state who voted for secession are now strongly for the Union."

"I've been hearing that Missouri, Tennessee, and Kentucky have large segments of their population who are for the Union," Alex interjected.

"That is so, but take Missouri, for instance. The state's become fragmented by internal fighting and guerrilla warfare. Those Unionists may find their timidity is keeping them alive. I certainly can't recommend going there. If you did raise a following, it could be fatal to the handful of Unionists there."

"What about Kentucky and Tennessee?"

He sighed. "Tennessee seems to be pretty much in submission to the Confederacy. From the reports I've heard, I don't believe they are all happy with the situation. Kentucky is divided between Union and Confederate. I believe things are under control right now, but there's been enough fighting in the state to indicate the people are strong in their individual loyalties."

For a moment the man was silent. Olivia watched his brooding eyes. Finally he sighed and sat up. Smiling gently, he said, "You are brave people; I know you've had to face opposition to do what you believe is right. I want you to know there are many who are suffering over this situation, and their hands are tied too. One of my acquaintances is a special friend of General Robert E. Lee. He told me of the agony the general faced.

"Lee has been against slavery for many years; in addition he's been a firm Union man. Now, since the secession, he's begun to realize his roots are embedded, even entwined in the state of Virginia. My friend tells me it was a matter of extreme agony for General Lee to realize he couldn't do any less than support the South. Long after calling slavery a moral and political evil, he made a statement that is now branded on my mind. Lee said, 'I foresee that the country will have to pass through a terrible ordeal—a necessary expiation, perhaps, for our national sins.' "

Reingold got to his feet and looked at Alex. "Young man, I understand your reluctance to fight in any way other than this, but don't let it be an excuse. General Lee is truly a man of God. I wish you could meet him and hear from his mouth the reasons he has for fighting. I don't fully understand it. Perhaps it's a calling—a calling to die for the things we hold most dear."

He turned toward the door and stopped. "I must warn you, the railroad beds are in terrible condition. No matter which direction you travel, it will be difficult. However, from the reports I've received from northern Virginia, it will be virtually impossible for you to get out of the state by traveling that direction. I suggest that you travel west. I have passes prepared for you. From Kentucky you'll be able to go north." He smiled briefly. "If nothing else, there will be time enough while you're waiting on trains to do a great deal of talking with the people you meet."

As he let them out, he said, "There's a final thing you should remember: The Unionists in the South largely hold Lincoln responsible for the war."

Olivia and Alex walked quickly back to their hotel. When Alex closed the door to their room, he said, "My dear, after listening to Lawrence Reingold, I don't believe it will be necessary to contact the rest of the people on the list."

Olivia whispered, "What do we do now?"

Alex paced to the window and back. "Reingold mentioned Kentucky. He also told us it's impossible to travel north through Virginia because of the poor condition of the railroads. There's enough military activity between here and Washington to make me doubt the wisdom of taking you that direction, anyway."

"It's starting to sound as if it's best to travel west," Olivia murmured. Flicking the newspaper with her finger, she added, "Nearly every day we hear of problems along the coastline or in the mountains in western Virginia."

She smiled and put her arms around Alex's neck. "It doesn't matter; we'll be together. Alex, do you think we'll ever be able to settle down to living a sedate, normal life?"

"Might be when we have several little ones, we'll be glad to settle down. I watched that woman in front of us as we came back to the hotel . . ."

Olivia laughed. "With the three children hanging on to her skirts and a baby in her arms? But she looked happy," she admitted. "And she was delighted when you fussed over the baby."

Alex bent to kiss Olivia and nuzzle her ear. "Don't forget," he murmured, "in the Lord's good time—" She tightened her arms around his neck and hid her tears against his coat.

———

At the train station the conductor fingered their tickets. "Going for a ride through the mountains? Mighty pretty; might even see a touch of snow." Returning the tickets, he said, "Good idea—you going this month instead of last. The Yankees were trying to take over the whole railroad line. Didn't last long though—it's mighty rough terrain to fight a battle on. No matter; travel in these times is hard. More'n once I've had to dump passengers so's the army can travel. Have a good trip."

Several hours out of Richmond, after they settled into their seats, Alex said, "This is the route I hoped Mother and Father would take, through Roanoke into the mountains. So we'll get to see the area, even though winter isn't the most desirable time of year for a visit."

"I wonder, would it have been different for your mother if they'd come here last summer?" He shook his head and took her hand in his. She observed the strong line of his mouth, the gold circle embedded in his ear, and the dark beard that hid his clenched jaw.

He leaned close. "Do you approve of what you see?" he teased.

"I was thinking how gentle your lips can be. Yet you look so stern right now."

His eyes twinkled. "My dear Mrs. Duncan, you surprise me! No matter, at least you know I'm putty in your hands. Now enjoy the scenery or I shall steal a kiss when no one is looking."

"What were you thinking?"

"That perhaps we'll run into a spot of trouble. There was a weary, ragged-looking detachment of Confederate soldiers marching—if it can be called such, through that cornfield."

A new awareness lit Olivia's face as she began to comprehend their situation. "We're getting into the area where there has been fighting. What happens if—"

"There are villages all along here; that's encouraging. The most that will happen is we'll be detained."

She nodded mutely, but somehow her heart was not reassured.

CHAPTER 17

The news Alex and Olivia gathered from talking to others on the train did not sound promising. Everywhere, the South seemed to be arming for battle, and traveling was nearly impossible.

It was late when they left the train at Bowling Green, but even in the dim late January light, it was easy to see that the largest number of people on the streets were gray-clad soldiers.

Alex turned to Olivia. "I'm going to inquire about trains. Much as I dislike traveling at night, if there's one going through to Paducah, I believe we'd be wise to take it." His mouth twisted. "Seeing those soldiers, I don't believe there's a forum for my ideas tonight."

She slipped her hand through his arm. "I'll come with you. I don't want to be left for a moment, and certainly I don't look forward to staying here tonight, either."

The station agent looked at them strangely. "Paducah? That section of the line isn't in operation north of Union City, by order of the army. The Yanks have taken over Paducah, and it seems the two armies aren't on friendly terms." A shadow of a smile touched his eyes and Olivia wondered why he was amused.

"If you want to get to Paducah, I'd suggest taking the local stage to the Tennessee River and ship down to the Ohio. There's a boat going down shortly after noon tomorrow. Stage leaves here at six in the morning."

They checked into the hotel. When they reached their room, Olivia looked wide-eyed at Alex. "How are we going to get home?"

"Doesn't sound like a problem to me." He patted her shoulder and gave her a quick hug. "If nothing else, the army will find a way to get us across the river. On the Illinois side we can take a train home."

Shortly after noon the following day, the stage reached the river. But when Alex and Olivia reached the wharf, the boat they were to have been on had become merely a dot in the distance downriver.

Olivia scanned the sleepy group of buildings and the two small boats rocking gently in the backwash of the steamer headed for Paducah. "Alex, I think we'd better find someone to talk to. There's neither a hotel nor a place to eat."

Alex pointed to the trim little tugboat docked just below them. "First I'm going to see if that fellow's headed toward Paducah."

At the end of the wharf a man leaned over the rail, smoking a cigar and staring upstream. Alex called to him, but the man didn't move. Alex walked to the end of the wharf. "Sir—Captain, may I come aboard?"

The man's head came up and he turned. For a moment he frowned at Alex and then he glanced Olivia's direction. "What's your business?"

"We need to ride to Paducah. I'll be happy to pay you double fare if you can take us this afternoon."

The man's eyebrows lifted. "Better double that again. There aren't any hotels around, and I don't see a wagon."

Alex grinned up at him. "You got me there. Name your price."

The man pushed his cap to the back of his head, leaped to the wharf, and sauntered toward them. He turned to drop his cigar in the water, then stepped closer. "Mind telling me what your business is in Paducah?"

Alex hesitated. "I understand the town is in Federal control. We want to contact some people who live about fifteen miles inland. A farmer named Stevens."

Slowly the man shifted his weight from one foot to another, then he reached for another cigar. "Do you have travel passes?"

"Yes." Alex took them out and handed them to the man.

"Been in Richmond, huh? You aren't planning on going across the Ohio, are you?"

Alex gave the man a quick look, and said evenly, "Certainly not right now. We've further business in Kentucky."

As soon as the words were out of his mouth, Alex regretted them.

Suddenly the tugboat captain became very interested. The gray eyes turned cold. He straightened his shoulders. "If I were to refuse you, I'd lay myself open to letting you slip through my hands. I—"

A thump sounded on the wharf behind them and Mike Clancy came across with an outstretched hand. "Alex Duncan! Olivia, ma'am, what a surprise!"

He turned with a grin. "So you've already met General Grant—" He fell silent as he looked from one face to another. "Did I interrupt something?"

Grant sighed softly. "Might say so. He's been beating the bushes trying to stay hidden. Mind introducing your friends? I'd decided they were spies. Maybe when you finish talking, I'll can you, too."

"Alex, Olivia, this is General Ulysses S. Grant of the United States Army."

Alex heaved a sigh of relief. "I thought my past had caught up with me."

"Sir, this is Alexander and Olivia Duncan. They sound Southern, but well—" Mike grinned. "Maybe I should explain. Sir, you didn't ask me what I did before the tugboat came into my life."

Grant's face was stolid. "I'm asking."

"We've been running slaves up into Canada. Part of the Underground Railroad."

"I suppose that makes you acceptable." There was a twinkle in his eyes. "But one thing. Don't get the idea I'm abolitionist. Those guys have been a pain in the neck—to both sides of the Mason–Dixon line. My job is to hold the Union together, and right now that involves fighting this war to the finish." His jaw jutted out.

"Sir, I'm happy to make your acquaintance." Alex said. "Also, I apologize for calling you captain." He glanced at the man's rumpled dungarees and oil-stained cap.

Grant turned. "We've got to get this thing moving. "Mike, is Foote ready?"

"Yes, sir."

Grant waved toward the boat. "Come along. We've got a mission to accomplish this afternoon. I have an idea it will be to our advantage to have the Duncans aboard, especially if Mrs. Duncan is very visible once we head up the river."

"Me?" Olivia cried.

Grant grinned. "Ma'am, you are temporarily in the employment of the United States government. I'm pleased to have you aboard. Come meet Commodore Foote, who is in charge of this expedition."

"Yes sir, General Grant," she smiled as Mike pulled the gangplank into position and offered his hand. "So you've been piloting this boat, Mike?"

Alex followed, dropping their trunk and valise on deck. Mike turned to point. "Take your baggage into this cabin. Fortunately it won't be as crowded as it was on the *Golden Awl.*"

Alex looked around curiously. "I'd heard the Mississippi was closed to traffic, and I wondered what you were doing."

"Been taking barges down the Ohio—oil, coal, whatever. Come up to the pilothouse. Foote's been looking over the charts while I've worked on the steam gauge. It was stuck."

Halfway up the stairs he paused. "You'll enjoy meeting Foote; he's a Christian gentleman, and a good seaman besides."

General Grant had preceded them to the pilothouse. He and Foote turned with a smile as Alex and Olivia followed Mike. Commodore Foote held out his hand. "You two are a very welcome addition to our crew. Let me get you some coffee and we'll explain it all." His eyes were still twinkling as he handed coffee to Olivia. "Sorry this isn't tea, ma'am, but you see, we just didn't expect you."

"If Mike hadn't come over the rail when he did," Grant rumbled, "I'd have fed them to the fish."

Alex chuckled. "Sir, if I'd any idea who you were, I could have saved us all a few tight moments."

Commodore Foote bent over the chart table. "Don't think you need to know anymore than this—" He cocked his head. "Full ahead, Mike. The steam's up, and there's no reason to delay."

As the boat moved away from the wharf, Foote said, "Alex, we were on our way up the Tennessee River. Need to take a look at Fort Henry."

"I'm in the dark," Alex murmured.

"Come here." Foote pointed to the map. "See these two rivers? The Tennessee and Cumberland, nearly parallel each other. At this point, just over the Kentucky-Tennessee line, the Confederates have built two forts—I should say, they *are* building two. Right now they are only partially completed and armed. We need to take a good look, see what we're getting into. Understand?

"The Tennessee flows north into the Ohio at Paducah. We're going upriver, away from the mouth."

Olivia nodded and returned his smile. She liked this man, who explained things clearly without condescending.

Foote glanced back at Alex. "Having your wife along will make it much easier to appear casual about this reconnaissance," Foote commented. "Not too often do pleasure trips transpire in tugboats. But then, attractively dressed women don't usually ride on such vessels, either."

"Whatever the reason," Olivia said, "I'm enjoying being back on a boat again. It's nearly like coming home."

"Are you by chance a pilot?" Foote asked Alex.

"I have my license, but not for large vessels." Before Olivia turned back to the window, she caught a glimpse of the studied expression on Commodore Foote's face.

General Grant moved from the window to the table. "We'll move full power ahead until we reach the border, then we'll assume the relaxed manners of sightseers."

"It's late now," Foote murmured, checking his watch. "If we don't have good daylight, we'll lay over until tomorrow."

Grant glanced up. "Might be a good idea. That would give us an opportunity to check out Donelson, too."

"What is Donelson?" Olivia asked.

The men looked at each other, and Grant answered, "Another fort, sister to Fort Henry. It's located about fifteen miles east of Henry, on the Cumberland River." Grant paused. He seemed lost in thought, then he turned to Alex. "I know you have questions. What I'm telling you is information that is not known beyond this circle. I feel it's better to answer the questions now rather than allow you both to speculate. Sometimes the most innocent information serves disloyal ears."

He paced the pilothouse, returned to the table, and faced Olivia and Alex. "Beginning last autumn, we've been making attempts to gain a foothold on the Mississippi and extend our control throughout Kentucky. Mike can tell you that our initial attempts to take over forts along the Mississippi were thwarted."

He paused and turned to look at Alex and Olivia with a crooked grin. "I don't suppose, since it wasn't a Confederate victory, that you've been advised of the fighting that's taken place during this month in the eastern part of Kentucky. Harris, Buell, and McCook have all had their turns. Harris pushed the Rebels back into Virginia, but he couldn't gain control of the railroad. General Thomas, a Virginian true to the Union, pushed back another group at Crossroads. And now it's our turn. We've got to gain control of the western section. We must begin to break open the Mississippi."

"And Tennessee?" questioned Alex.

Grant threw him a quick glance. "We must have all of it, but we'll take it as we can get it. Right now the Confederates are primed to defend Fort Columbus. We have other matters to handle first; our aim is to surprise them. You two are our guests this sightseeing cruise in

Mike's little tugboat, while we check out the forts on the rivers."

Olivia was in the cabin, shaking out her frocks and hanging them in the tiny wardrobe when Alex came in. She glanced up and asked, "Is it time to come out on deck?"

"No, it'll be another hour or so." He wandered restlessly around the cabin while she continued unpacking.

"Alex, being on the water again reminds me of all the wonderful times we've had in the past."

"Wonderful? We were risking our necks." He smiled down at her.

"What is it, Alex? Something's bothering you."

"Commodore Foote has asked me to pilot a gunboat. He said they're desperately short of pilots."

"Why, Alex, that sounds exciting."

He faced her. "Olivia, don't you realize what that means? I'll be taking a boat into battle. There will be fighting. My boat will be lobbing shells at those forts. I'll be indirectly killing men. That's something I've never been able to reconcile doing."

Slowly she folded Alex's shirt, straightened the collar, and buttoned it. She faced him and studied his troubled face. "I can't see you in that situation. But Alex, no matter what you decide, just be certain that it is what God wants of you. That's the only really important consideration." She stared at him a moment more and then flung herself into his arms.

CHAPTER 18

Alex stood at the wheel of the tugboat. The clouds to the west reflected the rosy dawn in the east. The "sightseers" had left Paducah, Kentucky, before daylight and Cairo, Illinois, lay directly ahead of them.

The door opened behind him and closed softly. Grant spoke. "Foote is impressed with the way you're handling the tug."

"It's good to be behind the wheel again, sir." Alex kept his eyes on the channel and listened to Grant's footsteps as he restlessly roamed the narrow quarters.

"Your wife is staying with friends?"

"Yes, sir. The Stevens were glad to have her. I guess I should have insisted she go back to Pennsylvania."

"A fair number of women follow their men around the country," Grant mused. "Personally, I find it distracting, and it's certainly dangerous. The battle of Bull Run proved that."

"Were there civilian injuries?"

"As far as I know, there weren't. But I wasn't there; General McDowell was, and also General Patterson." He was silent before adding, "But it was a miracle. Some saw it as a spectator sport. It was bad all the way around."

Alex heard the General's voice change and glanced at him. Head down, Grant stared at the charts. His voice was muffled as he said,

"You mentioned being involved in the Underground Railroad. I don't expend any energy caring one way or another about slavery, but one thing I have noticed is that the Negroes are more than willing to be in this fight. They seem to make good soldiers. I welcome the time they'll be allowed to join the army." He glanced at Alex. "I understand the navy is making a place for them right now.

"I came to tell you the Commodore wants to see you after we dock. He'll be up, so don't take off." The door closed, and Grant was gone.

Alex pulled the bell cord and began to ease into position at the crowded wharf. Mike stuck his head through the door. "I'm heading for the barracks; see you later."

Alex had finished putting the cabin in order when Commodore Foote came through the door. With a weary sigh, he dropped into the nearest chair and asked, "Is there coffee in the pot?"

"Yes, Commodore Foote; I'll bring it. General Grant said you wanted to see me."

"Mostly wanted to tell you I appreciate your cooperation. I was very serious when I asked you to consider joining us for this next offensive. I like the way you handle a boat. There's a permanent slot open for you—if you want it."

"Mike mentioned you were having a problem getting pilots," Alex murmured as he poured coffee and sat across from the commodore.

"Right now we're nearly desperate." Foote looked at him intently. "Your wife mentioned that you've been making your home with a Quaker family. Certainly I know the Quakers are deeply involved in the abolitionist movement, but they're also pacifists. Does that have anything to do with your reluctance to pilot a gunboat for us?"

"I'm struggling with it," Alex replied. "Commodore Foote, Mike tells me that you are a Christian. How have you dealt with this?"

"Son, I became aware of the slave problem as a navy man back in 1849. After stopping a few illegal slave boats, I found myself hating the institution of slavery. You can't grasp the ugliness of it until you've seen black people pirated from home and freedom to be stuffed in the stinking holds of ships and sold as merchandise—if they survive the torture of the trip. The degradation is total, both moral and physical."

He shook his head. "From beginning to end, it's dehumanizing—not only for the slaves, but for those who traffic in their flesh. A man cannot treat a fellow man like an animal without becoming an animal himself."

"Sir, that's strong talk for a Southerner to hear."

"Then tell me why you call yourself an abolitionist?"

"When I came crawling to God, slavery passed from being a slightly distasteful situation to a condition I had to do something about." Alex stared into the distance, remembering. "For years I saw only their shiny, happy faces and heard their quaint songs. At Christ's feet I learned to see past the smiles to the soul agony, and I began to hear the heart behind the songs."

Foote fastened him with a stern eye. "And having begun, now faced with the ugly part of the task, you're going to be a quitter?"

"That's not so!"

"Then, pray tell, what is it? Alex, have you foreseen the future these people will have if the North loses this war? So you don't like putting a bullet into a man's head. Neither do I. When this all began, I didn't consider the outcome of my action against the men promoting slavery, either. But having begun the fight, I dared not back down." He was silent for a time. Then, looking at Alex, he said, "I must face my Maker some day, and I know the first words I'll be hearing are those from the book of John when Jesus said—"

" 'Greater love hath no man than this, that a man lay down his life for his friends,' " Alex quoted.

"No," Andrew Foote said gently. " 'He that loveth his life shall lose it; and he that hateth his life in this world shall keep it unto life eternal.' "

"Are you saying my problem is self-love? I honestly thought I'd done all that was expected of me."

The men sat in silence for a long time. Alex drank his cold coffee; Commodore Foote raised his head and reached for the map. He touched Cairo and drew his finger down to Fort Columbus. In an easy conversational tone he said, "Earlier this month, reconnaissances were made all over the place. The cavalry moved toward Columbus; General Buell has made motions in the eastern part of the state, and we understand Johnston has responded by drawing his forces into Knoxville. You see, Alex, things are drum tight around the whole area, including Tennessee. We've made feints until we dare not make another."

He got to his feet. "Grant has called a meeting for tomorrow morning. I won't pressure you, but if you want to move out with us, be at the meeting."

———

The next morning, when Alex walked into the conference room, Grant was seated at the table in the front. Commodore Foote sat beside him. For a fleeting moment, his eyes met Alex's, and then General Grant got to his feet.

"Briefly, men, this will be the order of action. The gunboats will proceed up the Tennessee, destination: Fort Henry." He paused briefly. "So we'll go upriver with the gunboats. They will be followed by ten regiments, transported with artillery and cavalry. On the morning of February fourth, the fleet will assemble nine miles below Fort Henry. Troops will be dispatched from there."

———————

On Tuesday morning, when Alex took his gunboat up the Tennessee, the dawn was grayed by fog. Unseen marsh birds screamed protest while owls surrounded the flotilla with hoots of inquiry. The distant answers had Alex moving uneasily about the pilothouse, wondering if by chance the bird voices were human.

Foote came in. "The *Essex*, the boat in front of us, has been ordered to continue upriver. We want to draw fire from the fort, to see what their capabilities are." He turned abruptly. "Don't be alarmed if there's a problem. We're sending in the *Essex* for a reason. Of all the boats, it's the most expendable. The tub started out as a ferry in St. Louis. They converted it for us by slapping on some thin iron sheathing. If it holds together, it'll be a miracle."

He came to the wheel; Alex, holding the glasses, said, "Don't see a thing. Wish those owls would lay off; I keep feeling something's creeping up on us."

"Could be," Foote murmured, taking the glasses. The fog began to lift. They watched the *Essex* bring up her steam and slowly push up the Tennessee.

Foote instructed, "Pull in behind her. Prepare to move in if necessary, but keep plenty of distance for now." He settled down with a mug of coffee.

The sun was overhead when they sighted the fort. Foote had his field glasses on it when the firing began. Shells hit the water on either side of the *Essex*. The explosions rattled the pilothouse while water shot up like geysers around them. Alex reduced his speed, but the boat continued to rock.

Giving an exasperated sigh, Foote dropped his binoculars. "Well, that did it. She has a hole in her plating. She'll make it back, but won't be good for much."

The *Essex* limped past them and headed back downstream. "We're out of range. Let's keep it that way for now," Foote murmured. "We saw a pretty sizable group of men the other day. We'll work on the assumption they're still in the fort." He walked to the opposite window. "The transports behind us will be unloading as soon as it's dark. The troops will encamp along that ridge. If you noticed the position of the fort during our little sightseeing trip, you've probably guessed it won't be difficult to take. It's built too low to avoid the rising river water."

Throughout the day Alex stood at the wheel, watching the fort and surrounding terrain. Late in the afternoon, Commodore Foote reported, "General Grant has called for action tomorrow morning. The Confederates, soggy feet and all, are abandoning their rifle pits," he added. "The water's coming up."

Early the next morning, Commodore Foote stood beside his men on the deck of the *Cincinnati*. He nodded toward the gray hulks surrounding them. "You four ironclads move out in front. Flagship is *Cincinnati*. Watch her signals. You other three keep in as close as you can."

He stressed his words. "It is of absolute importance for you to keep cool. From pilot down to each gunner, keep every action controlled and deliberate. We don't have ammunition to waste. Furthermore, if these guns get too hot, you'll blow them up. Remember, we're here to give the troops coverage and support. Now to your ships, and God bless you and keep you safe."

Alex took his boat into position. Moving slowly to the pace of the marching troops on the banks of the river, they began a slow advance.

Grasping the wheel, trying to watch the channel and the signal flags from the *Cincinnati*, Alex was caught off guard when the gunboats behind him began firing. Hanging on to the wheel, he heard the whistle of shells passing over the pilothouse from the boats in the rear.

The skipper came through the door. "Hold it steady," he shouted, "my men need all the help you can give. Line it up straight and keep it facing the fort."

Another shell whistled overhead. He heard the explosion, and the skipper shouted, "Got 'em! Hold on now, it's our turn." He ran for the stairs. There was another explosion.

Alex yelled, "Skip, that's the *Essex*!" The door banged behind the skipper. Alex watched the *Essex* founder and list sharply. Then her boilers blew.

He threw a quick glance at the fort. As the smoke and dust cleared, he saw a section of wall was beginning to cave in. There was a double explosion, and this time as the smoke and dust drifted away, Alex saw only rubble where cannon and men had stood a moment before. Within minutes, Alex saw the Confederate flag come down. A white flag was quickly lifted.

The *Cincinnati* signaled a stand-by and Alex hit the gong to cut the engines. Foote had taken a skiff to shore, and Alex watched with his glasses as the commodore was greeted by the gray-uniformed man leaving the fort.

The door opened and Alex turned. "Skipper wants you below," the seaman said. "Take your gear; you're piloting the *Conestoga* upstream.

Lieutenant Phelps has asked for you. His pilot is wounded, and they're moving out now."

Alex grabbed his bag and sprinted down to the waiting skiff. Boarding the *Conestoga,* he headed for the pilothouse. Phelps met him. "Move it out as fast as you can. We're going south on the Tennessee. We're going to chase down those Confederate gunboats."

When Alex had put Fort Henry behind them, Phelps returned to the pilothouse. "Twelve miles south of here, the Memphis and Ohio Railroad crosses the river. We've got to cut that line. It's the link between the whole works. From Bowling Green south and west to Memphis, and then north up to Fort Columbus, it's the Confederate lifeline. We destroy this railroad, and we have their bread and munitions line."

He picked up the binoculars and moved to the window. "Push it; the *Tyler* and *Lexington* are behind us. I figured we'd need help."

As they approached the railroad bridge, Phelps muttered, "The draw is closed; they've probably jammed the gears. We've got to get through."

It took an hour to open the draw. As the bridge creaked open, Phelps sprinted for the boat, yelling, "Men, pour on the steam, we're gonna catch those Rebs."

Back in the channel, Phelps finally caught a glimpse of the Rebel boats ahead. He kept his glasses on them, announcing, "We're gaining." As he spoke, there was a muffled explosion from behind.

"The *Tyler* has taken care of the railroad bridge," he said. "Can you raise more steam? I'd like to force those boats over."

Alex nodded and reached for the bell cord. They were gaining on the lumbering transport when Alex heard the first rumble. The explosion seemed to turn the vessel in front of them inside out. He grabbed the bell cord just as the concussion knocked him off balance and threw him against the wall.

"Alex!" The sound reached him from a distance; with a groan he shoved himself upright.

Phelps had the wheel. Alex shook his head and felt blood on his face. "What happened?"

"They've blown up the ship; guess they didn't want us to have their gunpowder."

When they reached Florence, Alabama, they found a delegation of citizens waiting. Alex looked from the flag flying above his head to the line of people on the wharf. They were smiling, but they seemed apprehensive as Phelps approached. Alex leaned over the railing to listen. The spokesman of the group gestured toward the railroad bridge, pleading, "Please, sir, don't blow up our bridge."

When Phelps returned to the pilothouse, he said, "Matey, let's go home. Mission accomplished."

"Going to leave the bridge?"

"No reason to destroy it. Strategically, it's not important to either side."

After they were back in the channel, Phelps sat down at the chart table to write his report. For a while there was silence in the pilothouse. Finally Phelps came to the wheel. "Alex, I've been sitting here thinking, trying to decide what to put in my report. Know what sticks in my mind with significance? It's the people we've met every place we've stopped. It nearly tears me up to see how eager they are—not only to see us, but to tell us of their loyalty to the Union. Alex, at first I was skeptical, but it's happened over and over. These people are sincere."

Alex nodded. "Several places the crowds have numbered in the hundreds. Instead of shouting like we're heroes, they could have swarmed aboard and overpowered us. Think of the accolades they would have received from Richmond."

"But instead they were hailing the flag with genuine love and respect," Phelps added.

When the *Lexington* and *Conestoga* reached Fort Henry, it was deserted except for stragglers moving east.

Phelps took the glasses. "Grant said he was going to push on to Fort Donelson, just twelve miles east of here. I've a feeling they started marching immediately."

"Think we'd better stop for information?"

"No, let's not waste time. We need to move on Donelson as soon as possible. Let's head for Paducah. We'll take on supplies and proceed upstream to the Cumberland."

At Paducah, they discovered the flotilla hadn't arrived. Phelps returned with information. "Foote has the gunboats in for needed repair. They said he's apprehensive about going in at all because of the condition of the boats."

Late Wednesday night the flotilla headed for the Cumberland River. Alex was at the wheel when Mike came into the pilothouse. "Buddy, I haven't seen you since we left Cairo over ten days ago. You been hanging on that wheel the whole time? You look exhausted. I'm relieving you for now. Go down and get some rest."

The following morning when Alex arose, the riverbank was lined with people shouting and waving. They pointed toward the flag on the boat. A gray-haired man snatched his hat from his head. "Hurrah,

hurrah, hurrah for the Union!" As the boat left the man behind, Alex heard him shout, "God bless you, soldiers!"

"Six gunboats and fourteen transports, and they're greeting us like liberators. Is that what we are?" The lad looked at Alex with awe.

"I hope we are," Alex muttered, heading for the stairs.

———————

By Friday the gunboats were in position for attack. Foote faced his men and said, "We hoped this would be a combined assault, however, the terrain has slowed the army and we can't wait any longer. We'll clear the way for them. Take the position you had before. Remember, this isn't going to be an easy task. Fort Donelson is entrenched and ready for us. They are positioned higher, and this gives their guns the advantage. Take it cool and easy. God bless."

Slowly the gunboats began to move. In accordance with Commodore Foote's command, they didn't stop at a thousand yards and position for firing as they had at Fort Henry. Alex continued to advance. The tension mounted in the pilothouse. Wiping perspiration from his face, Alex wondered about the men on the hurricane deck, poised behind their guns.

Finally the firing began. A few shells struck the fort, but the watchful silence continued. Alex shifted from one foot to the other, uneasily studying the fort. Looking down the channel to the flagship and back to the fort, he muttered, "We're putting ourselves right under their guns."

Lieutenant Adams, who was standing beside him, lowered his field glasses and looked at Alex. "Bunch of jumpy men! The *Tyler* and *Conestoga* are firing over the fort. Our men have got to slow down. They're shooting like scared idiots."

"They don't like being this close."

"Orders, not choice. Keep on course," snapped the officer as he left the pilothouse.

Feeling as if he were peering into the depths of the heavy artillery pointed toward them, Alex grasped the wheel and watched the Confederate guns move into position. Abruptly the first line battery fired. Immediately, another battery position fired and the gunboats began their barrage.

He felt the vessel beneath him reel with the explosion.

Alex tested the wheel. The gunboat responded, but sluggishly. The lieutenant appeared in the doorway, his face was white with concern. Alex said, "We're still operational."

"We've taken some bad shots. So far it's surface damage." He lifted the glasses and said, "But we're getting in some good strikes. Give us fifteen minutes more and we'll have them. Will you look at that!"

Alex looked at the fort. The first gun and its crew had disappeared; there was only a gaping hole in the wall of the fort. The gun beside the hole had exploded, fire streaking the air. Then they took a hit. The *St. Louis* was listing, moving downstream out of control. Another explosion sent the *Louisville* to join her sister ship, and together they drifted with the current.

"Two out of six," Adams muttered. Another explosion had Adams out of the pilothouse at a run. He returned briefly, saying, "It's the *Carondelet*. Looks like their gun exploded. There's going to be heavy casualties."

"We're being signaled to withdraw!" Alex exclaimed.

They moved downstream. Hidden by the island, the boats regrouped and waited for General Grant to board the ship carrying Commodore Foote. Lieutenant Adams came to the pilothouse. "Commodore Foote has sustained a foot injury. Looks like our job is completed; we'll be moving back to Cairo."

He left the cabin, but returned immediately. "Phelps has been ordered back up the Tennessee to finish off the railroad bridge," he told Alex. "Seems the job wasn't completed last week. They're taking the *Tyler*; he's asked you to pilot. Take your gear; you'll rejoin us in Cairo."

On deck Alex looked at the damage the fort's guns had inflicted. He touched the deep dents in the iron plating, fingering the fractures and sections where the armor had separated from the hull. "Makes a person mighty glad we were in an ironclad," the seaman beside him said. "It's a scary thing to watch them point those big guns your way."

The skiff from the *Tyler* was approaching. The cold wind swept downriver and Alex clutched his cap and muttered, "Can't see the men from here, but we know they're in the heaviest part of battle right now. It's going to be a cold night out there on the hillside. I pray to God that they get the wounded in before nightfall."

"Aye," the sailor murmured, moving to catch the rope thrown at him. "And finish that bridge off this time."

Late the following day, their mission completed, the *Tyler* returned down the Tennessee, crossed over to the Cumberland, and began moving upriver toward Fort Donelson.

"Aren't we heading for Cairo?" Alex asked when Lieutenant Phelps gave him the order.

"No, Grant wants to keep the *St. Louis* and the *Louisville* here. We're to serve as backup." Phelps added, "They lost the pilot on the *St. Louis*. The bombardment wiped out most of the pilothouse. We're short of pilots again."

The sun was setting as they drew even with Fort Donelson. At first the place seemed deserted. Alex saw a hint of movement from the batteries. Light touched the barrels of a few guns. Phelps studied the fort through his field glasses. Slowly he said, "Something major has happened here. There are mighty few men around; certainly not the troops we saw Friday."

Then he caught his breath. With a low, incredulous oath, he dropped the binoculars and faced Alex. "That field over yonder is covered with men," he whispered. "They appear to be dead." He wiped a shaky hand across his face. "I've never seen so many!—Alex, take us down around the bend, out of shell range, and let's see if we can give a hand."

The crew was on deck waiting when Alex reached the shore. Phelps said, "Approach the battlefield from the back side. Daylight is nearly gone; hurry, fellows." The cold wind whistled through the tops of the trees, pelting Alex in the face as he rushed to join the crew.

Phelps and his men stood in silence on the edge of the field. With caps in hand, they began to look for signs of life. Then the wind reversed, sweeping the scent of death across their faces. Alex turned away, reeling from the smell and the impact of the scene.

"Help! Oh, God help me!" The voice was faint.

Shaking his head slowly, Alex muttered, "Oh, my God, what are we doing?" The scene sickened him. "Is the preservation of the Union more important than the lives of *people*?"

A hard hand came down on Alex's arm. Alex saw the general's insignia first, then the man's face, deeply furrowed with fatigue, his eyes blazing. "Lad—" His voice was deliberate and slow. "The Union *is* people; the *slaves* are people. Our business is to cause freedom to happen for *all* people." The general jerked his head toward the bloody field covered with twisted, ruined bodies. "Lad, if the Union isn't worth dying for, what is?"

"But to pull a trigger and take a life?" Alex muttered, wiping his face with a trembling hand.

"Even then. These lads didn't back out of pulling a trigger or dying." The hand released Alex's shoulder and patted him on the back.

Gently the general said, "Over there. Boy, the two of you get over there together." He thrust a seaman toward Alex. "See what you can do. We've got to get these men out before they freeze."

"Water! Help!" Alex looked across the field and ordered his numb legs into action. Alex and Tim, the seaman, worked throughout the night. Where there was a sign of life, they stopped to give water and carry the soldier to the riverbank.

It was nearly dawn when the old general stepped in front of Alex again. "Take some coffee and hardtack; you need it." Alex eyed the uniform and the man continued in a gentle voice. "It's ugly, but it's war." By the light of the fire, the general's eyes examined Alex. "I'm Lew Wallace."

"General Wallace," Alex murmured. "I've heard about you."

"Don't turn away from a man if he's wearing the wrong color uniform," he warned. "We're all brothers."

"I know, sir." Alex stopped beside the fire, took the cup of coffee and hardtack. He glanced at the tired, drawn face, and impulsively said, "Sir, it's hard to see God in this."

"But He's here. For some of these fellows, He's closer than He's ever been before in their lives. They need to be reminded of that. Don't judge God by the ugliness man creates."

At dawn the last shovel full of earth had been thrown into the last shallow grave. Wallace faced the soldiers clustered around him, "Return to your positions. We must prepare to take Fort Donelson this morning."

For an unbelieving moment Alex stared at him. But with another glance at that face, he knew General Wallace meant what he said. The lines of fatigue had deepened into lines of determination. Alex headed for his gunboat.

Back in the pilothouse Alex ordered the steam up. He waited until he felt the engines send a shudder through the ship. Deeply conscious of the wounded lined on the riverbank, he signaled to reverse the gears and slipped in behind the *St. Louis* and the *Louisville*.

Phelps stuck his head through the door. "We're going to join them." He closed the door behind himself. The morning sun touched the ruined entrance to Fort Donelson. Light bathed the Union troops, guns ready as they flanked the fort. Alex's eyes swept over the waiting men. In that moment, when it seemed as if life itself held its breath, the flagpole inside the fort quivered, and slowly a white flag was lifted.

The sun touched the figure of a man poised in the entrance to the fort. Light picked at the glory of gold braid on his uniform and the white flag he bore as he made his way across the field toward General Grant. Hardly believing his eyes, Alex sighed and muttered, "So they're tired of fighting, too."

As Alex waited to receive the prisoners, Phelps stood at his side with the glasses trained on the men. "There are at least ten thousand men," he murmured. "Look at them, dressed like farmers. What a contrast to all the gold braid the officers are sporting."

Alex watched the weary faces, lined with defeat. He felt a strange kinship, wondering, *Are Olivia's cousins in that group? Have any of my kin been taken captive? Someone has called this a brother's war, and how real it is. I look at those defeated, hungry, weary faces and see my own.*

CHAPTER 19

Olivia paced between the window and the Stevens' cozy kitchen. "It's been so cold lately," she murmured. "I keep thinking of all those men out there. Louisa," she turned to Mrs. Stevens, noting her serene face and the gray knob of hair on her neck, "why do men fight? I mean, they could just refuse to fight."

Louisa Stevens shook her head as she turned the freshly baked bread out of the pan. "All the men I've known wouldn't do otherwise."

For a moment Olivia's heavy spirit lifted and she laughed. "Oh, Louisa! How Southern you are, and how much I've forgotten. Of course, it's male pride. But don't you get extremely tired of it?"

"Don't know anything else." She looked at Olivia with serious eyes. "It's hard on the folks around them. I'm right sick of duels and swords. For one thing, I don't believe the Lord intends people to be living out the Old Testament nowadays, otherwise there'd be no need for a New Testament."

"Love rather than fighting?" Olivia nodded. "Alex would say we're to live the New Covenant; the Old is dead."

"But love doesn't seem to come natural. Guess a body's forced to listen to the Lord before he's willing to change his way of life." Louisa wrapped a loaf of bread in a clean towel and added, "Now let's walk this bread down to Lily Mae's place. She's in the dumps, too. Hope this war's over before they start taking old men like mine."

Olivia handed the shawl to Louisa, and together they left the house and turned down the path. "It's only February; it's going to be an early spring." Olivia pointed to the dogwoods and willows with their beginning buds. The grass along the creek banks held nestling bunches of violets. The wild geraniums had unfolded their leaves, revealing a promise of buds.

Olivia sighed deeply. "It's good to see nature responding just as it should. Everything else in life is starting to appear twisted and unreal. War, war, that's all we hear." Impulsively she turned to Mrs. Stevens. "How good of you to let me stay with you. I couldn't bear going back to Pennsylvania without Alex."

"He's a dear lad; I'm glad to see you both so happy with each other," Louisa said. There was a troubled frown on her face.

"What is it?" Olivia whispered.

"Wondering how you feel fighting against the South like this. Kentucky is my home, there's no way I could ever see myself taking up arms and shooting my neighbors."

"Alex says we aren't fighting against the South, but against slavery. In addition, we fight for the liberation of the people."

"You mean the slaves?"

"No, everyone. There's a frightening feeling that until slavery goes, there's little chance of growing up to be the nation we should be. Alex explained it by saying it's like keeping a child forever a baby by depriving him of the opportunity to grow. A small stomach can't eat bread and meat if we insist on giving the child only milk. A baby will never walk if we carry him constantly."

"And you think the South is like that?"

"It seems there's an unwillingness to grow beyond what they are. We heard a man talk about the lack of industry in the South. He also mentioned the lack of education for poor white people as well as for the slaves."

"My children never had much of a school to attend," Louisa said slowly. "I always thought it was just wishful thinking to want more. 'Specially since the slaves around us had nothing in the way of teaching. So you think the South needs to be forced to grow?"

"No, not forced. That goes against the grain. Alex says sometimes we have to feel pain before we want to learn a better way of living."

"Do you regret that Lincoln didn't just let the South go?"

Olivia sighed heavily. "I think I will before this is over. At times I think anything is better than war."

Together they walked silently up the path to Lily Mae's house. The woman who opened the door was red-eyed. She twisted her apron and stood back for them to enter. "Aw, this war," she sniffled as they sat down at the kitchen table. "Why God doesn't just blow the North off the earth, I'll never know. Surely this war is judgment against them, but it's hurting us all."

Olivia winced as Louisa placed the bread on the table and asked, "What's troubling you today?"

"The cow's gone dry and I can't get no one to plow for me. My pa would, but he's just too old."

"Why don't you and the young'uns do it? I've handled the plow for Mr. Stevens. It's hard work, but it's better than going hungry."

"How do you plow?" Both women turned to look at Olivia. Feeling foolish, she said, "I've never been around when there's plowing going on. Seems it ought to be a thing for a woman to learn."

"Well, it isn't easy," Lily Mae said shortly. "You've got to work the mule and that stubborn hunk of metal at the same time. Of the two, the plow's more apt to take off in the wrong direction."

"Well, let's give it a try," Olivia got to her feet. For a moment Louisa's eyes sparkled, but with a sober face she stood up.

When the afternoon sun sloped toward the west, nearly three furrows had been plowed. Olivia surveyed her crooked furrow, looked at her blistered hands, and sighed wearily as she said, "Can't you just plant corn where the plow *did* go?"

"Might," Lily Mae admitted.

"No," Louisa said. "We'll be back tomorrow to help. And Lily Mae, if my man ends up going to battle, can I count on you to help me?"

When they entered the Stevens' kitchen, Mr. Stevens looked up from his newspaper. "Saw you down the road. Most fun I've had for sometime."

The merriment died out of his eyes as Louisa grabbed a spoon and shook it at him. "Harold Stevens, are you laughing at three helpless women plowing behind that lazy mule? I'm ashamed of you!"

"Louisa, might be it won't hurt you women a bit. It's better'n going hungry. Read in the newspaper where there's shortages of food down in the cotton belt. Can't get things moving smoothly enough to get crops in." He paused. " 'Tisn't the women's fault. Some of the farmers are still planting cotton when they should be planting corn, wheat, and 'taters."

"Cotton brings more money, if they can sell it." Louisa slowly put the skillet on the stove. "Are you saying that we need to learn to do for ourselves, because you men may not be around to do it? It's that bad, huh?"

"It's bad and getting worse." His jaw tightened. "Might be when the South gets organized it won't be, but right now—" He sighed and bent over the newspaper. "Last week we read that while General Grant was taking Fort Donelson, other Federal troops were moving against Bowling Green and then Fort Columbus. Now today's paper says here that General Grant's headed south. Next he'll probably push into big places in Tennessee, like Nashville, Memphis, and Clarksville."

"Why are you sighing like that?"

He looked up at his wife. "I was just thinking how much trouble we'd have saved ourselves if we'd been a little more outspoken when the matter of secession came up before the state legislature. You know it was like a stack of cards. One strong push from either direction would gain the vote. The Confederates pushed the hardest."

"Why, Harold, do you mean to tell me that you honestly think we'd have gone Union that easy?"

"Certainly. I told myself it didn't matter too much. Seems the idea of war wouldn't linger too long. But I forgot one thing."

"What was that?"

"Southerners aren't known for giving up easy on anything. They've demanded their slaves, and they're determined to keep them. Also, they've been pushing this idea of the North being a patsy. Wanted people up north to believe one hard threat with a few guns, and the North would give them slavery forever. Didn't realize the North has a lot of the same kind of blood in their veins. It's a hard-nosed bunch we're up against. I'm thinking now that we're going to be forced to fight until this problem is resolved once and for all."

He paused for a moment, then continued. "I've been listening to the fellows talking around town; these aren't my ideas. Might say I'm scared to admit it, but this is one of those situations where there's no backing out of the situation we've helped cause."

———

Each day Olivia and Louisa walked down to Lily Mae's field and took their turn at the plow. Louisa said, "Olivia, we might as well look at this as a good opportunity. Never know when we'll need the experience. Besides, it's keeping you from wearing out my floor by pacing to the window to see if your man's coming up the path."

For a moment Olivia was embarrassed, and then she laughed. "I wasn't aware of being so—silly." She kept her voice light. "But if I'm able to plow a field all on my own, might be I'll talk Alex out of being a lawyer so we can buy a farm instead."

Unexpectedly Louisa hugged her. "You ought to learn to plow straight before you do much talking to Alex."

On the first of March Lily Mae's sister arrived from Nashville. On that same day Olivia and Louisa carried a sack of seed corn between them when they arrived at the farmhouse.

Louisa dropped the sack of corn just inside the door, out of the reach of persistent hens. Lily Mae, flanked by her children, pressed Louisa and Olivia into the kitchen. "This here is my sister, Hannah; she's from Nashville, and she has the tales to tell! The Yanks have taken Nashville, and she's escaped with her life!"

"Oh, Lily Mae!" Hannah turned from the stove with a wide, easy smile. "Don't you believe half of what my sister says. I did not say that. Actually, it's quite the opposite. They gave us a bow and said, 'Pleased to meetcha, and please go back to doing what you were doing when we came.' No, I'm serious. They were just as nice as they could be. See, we were shaking in our shoes when we heard the Yanks were coming. General Beauregard had said about those Yanks that 'beauty and booty' was their motto."

She came to the table and sat down. "But it was a blow, I tell you. On Saturday night, pretty close around midnight, the word came that General Grant had been defeated and that General Pillow was victor. My, there were church bells ringing and people dancing in the streets. Never did we feel so confident and secure—then came Sunday morning."

Hannah stopped to drink her coffee. Olivia eased forward on the bench. "Mind you, we were at church, celebrating the victory, when the blow fell. All peace and quiet one minute and the next, Governor Harris came galloping through town yelling that Fort Donelson had fallen, the army had been captured, and the Yanks were moving in on us. He gathered up the state legislature, jumped on a train, and headed for Memphis. And the confusion he left behind him!

"That was the end of church and rejoicing. Men were throwing bags and trunks out windows, while the womenfolk were walking up and down, wringing their hands and weeping. Johnston was telling us there's not a way on earth Nashville can be held against the enemy. Down in Nashville, there's hardly an anthill to hide behind. So he took off, and here came the Yanks.

"Sure, the Yanks would rise up and call us blessed for giving them the river and a bunch of good roads." She twisted out a wry smile. "But after all the things Beauregard said about them, we didn't want to stick around and greet them. But most of us realized there wasn't any place we could go, so we might as well sit tight and hope for the best.

"My, those Yankee generals were something else. They were gentlemen. Came into town, and the first thing they did was to put down rules, saying the soldiers weren't to enter any home without being sent out to do so. Then they all went and called on Mrs. Polk—you know, she's the old lady whose husband was President of the United States." She sipped her coffee and then added soberly, "It's fearful how fast life can change. Last month the South was spreading out all over the place— half of Kentucky and all of the Tennessee was in their hands. Now every where you look there's the Yanks."

Olivia couldn't control her sigh of relief. Hannah grinned at her. "I kinda feel the same way. Not much in favor of war in the first place. I guess at heart I'm really for the Union."

The corn didn't get planted that day. But when Olivia and Louisa left the house late in the afternoon, Lily Mae eyed the corn sitting just inside the door. "We could come back tomorrow morning and plant," Louisa said. "We'll have you a crop coming up before your husband gets home."

When Louisa and Olivia turned into the Stevens' lane, they saw a strange horse tied to the fence. A man on the porch got up from the rocking chair and Olivia recognized Alex.

She moved toward him, nearly doubting her eyes, as he came down off the porch with a leap. His arms were hard, warm and familiar. "Oh, Alex, you have a bump on your nose."

"Olivia, let me see your hands. What have you been doing?"

She sighed happily. "Nothing, just waiting for you."

"And I've come to take you home, back to Pennsylvania."

"Alex, you don't need to convince me. I've no desire to do more traveling except back to Pennsylvania. And we'll stay there forever."

She leaned back to look at him. He was pale, and his eyes seemed sunken, shadowed. She put her arms around him. "Oh, Alex, you don't need to tell me," she whispered. "I can see it was horrible."

CHAPTER 20

S pring has come to Pennsylvania, too." Olivia glanced at her husband and slipped her hand into his. "Did you notice, Alex? The hickory trees and the willows look as if they're wearing green clouds."

She turned to look at the Coopers' house, rising like a pale gold shaft in the middle of plowed fields, barren orchards, and empty flower beds. "For us, the Willows is home, isn't it?"

"Yes, my dear, it is home," he murmured, looking toward the dock. "And now I need to check out the *Golden Awl*. See what needs to be done before she's ready for the river."

"We've only been home two days, and you can't wait to get into that boat," Olivia murmured. He glanced at her and she smiled. "I'm teasing. But Alex, after your stories—"

He wrapped his arms around her and snuggled her head under his chin. "Olivia, I awaken in the night and have to touch you to remind myself—"

"I know; I've felt your restlessness. Alex, what must it be for the others?" She felt him flinch and she tightened her arms. *Is he thinking of going back—back to the battle, into the danger?* she wondered. "Alex, it will soon be over," she insisted. "You've done your part. Amos has given you a list of projects you can do to help the slaves and the soldiers."

"I wonder why Caleb hasn't come?" Alex questioned. "Not a one of us has heard from him since we left Canada."

"I've written again," Olivia murmured. "But Alex, even more than worrying about him, I can't stop wondering about Crystal and Matthew."

"I hope you're praying for them."

"Yes, and it seems strange to me that I constantly think of them together. I do pray that God will keep them safe and bring them back together. Is that too much to ask? Oh, Alex, both of them were so torn I can scarcely believe they'll ever see each other again."

"Let's pray they'll try to settle their problem. Our God is a God of miracles, and if we want a miracle in their lives—"

"We must believe God wants it, too."

Alex kicked at the stone in the path and Olivia asked, "What are you going to do with the boat?"

"I don't know. Perhaps look around for someone needing my services."

"Sadie said Mike did hauling on the river until the war closed it to traffic other than military." She hesitated. "If something's happened to Mike, will they let us know?"

He shook his head. "But I understand the newspapers publish lists of casualties, and they're also posted in each city and town." A shadow passed over his face like a cloud over the sun. "After seeing a battlefield such as the one at Fort Donelson, I can't believe it's possible to deliver a correct account of the men."

They stopped where the path forked. One trail led down to the river and the other up to the house. Olivia said, "Go see to the *Awl*; I'll help Sadie prepare for Sunday dinner. I understand Beth has invited her young man."

"Such a child," Alex muttered. "How can she be considering marriage to that fellow?"

"But Alex, she's as old as I was when we were married." She laughed up at him. "We've been married nearly four years; have I aged that much?"

"No, but you've mellowed considerably!" he teased. He cupped her face in his hands and whispered, "Olivia, what would I do without you? How I thank the Lord for you."

The smile disappeared from her face. "Even when I can't give you the child you want?"

"I don't want a child nearly as much as I want you. Please don't feel as if you've failed me." He wiped the tears from her eyes and kissed her tenderly. "You are my only love, my only sweetheart."

"Alex, let me go before the neighbors see!"

Beth dropped the corner of the curtain and turned away from the window with a sigh. Sadie looked up from the dungarees she was mending. "What is thy trouble, Beth?"

"I was just thinking, maybe I don't really understand what love is."

"If that's the case, thou had better put aside any talk about getting married until thou dost. Afterwards, it's too late to change matters." She bit the words off, pausing to snip at the thread on the dungarees. Snapping the scissors together, she added, "Some people are constituted to learn to be loving, and others would rather run than settle with what they've bought into. Now, take that little miss down at the schoolhouse. She's the type to settle in and be grateful for any kind of a man."

Beth snorted. "And you're saying I'm not? Well, Mrs. Cooper, I'm inclined to agree." She eyed Sadie curiously. "What kind are you?"

Beth watched Sadie's eyes dance as she chuckled and said, "I'd sooner be not married than to be saddled with a man I didn't love." Hastily she added, "But I knew long before I settled for Amos that we'd be happy."

"Funny," Beth said slowly, "I don't think of older people caring much about love. Seems after the children come along most people hardly pass the time of day with their spouse." She hesitated, picked at a stray thread on the rug, and then sat down beside Sadie. "To tell the truth, I can't imagine the people at meeting even knowing what love is all about. Take Mattie and Jake Thomas. She's so fat, and he doesn't look like he could keep his feet under him in a windstorm."

Sadie slanted a glance at Beth. "Well, they have a houseful of nice tykes. Thou couldn't do better than to follow her—in behavior more than eating patterns. The mister doesn't look like much, but I've caught him patting her hand on the sly, and it didn't seem to me that she minded too much. Might do thee good to go talk to her."

————

During the night Olivia turned and reached for Alex. The cold sheet under her hand brought her bolt upright in bed. Moonlight outlined him against the window. Olivia sank back against the pillows and pressed her hand to her racing heart. Finally she asked, "Can't sleep?"

He turned. "Did I disturb you?"

"No, I missed you." She slipped out of bed, reaching for her shawl. Shivering, she went to stand beside him.

"Olivia, you'll catch cold." She shook her head. Impatiently he said, "Then come, let me hold you in the rocking chair."

"Alex, what is it? Since we've been back, it seems you toss and turn most nights. Are you thinking of the battle at Donelson?"

"Partly," he murmured, snuggling her into his arms. "Your feet are icy."

Hesitantly Olivia said, "There's much you can do to help without going into battle yourself. Sadie told us about the Sanitary Commission, how the nurses and doctors work on the fields to care for the wounded, and of the hospitals they've organized. There are also factories and foundries needing manpower." He didn't answer. Desperately she said, "Alex, you know I'll go anywhere you say. And I want you to do what you feel is necessary."

Slowly he said, "It's the burden of war. By helping slaves escape, I've done my share toward making it a necessity. I guess I've just begun to see the enormity of it all."

"Do you mean you'd never have become involved with the slaves if you'd been able to have seen the consequences?"

He hesitated. "When you put it that way," he mused, "the idea seems ridiculous. The job needed to be done, without a doubt."

Olivia sighed, moved her cheek to rest against his, and admitted, "I've thought of it all, too. Wandered down a hundred paths, wondering what avenue we should have taken instead of just simply secreting the people out of the South. I know we saved lives, but now we face this terrible war. What do we do? Alex, I really do feel horribly responsible. But fighting doesn't seem to be the answer. Why can't people resolve these situations without bloodshed?"

He shook his head. "We've all gone over this a hundred times. I suppose the closer one lives to God, the more horrible the consequences of war seem. Especially when we don't know whether or not these men know Christ as Redeemer."

He paused, thinking. "Olivia, I can only take courage from some remarks General Grant made. In Tennessee he said that he believed one more big Union victory would give us the war. I believe the man; I think he knows what he's doing. God knows we can't take much more of this. Acres of dead or dying men can't support a war, and that's what we're seeing."

———

The next evening when Beth walked into the barn, the packed earth floor had been swept smooth. Benches lined the walls, and wagons were loaded with barrels of cider and baskets of pastries. "Roald, it really looks like a dance hall, all cleared of hay and tackle."

He chuckled. "A barn party!" He looked down at her. "I understand it was to have been on the common, but because of rain—"

"They moved it inside." Beth looked up at him. "Oh, Roald, I can't forget all the frightening news," she whispered, clutching his arm. "I keep wondering how much longer I'll be seeing you. Some of the fellows who were at the last frolic are—" She gulped, unable to say the word.

"Beth, don't think about it." He bent close and she blinked tears from her eyes. "We have to snatch at life as we get it. As far as I know, I'll be here training troops forever." His smile teased her. "Unless you're in mourning for those other fellows, come dance with me."

She lifted her hands and smiled roguishly. "I love the uniforms; they make men out of country bumpkins."

"So that is what you think I am," he murmured in her ear. "Come into the tack room, and I'll prove otherwise."

She laughed and spun away from him. "No matter; right now it's all exciting, and I can forget the war."

For a moment he was serious, frowning down at her. "I can't forget it for one moment. And Beth, when I hear you speak, I can't forget we're on opposite sides of the battle."

"I've heard that several generals with Northern politics have married Southern women," she taunted. "I wonder how they manage?"

"Are you suggesting it's feasible?"

"Only that it's happened to others." He steered her toward the tack room. "Roald, please—someone will see us."

"Does that matter?" He lifted her chin, kissed her quickly, and said, "Beth, you know that I'm terribly in danger of falling in love with you. What shall we do about it?"

"Roald—" She paused and smiled up at him. "I seriously think—"

"What?"

She patted his cheek and in a rush finished, "We should go have some cider." She laughed as she whirled through the door.

"Beth, you are a tease," Roald said over cups of cider. "I suspect that you've got forty beaus hiding in the bushes. I suppose there's only one way to secure you for myself if I must march off to battle."

"Since you won't be marching anywhere except around Mr. Cassaway's meadow, I suggest you don't worry." With a smile she walked back to the packed earth dance floor.

The cool March wind had become brisk by the time Roald took Beth home. The wind cut at the light buggy, making it sway on its high bed. Beth tightened her shawl around her shoulders and moved closer to Roald. "If this thing tips over, I shall land in the middle of you," she said with a giggle.

"Then I suppose to be safe, I should tie it to the first tree I find." Beth was silent, and Roald flicked the whip over the horse's back. He glanced at her. "I'll take the back road; it isn't as windy."

They were nearly to the Willows when Roald pulled the buggy into the shelter of the trees and stopped. "Beth, you tease until I never know just what you do think of me. Is there any possibility you'd give me a serious thought?"

"Most certainly, Roald. I give you much serious thought. I wonder if you're happy, if you like being a soldier. I wonder what you really think of Southern girls, and I wonder—"

"Too much." He tugged her hand and bent close in the moonlight. "Now, would you like to know what I'm thinking? Beth, I don't want to obligate you with any promises, but when this war is over, I have some serious questions to ask." She sighed, lifted her face, and let him kiss her.

"Roald, I know so little about life," she said slowly. "Sometimes I have this desire just to grab on—anywhere, just so life won't go off and leave me alone."

"Grab on; you're not alone, Beth." He pulled her into his arms and Beth touched his face as he kissed her.

———

When the sun streamed through her window in the morning, Beth's first thought was of Roald and his ardent kiss. Moving her shoulders uneasily, she questioned, "Why do I feel guilty?" But with a determined whisper, she added, "After all, I'm going to marry him someday." Slowly she got out of bed, warming her feet on Sadie's braided rug for a moment. *Do you marry someone,* she wondered, *when you don't even like their kisses?*

CHAPTER 21

Mike dropped his duffel on the barracks floor. "So General Hallack is now commander of all the Union troops in this section of the country," Mike mused. He sat down on the wooden bench and unlaced his muddy boots. "How come they didn't make Grant commander?"

"Guess he's still on probation," Deaver muttered. "Heard there's talk about him drinking and so forth, but I sure haven't heard anything about it personally. He's always right there in battle." Deaver scrutinized the red slash of fresh scar tissue on his arm.

Tom sat up. "Naw, it's just that he's new at it all. Give him time. I'm putting my money on Grant, even if he's a nobody right now."

The door at the end of the barracks opened, and a gust of windborne rain rushed in with the seaman who entered. He consulted the paper he pulled from under his jacket. "Deaver, Thompson, Jacks, Shultz, Maxey, and Rohner. Report to building seven at 9:00 A.M. sharp." He paused. "Clancy, General Grant wants to see you in his office at six in the morning."

"What have you done now, Clancy?"

Mike sighed. "Nothing. Just means they're still short of pilots. There goes my trip home."

"Give me that pretty little gal's name and I'll drop in on her next week when I'm on leave," Thompson leered.

"If I had a pretty little gal, I'd heave my boot at you for the invitation," Mike countered with a grin as he reached for the boot brush.

"When are you and Duncan going to join up with the rest of us?"

"Why join? We've been doing the job without being in the navy."

"Guess so's you'll get a pretty uniform like the rest of us and then leave," Thompson retorted. "Duncan went home, didn't he?"

"I think so. His wife was with him. They'd planned on going down to Natchez, Mississippi, to visit her folks, but things are too hot down that way. Some are saying New Orleans has been harassed by Farragut."

"Bet the Rebs'll hang that guy if they get their hands on him. He's Southern. Not a good example of Southern loyalty, sticking to the Union like he has, and then giving it to New Orleans."

Deaver chuckled. "When they tried talking him into going against the Union, old Farragut told them the Confederates'll catch the devil before they're through with it all. Guess he's going to see that they do! He's been trying to take his boats into the Mississippi from the Gulf of Mexico for nearly a month now."

At six the next morning Mike walked into Grant's office. The general raised his head and dropped his pen. "Morning, Mike. You can probably guess we didn't get any naval pilots. Foote has a good share of the pilots and they're pushing against Fort Columbus. If you will, help us out again. We've got two transports, two gunboats, and at least one dispatch boat going up the Tennessee."

"That doesn't sound like a very big job."

Grant threw a quick look at Mike. "That's just my personal contingent. Smith, McClernand, Wallace, Sherman, and Hurlbut will be joining us." He straightened. "These divisions are following us from our supply depot."

"From your map the depot looks a fair piece downriver."

"It is, unfortunately, but it can't be helped." His grin twisted. "Taking eighty-two transports upriver is like blowing a bugle to announce our arrival. We're ready to start our push to take Corinth, Mississippi." Grant continued. "I want to be moving out tomorrow morning." As he spoke he pushed a pencil across the map in front of him, touching the Tennessee and following the river south to Corinth. "I'm heading out first. General Buell and his men will be behind me a day or so. General Wallace will be coming in with the final group. In the field, we should have a force of around ninety thousand. Our plans are to move out from Pittsburgh Landing, twenty miles above Corinth, Mississippi.

"When we reach there, I'll lay over and wait for Sherman and Buell."

He paused, adding slowly, "The only thing that bothers me right now is the green divisions. Just plain raw recruits make up the divisions of both Sherman and Prentiss. Unfortunately, they'll be the first to go in."

He got to his feet. "Here's your boat assignment and instructions. You'll have the *Tyler*. The other boat is the *Lexington*. See you in the morning."

At dawn the gunboats pulled away from the wharf at Cairo with the transports following. Before noon they turned up the Tennessee.

Skipper Jones came into the pilothouse. "Well, Clancy, are you expecting the best on this trip?"

"Aye, sir," Mike said with a nod. "Seems people are beginning to look on us with favor, like family. Hope we get the same response at Corinth. Looks like we're expecting a big battle."

"Don't see how it can be avoided. Corinth is mighty important. It's the crossroads of the Confederate's main railroads. We get the railroads, and we've crippled them all along the Mississippi." He paused. "I see you have instructions, but I need to add that both gunboats will be positioned just above Pittsburgh Landing. Grant's troops will be west of the landing, and Wallace will be over here, near this little church, at a place called Shiloh. You need to know these positions in order to keep track of the action going on. Don't want one of those eight-inch shells landing in the middle of our camp." He gave Mike a friendly poke in the shoulder and left the cabin.

By the end of the day, the transports had unloaded their men near Corinth and retreated downstream. Using the field glasses, Mike watched Grant's men bedding down. The skipper came into the pilothouse and Mike lowered the glasses. "Jones, isn't Grant going to entrench his men? They're lined up like birds on a fence."

"No. Doesn't want them too comfortable. They'll be marching the twenty miles into Corinth as soon as Buell arrives, so it didn't seem necessary to dig in for so short a time."

"Guess I shouldn't be questioning," Mike said slowly, " but is there any possibility the Rebs will come creeping up on our men?"

The skipper chuckled. "I think we're safe. They don't know we're in the area. Johnston's so demoralized that he won't be looking for trouble again soon. No chance of him popping into Tennessee now."

For the next two days, Mike listened to the sounds of camp and watched the river traffic. Buell still hadn't arrived and the men appeared bored. They were even relaxed enough to pull in a good string of fish for their supper.

On the following morning, Mike took his own restlessness to shore. The early sun had not yet burned off the river mists and the silent sleeping camps had lent encouragement to the foraging deer as well as the cranes and ducks. Mike had just settled himself on a log when he heard a horse. "Who's there?" he called softly.

The man turned his mount and rode toward him. "What are you doing here?" The soldier's voice was tense.

Mike glanced down at his dungarees. "I'm Clancy, pilot of the *Tyler*." The fellow relaxed.

"I'm Prentiss' picket," he spoke rapidly. "Reconnoitering. I've found troops moving this way. Think it's Johnston." He wheeled his horse and took to the trees.

Mike jumped in the skiff and headed back to the *Tyler*. The engineer saw him coming. "Alert the other gunboat," he muttered, heading for the skipper's cabin.

With the field glasses, Mike stood at the railing of the *Tyler*. For the next hour he scanned the shores of the Tennessee River. Standing with his back toward Shiloh church, he had begun to relax. But as he watched the terrain sloping toward Owl Creek, screaming Confederates burst out of the woods surrounding the church. Stunned by the Rebel yell, Mike spun around.

Skipper Jones charged into the pilothouse. Reaching for the field glasses, he groaned and dropped them. "We're too far away; we won't reach them with the guns. We'll have to let the army take the field until we can get the artillery in position. I'm going to send my men down to help with the guns we have unloaded. To think Buell's headquartered at Nashville! We'll never bring him up in time. The others better get here pretty soon, or we're in trouble."

Throughout the day Jones stayed in the pilothouse, looking for an opportunity to move into position with his guns. Mike watched him periodically drop the binoculars and pace. "I can't believe this," he muttered. "How can that many men sneak up on an army? And look at them! They've thrown every man into the battle at once."

At noon, Mike had the binoculars. He watched the ranks break and exclaimed, "Oh, no! Skip, look at this."

Jones looked. "The green ranks are fading out of the picture." He swore and thrust the binoculars toward Mike. "Only good thing is that half of those men are dressed in gray."

Mike held the field glasses on the bluff lining the edge of the Tennessee. "Poor young'uns! I can see the terror on their faces even from here." Mike shook his head. "It's a shame, sending them into a battle this fierce."

"We gotta do it, Mike. We get this far and there's no turning back."

Later they watched General Prentiss march his troops out along a sunken road leading toward the creek. "Those lads have guts—that's a bad position," Jones muttered. "Go to it, boys. We're rooting for you."

"Those boys are going to be slaughtered," Mike said. "Even from here, it's evident they're outnumbered. Why aren't Buell and Wallace here?"

Jones shook his head. Mike paced the deck and watched the shoreline. "It's bad. They're dropping like flies."

Just as the sun slipped behind the trees, Jones exclaimed, "Now's our chance. Mike! The Rebels are moving into position. Take the boat in as close as you can. They're sitting ducks!"

———

When the roar of their guns finally ceased, Jones came upstairs. Mike turned from the wheel. "Shall I take it midstream?"

"No, let's keep this position; we're not plugging the main channel."

"Good job," Mike said. "You forced them to withdraw from the field."

Jones gave a tired sigh. "The Confederates are still pounding that lane with field guns. There's no way Prentiss can take it. Looks like he's surrendering," he added. "There aren't many lads still on their feet. At least—" He dropped the binoculars and pointed to the ridge. "They gave Grant time to line that ridge with his men."

Mike took a look. "Is that General Beauregard?" Jones nodded. "Looks like he's pulling out," Mike said. "Strange; I didn't expect that. There's still daylight left."

"I've been watching them for the past hour. Looks to me like those fellows are about as low as a fighter can get and still stay on his feet. For us, maybe it isn't as hopeless as it seemed. I expect Buell to be on the field in the morning."

Mike checked through the binoculars again. "Ah, I see! No wonder they quit. Those Rebs have a ravine at their back." Slowly he added, "Skipper, if you don't think we'll need to move this boat tonight, I'll go down and lend a hand. Things look pretty bad."

"I'll send my men down there too," Jones muttered, heading for the stairs.

Mike reported to the grim-faced team on the river bank. An officer came to him. "We've got one doctor. Get a helper and a stretcher. Try to give them water if they're conscious. Be careful, or you'll be stepping all over the wounded."

"Name's Art," the youth beside him muttered. They started out at a trot. But when they reached the battlefield, they both stopped. "Lord, have mercy," Art muttered. "Look at 'em. Blood boot deep, and—" he stopped gulped.

Mike continued to stare down at the mangled bodies, tortured faces. "Those field guns blew them apart. Just boys."

"The most horrible part is that they can look like that and still move."

Art's teeth were chattering, and Mike straightened up. He took a deep breath. "Art, we've got to get out there. Come on, buddy."

"Help, please help me!" A piteous voice called, nearly under their feet. "Water?" The man's arm was gone, and Mike hesitated, wondering how they would lift him.

"Sure, buddy, here's water." Art knelt and lifted the man's head. He hesitated, then looked up at Mike. "Guess he won't need this water." His voice was choked with tears.

Mike had made two trips carrying the wounded from the battlefield when Grant came onto the field. With his officers clustered around, Mike watched the man's face sag in disbelief and sorrow. "We've got to get the living out of here as fast as possible. Bring up the transports."

"Are we retreating, General?"

"Retreat?" Grant rounded on the officer who had said the word. With a steely-eyed frown, he stressed the words, "I don't intend to retreat. I'll be on the field at daybreak tomorrow, and we're going to whip them."

Mike looked down at his blood-stained hands and clothing. "God bless you, General," he muttered toward the slouched form moving among the injured. "You're going to need every bit of blessing you can get."

Until well after dark, Mike continued to fumble his way through the field. The moon was rising when a soldier stopped him. "You Mike Clancy? Grant wants to see you; he's over there."

General Grant turned as Mike approached. "Mike, I've just been told Buell is across the river. Take the *Tyler* and start ferrying them across. We can't spare the other boats; we're moving the injured into them as fast as we can."

Mike headed for the boat just as it began to rain. He lifted his face to watch the heavy clouds swirling across the moon and shook his head. "God, bless the men out there; it's a horrible night to be out in this cold rain." For a moment he hesitated. Thinking of the wounded and the rain, bitterness welled up inside of him. Carefully he bit back the agony of all the "whys" he wanted to shout heavenward. Turning his back on the bloody field, he doggedly set his feet in motion.

Olivia stepped out the front door and watched as a man climbed out of a wagon, shouldered a bag, and turned. "Mike!" she gasped, staring into the pale, unsmiling face. "Oh, my dear! What has happened?"

Alex came down the steps as Mike said, "Nothing—at least nothing more than has happened to all the others."

Alex looked him in the eye and took the bag from his shoulder. "Welcome home, Mike. It's good to have you back."

Sadie rushed out the door, wiping her hands on her apron. "My boy—oh, Mike! Come in right now and let me take care of thee."

When Amos and Beth came into the house, the group was still sitting at the table with Mike. The rhubarb pie was untouched, but the coffee cups were empty.

Amos shook Mike's hand while Beth lingered in the doorway. With her eyes wide in her pale face, she whispered, "Mike, you are so thin. Your face—"

He avoided looking at her as he made room for her at the table. Amos asked, "Hast thou been on those gunboats all this time?"

"Yes, sir." He glanced at Alex. "After you left I helped out at Columbus. I was ready to take leave when Grant asked me to go up the river again. We were headed down to Corinth, Mississippi. Johnston and Beauregard met us at Pittsburgh Landing, about twenty miles out of Corinth. We had quite a battle."

"We read about it in the papers," Alex said. He squinted at Mike. "Pretty bad? A day and a half of fighting and twenty thousand killed and wounded. I pray the dear Lord nothing like that happens again."

"Alex, don't kid yourself," Mike interrupted roughly. "We were saying the same thing until Grant changed our tune. I guess he's the only one with the nerve to lay it to us straight." Mike stared down at his coffee cup for a moment before adding, "Grant admitted that before this encounter, he'd predicted one more battle and the rebellion would be over. Now he's admitting he's given up all idea of an easy victory, saying there's no way the Union can be saved except by a complete conquest. Shiloh is just the beginning battle of all out war. We'll fight until there's no one left to fight."

He got up from the table, stumbling as he walked to his bag. "Mind if I just go up and sleep? I haven't had much lately. As good as Sadie's cooking is, I need sleep worse."

As he moved past Beth, she stretched her hand toward him and then hastily pulled it back.

The group around the table listened to Mike's unsteady footsteps on the stairs. Beth whispered, "Roald—will he be like that?"

Olivia looked at Alex but he avoided her eyes.

"It isn't right," Amos said, "this lifting a gun against another human being."

His voice heavy, Alex asked, "But is it possible to reverse, to go back the way we came, to allow slavery and say it is not a worse evil than to pursue the course set before us now?"

"One innocent man killing another?" Amos asked.

"Or one powerless black man being killed through oppression? I think it is impossible to answer for them."

Olivia caught his eye. "Haven't the slaves given the answer? They've risked their lives for freedom. Some of them didn't make it. Oh, Alex, I hate war, but what choice do we have beyond being true to our inmost being, and to God?"

"That's the part bothering me," he said slowly as he got to his feet and left the room.

Beth watched him go and turned to Olivia. "Why can't we just leave things as they are? Why must we stick our noses into this?"

Sadie winced and rubbed her red eyes. "It is impossible to roll back time and circumstances. Dost not God expect us all to live honestly, even if it is painful?"

CHAPTER 22

Amos came into the kitchen to find Mike, Alex, and Olivia sitting at the table. As he dropped the newspaper in front of Mike he said, "Here's more about Farragut taking New Orleans. He didn't exactly get a hero's welcome when he marched into the city."

"According to the last newspaper," Olivia said, "it sounds as if the South isn't too happy about Beauregard's actions in Tennessee. Mike didn't tell us this, but it says here Beauregard not only surrendered the field in Tennessee, but he also left Corinth, Mississippi, saying it wasn't important enough to fight for. And the railroads junction there!"

"The situation in the South is changing," Mike interjected. Slaves are coming out in droves. We saw caravans of them, traveling with a few old broken-down wagons and horses in pretty sad condition. They were headed for the Union lines as fast as they could go."

"Why?" asked Beth.

"They were freeing themselves by escaping into Union territory."

"And no one tried to stop them?" Beth cried in amazement. Mike studied her face for a moment before he answered, "Not very hard. In some parts of the South, living conditions are getting bad enough that I honestly believe the owners are glad to have them go."

When Beth lifted her face, she looked around the group with a bewildered smile. "Why is everyone looking at me?"

"I suppose it's because you didn't say anything," Olivia said hesitantly. "Beth, I can't help thinking you're very homesick."

"Homesick?" Beth laughed shortly as she got up and began to clear the newspapers from the table. "Sadie," she called toward the kitchen, "I won't be here for supper. Roald is taking some of us downriver to Stubbensville. There's some kind of fair to honor the soldiers and raise money for them." With a smile, she added, "I think the fellows will be honored and the girls will be worked!"

She started to leave the room and then turned. "Mike, would you like to come?"

He dropped the newspaper to look at her. Olivia saw his jaw tighten before he forced a smile and said, "Thanks, but I don't care to go."

Late that evening as Alex and Amos carried pails of milk back to the house, Alex heard his name called softly. He stopped in the path, recalling another night when a voice had called from the shadows—the night the *Golden Awl* had returned with a load of slaves. The call came again.

"Who is it?" He called, but as soon as he saw the darker shadow move out of the trees, he knew. Carefully setting the pail of milk in the path, Alex ran forward and caught his old friend in a warm hug. "Caleb! We've wondered about you—and worried. Come into the house."

Inside, Alex looked at Caleb's tattered clothes, noted the lines on his face, and gently took him to the table. Sadie hurried into the kitchen, and Amos poured coffee for Caleb. Alex said, "I thought we'd lost track of you. We've been home for over a year. Mother died last December."

Caleb lifted his head, focused on Alex and said softly, "I'm sorry; she was a nice lady." He paused, then the words came in a rush. "I have bad news, too. Lost Bertie and the baby—a little boy; we named him Alexander." For a moment his face twisted. "Things seemed to be going fine that winter after he was born, and then something came along—a plague. Took out lots of the people." Looking at the floor, he rambled, "Seems us people accustomed to the heat can't take the cold."

Olivia had come into the room, and she listened as Caleb finished his story. Sitting down beside him, she whispered, "Oh, Caleb. I'm so very sorry. Please, will you stay here with us?"

Sadie came over and said, "Thou art welcome. Just take the room next to Alex and Olivia. Now, Amos and I will be going to meeting. Make thyself at home."

"Thank you. I'll tarry for a day or so, then I must be off." He shook hands with Amos, adding, "Been seeking out our people. Now I'm hearing the Union navy is taking on black folks. I aim to join up."

After Amos and Sadie left, he turned to Alex, his eyes lingering on the gold earring. "Getting a taste of freedom gives me a need to work it out for the others. Alex, you think Lincoln will free the slaves? Down South that's all they talk about—how Lincoln's going to save the slaves and deliver them out of bondage."

"I think he's going to need to win this war first," Alex said slowly. "There's talk of freeing the slaves, but Lincoln says he's only trying to save the Union, and he'll do what must be done for the Union's sake."

"He doesn't care about the slaves?"

"Lincoln cares very much. He thinks slavery is wrong, but freeing the slaves isn't the issue right now. It's preserving the States as a whole, united body."

Caleb hesitated, picked up his fork, and asked, "What do the people in the North think would happen if the South were just let go?"

Alex shook his head. "Most think it wouldn't work. It's like a married couple deciding they aren't going to be married any more, but will live next door to each other as neighbors. There's no way, after being married, that they'll ever be *just* neighbors. Some things can't be undone."

Caleb chuckled. "There'd be a heap of fighting going on." Olivia watched the shadows in Caleb's eyes as he picked at his food. Finally Caleb asked, "Alex, you gonna fight?"

Olivia held her breath. "Not if I can help it," Alex said. "Goes too much against the grain, taking a gun against another human."

Caleb nodded. "But you're different. Since we were little, you've been different. Not like other Southern boys, always scrappin', trying to be the hero and out-brag their buddies. Them duels and fisticuffs!" He shook his head. "Alex, against the grain or not, maybe you'll have to get in there and help Mr. Lincoln. You'd do that for him, wouldn't ya?" Alex drank his coffee as Caleb continued. "Might be the Lord's sayin', 'Looky here, you fellows down there started this, now finish it. You wouldn't listen to me in the first place, why come beggin' me to take over now?' "

"You think so?" Alex looked up. "Caleb, do you think there are some things in life which the Lord won't change? Maybe the problems we pull down on ourselves?"

"Alex, you told me yourself that the Lord will never force us against our will. You said that it rains on the just and the unjust. The North wouldn't give the South what she asked for, so the South, she starts a war. Guess the North fights back or decides a *United* States isn't worth keeping."

"But Caleb," Olivia protested, "you've told us over and over that the slaves have been crying out to the Lord for deliverance. Won't God deliver them?"

"If He answers prayer, then He'll deliver, one way or another. Maybe he wants people to help deliver, Missy. Why do some prayers get answered and some don't?" She saw a deep pain in his eyes, and she could only shake her head.

"At times," Alex answered, "all we can guess is that God has plans and purposes we know nothing about, and His greatest desires for us are that we truly become people of God."

He toyed with a spoon, then finally looked up reluctantly. "It's very likely God will ask of me something I don't want. Life has almost been too easy. This might be that call which will enable me to become what He wants."

"Even so far as fighting and dying?" Olivia whispered.

Alex opened his mouth to answer when they heard footsteps come through the hall. It was Beth. She seemed bewildered as she looked around the room. At last she focused on Olivia and cried out, "Roald is going to Washington. That means he'll be fighting."

"Oh, Beth, I'm sorry. But just because he's going to Washington doesn't mean he'll fight."

"There's men being killed by the thousands!" she cried, pacing to the table.

"And Lincoln's plea for men has turned out hundreds of thousands," Olivia countered. "Beth, can't you see, it's going to take this kind of army to win the war?" She stopped abruptly. Alex was watching her.

Ashamed of her duplicity, Olivia turned, but Beth had already left the room. Olivia watched Mike coming down the hall. Without speaking, Beth hurried past him and up the stairs.

He hesitated in the doorway and Alex called, "Come in, Mike. Here's someone you need to meet. This is Caleb."

He came forward with a grin. "I've heard plenty about you. Good to have you here."

Caleb nodded. "I'm on my way to join up with the navy."

"Man, am I glad to hear that! I've been filling in because they can't get enough pilots. I'll let you have my job any day."

"You're not going to stay with the navy?" The smile faded from his face. "You and Alex." He shook his head. "My mother used to say to me, 'Caleb, you started this, now you finish it. It don't matter you didn't give it a moment's thought before getting in over your head, dat's yo' problem!' I don't reckon I like fighting any better than you."

"But you're going, Caleb," Mike protested. "I can't reconcile Jesus Christ and his gentle ways with killing."

"Then I guess I'll have to ask for you to know His will."

"What if you find out He says it isn't my job?"

"Then I'll be going for you. I feel it's what the Lord wants me to do."

During the night, Alex awoke sweating and shaking. He had dreamed a man had been attacking Olivia, choking the life out of her. As his racing heart slowed, he recalled his part in the dream. He hadn't delivered just one smack to the head of the intruder; instead he had methodically pounded the man to death. The man's blood ran boot deep around Alex.

He took a deep, shaky breath. *You can fight for anything*, he thought, *if it's important enough to die for.*

CHAPTER 23

"Alex," Olivia said as she turned from the bedroom window the next morning, "how would you feel about becoming a father early next spring?"

"Is that a promise or an enticement?" he murmured, nibbling her ear.

"I think it's a promise." He looked intently into her face before pulling her close, rocking her gently in his arms. Pressing her face against his shoulder, he fought the dismay he felt. *Lord, I was ready to tell her I must go to war. What do I say now?*

"So that's why breakfast is suddenly uninteresting. Olivia, my dearest, I'll put you to bed and personally wait on you for the whole nine months."

"No, you won't, I'm perfectly healthy. And it won't be nine months. This is the middle of August. Sadie says it will probably be in March."

"Olivia, God is in control of this child. I promised you we'd have a baby in His time."

"His time," she whispered wonderingly. "And His time is at the worst possible time for the Union. Oh, Alex, last year the Union lost that terrible battle at Bull Run. Now it is starting to look as if they'll be repeating it all again."

"It doesn't look good," he admitted, "but Lincoln and the army have learned plenty during the past year." He snuggled her closer. In an article I read recently, one newspaper man said part of the North's problems now stem from their defeat at Bull Run."

"What did he mean?"

"That the North lost their confidence because they were whipped. And the South has a high level of confidence because they won. The writer didn't feel it was going to work to the South's favor in the end." He paused, saw her puzzled expression, and added, "Overconfidence. Guess what we need to do for our fellows is to pray they'll do their best—better than they think is best right now."

"Alex, we were in Charleston when the war began. I remember how terrible it was—the agony we felt listening to reports, hearing it called a blood bath."

Alex lifted her chin and kissed her. "It's getting late. Today is the Sabbath. Will your stomach allow you to participate in breakfast and meeting or would you rather stay home this morning?"

"Let's try the questions one at a time, starting with breakfast. Right now I'm starved."

At the breakfast table, Sadie eyed Alex's grin and said, "So thee knows. Might as well make an announcement; it'll be easier on Olivia."

"Why?" Beth asked.

"Because Olivia turns green when she smells bacon," Sadie said with a twinkle in her eyes. "Well, Alex, if thou art just going to grin, I will say it. Olivia and Alex are going to have a wee addition to their family." She nodded to Olivia. "Now thou can just let Beth wait on the table. I've made some nice cooked oats for you this morning. Oats sit lighter than cornmeal."

After breakfast Amos turned to Beth. "Beth, if thou goes to meeting this morning, it might be easier to face the week."

She lifted her chin. "You are saying you don't think I'll be getting a letter from Roald this week. How can meeting help that?"

Sadie nodded, "True, it doesn't. I know I'd like a letter from Mike, telling us what's happening to him. But it helps to know thy kind heavenly Father cares when thy heart aches, Lass."

———

Meeting had just begun when Mike slipped into the pew beside Alex and Olivia. While Alex clasped his hand and Sadie beamed at him, Olivia examined his face. The stark, stunned look of pain he had worn home last time had vanished. She sighed with relief. As the brethren rose one by one to share with the congregation, Olivia silently thanked God for Mike's return, and then fell to musing over the expression on

Alex's face when she told him about the baby.

He couldn't hide it. Joy, yes—but he still had shadows in his eyes. Did they have something to do with the cautious statements he's been making since Caleb left to join the navy?

The voices around her faded, and Olivia faced the solitary thought. Alex would go to war, and she must not cling to him. Carefully she bit down on her lip until the desire to cry fled under the pain.

While they were climbing into Amos' carriage, Mike said, "This far inland, the heat gets to you. Guess I'm going soft, spending so much time on the water."

"How didst thou manage to find us?" Sadie asked.

"Where else would I look on Sabbath morn?" Mike asked with a laugh. "I took the train into Martinsville, found a ride coming this way, and knew I'd find you here."

"Going to be with us for a time?" Amos asked as he flipped the reins along the backs of the team.

"No. Things are slow right now; there's regrouping, and we're waiting for troops to come from out East." He took a deep breath. He threw a quick glance at Sadie and continued. "I've joined the navy. As long as I'm going to spend all my time piloting boats around, I might as well be part of the crowd."

Sadie sighed heavily. "I can't say it surprises me, but Mike, thou art so young—"

Words failed her, and Amos added, "And he'll be young when he comes back from battle, too."

Mike looked around. "Beth isn't here. Did she leave?"

"No." Sadie eyed him sharply. "After thee left, that young man, Roald Fairmont went back East with his regiment, the Pennsylvania Volunteers. He didn't know much about where he was going. Beth's had letters from him up until the last month. From what they've been saying all over, the mail just isn't getting through. Heard Lincoln's cut off the mail service into the South. But thou can't believe all thee hears, especially during times like this."

"Where is she?"

Sadie looked startled. "Beth? She stayed at home this morning. Didn't seem to be willing to let the Lord bless her at meeting."

When Mike walked into the house, it was filled with the aroma of roasting pork, apples, and onion. Beth had the table set and the fragrance of coffee was beginning to mingle with the scent of meat. Mike went into the kitchen, grinning at Sadie. "I'd forgotten what real food smells like."

He found the tray of cookies. "Hello, Beth," he said casually. "So you're chief cook today."

For a moment she stood blinking at him. "Mike . . ." she said slowly, "I'm surprised to see you. How do you manage to get leave so often when none of the others do?"

"Well, thanks for making me welcome," he said dryly. "Until this past month, I was my own boss. Now I'm part of the Union's navy. I'll inform them that you'd rather I didn't pester you with my presence."

She flushed. "I'm sorry, I didn't mean that. I am glad to see you. It's just that I was thinking about Roald and wondering why he can't come home. You know he's been gone for over two months."

"I understand that's the military life. Hear it happens to most of them."

"Did you—" She rushed to stir the contents of the kettle. Sadie came into the kitchen. Tying on her apron, she said, "Beth, it smells like thou didst make a wonderful meal. Would thou get the milk and buttermilk from the springhouse? Olivia needs a mug of milk now. I'll dish up the dinner."

"What's the matter with Olivia?" Mike asked.

Beth turned pink and Sadie said, "She's in a family way. If thou goest to help Beth, thou can carry the jugs." She gave him a stern eye. "And hurry."

Silently Mike followed Beth as she quickly crossed the kitchen and headed for the springhouse. In the cool earthen depths, Mike breathed deeply of the mingled odor of fresh butter, ripened cheese, and mellow apples. He dodged the side of bacon hanging from the rafters and made his way through the dimness to the far corner where the swift-moving stream dipped in and out of the building.

Pulling out jugs of milk cooled by the water, he wiped them dry with the towel Beth handed him. "Get the tub of butter too, please." She pointed to the crock in the water.

"Sadie's springhouse is another memory I'll cherish," he murmured.

"You don't expect to be back?"

"Haven't any idea," he muttered, selecting an apple from the basket. He faced her in the dimness. "I'm just storing up things to remember. Don't most people do that?"

"What will you remember about me?" Her eyes were wide and dark. He touched her cheek with a fingertip, grinned slowly and admitted, "That you are a puzzle and a tease. That you are beautiful and promised. Other than the bedraggled child I pulled out of Mississippi, what more could a fellow remember under the circumstances?"

"We've had good times together—the hayride."

"And when I kissed you in the hay, Sadie scolded me."

"You let me dump my problems on you."

"And you let me kiss you again. Pretty Beth, china doll."

There were tears on her face. "Oh, Mike; I'm afraid Roald won't come back. He could be wounded or even dead. It's been over a month since I've had a letter."

"Beth," he said heavily, "have you checked the lists in town? It's silly to mourn when you've nothing except your own fears to feed your troubles."

"Will you go with me? I need a big brother."

He chewed his lip as he looked at her and thought, *Big brother, as usual*. He squared his shoulders, "Certainly, but now let's get this milk up to Sadie. So old Alex is going to be a papa," he mused as he followed Beth.

The evening settled in hot and muggy. It was too hot to sleep in the upstairs bedrooms. With doors and windows standing open and the mosquitoes coming in, everyone went out to sit on the veranda and steps. They watched moonlight bounce shining paths of light off the Ohio while clouds slid across the moon, one by one like silent troopers. They listened to frogs croaking and crickets chirping.

Amos said, "Mike, the newspapers make it sound as if thy boats are cleaning up the Mississippi right sharp."

Mike said, "Have you heard of Charles Ellet?" Amos shook his head. "Well, I've told you about the gunboats; now there's another tale to tell. Ever heard of the *rams*?"

Amos said, "Read in the newspaper about some on the east coast. Also said the Confederates had a few on the rivers in the west. Sounded like their effect is deadly. I'm not certain how they work."

"It's an old concept, used in Europe back before big guns. Steam-powered boats have made it practical again. Even more so since they've improved the boats, giving them more power.

"When I went back to Cairo, I found my bunch had an encounter with Confederate rams down by Fort Pillow. Our fellows didn't fare too well. Came back with their tails between their legs, with the Rebels bragging the Yanks wouldn't penetrate any farther down the Mississippi.

"Later I ran into Charles Ellet. He found me inspecting his rams and gave me a first-class introduction to the whole idea. Turns out he was getting ready to send them down the Mississippi, and said it was time to prove their worth. He was in the middle of hiring riverboat pilots to man these rams, so I got the job.

"It was June before we took them out. The theory is that a boat with a heavy reinforced prow can do more damage than shells. It's a hit and run kind of operation—you just plain ram your boat into the enemy. Not the kind of maneuver you go into without first clearing all the dishes off the table."

Amos chuckled. "It sounds like an idea young'uns would hatch just for the fun of it. The government is taking this seriously?"

"Mr. Ellet couldn't interest the Union navy in his idea, but Secretary of War Stanton liked the sound of it. He made Ellet a colonel and sent him west. Well, Ellet rebuilt nine steamboats according to his plan. He loaded four of them up with us riverboat men and headed down the Mississippi. Might say we were looking for trouble."

"So you were in it, then," Alex said. "It does sound interesting."

"More'n interesting," Mike admitted. "The Confederates were in Memphis, moved in there with their fleet. Then Ellet arrived on the scene. There were five Union ironclads and four of Ellet's boats.

"Just before we entered the harbor, the Rebels steamed out to meet us. And we had an audience. Above us on the bluff, most of Memphis came to cheer on the Confederates." Beth was watching Mike, and he paused to grin at her.

"It was something," he admitted. "Ellet started his boats downriver at about fifteen knots. They were holding that speed when they met the Rebels. We heard later that the shock of the collision between Ellet's boats and the Confederate rams could be felt up on the bluffs.

"Colonel Ellet, in the first boat, collided with a Confederate ram. His son Alfred squeezed his ram in between two Confederate's heading for a hit on the old man. This caused them to collide with each other. Alfred circled around and hit the Rebel boat that survived the crash. About then the gunboats finished off the damaged Rebel boats, sank another, and captured three others."

"You make it sound like a lark," Beth whispered. "Was it really so?"

Mike shook his head. "No. It was a tragedy. Charles Ellet was shot and later died."

"Oh, the poor man. It's a shame to lose such a one." With a sigh, Sadie got to her feet. "I'm going to bed before thee starts on another yarn. One more like that and my eyes'll be stuck open all night."

One by one the others followed. Mike continued to sit on the steps and Beth moved down beside him. He surveyed her sad face and waited.

"Are they still drilling recruits out in the pasture?"

"Yes, they bring fellows in from all over this end of Pennsylvania. Roald said the Pennsylvania regiments are getting a good reputation. Known as good fighters."

"Where was Roald sent?"

"To fight with Fremont. Roald didn't say where, but his letter was written from the East." In a moment she added, "There was a Southern raid against Fremont in the Shenandoah Valley. I haven't heard anything since."

"Beth, I'm sorry. I suppose there's nothing to be done except to tough it out. I'll go with you tomorrow to check the lists."

"Mike, why does God let all this happen? You know what Amos said to me this morning? He said I'd feel better if I went to meeting. How is that possible when God has been allowing this to happen? If He's God, then He can stop this."

"Beth," Mike said helplessly, staring down at her tear-streaked face, "you've got to believe there are lasses on the other side of the line praying just as hard as you are that their men will come home."

"Mike, you're no comfort at all," Beth cried. "Why men insist on fighting—why it is so enjoyable to them, I'll never be able to understand. While you were talking about that battle with the rams, you and all the other fellows acted as if it were a great romp." She jumped to her feet and headed for the door.

He reached the door first and blocked the way. "Beth, that isn't fair. Come talk with me; at least let me explain my feelings about war."

She shook her head and tried to push past him. He resisted for a moment, and then with a sigh, encircled her with his arms. "Okay, come on. I—"

Suddenly she threw her arms around him and cried against his chest. "Oh, Mike, don't be angry with me; I can't take much more of this."

"I'm not angry. Right now I'm trying to behave like a gentleman," he muttered, "and it doesn't help a bit to have you, an engaged girl, draped all over me."

She leaned back and stared up at him. "Mike, I'm not engaged to Roald. We've only talked about what might happen when he comes back."

His arms relaxed. "You mean I still have a chance with you?"

She caught her breath. "Oh, Mike, please, let's not talk about us. I'm too confused to know anything except that I'm worried about him. What I really need is—"

"A big brother," he said dryly, dropping his arms.

"Well, I suppose now I'll have to worry about you, too."

"That would be nice."

She hesitated, then stretched on tiptoe and put her arms around his neck. "Mike, you are really the dearest person on earth. I like you so much, but please—"

Her soft warm lips were close. He groaned, turned his head, and found them. "Beth, I want you. I know I shouldn't be talking like this now with Roald gone."

She wilted into his arms, and with her tears drenching his shirt, he carried her to the rocking chair and held her on his lap until she stopped crying. When she finally smiled up at him, he wrapped his arms around her. "Beth, what are we going to do?"

She sat up, pushed away, and looked at him, "Do, Mike? You are a dear, sweet friend, a *brother*, and we'll continue to be friends as long as we live. You rescued me. I won't forget it. Thank you for letting me cry on you." The door closed behind her.

Slowly Mike sat down on the steps, still overwhelmed with the memory of her softness, and muttered, "Brother!"

He wiped his hands wearily across his face. The crickets began their cheerful chorus. He thought about the kiss. *Lord, I did it again.* He thought of his resolve, and shame swept through him. *Poor Roald.* "As sure as I know my name, Lord," he muttered, "I know You want me to concentrate on helping this girl, not kissing her and carrying on like a love-sick kid. When she gets close, I seem to forget all my good intentions." He stood up and shoved his hands in his pockets. "I sure wouldn't want a fella trying to take over my girl." He stomped up the stairs to his room.

CHAPTER 24

Olivia watched as Beth walked up the lane to the Coopers' house. With her head lowered, it seemed every step was an effort. She stopped at the gate and looked up.

"Missing; presumed captured," Beth said briefly as she leaned wearily against the gate post. "For two weeks I've lived with it, and still it seems like an ugly dream."

Olivia stood up. Clenching her hands, she fought with her own emotions and glanced quickly toward the *Golden Awl* before she left the veranda to walk out to meet Beth. "I'm sorry this has happened, Beth. But you mustn't give up hope," she insisted. "To be captured is at least a promise of life."

"Mike said there's a chance he'll be exchanged."

"Beth, I've read just recently that the cartel governing the exchange of prisoners has been renewed."

"Why would they have to do that?"

Olivia shrugged. "I suppose it's better that way. This cartel is based upon the agreement made between the United States and Great Britain in 1812. Prisoners are to be held no more than ten days, and exchange is made soldier for soldier, officer for officer." She looked at Beth. "If he's alive, you'll probably hear from him very soon."

"It's been so long. There are only two days left in August, and I haven't heard anything from him since the end of May."

Olivia nodded slowly. Over Beth's shoulder she saw Mike and Alex coming up the path from the boat. She fingered the brooch at the neckline of her frock as she watched Alex.

"Are you selling the boat?" Beth asked, turning to look toward the river.

"If we can find a buyer. There aren't many who have money to spare, especially after the taxes Congress levied last month." She wrinkled her nose and looked down at Beth. "Seems everything is taxed and over-taxed, but I suppose that's to be expected. Something must be done to pay for this war."

"I can't find any virtue in war," Beth said darkly.

"None of us can, not in any war. I don't know how the men can face fighting." Olivia sighed. "We can only hope there will be such a brokenness and healing that the country will survive."

"What do you mean by that?"

"We're a sick nation, selfish and uncaring," Olivia said slowly. "At times I wonder if we'll fight until we are nearly ruined. Certainly we deserve little help from God."

"Do you think God cares much about what happens here?" Beth asked bitterly. "I don't think He does. They talk about Him being a God of love. I have a very hard time believing that."

Gravel crunched behind her. Beth turned and saw Alex and Mike approaching. She watched the expression in Alex's eyes as he looked at his wife. When the two of them turned up the path to the house, Olivia tucked her hand through Alex's arm and pressed her cheek against his shoulder. A knot twisted in Beth's stomach.

"Look at them," she said to Mike. "They act as if it's been a week since they've seen each other."

"Seems to me they must have almost a perfect marriage," Mike said. "Been married four years, and they're still like sweethearts. Guess it isn't common to have that kind of marriage, but it makes a body wish it were."

Beth nodded. "A fairy tale marriage—they live happily ever after. Sometimes I think it isn't fair; people like that never have troubles."

Mike's glance was level, questioning. Abruptly he asked, "When are you going to sit down with me and tell me how it was to be raised in the South in a rich plantation family?"

She caught her breath. "I suppose when you can think of something besides kissing." Mike chewed his lip thoughtfully before he followed Beth into the house.

———

As he prepared to leave three days later, Mike noticed the first touch of autumn in the air. The crispness seemed proper against the background of changing leaves and glowing asters in Sadie's garden. He carefully closed the kitchen door behind himself just as Beth came out of the barn leading her horse.

"Thought I might as well give you a ride into town; that way you won't need to worry about getting the mare home."

"That's mighty nice of you, Beth," he said soberly, examining her face in the pale morning light. "But this means you'll be getting to work at a very early hour."

"I don't mind. This is my favorite time of year, and I'll just enjoy it."

"Let's get going."

She reached for the horse. Mike took the reins from her, mounted the mare, and held out his arms. "Come on. One last time."

After settling her skirts, she asked, "What do you mean one last time?"

"Well, I might not come back."

She turned until she could see his face. "Mike, that's nothing to joke about."

"I'm not. I'm just facing the facts."

"I've scarcely adjusted to the idea of Roald being gone, no doubt forever, and now you're talking this way."

"Do you care?"

"Of course I care, and you know it."

"Beth, I think a lot of you. I know I'd be second best, but with Roald gone I want to see you taken care of. What if I ask you to marry me?" Hastily he added, "If and when I come back."

"What if?" Her lips trembled.

"I'm asking right now. I want you to marry me when I come back— next month, or maybe the month after that. If I come back. How about it?"

"Mike, being married is for such a long time."

"Or such a short time."

She shuddered, turned, and rested her shoulders against him. He put his arms around her and pulled her close. "Beth, I guess I've loved you forever; at least it feels that way." He tipped her chin so he could see her eyes, and then he bent to kiss her.

"Mike, I'm nearly afraid to say yes. If I say yes, you won't come back. If we just leave it this way, then—"

"You will?" he finished her sentence. She nodded and pressed her face against his shoulder.

She waited at the station until the train gave one last, lonesome whistle. With a shiver she hurried back to the mare. Giving another glance toward the disappearing train, she sighed and murmured, "Forever is a long, long time."

CHAPTER 25

When Beth came into the keeping room that September day, the wind was blowing briskly. Olivia stood at the window watching the trees bending southward to release their leaves. She turned when the door opened.

Smiling at Beth, she said, "With that hair as red as maple leaves, I expected you to be airborne too. Bad day to be on horseback."

"Worse for some of those buggies. Saw one turned over in the ditch."

"Was anyone hurt?"

"There wasn't even a horse around. Might have had a broken wheel from going down the slope. I didn't look closely; I was too busy hanging on to Mag." She hung her shawl and pulled a crumpled newspaper from her satchel.

Going to the table she said, "I heard people talking about fighting in the East and decided to get the paper. Take a look for yourself. I've given up on Roald coming back—at least I think I have."

Sadie came out of her bedroom. "The men are coming from the barn; guess I'll push that roast over the fire and make some gravy."

"What shall I do to help you?" Olivia murmured, opening the newspaper.

"Nothing for now. Might tell me what you're reading," she commented as Amos and Alex came into the room.

"They're saying the lists of casualties are to be posted within the week," Beth said. She sighed heavily. "Will someone please go with me to read them?"

"Better give them a few days to get them posted," Alex advised. He sat down beside Olivia and looked at her, his eyebrows raised. She blushed under his scrutiny and said, "My clothes are getting too tight."

"Let's go shopping tomorrow."

"Oh Alex, they don't make dresses to fit me like this. Sadie's sewing a jumper for me."

His eyes twinkled and he peered over Olivia's shoulder at the newspaper. "Must be a significant battle."

Hesitantly Beth said, "I guess it's a victory for the Federal Army."

Amos lifted his head. "I hope so; after Bull Run, they need to start showing their mettle."

"It's McClellan again," Alex said, his eyes still on the newspaper. "Sounds like things have gone wrong for him once more."

Sadie came to the doorway. "What happened?"

"Seems, from the description of the battle, that something was terribly wrong."

"The Union soldiers are said to be totally demoralized," Beth interjected.

"I don't believe it's that. McClellan's army outnumbered Lee's with odds that should have brought victory." Alex shoved away the newspaper and jumped to his feet.

"Even a person without military training," he exclaimed, "can see the indecisiveness of the Federal Army. I can see nothing except that delay is causing losses that are horrendous."

"Here's a comment by a newspaper man describing Bloody Lane," Amos said, looking over the newspaper. "Says Confederate soldiers dropped like grass behind a scythe."

"Thee had best put away the newspaper for now," Sadie gently said, "or thou shalt not have a stomach for thy supper."

Amos caught her eye. " 'Tis already that state. We need to bring this terrible war to the God of the universe and let Him hold it. 'Tis a gentle, untouched land we have right here, and we're to be grateful for it—but let us not forget."

———

A week later, Beth came into the house, her face ashen. "Olivia, they've posted lists of the dead and injured. It is terribly long. Tomorrow the stores will be closed so that everyone can hear the names read."

"We will go," Olivia murmured, touching the girl's shoulder.

When they rode into town the following day, they found the green around the church packed with people. There was a cold wind blowing, and the crowd pressed close to each other as they pushed against the crude platform.

Beth looked around sadly. "And to think less than a year ago we were having a frolic here to raise money for the soldiers going to fight. Now look at this crowd. They're all old, and very sad."

As she spoke, Olivia noticed two ragged youths pushing in through the crowd. Hearing the excited voices surrounding the lads, Beth stopped and strained to hear. "I recognize that fellow," Beth whispered. "I thought he was in the army."

The youth was speaking. "We were there. But that was enough. Soon as it was over we skedaddled. No more war for us."

"Me and Tim here were right up front," his companion said. "It's God's miracle we weren't killed. Sure wasn't anythin' that McClellan or Burnside did."

"Tell me," came a tremulous demand, "how do you think we're going to win this war if you lads don't stay in there and fight?"

"How we gonna win unless we get a general who's not afraid for his skin? McClellan's afraid of his shadow. Fiddles around with his papers but never gets down to fighting. You don't win a war without getting in there and doing something besides talk."

"Now Mac," his companion admonished, "that's not the whole story. They're saying sometimes he gets information in those papers that scares him outta trying."

The old man shook his finger at the youths. "A body without the gumption to go out there and charge right in and give it to them don't have no business undertaking anything more serious than milking cows."

"Tell me," another voice rose, "is it true the soldiers are demoralized?"

"We were like whipped dogs after Bull Run," answered the first.

"But not now," the fellow called Tim replied. "We were ready and impatient. Man, if they'd just taken the stops out, we'd have let them have it."

"That so?" The man looking at them had an empty sleeve, and the scars on his face were still red. "I didn't share your bravery; neither did the men around me. Sure, I know we had a reputation of going into battle eager to kill all the Rebels, but that's not so, at least not in the regiment I was in. There was plenty of brave talk, but when it came down to having bullets flying around our heads, we spent more time ducking than shooting.

"There's an additional fear—" The man paused and his lips twisted. "A fear that our buddies would see us as bellowing babies. It does something to a fellow when those bullets get mighty close. Might say it makes the trigger finger work better."

"At least," Tim said, "those Confederates weren't in any condition to fight. They were walking skeletons; their uniforms were in rags and some didn't have shoes. How they managed to fight is more'n I know."

A woman spoke up. "You men are harsh. I believe McClellan is kind and considerate of his men."

"Lady," the man with the scars said, "McClellan isn't hired to tuck his men in at night; he's hired to whip the Confederates. Personally, I'd like to get this war over and get on with living."

Three men wearing black suits marched to the platform. Beth watched them divide the long sheets of paper. One stepped forward. "The following is a list of the missing and presumed dead or held as prisoners. If your loved one has not been exchanged within one month's time, you may conclude that he is a part of the group deceased."

Beth's face grew pale as she considered what the grim man's statement meant. She hadn't heard from Roald in over a month. *He's dead*, she thought, her hope completely gone.

Later, after the sun had set, the final list of names was read by the light of a lantern. The reader concluded by saying, "With God's help, we'll never again find it necessary to read such a long list."

That night Alex held Olivia as if he would never let her out of his arms again. "Alex," she whispered, "I know it's getting more difficult for you. I want to hold you here forever. But women do have babies without their menfolk around. Go on, deliver your soul, and I'll be here when you come back. *We* will be here."

"It's a burden," he admitted, "an obligation that becomes heavier. But also, it's as if the deciding step was taken when I picked up the first load of slaves on the *Golden Awl*."

She nodded against his arm. "You struck a blow at the institution of slavery. Now you must finish what you've begun."

The next evening Beth came into the house and dropped the newspaper in front of Alex.

"A proclamation of emancipation; Lincoln's issued it. Now what's going to happen?"

"You don't sound very happy about it," Alex said as he picked up the paper.

"Of course I'm not. Never did I believe it would come to this."

"What did you expect, Beth?" Alex asked with a puzzled frown. "The North has never denied that Lincoln doesn't believe in the expansion of slavery."

"Expansion?" Beth exploded. "This is freeing every slave in the states where the people are said to be in rebellion. They aren't in *rebellion*; they're trying to be *free!*"

"And you've had hopes for them, haven't you?"

"Most certainly," she snapped.

"If that is the case, then the proclamation is just about the worst thing that can happen for you, isn't it?"

Suddenly Olivia straightened in her chair. "Beth, how could you have considered marrying a man fighting for the Union? If you feel this strongly about slavery, how could you marry someone who feels just the opposite?"

She lifted her chin. "I don't believe that love is impossible under these circumstances."

"Unless you believe that love is more than romance—regardless who you marry, Beth, you'll have to live with his values. I don't believe I could do otherwise, without feeling I am compromising myself."

"Compromising? I don't understand what you mean."

"Violating a principle inside that is more important than my personal happiness."

"I suppose," Alex said softly, "each one of us has something which we would be willing to die for. She's talking about that."

Beth glared at him. "You'd be willing to die for the slaves?"

"And the Union."

"How can you say that? It is impossible to make such a choice and really mean it. I'd never willingly die for anything."

Alex frowned. "For a soldier in wartime, it seems there are only two alternatives. You either choose to die for a cause, or you die unwillingly without a cause."

———

The day before Alex left for Washington, a letter came from Crystal. She had written:

Dear Ones,

This will be brief, because I'm in a fuss over packing, and also because I don't know whether there's any possibility of your

receiving this letter. Matthew and I will be coming to Pennsylvania as quickly as possible.

We love you,
Crystal

Olivia dropped the letter and flung her arms around her husband.
"Oh, Alex! Our prayers have been answered. Matthew and Crystal are
together again! I can scarcely wait to see them."

She buried her face in his chest. *Our prayers are answered*, she
thought, *but Alex won't be here to see them*. He kissed her and said,
"That nearly makes it possible to leave you without a worry. How good
God is to give us this!"

CHAPTER 26

Outside the farmhouse bare branches whipped in the wind. Slowly Olivia wrote:

My Dear Husband,

How I long for the sound of your voice. It seems forever, but I suppose it is the same for you. October is nearly finished and our baby is growing. I am starting to feel his little fists and feet pushing against me. How I wish I could share this time with you!

Olivia dropped the pen and got to her feet. Sadie glanced at her and continued to count stitches. "Thou art restless?"

"I wonder if Alex is well," Olivia mused. "Why have they sent the men so far away? I'd hoped to have him training at home, although he says they are doing little training. They talked about building fortifications, but he didn't say where. Sadie, do you get the idea that they must be moving all over?"

Sadie nodded. "Likely. When he mentioned being in Washington for a time and then talked about New York state, I felt that way." She eyed Olivia. "If thee feels like sewing, there's bits of flannel in my room. 'Tis enough for several little gowns."

"I need to move around. Shall I peel potatoes?"

"If thee wishes—" She cocked her head. "I believe I hear a carriage."

Straightening her full, loose apron, Olivia walked toward the front door just as the rap came and the door was pushed open. For a moment Olivia stared at the laughing face. "Crystal!" She grabbed her, reaching a hand to Matthew as he came through the door. "Oh, how wonderful!" She leaned back to look at Matthew's smiling face; quickly kissed him and turned back to Crystal. Hugging her again, she whispered, "Oh, how beautifully God has answered our prayers! Please come tell us about it."

Crystal's eyes widened. "Olivia, you're going to have a baby! I shall be an aunt. Oh, Matthew, isn't it wonderful?"

He grinned, hugged Olivia, and asked, "Where's Alex? I must congratulate him."

Olivia caught her breath. "He's left to join the army. Last month. He's in Washington now. At least I think so. Every time I get a letter it's from a different place."

Matthew's face was grave. "Has he been in battle?"

"No, not really a battle. There have been scouting expeditions and other—maneuvers, he called them. I have the feeling they're headed for battle, simply because he said so little." She sighed, smiled at the two of them, then said, "Crystal you look wonderful. And Matthew, you are so thin."

"He's been in battle. He's still recovering from a terrible injury to his arm. Remember Amelia? Her daughter and husband rescued him. I'll tell you all about it later. Where are Sadie and Amos?"

"Sadie's probably gone to the barn after Amos. Come back here and I'll fix tea." Olivia paused. "Did you say Amelia's daughter? Well, you can tell me later. I want to hear all about *you* two."

Sadie and Amos came through the kitchen door just as the others reached the keeping room. With Sadie beaming and blinking through tears and Amos thumping Matthew on the back, they sat down at the table.

"Thou art refreshing to weary hearts," Sadie said. "And thou must tell us all about thyselves."

Crystal threw a glance toward Matthew, and he nodded and smiled at her. "You tell it, my dear."

"I know Matthew's story as well as my own," she said softly. "He was coerced into joining the Confederate Army. He was sent to Texas and later was involved in the one battle that took place in the Far West, in New Mexico. He was injured and simply walked away from the army. Later he traveled to the Colorado Territory with some people he met in New Mexico. By the Lord's providence, he was in Denver while I was there."

"Just after we were married we'd discussed the possibility of moving to Colorado Territory," Matthew added. "When I ended up in the Confederate Army in Texas, I thought of those talks, little knowing Amelia had provided the pull to get Crystal there."

Beth came in as the evening shadows began to darken the room. Amos put another log on the fire, and Beth rubbed her cold hands as she stood close to the fire and listened.

Crystal finished her story and said simply, "I suppose being separated as long as we were helped us sort through the important and unimportant things in our lives. Knowing God in a deep way made it possible to forgive each other, and this also helped us make the decision to come back. It just seemed to be the thing to do."

"I intend to join the army," Matthew interjected, "this time on the Federal side. I feel I have a double portion of wrongs to right."

"Matthew," Olivia protested, "you must not feel that way. You didn't willingly join the Confederates. You never told our parents about this, did you? I've questioned them about you in letters, and they were very evasive. Mentioned only that you'd left home early in 1861 and they hadn't heard from you since that time."

Matthew flushed. "I suppose it's best to say I was bitter, and just leave it at that. Certainly, once this situation has been resolved, I'll try to make amends."

He moved restlessly around the room, and Amos asked, "So you had a stint with the Confederates. Do you think you can easily join the Federals now?"

"It hasn't occurred to me that they won't have me," Matthew said. Grinning suddenly, he added, "I doubt they ask very many questions when they sign a fellow up. I'll just be happy to serve anywhere, doing anything."

Olivia glanced at Crystal and saw the yearning in her eyes. "I know," she whispered. "Oh, Crystal, I feel the same way. I'm so lonely for him, but it will help to have you here."

"I really want to stay with you," Crystal said, biting her lip, "but right now I have another worry. I haven't heard from my mother for several months. I know that the Union captured New Orleans in April of this year. Mother wrote quite a detailed letter then. It sounds as if it's a very difficult situation down there. Neither the Federal soldiers nor the people of New Orleans have been happy with each other. Mother's last letter indicated she isn't well. I'm going to make an effort to visit her as soon as possible."

"Crystal, my dear," Matthew protested, "give yourself time to rest after this trip. Also, we need to be absolutely certain travel will be safe for you."

"You aren't going, Matthew?" Olivia asked.

"No, we've agreed it's best I join the army as soon as possible. But there's another reason." He threw a quick glance at Olivia. "Frankly, I don't want to head down the Mississippi. The fellows in my regiment were from that area, and considering the way I walked out of the battle, I'd just as soon not see them right now." His grin twisted as he added, "I've already spent more time in the Confederate Army than I've cared to."

Sadie appeared in the doorway. "Matthew, carry your bags to the second room down the hall on the west. Olivia is in your old room. Crystal will want to freshen up, and supper is nearly ready to serve."

Beth followed Sadie into the kitchen. As she sliced bread, Sadie commented, "Beth, 'tis the first time I've seen the cat get thy tongue."

She looked startled. "Oh, I was thinking about Crystal. She's not all white, is she?"

Sadie turned to stare at Beth. "So? Dost thou think that makes a speck of difference around here? Missy, it will make thee appear much more charitable if thee fails to notice color in this house."

Carrying their luggage, Matthew led the way up to their room. Crystal hesitated when she reached the top of the stairs. She turned slowly to look at the railing, then glanced down the steep pitch of stairs. Matthew carried the bags into the bedroom and returned to the hall. "You're thinking of that day I left you?" he asked gently. "I'd give anything to spare you the memory of that day," he murmured.

"I'm sorry, Matthew," she whispered. As she turned, he touched her cheek. Looking up, she saw the dark shadows in his eyes. "Please, my dear Matthew, don't look like that. I'm not blaming you. It was my fault from beginning to end. I was deceitful, and I can only blame myself for the pain both of us have endured. If I had only told you the truth about myself from the beginning—"

He opened the door to their room. "I knew if we came here we'd be dragging at painful memories. But Crystal, the past month has been beautiful. Do you suppose it will help us get through the bad times now?"

Running her hands down the lapels of his coat, she smiled up at him. "One of the things I was thinking out there in the hall is that if the foolish girl I was back then could have seen where her deceit would lead, she would never have acted in that manner."

"My dear, I believe you are too hard on yourself. But that's behind us," Matthew whispered. "We can't waste time thinking about it. Perhaps we ought to promise to never again refer to that painful time. With the war facing us, you know as well as I that the present is going to be difficult enough. But someday—"

"The war will be over and life will be normal."

———

One afternoon the following week, Crystal came out of her room, hesitated before Olivia's closed door, and tapped, "Olivia, if you don't want to be disturbed, I'll come back later."

"Come in, Crystal; I can't sleep."

Crystal looked at Olivia's reddened eyes and went to sit on the edge of the bed. "What is it?" she whispered.

"Just feeling sorry for myself. It's been two-and-a-half weeks since I had a letter from Alex. I suppose he's simply without means of getting a letter posted. But I worry."

"I would, too." Crystal brushed the hair away from Olivia's face. "I'm afraid that's how it's going to be for all of us. Waiting. I'm glad you'll be having the baby. That will help make time pass quickly.

"Oh, this terrible war." She sighed and looked at Olivia, who sniffled and nodded half-heartedly. "In Colorado it seemed frightening enough; but here, with soldiers talking about battles and women looking for information from the battlefields, it is horrible. Even reading the newspaper accounts is frightening. It is so near! That's why I wanted to talk to you. Matthew's nearly promised I can go with him. He said for a month or so we'll be together, and then I'll go on to New Orleans.

"I've been thinking about the baby coming, but also about you. Olivia, would you rather I stay with you now, or come back just before the baby is born?"

"Crystal, I think I'd like you to be here when he comes. I'd love to have you stay now, but I understand. You were both separated for such a long time; I wish for both your sakes that Matthew didn't feel obligated to join the army so soon." She sat up and smiled at Crystal. "Your going with him sounds like a good idea. I understand there are many women joining their husbands, following their men from camp to camp, just to be near and help take care of them.

"If it hadn't been for the baby, I would have insisted on going with Alex." She tried to smile. "He's pretty self-sufficient; I imagine he can even manage to keep his socks clean."

She caught her breath in a ragged sob. "I'm sorry, Crystal. Sadie says pregnant women are tearful and moody, but it makes me ashamed. I do all this preaching at myself about being strong and trusting in the Lord, but sometimes it doesn't help."

Crystal fingered the brooch pinned to Olivia's dress. "This is a lovely piece of jewelry."

"Alex gave it to me just before we left Canada. Both of us see it as a symbol of the times in which we live. Alex read me some verses in Isaiah. He said that he thought of them when he first saw the brooch."

"Tell me the verses; what do they say?"

"That just as a bride is adorned with jewels, in that same way the Lord God will cause righteousness and praise to spring up before all the nations. Alex said the brooch signifies the way Christians are to shine against the darkness of this terrible war." She gulped, touched the gold filigree, and added, "I don't think I'm doing much shining right now. But I'm praying constantly. No matter what happens, Crystal, even if he's injured and we lose the war, I'll be happy if only he comes back."

CHAPTER 27

"Private Duncan, report to your division commander immediately."

Alex glanced down at the stockings floating in the basin of water. "Yes, sir, just as soon as I hang up my stockings, otherwise I'll be going barefoot like the Confederate soldiers."

The lieutenant grinned and walked away.

The private leaning against the pine tree shifted his back and looked at Alex. "Duncan, only a hulking smart mouth with a Southern accent could get by with that."

"Washing stockings?"

"No, explaining so's it looks like it isn't important to be in a hurry around here."

"Since I joined McClellan's army, I haven't seen anyone here in much of a hurry. Guess the lieutenant agreed, since he didn't object." He turned to look at the pleasant countryside. Their camp was spread along the banks of the Potomac, within sight of Harper's Ferry. "Nearly nice enough for a picnic," Alex said, grinning at the youth as he rinsed his stockings and draped them on one of the currant bushes surrounding their camp. He studied the effect of the black against the autumn red leaves. "Mighty nice effect, don't you think?"

"Whole place is mighty nice if we were doing something besides fighting a war—trying to fight, that is," he added, looking at the horses chomping the lush grass along the river. As Alex walked toward the commander's tent, he studied the scudding clouds weighted with mois-ture and moving in from the Atlantic. Sighing with regret, he decided this mid-October day seemed to signal the end of autumn.

He headed for the largest tent. "Lieutenant Jacobs," Alex saluted. Jacobs touched his cap.

"Duncan, be seated, breaks my neck looking up at you." Jacob's sardonic grin held as he leafed through the papers in front of him. "I need someone to carry a dispatch into Washington, thought you'd enjoy getting out of camp for a day or so."

"Yes, sir. Telegraph down again?"

"No. What I say'll take all night to transmit. Help yourself to the coffee and sit down."

The man continued to write quickly. Alex studied his grim face and went to the fire for coffee.

When he sat down, Jacobs dropped his pencil and looked up. "Give it to me straight. What's your impression of this regiment?"

Alex chewed his lip. "I haven't been here long enough to be qualified to judge. But it seems we're not getting anywhere, or doing anything. I'd almost rather be digging ditches."

"I'll remember that," Jacobs said with a smile. "No, honestly now."

"Sir, I've been in the army since the last week in September. I came in expecting to be handed a musket and told to go to it. That hasn't happened. I've been sent on a few little jaunts with a piece of paper in my hand, and told to size up the road I traveled. Might be this is the way wars are run, I don't know, but I can sure think of things I'd rather be doing. My wife is going to be having a baby next March, I'd like to see this whole situation cleared up by then."

"Congratulations," Jacobs grinned, "but your wife and nearly every other soldier's wife is in the same situation. You a farmer?"

Alex shook his head, "Going back to the question. I'd read some pretty sour statements about McClellan in the newspapers. From Pres-ident Lincoln on down there seems to be considerable irritation with his leadership. But here in camp I see the fellows nearly idolize him."

"Why do you suppose that is so?"

"To tell the truth, I honestly don't know. But in addition, I'm sen-sing an underlying discontent with the whole war effort."

"They're bored with it all," the young lieutenant said. Tenting his fingers, he stared down at the paper in front of him.

Reluctantly, yet feeling the need to be honest with the man, Alex added, "Sir, when a bunch of fellows give up on bragging about what they did in the last battle and start questioning the right or wrong of the whole war effort, I think there's serious trouble."

"What do you mean? The North has never had the wild enthusiasm for fighting that we've seen in the Confederate army."

"I wasn't here when the battle of Antietam was fought," Alex said, "but it's been brought to my attention several times that the fellows feel absolutely nothing was accomplished by the battle. They said both the Confederate and the Federal forces are holding the same positions held before the fighting began. Sir, these fellows are saddened by the loss of life which seems unnecessary to them. Back home I saw nearly the same reaction. Six thousand men killed, seventeen thousand injured, and nothing gained. Even the Quaker farmers in rural Pennsylvania were pretty upset about the loss, and it usually takes a lot to make them speak out against authority.

"While we were gathered around the reports of the dead and wounded, we tried to add up the merits of the battle and there didn't seem to be any. Particularly when it became known that McClellan finished the battle by refusing to track down Lee. It was even more upsetting when the final count showed the remaining Federal force was twice the size of Lee's, and his fellows were exhausted and sick."

Finally Jacobs spoke, "If it will help, there's something good coming out of it all. News coming out of Great Britain indicates that Antietam sealed the question of whether Britain should support the South's bid for recognition as an independent nation. They have closed the door on it."

"Well, that's certainly encouraging. I know the battle was considered a draw, but perhaps the British read something else into it." Alex added slowly, "Something else I didn't realize is that some of the men are tired of the war, tired to the place where they are desperate for any kind of a compromise. Not all of them feel that way," he admitted, "but enough do, and that's frightening. It's bad enough to die, but to not be convinced the cause is worth dying for makes battle a travesty. In parts of the North I don't suppose there's ever been strong feelings for or against slavery. That doesn't surprise me—"

Jacobs interrupted, "The war is for the purpose of saving the Union, not the slaves."

"But now I'm wondering if the soldiers have lost confidence in the Union."

"Why do you think this?"

"One of the subjects coming out around the campfires is that they feel they are being held back from the kind of fighting they feel is necessary for this war to be settled."

"What kind is that?" Jacobs asked heavily.

"Fighting until the job is done; pushing until they conquer. Almost to a man they seem to feel they are being unnecessarily restrained. Sir, these fellows impress me. I think they know what they're talking about, and I sympathize. These men want to get this war over and go home."

"Duncan," Jacobs said thoughtfully, "thanks for talking. You've confirmed things I've sensed and heard." He tapped the paper in front of him. "This dispatch reflects my feelings, now they're echoed by yours. And I heartily endorse the men's statements. I want to see this war finished. Right now I doubt these men can continue this conflict for another year. And God help the poor Confederates, they are about the most miserable bunch of men I've ever seen, but they fight like nothing human. It's as if they have nothing to lose and everything to gain."

Jacobs got to his feet, folded the paper and placed it in a leather case. He hesitated, then pulled out a folded newspaper. "This newspaper was passed on to me by an Englishman who has come to the United States for the purpose of taking our pulse. I felt the need to pass it higher. Let me read snatches to you. In this editorial, the writer says:

> Great Britain sees the American war with two faces. Our aristocracy has long considered the Yankees as uncouth bumpkins, putting them on a par with the slaves. The English revere the manner of living embodied in the Southern structure, to the place where there has been a conscious effort to overlook the means by which this life is supported. Of course that is slavery, the institution the British profess to abhor.

He glanced at Alex. "There's more in the same vein. There's one snappy phrase I like, by a man named John Bright. He says, talking about the United States, there's never been a country where the people have been so free and prosperous. He goes on to say Confederates 'are the worst foes of freedom that the world has ever seen.' Here, Duncan, take it to Washington. The name of the man who must receive this is on the inner flap."

Olivia took the letter from Amos and carefully turned it over. It was Alex's handwriting. "I can nearly hope again," she breathed, holding it against her face for a moment.

Sadie touched her arm, "Sit down, thee will be sick with hope as thou hast been sick with worry. Now, read thy letter."

> Olivia, my dear wife. I write in haste, filled with the need to urge your continued faith and hope. I haven't had a letter from you since the middle of October and guess the situation to be the

same with you. As you can see this is written and posted from Washington. Right now it appears we'll continue to be in the same impossible situation, sitting out the war on the banks of the Potomac. Please, don't worry. It may be months before you hear from me again. For some reason we have a bottleneck in the outgoing mail, and I don't know what to expect coming in. I'm well, but concerned for you . . .

Olivia held the paper to her face and fought to control the tears streaming down her face. Sadie came into the keeping room. Blinking at the tears, Olivia saw the concern on Sadie's face. "I'm not ill, it's just that—" her voice failed and she leaned against Sadie's shoulder.

"Olivia, thee must break this tide of sadness. It isn't healthy for thy babe. Come now and eat. Thee has scarcely had a decent meal for the past week."

She sat up and mopped at her eyes. "Now I'm crying because it is so hopeless to send him a letter. He's worried and I've no way to tell him that everything is fine. Oh, Sadie, I wonder if he has enough to eat. In the last letter he mentioned salt pork and cornbread. That doesn't seem like much for a man as big as Alex."

"Now Olivia, thee knows the Union feeds their men better than that. I think thee frets too much. Come, let's take it to the Lord, and then thee can enjoy thy dinner. Since Crystal has gone east with Matthew, thee has not had the appetite thee should have for the babe."

CHAPTER 28

Early one misty October morning Alex was awakened by the bugler. He lifted his head to listen and his eyes met Dowd's. His tentmate said, "That's a call to assemble. I wonder if we're being attacked?"

Alex rolled out. "I doubt it, but we'd better move."

Standing in parade formation, Alex counted regiments. As far as he could see, blue-uniformed men covered the banks of the Potomac.

General McClellan and his staff passed down the ranks and turned to address the troops. "Tomorrow," he proclaimed, "October 26, 1862, we shall began our march against the enemy. Due to the size of our army and in consideration of the seriousness of the task that lies before us, it will be to our favor to refrain from moving with undue haste. Today I shall dispatch scouts to reconnoiter and report back. All regiments shall be in a state of readiness to begin our march tomorrow."

Alex's friend Wade came into the tent after breakfast. "Well, old buddy, I've a feeling our divisions won't be this close together again for a long time."

"I'll miss our talks," Alex said, getting to his feet and holding out his hand.

"I'm hoping this whole affair will be resolved early into the new year. Alex, I'd like to have your address. When this is over, let's try to get together. I'd like to meet your wife and see that little fellow. I know my wife will feel the same way."

"Sounds fine to me," Alex said, ducking into his tent to hunt for paper. "I'll write it out for you. It'll be interesting to see you again and talk over our experiences. God grant this will soon be settled," he added.

Late the following day, while Pennsylvania troops waited by the Potomac for their turn to cross, word rippled through the ranks. Standing beside Alex, Wade said, "We're sure not sneaking up on them. They say Lee's positioned Longstreet between us and Richmond. We'll have to fight every inch of the way. Have a feeling Lee'll be escorting us back here by next week. We might as well leave the fires burning and the soup on."

"Ah, sour apples!" retorted his buddy. "We sent them running after Antietam. The Union is doing its stuff now."

"It's to be move, halt, move, halt," Wade told Alex. "No wonder President Lincoln is getting impatient. We have lots in common, Lincoln and me. I'm impatient, too. How much longer is this going to last?"

"Well, sounds like things are moving again," Amos said when he walked into the farmhouse. "General McClellan has been relieved of his command and General Burnside is in as commander of the Army of the Potomac."

"Potomac," Olivia repeated. "That means Alex will be moving." Slowly she added, "I suppose all I can do is wish him godspeed and continue to pray for him." She sighed and pressed her hand to her side.

Dense fog blanketed the battlefield. Alex stepped out of his tent and tried to peer through the swirling haze. He moved his shoulders uneasily, more alarmed by the distortion of sound than the blanket of moisture surrounding them. Distant oars seemed to splash within camp.

It was mid-morning before the eerie gloom began to lift. Slowly the landscape reappeared, and the phantom oars and thready voices disappeared.

Even before the fog was gone, the commanders issued orders. The word was passed down the line, "We're doing battle today."

Shivering in the cold dampness, they were given instructions. Meade's men were to march toward Stonewall Jackson's position. Alex was with General Franklin, and their contingent was ordered to cross the open plains.

Just as the sun pierced the fog, Alex saw they were below Lee's position. They heard the command, "Company halt!"

"Ain't we going up there?"

"Can't go nowhere until ordered. That's Meade up there."

"Well," drawled the soldier beside Alex, "at least we've got a good view of the battle. See, the fog's finally lifting."

Alex turned to watch Meade's men dash toward the hill where Lee's men were positioned. The lifting fog revealed two columns of blue marching rapidly toward the stone wall at the base of the hill. Alex found himself gripping his gun until his hands ached. "Our men are moving out!" he muttered.

Sweat dripped onto Alex's musket as he watched men crash through ravines and leap across marshy ground before plunging toward the stone wall running the length of the hill. "Dear Lord, that's impossible! They'll never survive," he exclaimed, watching the fragile line of blue.

As the men reached the stone wall, Alex saw the gray mass rise beyond them. He groaned helplessly as the rifles began to fire with the steady precision of drums, pounding out a staccato barrage with deadly results. The blue uniforms hesitated, then crumpled away from the wall.

The hours of the afternoon ticked by slowly as Alex watched mass after mass of blue uniforms assault the wall and fall at its feet. "Oh God," Alex groaned.

"We'll all be in there, unless Burnside calls a halt to this suicide," muttered Henson. "Look at that, our men keep coming out of that ravine, and the Confederates are mowing them down as fast as they appear!"

"And there's no way our fire will reach that far," Alex muttered sadly. "From that position, we could send all our men in there with the same results."

"You're right; it's foolhardy to continue this massacre," snapped the man standing beside him.

Alex turned, saw the man's insignia, and examined his face. He recognized General Hooker from the next regiment. A young lieutenant came forward, "General, here's your reply from General Burnside."

Hooker took the paper and glanced at it, then frowned. "I'm going in for a conference. He's too far away to see what's going on."

It was nearly nightfall when the fresh assault began. Alex spotted Hooker and his men one moment before they shouted their battle charge and rushed toward the hill.

In disbelief Alex exclaimed, "They're going in! Burnside's sending them." He watched the charge up the mountain.

The Confederate guns were silent, and for a moment it looked as if the men would gain the wall, but then the rifles blazed point-blank. One after another the men dropped.

As Alex watched his comrades storm the hill and fall back, one of the men in his regiment clapped him on the shoulder. "Rumor is, we're next," he whispered savagely. "Don't look like Burnside's giving up."

"We'll all be dead by morning," Alex muttered despairingly. "Dear Lord, stop this madness!"

———

The next morning a cold December wind swept in from the north. Life moved with a blur of blood and torn bodies. Those who had carried muskets the day before now carried shovels. Moving among the silent ones, shivering under the howling wind and the sight of death, soldiers quickly searched their comrades' pockets for identification before lifting the frozen bodies into the shallow graves.

One private fingered the scrap of paper he had found in a bloodied pocket. He stared into the mangled face of the dark-haired man. "Good thing he left some identification, or no one would recognize him. He's from Pennsylvania—Martinsville. Name's Alexander Duncan."

CHAPTER 29

Amos came into the house carrying a newspaper. He held the paper while he looked at Olivia's face, then slowly he put it on the table. "There's a story about the battle of Fredericksburg." He cleared his throat. "Must have discouraged the Yanks powerfully. It wasn't a good battle."

It was only the first of many newspapers describing the battle in cruel, graphic detail. Olivia had only one thought in her mind—Alex. Because of him, the words became pictures stamping themselves on her mind. She read, "Federal losses are thirteen thousand. . . . Slaughter . . . If McClellan is incompetent, what is General Burnside?"

For two weeks Olivia paced the floors of Sadie's house. Sadie followed behind with imploring words and outstretched arms, saying "Thou art worrying when thee has no real reason. Take thy peace from the Lord, for the sake of the babe."

Olivia faced Sadie. "It was the Army of the Potomac, Sadie. How could he possibly have escaped?"

"According to the newspapers," Amos said, "thirteen thousand was a very bad loss. But there was a big army of healthy men still left." His gnarled hand stroked her hair. "Lass, don't go to grieving when thou hast no confirmation."

"Thou dost not know that our Alex was even there," Sadie added.

———

As the days passed, the winter darkness became increasingly oppressive with the threat of more snow. One evening Beth came in, her hair tumbled and her eyes dark circles in a too white face. Her words rushed out. "The list. Olivia, I saw it. Alex—"

"No, I don't believe it!" Olivia grabbed Beth and shook her. "Tell me it isn't so. Beth, tell me—"

Amos came into the house. He walked slowly, like a very old man. He dropped into the rocking chair, and Olivia waited, feeling as if life itself was holding motionless. With the sensation of stepping off into an endless void, Olivia asked, "Did you see the list?"

"Aye. Olivia, I don't know where they come up with these lists. We can't have total confidence in them."

She took a deep breath. Carefully she said, "What did the list say?"

"It gave his name and the town . . . and '*Fredericksburg.*' "

Her voice was cold; she heard it coming from a great distance as she asked, "And you tell me I shouldn't believe a list with details that complete?"

"Alex himself said they weren't reliable." The dark shadows still lined his face. She turned away from him and ran to her room.

During the night the pain began; at first Olivia thought of it as a blessed relief from thinking. But by early morning, before daylight, she understood the meaning of the pain. Struggling out of bed, she staggered into the hall.

Darkness, without a sound of life or a hint of light, surrounded her. She groped her way to the railing. The polished wood was icy and alien under her hand. As the pain moved up and tightened like a vise, she gasped and staggered against the railing. "Alex," she whispered. Then in the emptiness, with the vise tightening again, she screamed, "Sadie!"

The names echoed through her mind during the hours of pain. And when the pain fled, she knew total release.

Sadie came with a glass of milk. Olivia took it absently and carefully said, "I don't have a baby now, do I?"

"No. A tiny girl, much too small to live. But Olivia, don't give up hope; there's—" They stared at each other.

"Not without Alex. Sadie, he said I would have a baby in God's time. Right now I think I hate God."

Sadie's arms were warm and soft; a strangled sob came from her throat. "Olivia, my dear child, how I wish I could carry thy hurt! But I can't. Somehow the Lord intends that we learn to hold the hurts in such a way that the wounds make us stronger, not weaker. But until thou art strong, I will be thy shadow of rest, and then thou can pray again."

When Amos came to comfort her, his brusque words were as abrasive as his work-worn hands, but both were very real and earthy. They bridged the distance and reminded Olivia of life. He patted her hand and rambled on about the cow getting out of the pasture and how the neighbor's dog nipped her home.

Once she interrupted him. "Are you certain—did you really see his name?"

"Yes, lass."

She turned her face away, wishing he would leave. "Olivia, a body gets to thinking he knows what God's will is, and then a problem comes along. It's like finding the road has a crook in it. It's best to not fight the crook, it makes life easier."

———

When Olivia finally came down to the parlor, deeply conscious of her dress hanging limp and straight, she found the room flooded with light—that pale opal light, reflected by the snow padding the world and lining the windows with crystals. Keeping her eyes on the light, she asked the most difficult question, the one that she needed answered. "Sadie, was it because I didn't listen to you that I lost the baby?"

Sadie said nothing. She counted stitches and rocked in the chair beside the fire. The pink yarn had been replaced by dark blue. Olivia asked, "Are you making mittens for the soldiers?"

Finally Sadie nodded and put the knitting aside. "Olivia, it won't do thee a bit of good to try to mull over what might have been. Thou needs to get on with life. Thou art strong inside because the Lord does that when He puts His Holy Spirit in us. Thou art strong enough to do whatever the Lord wants thee to do."

"What does He want of me?"

"That is a question ye must ask of Him."

Olivia knew Sadie was right, but she had no heart for the fight. Alex was gone. The baby was gone. What could possibly be worth living for now?

———

At last a letter came from Crystal. "She's been all this time in Maryland with Matthew," Olivia told Sadie. "It finally looks as if she will be able to get a pass to travel south. She begs me to forgive her if she isn't here when the baby is born."

Sadie rocked in silence, and Olivia struggled against the black cloud of melancholy that enveloped her. Amos came into the room, looking from Sadie to Olivia, who still sat with the letter clutched in her hand and tears filling her eyes.

Sitting down beside her, he patted her hand. "Olivia, ye must see life differently now. I cannot tell you how it will be; that will be for thee to discover. But God is thy Father, and he loves His children and will help make a new path for thee which will bring healing. In the book of Hebrews, we're told to run the race before us with patience, all the time looking to Jesus."

Sadie said, "Husband, thou art preaching."

"No, wife; I am mentioning the fact that if we're told to run, then there's a place to run."

A place to run. The words stuck in Olivia's mind. But still she could not overcome the inertia that held her down.

———

It was Mike who unwittingly forced her back into life. His return to the Coopers' threw the whole household into an uproar. In February, just after the ice began breaking on the Ohio, he walked into the house in his uniform, with his soft, dark cap slanted over one ear and a new red scar slanting under his eye. Olivia met him at the door and hugged him.

Stepping back, he looked at her and said slowly, "It isn't March yet."

Olivia took a deep breath and faced the pain inside. *Now is the time,* she thought. *They said I must be the one to take the step, to accept.* She lifted her chin. "Mike, I've lost the baby—and Alex, too."

"Dear Lord," he murmured, following her down the hall.

She looked at his stricken face. Her voice was dull, not bright as she intended. "It's been a terrible time, but Sadie and Amos keep reminding me that God is still here."

Sadie came out of the kitchen, she looked at them both and went to Mike. "Thee has had some hard experiences, too."

He nodded. "But Alex?" He gulped and choked back his tears. "Please tell me about it."

"We know nothing," Olivia said. "I had an idea where he might have been—Fredericksburg." Mike winced and shook his head. "We know nothing except that his name was posted as killed in action."

"Olivia, sometimes they make mistakes."

Fingering the brooch on her dress, she shook her head. "I've tried to tell myself that. But it's impossible to believe when they had a name, a town, and a battle. I'll simply have to accept it. And I think I'm learning to accept."

"Mike, better come back and let me find thee something to eat," Sadie said. "Thou hast a lot of talking to do. That scar tells us much."

"Just coffee." Mike hesitated, shoved his hands into his pockets, and said, "Did Beth tell you that we're planning to be married while I'm here?"

Sadie stopped in the doorway. Without turning she slowly said, "Too bad ye didn't say so beforehand; I'd have prayed the air clear."

"What do you mean?"

"Mike, thou knowest how I feel about thee and Beth," she said as she hurried into the kitchen.

Mike shrugged awkwardly and said to Olivia, "I suppose you feel the same."

"I'm not certain, Mike." She went to sit beside the fire. "Beth seems like a child to me. I shudder to think of—"

He finished the thought, "Of what Beth would do in these circumstances?"

They were both staring into the fire when Sadie returned with the coffee. She put down the pot. "What happened to you? We've been hearing about the troubles in Mississippi."

"Aw, not much. I took a transport down the Mississippi for Grant. He's been jabbing at Vicksburg, trying to find a way to get in there. This time we dropped the troops off upriver. They marched in, and we decided to see if we couldn't move downstream. Some of the Confederate gunboats took after us. That's when I picked up this scar. A shell shattered some glass, and I happened to be standing too near the window when it went."

He stood up. "I think I hear Beth's horse. I'll go meet her."

Beth was pulling the saddle off the mare when he walked into the barn. For a moment he stopped in the doorway, watching her and thinking of Sadie's reaction. *Now isn't the time to figure out all Sadie's objections. Anyway, I'm the one who will be living with Beth.* As he walked toward her he moved his shoulders uneasily, wondering at his reaction to Sadie's dismay.

Beth turned from hanging the bridle, and he caught her in his arms. "Lady, are you the one promised to that Mike Clancy?"

She gasped, "Mike, oh, Mike, you're back! If only you knew how terrible this winter has been!" She flung her arms around him and tightened them, clinging desperately to him.

"I'm here," he murmured, reaching for her lips. "Are you ready to marry me now?"

"Marry you?" she hesitated, shuddering. "I'm afraid, Mike. I'm not sure. Will it turn out like Olivia and Alex?" He released her and looked into her eyes. She saw the scar, then touched it. "What happened?"

"Just a window shot out. You know sailors are safer than soldiers."

"Safer?" She studied his face carefully. "I believe you really are serious. I couldn't take what happened to Olivia." Abruptly she smiled and snuggled into his arms. "Oh, Mike, are you serious about getting married now?"

"Most certainly. Didn't I say so in every letter?"

Slowly she replied, "Then I guess it's the thing to be done right away, before I change my mind."

CHAPTER 30

Beth and Mike walked into the house hand in hand. Beth tilted her chin and announced, "We're going to get married now, while Mike is here."

Amos spoke first. Heavily he said, "Well, can't say thou doesn't know each other."

Sadie said, "I'll bake a cake. What'll you do for a special frock?"

Beth smiled sheepishly. "I have one you haven't seen. I wondered when I'd ever wear it."

Mike looked down at her. "Then why did you buy it?" For a moment Beth looked confused; she blushed, and Mike patted her shoulder. "That's all right, just as long as you wear it now."

"Then you'll go with Mike?" Olivia asked.

"No," Mike answered for Beth. "She's going to stay here. I'd be gone most of the time, anyway."

Beth's eyes were big. "I—I hadn't thought about your leaving. Oh, dear!"

"When?" Olivia looked at Mike.

"I have three weeks here, then I'll be heading out again."

"No, I meant when are you two getting married."

They looked at each other. Tentatively Beth said, "Day after tomorrow?"

Sadie gasped. "Better get supper on the table so I can start working on that cake."

"I'll help." Olivia followed her to the kitchen. She saw Sadie's troubled frown. As she reached for the plates and forks, she asked, "You don't like this, do you?"

Sadie sighed. "No. Way down in my bones I feel it's wrong. Don't have no reason for feeling thus, except that I don't feel that girl's spirit is right with the Lord." She stirred the gravy and poked at the potatoes. "Olivia, 'twas so different when thou and—" she stopped suddenly, patting Olivia's shoulder. "Can't reconcile all this," she finished lamely. "But Mike Clancy will have to make his own decision, between himself and his Lord."

Olivia carried the dishes to the table and came back for the butter and pitcher of water. When she returned for the bread, she managed a smile.

Late that evening as she walked slowly up the stairs to her room, she saw Beth and Mike in the parlor. They were talking and laughing, their heads close together.

In her bedroom, Olivia removed the brooch from her frock. By lamplight the gold stood out in stark contrast to the onyx. She could nearly hear Alex's voice reading the Isaiah verse. Closing her eyes she murmured, " 'As a bride adorneth herself . . . so the Lord God will cause . . .' God . . . ," she murmured, "it comes from Him. All of it. The Lord giveth and the Lord taketh away." Her tears dropped on the brooch, making the gold shine more brightly.

That night the dream she had had before she married Alex returned. When she stirred and opened her eyes, morning was a touch of pink in the sky. Still half asleep, she stretched, seeking Alex's familiar form beside her. Realizing what she had done, she abruptly pulled her hand away from the cold sheets on the far side of the bed.

She turned on her side to look at the vacant place. The dream blossomed complete in her mind—the rolling hills, falling away endlessly toward the horizon, with Alex and Olivia walking hand and hand. The same warm, loving glow filled it all.

"It's the dream I had when I understood it was Your desire that I marry Alex, Lord," she whispered. "Why are You reminding me again? Is it the brooch? Are You telling me that my life is still here, and I must shine like gold?" She touched the cold tears on her face and admitted, "But, Father, it is so difficult."

———

While Sadie beat sugar and eggs together in the kitchen, Olivia shelled and chopped nuts. Casually she said, "Sadie, you've been talking about the Sanitary Commission for the past three months, telling me all about their work for the men fighting this war."

Sadie's spoon slowed. "Yes, that is why I knitted the mittens and the stockings last winter. We pack boxes of cookies and clean underwear. Sometimes we have slickers and rubber mats to put in the bundles. Sometimes we just send ointment and bandages to the hospitals."

Olivia took a deep breath and the words rushed out. "Sadie, I've been thinking . . . I should become a volunteer. I could take care of the wounded boys."

Sadie's spoon stopped and slid down the side of the bowl. "Thou art not that well yet."

"Yes I am. You're pampering me; I have to be of use in this world. Sadie, I'm beginning to feel this is what God wants of me."

The next morning Olivia stepped out of her room to find Beth looking shy and uncertain. Suddenly conscious of how often Beth had avoided her during the past months, Olivia smiled and said, "Do you have time to talk?"

"I—Olivia," she stammered.

Gently Olivia said, "Beth, I'm not distressed because you and Mike are getting married. I feel you've been avoiding me, and I think I understand. Sometimes being wonderfully happy when those around you are sad nearly makes you feel guilty. That shouldn't be."

"I'm sorry, Olivia, I'm truly sorry," Beth whispered. "I suppose I'd be more honest to say I've avoided you because when I look at you I keep being reminded it might happen to me. It's easier to not think about it."

"Oh, Beth!" Olivia caught her breath. "I guess it's nearly a relief that I've faced the worst possible and have discovered I can survive even with him and the baby gone."

"How?"

Her heart pounded in her ears until Olivia could scarcely hear the question; she looked at the girl's troubled face. "If it weren't for God, life wouldn't be worth living. Beth, only that is important to me—to know God is there, loving me and gently urging me to get on with living."

Olivia started to turn away, and hastily Beth said, "Please come tell me what you think of my dress." Beth led the way and pointed to the dress lying on the bed.

Olivia fingered the fabric. "It's beautiful, Beth. Very costly, and obviously a wedding gown." She turned and looked curiously at the girl.

Beth looked confused and at loss for words. "I—then you think it will be the thing to wear?"

"Most certainly. Perhaps a little more elegant than our humble Quakers will expect, but certainly acceptable. This lace is exquisite." Again Olivia glanced at Beth, who was examining the lace. Beth looked up, and Olivia asked, "Do you have shoes to match?"

"Match? No. Oh, dear. Will these green slippers do?"

Olivia studied the anxious frown on Beth's face, and slowly said, "I suppose so. But I do have some white satin slippers. Shall we see if they fit?"

Beth nodded and followed Olivia. "You know," she whispered, "I can scarcely believe this. I mean, I'm getting married tomorrow—just like that!"

She took the slippers and sat down to try them on. "They are slightly long, but I can stuff cotton in the toes. My mother did that when I was little. She'd buy my shoes large. That way I could wear them—"

Abruptly she broke off and jumped to her feet. "I must get busy; the dress needs to be ironed."

"Do be careful; the fabric is delicate," Olivia said as Beth gathered up the dress and left the room.

Watching Beth walk downstairs, Olivia wondered, *Why did I say that? Surely a plantation girl with such a dress knows how to care for her clothing. But why would a plantation girl stuff cotton in the toes of her shoes to make them fit?*

———

Hands in pockets, head down, Mike walked slowly toward the barn. He expected to meet Beth as she led her horse to the barn.

Stopping beside the apple tree, he lifted his head to sniff the air. Hay mingled with the scent of barnyard and dampened, decaying foliage reminded him spring was yet to come.

Looking at the clouds drifting across the sky, he took a deep breath. "God, seems I've paid You no mind since coming upriver. Everything's been moving too fast for thinking."

He leaned against the tree and uneasily considered the heaviness in his heart. "I'm sorry, I really am. Seems the excitement—" He thought about his feelings. "I ought not to be going this fast; I can't really think." He recalled the times he had thought about Beth, how she needed to know more about God.

He sighed. *Another day and we'll be getting married. It still seems strange. Seems it ought not be that way.* He heard the mare whinny and turned.

Beth drew close to him and lifted her face for his kiss. He hesitated, and her eyes opened wider. "I wonder why I feel as if you are a butterfly ready to disappear if I should reach for you," he said.

"Mike," she whispered, "what do you mean?"

"I don't really know," he said slowly. "I guess I expected—" She pressed her face against his shoulder. "Aw, Beth," he muttered, "I suppose a man never feels he really knows a woman, even when he marries one."

Linking her arms around his neck, she looked up at him. "It just might be the same for women. It seems men support families, go hunting and fighting and then, what else is there?" Soberly she examined his expression before she whispered, "Mike, if we ponder it too much, we—I mean, it's scary. I suppose girls always think of marriage as a high point in life. But that isn't the end of the story, is it? Sometimes thinking about cooking and babies and worrying about money, it just doesn't seem all that—secure."

Lamely she finished, "I guess we women are too prone to worry about being taken care of."

Mike tossed, turned, and pounded his pillow. Sleep was impossible. He sat up, shoved the pillow behind his back and watched clouds race across the face of the full moon. He had gone to bed with his thoughts on the final kiss Beth had given him. The lingering memory of her soft body returned for just a moment. But as he watched the moon, his thoughts took him elsewhere.

He contemplated the presence of God; the steady unremitting pressure was a searchlight on his careless life. "Lord," he murmured, "I've neglected You, and yet You're constantly with me. I sense Your presence in a way I can't fully understand. I want to ask You to forgive me for not staying close to You."

He slipped to his knees beside the bed, rested his face in his hands, and waited. Nothing. No brilliant illumination—simply the firm conviction that God was speaking, and he could no longer fail to listen.

Finally he rocked back on his heels. The moon had slipped beyond his window, and the faint luminescence indicated the approaching dawn. With a sigh he got up and looked at the uniform hanging just inside the door. *Sadie doesn't approve of my getting married, yet she's*

*brushed and pressed my uniform, probably frowning and shaking her head
the whole time she worked.*

Still he hesitated. In the midst of shaving, he flung his razor aside
and paced to the window and back. "I am the world's biggest ninny.
Scared of a couple of women; scared more'n I ever was of shells flying
over." He picked up the razor, shook it, and sighed. "Lord, I hear You.
No doubt, it is You. I don't understand it all, but I will obey, no matter
what the cost." Now he knew—perhaps for the first time—what the
cost of his commitment would be.

When Mike went down to breakfast, the room was deserted except
for Amos. Looking around with a puzzled frown, he said, "Did she
change her mind?"

Amos chuckled. "Don't know much about weddings, dost thou?
The three of them headed for the church nearly a half hour ago. Hast
thou not heard all the stories about it being bad luck to see thy sweetie
before the wedding? Well, those women are making sure thou don't.
Now I suggest thou load up on ham and eggs and at least a pail of
coffee. Getting married is hard business." Hastily he added, "At least
until thou gets past the preacher man and the crowd of fussing women."

When they were ready to leave for the church, Amos pulled out his
pocket watch and considered it. "If we leave right now, thou'lt have
women fawning over thee. If we leave in ten minutes, thou'lt be able
to sneak into the church without any trouble."

"Amos—" Mike's voice squeaked, and he stopped to clear his
throat. "What will happen if we leave in five minutes?" Amos cocked
his eyebrow, and Mike added, "It's terribly important that I talk to Beth
for a couple of minutes."

"Better go now." Amos paused. "For the next hour or so it won't
get any better."

When they arrived on the meetinghouse grounds, Amos pointed
with his buggy whip. "I suspect the women are over there in that house.
One of the church women lives there, and it's a likely place for the
womenfolk to congregate." He eyed Mike. "Want me to go clear the
way?" Mike nodded. From the buggy he watched the conversation
taking place; Amos had his foot on the step as his arm gestured toward
the buggy. Finally he turned to beckon to Mike.

"They'll skedaddle. Sadie and I'll go inside the meetinghouse."

Slowly Mike stepped down and headed for the cabin. He stopped
just inside the door. "Beth, you're beautiful." With his throat knotted,
he gulped and looked at her gown. "That's the most beautiful gown
I've ever seen." He continued to look at the ivory satin with its panels
of heavy lace across her shoulders and down the sleeves.

"They didn't want to let you in. But Amos seemed to think it was a matter of life or death." Her blue eyes were curious.

"Beth, please come sit down with me."

"I can't; I'll wrinkle this dress." She stood waiting, and Mike turned to pace the room. "In five minutes the parson will begin the service," she said.

He came back to her. "Beth, you won't believe this, but I love you with all my heart."

"Mike, is that all you came to say? I know it. I—"

"Beth, please hear me out. I can't marry you."

She caught her breath. "Mike, are you married?"

"No, it isn't that. I don't know how to say this to you. But I'm—"

"You want out." Her voice rose, ending in a wail. "This is a fine time to change your mind!"

"No, you don't understand. I haven't changed my mind. It's simply that God doesn't want me to marry you."

"Did you say *God*?" Her face sagged in astonishment. "Oh, Mike, I've heard of excuses, but to blame God! This is ridiculous. Most men get cold feet. I'm shaking too. But let's just go through with it."

"Beth, that would be wrong. We can't face that preacher and God and all the people to promise ourselves to each other, when we know it's wrong in God's sight."

She scrutinized his face, then slowly she wilted and burst into tears, covering her face with her hands. He touched her shoulder. "Please Beth, I don't mean to shame you; I'll do anything I can to make it easy for you."

She lowered her hands and looked at him, whispering, "You really do mean it, don't you? Mike, I can't believe this of you. I'd thought you so fine, honorable, trustworthy, and now—" She paced the room and came back to him.

He saw the blood had risen to her face; her lips were a taut line. Lifting her hand, she struck him across the face. "This is what you deserve," she hissed. "Go tell them that I refuse to marry you. I never want to set eyes on you again as long as I live."

CHAPTER 31

Olivia heard footsteps dragging across the keeping room floor. She turned to face Beth, watching with concern as the girl came into the kitchen. It was Monday morning, and Beth should have been on her way to the hardware store. Her face was blotched and swollen.

Beth tilted her chin, said, "I'm leaving. I know you and Sadie are trying to be kind, but I can't stay."

"Beth," Olivia said slowly, "my heart aches for you. I wish you felt free to talk to us. You know we want to help you." Hastily she added, "I'm not suggesting you tell us all about the situation. It's obvious it's heart-rending for both of you. Did you know Mike left immediately without talking to any of us? We let him go without questions, but with you it's different."

"I've explained." As Beth spoke, her fingers tugged at the handkerchief she held. "It isn't as if I'm running away, Olivia. When I came here with Mike, it was with the understanding I would go on to Washington."

"Washington?" Sadie cried, coming into the room. "That's no place for thee alone."

"I know people there who'll take care of me. Actually kin—a cousin. Nearly like going home. Sadie, you've been good to me, but don't try to keep me here. This will be best for all of us." She turned quickly, flashing a tremulous smile at Olivia and Sadie. "Amos says he'll take me to the train station."

Olivia sighed, glanced quickly at Sadie, and said, "Please at least leave us the address of your cousin. We'll want to write to you, and there's a good possibility I might go to Washington to work."

"Well, certainly." Beth quickly went for paper and pencil. "I'll feel better knowing you'll write to me."

When the door closed behind Beth, Olivia said, "She couldn't wait to be gone. Did you notice the strange way she spoke? Stuffy, as if she had planned out each word."

Sadie nodded. "Thou art serious about working for the soldiers, aren't ye?"

Olivia took a deep breath. "Yes. More and more I'm feeling it's necessary I do my part. But I'll admit the thought of caring for wounded soldiers is frightening."

"Thou art always welcome back here," Sadie said hastily. "I will miss thee sorely. But I understand, I know how I would feel." She started for the door and stopped. "Please write us letters. That will help us in our lonely times, too."

Olivia nodded and took a deep breath. "I suppose I need to tell you that I've already talked to the commanding officer in charge of the recruitment and training of soldiers in town. He told me they desperately need nurses around the Potomac. He didn't have an address, but he suggested I go to Washington and make inquiries at the Department of War."

"Potomac?" Olivia nodded, and Sadie said slowly, "Still hoping? Maybe going isn't wise."

Olivia's voice was muffled. "Perhaps not wise; it will be difficult, but Sadie, it's necessary."

It was March in Pennsylvania. Olivia stood at the window looking across Amos' pasture at the carpet of spring colors. "Crocuses, daffodils, tulips," she murmured. The colorful strip bordering the path was a line leading Olivia's eyes down to the *Golden Awl*, dry-docked at the end of the pasture. She touched the brooch at her neckline as Sadie came into the room.

It was obvious that Sadie had been crying, but she smiled and cocked her head as she looked at Olivia's dark suit. "Thee looks very grown-up and capable. I would hire thee myself. It might be those people will want a reference. I will recommend thee—"

"For being fairly good at cooking and making beds?" Olivia smiled. "That's possibly all they want to know. Sadie, why are you wearing your bonnet?"

"Because I intend to go with thee to the railroad station. I want to look over the train."

"I'm certain it will be loaded with young men going to war," Olivia said. As she turned away from the spring scene, Amos stopped the buggy at the front door.

Sadie eyed the bag. "Is that all the belongings thou art taking?"

"Yes. I've no idea where I will be staying, and I doubt I'll need much of a wardrobe."

"I'm glad thou art leaving some of thy belongings. It will be good to have something of thee around. With thee going it's like seeing my own flesh and blood leaving." Olivia turned, quickly kissed Sadie, and hurried out to the wagon.

When Olivia got off the train at Washington, she discovered a Washington that was sharp and bleak, a dismal contrast to the beautiful city she and Alex had enjoyed together.

She directed the hack driver to take her to the hotel where they had stayed, then settled back in her seat. Olivia's eyes blurred; she tried to swallow the lump in her throat as she recalled their time in the city—the rose silk frock, the dinner parties, but most of all, being with Alex.

The same hotel was now shabby, not quite clean, and the people—from the man at the front desk to the tired-looking cleaning girl—seemed somber and fearful. After Olivia closed the door of her room, she leaned against it and murmured, "Father, I had thought I was the only person on earth with this sadness in my soul. Now I see it has seeped into everyone. Please, deliver us from this evil!"

Slowly she pressed the brooch to her face. The empty, dismal room wrenched the words out of her. "My precious Alex is dead and gone, and I must learn to live without him."

Olivia walked into the long, barn-shaped building and stopped just inside the door. From where she stood, she could see long lines of cots and stretchers. Fighting the discouragement the dismal scene gave her, she started toward a woman at the far end of the building.

As she walked slowly, she looked at the patients. There were a few smiles, but for the most part the men seemed asleep or tossing in delirium. She saw blood-soaked bandages, stumps where there should have been arms or legs, flushed faces and faces deathly pale.

"Lady—" The whisper was urgent, feeble. "Lady, please, water." She hesitated, saw the jug of water, and carried it to the man.

A wound stretched across his face, festering, angry red. What she could see of his face seemed dry and feverish. There was only one eye. Strangely detached, she noted it was blue, his hair curly and light. The hand he stretched toward her was hot, the grasp frail.

Biting her lip, Olivia slipped her hand under his head and gently lifted him until he could swallow the water. His burning hand slipped across hers, and his head turned away as his soul fled.

Olivia caught her breath in a painful gasp and eased him onto the cot. A uniformed woman was watching. When their eyes met, the woman's lightened until there was nearly a smile. She beckoned Olivia toward the end of the room.

"I'm Maggie Thorner," the woman said. "Why do you want to be here?"

"I don't know that I want to." Olivia looked around the room. "But if my husband had lingered, I would have wanted him to have this kind of care. I suppose it's the only way I can feel right about all this."

"And can you care for *Southern* soldiers? There are some here."

"Yes." Olivia hesitated. "I'm just frightened—terrified."

"It won't matter, as long as you are willing. Come, I will show you our bedrooms. I trust you have a bag with you."

Suddenly overwhelmed by it all, Olivia wanted only to run. But Mrs. Thorner was watching. Carefully Olivia pressed her lips together and followed her.

That evening, after settling her belongings in the tiny room tucked under the eaves, Olivia sat down at the rickety table and began a letter to Matthew.

> Dear brother,
>
> I write this, not knowing whether you'll receive it. I beg your forgiveness for delaying my letter so long. Once I decided to come to Washington, with the intent of offering my services as a nurse, it seemed best to wait until I arrived to explain everything to you. Please, if you are still in the area, come and see me. I am desperately in need of your company.

Less than a week later, Matthew did come. Maggie crossed the long room to get Olivia. "There's a gentleman to see you; says he's your brother."

Olivia smoothed the blanket and took the cup from the soldier's hand. "Matthew," she said slowly. "I am so glad that he's come."

With a sympathetic glance, Maggie said, "There's only an hour or so left of your shift. You won't need to come back. He's waiting in the office."

Matthew turned from the window as she came into the room. He watched her face, and his lips tightened as he said, "Come tell me about it."

Clenching her fists, she said, "Alex is dead, and I've lost the baby."

Carefully he put his arms around her and held her while she fought back the tears. "Come on, Livie, give way." Slowly she wrapped her arms around him and leaned against him.

"Matt, I can't believe I have a tear left."

"This is the worst place on earth for you to be."

"I had to do it. To do something. This seemed best." She took a deep breath. "I suppose Crystal is with her mother now."

"I hope so. After she wrote, there was a long delay because of the trains. Not only troop movement having first priority, but also the Southern railroad has problems with their lines." He grinned a bit. "Seems someone is keeping them in a state of disrepair."

He released Olivia and paced to the window. "To tell the truth, I'm beginning to regret not having gone with her. She headed south with the intention of taking the first available route west. She talked a little about seeing a cousin in Greenville—mentioned it in connection with taking the Memphis-Ohio Railway." He turned. "Anyway, I'm frantic waiting to hear from her."

He watched the reactions on his sister's face. "I need to know what you've heard about Alex."

"Very little. I only knew that he was with the Army of the Potomac, and that they were waiting for assignment. He talked about McClellan. I was concerned when I heard about the battle at Fredericksburg, because I'd guessed he went that direction. And then his name was posted as killed in battle."

"There's no doubt?" he asked.

"How else would they have his name and location?"

He paced to the window and stood with his back to her. "Olivia, I'm devastated. He meant a great deal to me. As for you—I can't begin to express how I feel—about all that has happened." She heard him choke. "Is there anything I can do to make it easier?" She shook her head mutely.

"I'm trying to accept it. Amos and Sadie tell me that sometimes we don't see the whole plan, and that we humans are prone to write a different ending to life. That's where the difficulty comes. They tell me the hard parts like this become easier when we believe and accept God's control in it all. I'm still trying not to understand, just to accept." She took a deep breath. "At least I know God hasn't left me alone."

CHAPTER 32

Mike slumped in his chair and stared at the blank sheet of paper in front of him. He picked up the pencil and wrote:

Dear Beth,

I hope that you don't mind my writing. I miss you very much, especially considering the bumbling mess I've made of everything.

The pencil sagged in his fingers. Getting to his feet, he crumpled the paper and shoved it into the stove. Grabbing another piece of paper, he again began to write:

Dear Sadie and Amos,

I apologize for causing such an unfortunate situation. Someday I'd like to sit down with you and try to explain it all. Suffice it for now to say that I had not been living as close to the Lord as I should have.

I love Beth with all my heart. I also feel that I'm closer to the Lord now than I've been for a long time. Perhaps one of these days, if I survive this war, Beth and I will be together again. Please give her my regards and ask if I may write to her.

We've had a difficult time lately. Nothing seems to be working out. There have been several attempts to push the Confederates down the Mississippi, but so far we haven't had much success.

You've no doubt heard about the foray into Arkansas. We took transports up the White River and then into the Arkansas River. Landed troops, and with little trouble they took the fort.

Since then we've had more problems than success—I suppose you also know about Porter trying to take boats into the Yazoo River above Vicksburg.

I expect to be out of here any day now, but don't know where I will be going. It's hard to believe this war has been going on for so long.

The door opened and Adams came in. "For January, the activity is getting pretty heavy around here. Sounds like we'll be moving out tomorrow."

"What's going on?"

"We're to support Grant in his push for Vicksburg. Porter wants to see you as soon as you can get to his office."

———

Admiral Porter pulled the river charts toward the center of the table. "Clancy, I'm told the boat *City of Vicksburg* has been brought down to Vicksburg. Also, we understand that supplies are being taken into Vicksburg by transports. This must stop. You get the picture. We have two objectives—disable the transports, and capture *City of Vicksburg*.

"Colonel Ellet, the son of Charles Ellet, is going in with his ram *Queen of the West*. She looks a little heavy and awkward to me, so I want to send in a gunboat right on her tail."

"Awkward?" Mike questioned. "What have they done to her?"

"Ellet changed her steering apparatus, moved it behind the bulwarks of her bows. She's also carrying three hundred bales of cotton, positioned to protect her machinery."

"Sounds like Ellet's expecting trouble."

"He is, and I'm afraid his ship will provide most of it. But that's where you come in. I've ordered a gunboat and crew for you. It'll be difficult following Ellet past the batteries just above Vicksburg." He got to his feet, saying, "Trailing behind, you might need to pick up the pieces."

"Does she have an iron prow?"

"Yes, she also carries an eighty-pound Parrott Gun on her main deck as well as a twenty-pounder and three twelve-pound howitzers. Between the two of you, I expect the job will be done. He grinned as he returned Mike's salute. "See you when you get back."

———

The Mississippi River glistened in the waning light of the moon while the sky to the east hinted at dawn. Mike stood at the wheel of the gunboat, moving restlessly from one foot to another as he continuously checked the rapid current carrying debris and downed trees. In the dark, the trees looked like phantoms with grasping arms. The pilothouse door opened, and Lieutenant Gibbs came in. "What's the problem with Ellet?"

"I'm guessing," Mike muttered. "Admiral Porter told me the ram was a little unwieldy since she's carrying a load of cotton to protect her machinery; they've also repositioned the steering apparatus. I've an idea that's the problem. With the debris and the heavy current, she acts like she's fumbling in the dark."

"I'm afraid we won't make it past those batteries before sunup."

"If we don't, there could be problems. We may be the ones who are surprised." Gibbs sat down at the table, and the pilothouse was silent.

———

The sun was above the horizon when Mike muttered, "I'm bringing up the steam; the Vicksburg batteries are dead ahead."

Gibbs came to stand beside the wheel while he watched the two vessels move full steam toward the batteries. "They see us," Mike said. "I'm guessing there's a hundred guns up there. Better get down below."

The first blast assaulted Mike's ears, rattling the pilothouse. Then the guns fired one after the other. Mike tightened his grip on the wheel and tried to keep behind *Queen of the West*. He saw her shudder, veer to port, and then straighten her course. She put on steam, and Mike reached for the bell rope. He sighed with relief as they rounded the bend and *Queen of the West* turned for action.

"There's *City of Vicksburg*, and our *Queen* is headed for her." As he spoke, the ram slammed into the Confederate ship. "Well, we got one, but I don't think it's a direct hit." The ram was caught in the force of the current and Mike watched her swing broadside into the *City of Vicksburg*.

Lieutenant Gibbs ran into the pilothouse. "She didn't get her. Those iron guards are too large. I don't think the ram did more than graze her."

Mike saw the flash and gasped, "Ellet's firing! Are those incendiary shells?"

"Yes! Look at that!" Gibbs shouted. "The shells have set fire to Ellet's cotton bales!" They saw the bales being frantically pitched overboard. With a burst of steam, the vessel straightened her course, and

Mike sighed with relief. Gibbs laughed. "She sure threw on the steam! That Colonel Ellet is some tough guy!"

Two weeks later as Mike came into the bunkhouse, he was hailed by Adams. "Did you hear about your new love, *Queen of the West*? Ellet took her down river again. They captured the *Era, No. 5.* It was quite a haul; got fourteen Texan soldiers, twenty-eight thousand dollars in Confederate money, and a load of corn headed for Little Rock.

"On the way back, the *Queen of the West* ran aground right under the guns of Fort Taylor. Her gunboat was about a mile below, but before she could get there *Queen of the West* was riddled. Lost quite a few Negro deck hands. They drowned—seems they panicked and jumped overboard. Ellet was rescued. When the gunboat caught up with her, the crew couldn't handle the fire from Fort Taylor. Had to sink her and run for their lives."

"Aw, what a shame!" Mike exclaimed, shaking his head. "She was a great ram." He reached for his bag and began loading it.

"Heading out again?"

"Yeah, Porter's going down the Mississippi. Since I was with him once, he's decided I'm better than a green pilot," Mike said with a crooked grin as he shouldered his bag.

The Mississippi was serene that balmy February morning. With his hands relaxed on the wheel and his cap shoved back, Mike let his eyes roam back and forth, reading the river and checking her banks.

The door opened and Admiral Porter rushed in. Going to the window, he raised his binoculars. "I can't believe my eyes," he muttered. "That's the ram *Queen of the West* docking at Warrenton's wharf! I'd no idea they'd raised her and got her moving so soon."

He lifted the binoculars again and said, "She's afloat, looks pretty good—at least serviceable and ready to go." With a worried frown he paced the cabin, glanced at Mike, and growled, "It's the *Indianola* I'm worried about. She's downstream a ways and I heard fighting down there."

"Do you think they've used the *Queen* against the *Indianola*?" Mike asked.

Porter lowered his glasses, looked at Mike, and then lifted them to watch the boats. "I can't say for sure, but we can't spare a boat to send down river to get her back if she has been taken."

Porter turned to Mike and said slowly, "I've got an idea."

"What's that, sir?"

"Did you notice the battery of guns up there on the hill? The way they were firing, I have a hunch they don't know that she is Confederate. They about finished themselves off when that boat went past." He began to chuckle. "Looks to me like they've over-fired and burst at least five guns in their attempt to get her. It occurs to me that if I had something to draw their fire, I might help them finish off the others. That'd help Grant." He was still chuckling and shaking his head as he left the pilothouse.

Vicksburg was far behind them when Porter returned to the pilothouse. "Mike, see that old barge grounded over there in the bushes? Let's go tie on to it."

Mike gave him a quick glance. Porter's eyes were dancing with glee as he turned and headed for the stairs. Mike shrugged and pulled the bell rope while he spun the wheel.

After they had tied onto the barge, Porter ordered Mike to go upstream to the first sheltered inlet. "Get back in the bushes and tie on."

Porter had the crew busy by daybreak. For the first few hours of the day, Mike watched from the deck as Porter's crew began their task. Just before noon, Porter appeared with grimy hands and his sleeves rolled high. "You might as well get into this. We're going to make a boat; think I'll christen her *Decoy*. We can use more hands in the mud. I want to get this show moving as soon as it's dark."

With a sigh, Mike followed Admiral Porter to shore. "Bring more mud," Porter said. "There's two buckets. I'll show you how to shape the furnace."

A roustabout appeared at Porter's elbow, grinning with delight. "Suh, I found two old canoes over in the bushes. Nearly fallin' apart, but I think they'll work for quarter-boats. 'Spect we'll be finished before nightfall?"

"Get the canoes, Bud. I'm aiming for dark." He turned. "Mike, I need some oil for the furnace. Dirty oil, if you have it."

After supper, Porter put the finishing touches on the barge and the first mate came with a flag. "Looks more like someone's underwear," Porter commented.

He turned to Mike. "What do you think? Wanna pilot this downriver?"

Mike shook his head and chuckled. "Pork barrels stacked for chimneys, and that old man's woodpile nailed up to resemble a cabin. Good thing you filled the chimneys with mud. When you going to fire the furnace on this scourge of the Mississippi?"

"We'll break out of here before dawn, haul it down river. We'll light the furnace just before we let her go. Come on, fellows, let's get some sleep."

Long before dawn, towing the old barge with her new contours, Mike took his gunboat down river. Just as dawn began to lighten the sky, Mike could see the Vicksburg batteries like a dark blight against the hills. Down below, Porter signaled Mike as he leaned over to cut the rope holding the ghost ironclad.

Mike turned to the seaman beside him. "Hold her steady; I want to take a look." He ran to join Porter at the railing of the gunboat, and they watched the current take the barge. Porter muttered, "With currents running like they do, our boat ought to keep midstream and chug right along."

"It's moving at about five knots. Kind of an eerie feeling," Mike admitted. "Not a sound, but that smoke will get plenty of attention."

Porter chuckled. "Let's drop anchor in the bushes. We can cut across this spit of land and get close enough to watch it all. Grant's men are close to here. Might be we can haul them out of bed."

Mike took the boat into shore and the crew sprinted across the spit of land.

They reached the point just below the Vicksburg batteries and found Grant's men at breakfast. "Come see a naval battle," Porter called.

They headed for the bluff over the river and pointed. "There, keep your eyes on her."

"What is that thing?" the commanding officer whispered. Just at that moment the Confederate batteries opened fire. Shell after shell was lobbed toward the dark silent boat. The bluff under their feet vibrated from the explosions; the cannon balls whizzed and the silent boat moved serenely on.

"What in tarnation is that?" muttered the commander. "It's creepy; doesn't even flinch when those balls hit."

Porter leaned close. "That's because the bullets go right through the rotten wood!"

The men looked at Porter, stared at the boat, and began to laugh. The first morning light touched the dark hull. They watched her slow, determined course. The guns fired with increasing intensity. A shell hit the furnace, and a chunk of mud fell away. Steadily the boat moved on. The soldiers slapped their knees, laughed, and shouted, "Hurrah, hurrah! The Union stands."

Mike spotted the boat first. "Admiral Porter?" He pointed. "Isn't that the *Queen of the West?*"

Porter sobered. "Mike, you're right. She's left Warrenton and is headed for Vicksburg."

"So's the ghost monitor," Mike muttered, lifting the field glasses. "And sir, the ghost monitor is moving down on *Queen of the West*. Look!" Mike's voice was full of awe as he whispered, "Can you believe that? The *Queen of the West* is turning tail and running! She's headed downriver as fast as she can go."

The commander choked. "And that fool ghost boat is right on her heels at five knots an hour!" The men were still laughing when they heard the explosion.

Out of the stunned silence, Porter spoke. "That came from the harbor at Vicksburg. Men, I think we'd better get out of here. If my hunch is correct, the Confederates have blown the *Indianola* up. Soon they'll get a good look at our newest gunboat. We're not prepared to stand off the Confederates. So long, General, hope you enjoyed the show."

CHAPTER 33

Mrs. Duncan?" Olivia looked over her shoulder. Dr. Whitt and Maggie were watching her. She wiped the cool cloth across the flushed face of her patient and slowly got to her feet.

Turning, she asked, "You want me?" Maggie nodded and Olivia crossed the room to them. "What is it?"

"Maggie tells me you've been here over a month," Dr. Whitt said, "and you haven't left the place. Unless you want to be ill, you must begin to take more precautions. I'm ordering you to get out of the building every day. Take a walk, and be gone at least an hour."

"Doctor, we're too busy," Olivia protested in a whisper. "I could work twenty-four hours a day and still find more to do."

"If you do, you'll not last another month. Mrs. Duncan, that man you were bathing has a communicable disease. If you don't maintain your health, you'll catch it. Now wash your hands and go. Maggie tells me Miss Cable is coming right away."

"Very well." Olivia saw her patient watching. Quickly she went to him and tried to smile into his miserable eyes. "Lettie will be here shortly; I must leave." He closed his eyes and nodded. Blinking at tears, Olivia walked out of the long ward.

At the door she looked down at her soiled apron and began to remove it. Her fingers slowed on the buttons, and she touched her brooch. Lettie Cable came down the stairs. "Going out?"

"Yes, I was ordered to leave the building for some fresh air. I just now thought of an errand." She swallowed hard. "It's a girl I knew in Pennsylvania; I really need to see her."

"You'd better change your dress and comb your hair," Lettie said gently. "For us, you are fine, but—"

Olivia tried to grin. "I guess I am tired. About Roger—I'm afraid his temperature is up." Lettie nodded, and Olivia hurried up the stairs.

As she changed her frock, she thought about Beth and the strange reluctance she had to renew their friendship. Taking out the slip of paper with the name and address of Beth's friend, she read it, murmuring, "I do believe that is a very short distance from here, just beyond the Capitol."

She left the hospital, nearly giddy from the rush of cool, fresh air in her face. For the first block, Olivia hurried, panting with exertion. Realizing her agitated state, she stopped, sighed, and turned slowly. People rushed around her. She saw the pale blue sky with its rolling thunderheads. "It's spring, and I'd scarcely noticed." She saw the bright yellows, lavenders, and pinks of violets, lilacs, tulips, and jonquils. The city park was spotted with them; window boxes constrained them. Olivia took a deep breath.

An old gentleman sitting on a bench looked first at her and then the view. "Seems a right good sign that life's continuing even when we're a blotching it," he said.

She watched him warily. His familiar southern accent identified him. "You working in the hospital down the road?" he asked.

"How did you guess?"

He chuckled, "Your frock." His face sobered; he nodded toward the flowers. "After a winter such as we've had, it's nice to know God's in His heaven. Maybe spring is a promise. We need something unshakable." She saw the sadness in his eyes as he added, "My life is nearly over, but you young ones will be left to put it all back together again. Even the parts our thoughtlessness has ruined."

With tears in her eyes, she nodded. "Good day to you, sir."

Olivia checked the address on her paper and stopped on the sidewalk to look at the imposing entrance to the house. Slowly she walked up the flight of steps to the door and tapped. The woman who opened the door was tiny and withered. Like a drought-stricken apple still on the limb, Olivia thought. "I'm Olivia Duncan and I would like to see Beth Peamble, or if she isn't at home, Miss Cynthia Bowen," she said.

"Neither of them's at home," the woman replied curtly, eyeing Olivia with suspicion. "Miss Peamble will be here tomorrow; might try again."

Olivia left her name and walked away, feeling as if she had been relieved of a distasteful task. She walked slowly back to the hospital, wondering about her attitude.

———

When Beth and Cynthia returned that evening, the dour maid said, "There's been a female here looking for Beth or Cynthia. Looked to me like an abolitionist. Kinda strung out and wearing dowdy duds. Said her name's Olivia Duncan." As she left the room, she added, "I told her you'd be here tomorrow. Want I should turn her back?"

Beth stared at Cynthia. "Oh dear; I left your name with the Coopers in Pennsylvania. That's before I had any idea of what you're up to."

Cynthia laughed. "My, Beth! You act as if we're in danger of losing our heads. Dear, this is just a little game to help in the war effort. Our part to make things go smoothly." Still chuckling, she stood up. "After Mr. Adams and Mr. Stollen leave tonight, we'll discuss the matter. Now we need to be prepared for the evening; come and rest."

Beth tossed restlessly on Cynthia's guest bed and tried to think of a way to straighten out the tangle her life had become. *What do I say, how do I explain it all? She'll look right through me, and I'll be exposed!* Beth slipped her hand under her pillow and felt the tiny flannel bag. She fingered the rings, the emerald bracelet, the ruby brooch. Satisfied they were all there, she sighed and snuggled her head into the deep soft pillow.

Later she faced Cynthia and confessed, "Maybe I'd just better leave right now. I'll make a bumble of it. I'm just not smart like you are. Back home I'd never have guessed you'd end up like this."

"Beth, my dear, I'm not *ending*, I'm beginning. Of course, if you don't see this as challenging and fun—but even more important, as something you must do to help the South win this war—well then . . ."

"Oh, Cynthia," Beth gasped, "you make me sound disloyal. It's not that at all. It's just that I always say and do the wrong things. I can't—"

"Yes you can, if you so desire. Beth, if not this, what will you be doing with your life that's really significant? I can tell by your face that you've not given it a thought. Besides," Cynthia added, sipping her tea, "this puts me in a very awkward position. Because you indicated you were willing to help, I've put myself out on a limb. You have met some of our prime contacts—those men in the White House who are strong links to the South. Do you realize only a handful of people in this city know of their activities?" She paused. "Beth Peamble, it's time to grow up. If you are simply scared, so what? I am too. This is serious business, but the South can't make it without you."

In a moment more, Cynthia continued, "There's money too. I don't know what you've been doing, but your wardrobe makes me suspicious. I happen to know your family couldn't afford one pair of kid slippers such as the half dozen you own. I know the price of the clothing this new Beth wears, and it doesn't come cheaply."

"Cynthia, I—" she gulped. "I just can't tell you. But, honest, I'm not a—bad woman."

"Sweetie, I didn't say you were. Neither did I intimate you must become a lady of the streets to accomplish this task." She leaned forward and hissed, "This is not only honorable, but very, very necessary if we are to win this war and have our old life back—on a silver platter, if you please. Beth, I can assure you that in the end, we will be praised and amply rewarded for our efforts in this war."

Beth studied her fingernails. Of the thoughts that marched through her mind, one series of images stood out starkly—she and Mike standing in that shabby room while the white silk and lace gown billowed around her. "I cannot marry you, Beth."

The hurt and shame of the day swept over her. She examined the emotions churning around inside. *It's like butter*, she thought. *Pound the cream around and something solid comes out. Might be this is the most important thing that's ever happened to me—Cynthia and her project.*

She clenched her hands under the table. Taking a deep breath, Beth said, "Cynthia, you're right. I must be loyal. But I'm still scared. Will you help me?"

"Of course, dear. But Beth, you need to look at the cause as being something beyond yourself. If you can't commit yourself to this with a passionate zeal, then when things get difficult you may want to get out of it all. That must not happen. Do you understand? It is possible your life will depend on how you approach this task."

Slowly Beth nodded. "I understand, Cynthia. I promise I won't back down."

Cynthia narrowed her eyes. "You mean it? How can you jump around like a fish out of water and then get this sudden passion to help us?"

Carefully Beth evaluated the new thoughts that had been filling her mind since she'd come to Washington. They were beginning to be more important than fear. She looked up. "Number one, there's a Union fella I'd like to see dug under. Number two, I'd like to be a somebody. Cynthia, you know what it was like with Pa . . . just a poor tenant farmer. You know what it's like to have the plantation folks sneering at us hill folks. You know what it's like to *want*—it's a sickness gnawing out your insides."

"Yes, I know," Cynthia nodded. "That's why I'm here."

"Well, I want to be somebody, too. I want a fine house, and people thinking I'm worth spending time on. I want to be a real lady. I want pretty clothes and—" Cynthia's eyes narrowed again. *A minute more and I'd have spilled it all,* Beth thought as she jumped to her feet.

"I think you'll make it; those are all the right reasons if you don't happen to be Jefferson Davis' wife."

Beth frowned. "Are you implying I'm not loyal enough?"

Cynthia ignored the question. "Now, come eat your cakes; we need to dress. Maude is serving dinner at seven-thirty. I'm glad you have such a nice wardrobe; that's important."

"Back in Pennsylvania they didn't even notice it," Beth muttered as she swallowed the last of the cake. "But if you keep feeding me like this, I won't be able to wear my frocks."

"Having a few more curves will be to your advantage," Cynthia replied as she left the room, and Beth stared after her.

———

Mr. Timothy Stollen had a mustache which tickled Beth's hand when he kissed it. He also had gray eyes—cold, yet curious. Several times during the evening, she discovered him watching her. Uneasily aware of those calculating eyes, she decided she was frightened, not flattered.

Halfway through dinner Beth began to compare the two men. Nat Adams seemed devoted to Cynthia, but his restless eyes and impatient fingers seemed to be saying something else. When coffee and liqueur were served in the library, Beth began to sense an underlying pattern. *It's like a game; we act because we must.*

Nat Adams sat down beside her. "Miss Bowen tells me you'll serve as courier. Do you realize the importance of secrecy? The life of the Confederacy depends on our being able to keep the lines of communication open. Beth, you'll meet important men. This will call for confidence and discretion." He gave her a quick glance. "Think you can make a good impression on Richmond's elite as well as Washington's? Being a courier is a skill you can develop, if you're determined to do so."

Studying his shrewd eyes, she felt the stirring of excitement. She could see herself dressed in velvet and diamonds, attending balls in Richmond. "I understand," she said. "But it's hard making promises when I don't know what will be required. Why does the South need communication with Washington?"

"The South must know every important detail we can give them.

You realize numerically the South can't hope to win this war. But with knowledge of campaign plans, we'll be able to wear the enemy down. Already we're seeing the effects of good communication with Richmond. It gives our men a great deal of confidence going into battle, knowing what the North has planned. Beth, we intend to hammer away at the North, demoralize them, and in the end win. I do not think this war will continue much longer; I fully expect the Union to come begging at our doorstep. With our advantage, they'll be more than happy to give us just what we want."

"Slavery," she breathed.

Tim leaned forward in his chair. "It isn't just that. We must be free as a nation, and we're paying a terrible price for that freedom. On both sides men are dying like flies. Can you appreciate a fellow like me being concerned with people dying?"

"I thought only Quakers felt that way."

"Doesn't sound like you're too fond of them."

"They don't care for the good life. Never have any fun, and after a time they begin to come across as better'n anyone else alive. Always talking about *God*."

He chuckled, and Ned continued. "We have men close to those who make decisions and plan strategy. This information must be passed on. While you are in the learning stage, you will be making a trip with another courier to meet contact people and to see how this is handled."

Later that evening, as the men prepared to leave, Nat Adams returned to her side, saying, "I'll make arrangements for your first trip and advise you." She watched him leave and with a shiver she ran quickly up to her room.

———

The following afternoon Olivia came. Beth faced her across the tea table. "Are you well?" Beth asked. "You seem thin and tired."

"I am fine. The work is hard. But I feel as if this is what God wants me to do with my life, now that—"

Beth shuddered and said slowly, "Olivia, maybe for me the way things turned out was best. Looking back now I can hardly believe myself." She glanced up. Hastily she added, "I guess what I'm saying is that being with Cynthia has helped me grow up. I'm no longer as timid and uncertain as I was back there."

Olivia looked at her, puzzled. "That's strange, Beth, I didn't see you as being timid. Maybe uncertain, but sometimes it pays to be careful before we make decisions."

"I'm trying to say I think I'm growing up. Cynthia does that for a person. Makes me think about what I want out of life. What's important."

"What have you decided?"

"I suppose I'll want to make friends here. Get to know the city. Olivia, I really like Washington. It's exciting. I'd like to feel myself a part of the important things happening here. I'm not certain where I'll start. I suppose I need to think about earning some money first." She looked at Olivia's curious expression. "You know, for clothes and such. No one will look at me until I have a decent wardrobe. Since leaving Pennsylvania, I'm starting to see how dowdy and countrified the place is."

"Perhaps it is," Olivia replied slowly, "but I love the people. I learned to appreciate the deep spiritual side of them. They weren't afraid to admit the importance of having God in their lives. I learned plenty about Christianity and love simply from watching Amos and Sadie." She paused. "Have you heard from them?"

Beth nodded. "They didn't say much except they'd had a letter from Mike and he wants to write to me. But I don't want to hear from him." She shuddered. "Those stories he told, and that scar—it was close to his eye! I suppose I just want to enjoy life and not be reminded."

Carefully Olivia placed her cup and saucer on the table and smiled at Beth, who said, "I suppose you'll be too busy to visit me often. I miss the good times we all had in Pennsylvania."

"Beth, I don't intend to drop you," Olivia said quickly. "What are you going to do with your time while you are in Washington?"

"I don't know," she answered evasively, twisting her hands. "I'm hoping to be doing a little traveling, so don't be surprised if I'm gone. But I'm hoping you'll come visit me again."

"Of course. Dr. Whitt has suggested I get fresh air every day. He says I need it to stay healthy. Perhaps we can walk together."

Beth's face brightened. "Oh, I'd love that. Would you come tomorrow?" Surprised by the girl's eagerness, Olivia hesitated. Hastily Beth added, "That is, if you wish."

"Yes, that will be a good idea." Olivia stood up. "About this time?"

After Olivia left, Beth leaned against the front door and thought of life in Pennsylvania, before Alex's death, before Olivia had been pressed into this sad woman.

As she went to her room to prepare for the evening meeting, other pictures of Pennsylvania surfaced. She remembered Alex with the big Bible in his hands, saying, "Beth, religion isn't a matter of belonging to a church. It's all a matter of belonging to the Kingdom of God. When you become acquainted with God you know He's aware of every detail of your life, even the thoughts you think. Frankly, it was a wonderful feeling when I discovered we don't have to pretend in front of Him." *Why did he say that? I'd been so careful to fit in with the others.*

Later Beth went downstairs to discover that Nat Adams and Timothy Stollen had a guest. Beth entered the drawing room just as the dark-haired woman kissed Timothy. She turned with a pout. "You must be Beth Peamble. I'm teasing these gentlemen into going with us. How can they expect unescorted females to be treated with courtesy?"

With a mocking smile, Cynthia shook her head. "Beth this is Kathleen Cogall. You two need to get acquainted; you'll be working together." With a grin, she added, "Kathleen's been with us for the past year and, as you can see, is getting very saucy."

Looking at the men, Beth noticed Timothy Stollen's eyes were a degree colder than they had been the previous meeting. She turned to Kathleen. "I'm very happy to meet you, Kathleen. I need to hear all about this. It's—exciting." The men looked at each other while Beth chewed her lip and reviewed her words.

"Kathleen, I've no intention of going with you," Tim Stollen said. "It's important for me to remain in the background; otherwise you wouldn't have been hired." He smiled with his lips, but his eyes remained cold. "If you must play, do so after your work is completed."

Late that evening, after Cynthia closed the door behind the three, she faced Beth and asked, "What is wrong? You didn't look too happy this evening."

"Cynthia," she whispered, "to tell the truth, I just can't see myself doing this. I know I'll do it all wrong. I want out before this goes any further."

"It doesn't work that way, Beth. Carrying the messages is important, but protecting the people involved is much more important. Don't let us down now. It's gone too far for you to back out gracefully." Beth observed the hard line of Cynthia's jaw, nodded, and hurried upstairs.

When Olivia met Beth the next day, she eyed her carefully and gently asked, "What is it, Beth? You seem miles away this afternoon. Is there anything I can do to help you?"

"Oh!" Beth looked at Olivia and blinked. "I didn't realize it. I—the day's lovely and I've just been daydreaming, I suppose." She was silent for a while, then she said abruptly, "Olivia, sometimes I get confused. In Pennsylvania, at meetinghouse, they talked about loving God and doing good to your neighbor as if it were the most important part of life. Do you agree?"

"Jesus said so. He called them the two most important of the commandments. Keeping them," Olivia added slowly, "is a good indicator of whether or not a person is serious about being a Christian."

She slanted a look at Beth and was surprised to see the troubled look on the girl's face. Olivia's heart quickened with excitement. *Is this the opportunity I've wanted so badly?* she wondered.

"Let's sit down and watch the birds and squirrels," Olivia murmured, pointing to the park bench.

"Then if a person keeps these commandments he'll go to heaven?"

In a rush of words, Olivia asked, "Beth, have you accepted Jesus Christ as your Savior?"

"I don't know what you're talking about," Beth admitted. "In Pennsylvania I kept hearing the same thing. Even Mike said it, but what does it mean?"

"To become a child of God. We can't belong to God or even enjoy being in His company until we've done something about the selfishness in our lives. I know this for a fact. I had to face it in myself. But there's nothing we humans can do to be righteous."

"I don't understand," Beth murmured. "Since we've done the sinning, it seems we ought to be the ones coming forward and doing something about it."

"But what could we do?"

"It would have to be something significant, wouldn't it?"

"God is holy," Olivia said slowly. "And we are His willful, disobedient children. Did you know those Old Testament men were afraid of God? When Moses was up on the mountain getting the law, the Israelites were nearly frightened to death. They knew they were sinful and unworthy, and they knew God knew it, too!"

"Olivia, it's terrible just listening to you! I don't like talking this way."

"Beth, I didn't mean to frighten you. I just wanted to say that God working through Jesus Christ is reconciling the world to himself, forgiving our sins. Only Jesus could do anything about our record of sin; nothing we do could ever be good enough. And all we have to do is be willing to accept the sacrifice Jesus made for us."

Beth stood up suddenly. "It's getting very late, Olivia. I didn't mean to keep you so long."

Olivia got up. "Beth, I accepted that gift of salvation. Looking back at the difference that step made, the joy and happiness I gained through getting to know God, I tremble to think how terrible this past year would have been without the Lord to help me."

Beth led the way out of the park. She turned to Olivia. Stiffly she said, "Thank you for explaining it all to me."

"Beth, it takes more than knowing about it. You have to let Jesus Christ be your Savior, too."

She hesitated. "Please come see me again."

"I will, Beth. I promise."

As Beth walked slowly back to Cynthia's house, she was busy thinking of her new life. The vision of velvet and diamonds was sharp and clear in her mind. And Mike . . . her stomach knotted as she recalled his face, his serious eyes, his gentle kisses. She shivered, exclaiming, "Thank God that wedding didn't happen!" Then she quickened her steps, wondering why his name still brought a lump to her throat.

CHAPTER 34

Crystal, is my collar awry? You're looking as if—"

She smiled. "I'm filling my eyes and mind with you. Oh, Matthew, beg me to stay, and I will without regret."

"My dear!" He put his arms around her and looked into her face. "You know I wouldn't ask that. You need to visit your parents. If I hadn't felt the urgency of getting into the army, I'd have gone with you." He tried to grin as he added, "It would be easy to persuade me I'm failing you by not going." She silenced him with a kiss.

"It's just," she whispered, "after being separated for so long, I can hardly bear more."

"Crystal, I've been thinking the same." He pressed his lips to her temple, "I'll be moving out of here soon. Probably south. So we'd be separated even if you were to stay."

"Do you think of—what might happen?"

"All the time. But I'm learning to trust God. I'll come through this if it's His will. Crystal, you know how I love you, and how I value the time we've had together."

She nodded against his chest. "Matthew, we've talked about this, and now if you say it again, we'll both be crying. Remember, this separation is temporary."

"You'll soon be back." Matthew stroked Crystal's face as he looked into her eyes. "Crystal, it would be easy to worry about what could happen to you."

"But you won't." She smiled at him. "You'll trust the Lord to keep track of me. As soon as possible I'll mail a letter to you. And I plan to return to Pennsylvania by June." She moved away from him and picked up her hat. "If only I could have gone to New Orleans in February!"

Matthew shook his head. "With the newspapers accounts of General Butler's difficulties in the city, I'm glad you weren't there. Life seems nearly back to normal, if the newspapers can be trusted." He held her coat for her, kissed her again, and said, "We must go now."

"A strange journey it will be," she murmured taking his arm. "Traveling by train from Washington to Alexandria and then to Richmond. I'll be wise to keep my eyes open and my mouth shut—at least long enough to get me on a train heading west. I didn't dream it would be so difficult to travel."

————

After Crystal boarded the train, she watched Matthew from the window until she could no longer see him. With a sigh, she settled into her seat and looked around. A woman across the aisle nodded over her knitting, saying, "The situation these days makes you wonder about traveling, doesn't it? Going far?"

"Yes." Crystal hesitated and asked, "Where are you going?"

"Richmond. My children and grandchildren are there. I try to take the train down every spring before the weather is unbearably hot. War or no war, I intend to go. And you?"

Crystal took a deep breath. "New Orleans."

The woman pushed her spectacles higher on her nose and stared at Crystal. "Alone? Seems to me that's a risky trip."

"What can possibly be risky? Surely they take good care of their passengers."

"Well, I suppose. But you've heard about the Yankees tearing up track and such."

"No."

"Well, they do. Then when they get it loose, they shove logs underneath one side of the rails. When the train hits those rails at a slant, over it goes."

Crystal watched the shiny steel needles fly in and out of the soft yarn. "Maybe I'll just go as far south as I can before traveling west," she said.

"Maybe you'll just go where they send you. Some of the lines aren't that dependable." She glanced over her knitting, took several more stitches, looked at Crystal, and said, "I'm Clary Hamilton Trent. From the Richmond Hamiltons. My family goes back to the earliest settlers. I assume you are Creole."

Crystal hesitated. "Yes, my mother and father are of French descent. Their great-grandparents came before the Revolutionary War."

"My, what a diversified society we have!" Mrs. Trent murmured. "Now with the immigrants from Ireland and western Europe, soon we'll have absolutely no real identity." She gave Crystal a curious glance.

By the time the train reached the outskirts of Richmond, both Crystal and Mrs. Trent were peering out the window. "Look at the masses and masses of people!" Mrs. Trent gasped. "I'd heard many are fleeing the fighting and moving into Richmond, but I didn't expect to see this. It's a wonder the city can hold them all."

"It does seem crowded. Somehow it makes the war seem even more tragic."

As soon as Crystal left the coach, she entered the depot and inquired about a New Orleans-bound train. She listened to the ticket agent with dismay. "You mean I'll need to wait until next week?"

With a tired sigh the man shoved his cap back and said, "Lady, troop movement has top priority."

With a shrug of resignation, Crystal took a room at the hotel across the street. Days stretched into weeks and then extended even more. It was well into April before civilians were allowed travel reservations.

When she finally left Richmond, Crystal traveled for days. At one stop Crystal left the coach, looked around the bleak depot, and turned to survey the train with distaste.

It's like a wild creature, she thought, looking at its black sides quivering, steaming, and belching. She glanced down at her clothes stained with soot. Her head throbbed.

She saw the conductor and hurried toward him. "Sir, why must I keep changing trains?" He cupped his hand to his ear. Fighting to keep her voice calm, Crystal cried, "I've transferred three times since leaving Richmond. I traveled nearly to Atlanta, swung north, and now I'm in Tennessee."

"Ma'am," the conductor roared, "these trains are all different. Their wheels don't fit on each other's tracks. Now, they call this train narrow gauge. You left Richmond on narrow gauge, switched to a different rail at the junction, and now you're back to narrow. Come tomorrow about noon, we'll be on the Nashville line, and after that you'll transfer to the Jackson-New Orleans line, which is different yet."

With a nod and a sigh, Crystal picked up her valise. He called after her. "No matter what, ma'am, you'll have to travel this way to get to New Orleans. That's the way the train goes."

She nodded again and trudged toward the coach he pointed out. As she climbed aboard, she noticed that this train was different. Covertly she examined the occupants of the coach. There were few comfortable housewives. There didn't seem to be any soldiers. Most of the people looked worn to the bone, sunken into themselves like shuttered windows. From the number of bags around them, she guessed them to be part of the multitude she had seen in Richmond—those fleeing the war-ravaged areas.

As she looked around, she modified her first impression. The man coming toward her was obviously a soldier in civilian clothing. She eyed him cautiously. His grin was too friendly, and his right arm was in a sling. The train was still gathering speed, moving with jerks and bumps, when he sat down beside her. His eyes were frank, appraising. "Mind if I sit here?"

Crystal noted the number of vacant seats scattered around the car. She tipped her chin upward. "I'm certain you'll sit where you wish, but I do believe you'd find more congenial seatmates among the men."

"I doubt it." With a smile very near a leer, he sat down. "I've just come from Fredericksburg. Was banged up a bit, and I'm going home to recuperate."

She nodded. Opening her newspaper, she said, "I wish you well."

"Better off than them Yanks. We bested them again. Don't know why they don't just go home and stay there." She kept her eyes fixed on the newspaper. "Where ya going?"

"To visit my parents."

"Where?"

She sighed. "New Orleans."

"Better stay out of there. I understand Butler's out to ruin all the pretty little ladies."

"I've heard that misconstrued report," she said coldly. "He's no longer in New Orleans." She turned the page.

"New Orleans? I'd a guessed you a nigger instead of a Creole—not that it makes much difference."

She looked at him coldly. "Excuse me, sir. I think you'd better leave." She rose and waited for him to move.

"Ma'am, I beg your pardon." Crystal looked up to see an older gentleman bowing toward her. "I must apologize for my fellow Southerner. He seems to have associated too closely with those he has been fighting. Obviously he's forgotten his manners." He turned to address

Crystal's seatmate. "Sir, you shall remove yourself immediately."

The soldier jutted his chin at the man addressing him. "Since when are we to treat them as equals?"

"You treated the lady as an equal when you sat beside her. I recommend that you continue to do so." The soldier slowly started down the aisle.

"Thank you, sir." As Crystal returned to her seat, she noticed the woman traveling with her benefactor. Her eyes were cold, and she turned away without acknowledging Crystal's presence.

It's finally begun, she thought miserably. *Matthew's built me up until I really believed I am as worthy as they. I wish Matthew were here!* As the thought was born, she felt a gentle nudge in her heart and smiled. *I'm sorry, Father; having once begun, I'll continue to believe You love me too, just as much as You love that beautiful white woman and her courteous husband.*

When Crystal purchased the ticket for the Mobile-Ohio railroad line, the ticket agent produced a map and marked the route. "You've made a long trip," he admitted, "but it has been to your advantage. This section in Georgia is in disrepair. Your trip has been long, but it has been safe.

"Now you'll need to transfer to the New Orleans-Jackson line at Jackson, Mississippi. With this transfer you'll be making the last change." He smiled at her obvious relief.

With a nod she took her ticket and hurried to the train. As Crystal entered the coach, she sensed tension in the atmosphere. Nearly all of the men were in uniform. The low conversation, serious faces, and watchful expressions made her uneasy.

Mid-afternoon the train arrived in Macon, Mississippi. It seemed to Crystal that the town was deserted with the exception of small groups of soldiers positioned along the streets near the railroad station. When the train ground to a stop, some of the soldiers left the coach. Another group of soldiers loped toward the train.

Crystal leaned forward. The men met nearly under her window. She watched them gesture toward the telegraph lines. One soldier knelt in the dust and drew diagrams with his finger while the others bent over him. When he stood, he pointed toward the engine, glanced at his watch, and backed away. The steam engine began to quiver; its bell clanged.

The granite-faced men returned to the coach and sat down. Crystal heard the murmur of their voices, and picked up the book in her lap.

Later, when the train slowed nearly to a crawl and began to curve westward, she put away her book and leaned against the window. The

Mississippi landscape of pines, dense thickets, and scattered bogs moved past the window. Trails, nearly overgrown with fern and marsh grasses crisscrossed the ground close to the tracks.

Just as she noticed the trails, the train stopped. Horsemen wearing Confederate uniforms broke out of the trees. Crystal's hands tightened in her lap as she watched three of the men dismount. The soldiers who had boarded the train at Macon beckoned to them.

Conversation came to her in scattered words. "Don't risk it." "Supplies, guns." "Can't chance losing it." "His gang is headed south." "Not Jackson, too risky."

The horsemen left. One of the soldiers stepped into the aisle. Crystal saw the gold braid on his shoulders. "Ladies and gentlemen—" He spoke with an authority that made Crystal shiver. "I regret the necessity of having to do this, but because of a band of desperadoes, namely Union raiders, we are taking immediate, defensive action. I'm canceling our scheduled stops; we're heading straight into Vicksburg. The natural fortifications of the city are nearly impregnable."

"Sir," Crystal cried desperately, "I must transfer at Jackson. I have to go to New Orleans; my mother is ill."

"Ma'am," he advised her, "today you aren't going that way. These Union raiders are none too careful about whose lives they disrupt. They've destroyed warehouses loaded with supplies and carloads of ammunition, and they are passing this way, headed south. We'll be hard pressed to get this train over the last bridge before they take it out, too. Ma'am, we'll work at getting you out of Vicksburg and into New Orleans when they've left the territory, but right now it isn't safe." He gave her a thin smile and sat down.

The train began moving, gathering speed until the coach rocked. Crystal clenched the arms of her seat and watched billows of dark smoke sweep past her window. The depot at Jackson appeared and retreated in a blur of faces and buildings. They thundered past a train waiting at the station. Guessing it to be the train she should have taken, Crystal bit her lip and thought, *What irony! I slip across Southern borders and become a victim of the army my husband serves.*

It was dark when they reached Vicksburg. Weak with relief, Crystal stepped out of the train into the mist swirling inland from the Mississippi River. Carrying her valise, she trudged wearily down the street to the nearest hotel.

"Read all about it! Grant retreats to Memphis!" A young boy cried, hawking his papers. Crystal shoved coins at the boy and took the newspaper.

Inside the hotel, the man behind the desk smiled at her. "You've come for the ball?"

"I didn't know there was a ball," she murmured. "My train has been delayed, and I need accommodations until I can leave Vicksburg." He picked up the pen and hesitated, looking from her face to her traveling costume. "I'm from New Orleans," Crystal explained carefully, feeling tears burn her eyes. "I must return home to see my parents."

"I understand," he murmured, pulling forward the guest register. As she followed the porter, she thought, *He understands I am Creole, not nigger.*

After dinner in the hotel dining room, Crystal returned to her room to read the newspaper. Halfway down the hallway she met the maid. "Good evening," Crystal nodded to her.

"Ma'am, will you be wanting assistance? Have you a ball gown to be freshened?" The black woman waited.

"Ball gown? Oh, I do remember the clerk mentioning a party. Tell me about it."

"Downstairs, starts in another hour. Gonna be a fancy affair, with dancing." A shadow crossed her face as she added, "Celebrating Grant being pushed back. If you want, I'll take a frock for you."

"I don't plan to attend," Crystal said. "But it would be nice to have some of the wrinkles removed from my clothing. Yes, come with me."

After the maid had left, her arms loaded with dresses, Crystal found the *Vicksburg Whig* and sat down to peruse the newspaper.

"Oh, this is terrible," she murmured. "Gunboats! Mike Clancy was probably with them; I wonder what has happened to him?"

She read the article aloud. " 'We have cause to rejoice today. After tolerating the Union's ineffectual jabbing at the glorious city of Vicksburg for the past ten months, tonight we celebrate with a ball in the grand ballroom. General Grant has withdrawn his army. Reports are that he has retreated to Memphis. Apparently the enemy's gunboats are all more or less damaged. It is not surprising to hear the Yankees are demoralized and dissatisfied. Shall we promise them, upon taking the suitable pledge, employment with the winning side? Certainly they offer us no terrors now.' "

Slowly Crystal folded the newspaper and opened the door to the maid. "They look lovely," Crystal murmured with a smile. "Perhaps I'll change my mind and go down to the ballroom for a short time."

She hesitated, arrested by the woman's haunted expression. "Are you celebrating, too?" Emotion flickered through the woman's eyes. "I'm also disappointed," Crystal said.

The maid gave her a quick glance. "Ma'am, I be glad to help you." Crystal looked into the dark, anxious eyes as she pressed coins into her hands. "Thank you, ma'am. Call if'n you need me." She pointed to the bell rope, bobbed her head, and left.

Crystal pursed her lips and stared at the door, addressing the now-absent maid. "It's nearly as if I've denied the bigger part of myself," she whispered. "I didn't answer your unspoken questions when you looked at my skin. And just knowing your question makes me feel guilty, guilty. If something doesn't happen to reverse this war, my sister, we'll all be in the same boat—slaves. And I deserve it no less than you."

Crystal dressed and went down to the ballroom. Lifting her chin just a bit higher, she managed a smile as she started toward the far end of the room. The last strains of the waltz faded away. She looked at the young women smiling and laughing with their escorts. Delicate gowns blossomed in spring colors, made even more beautiful against the background of gray uniforms, gold braid, and medals.

Crystal saw a line of chairs just beyond the dancers, filled with dignified older men in black, and silver-haired matrons in velvet and satin.

There didn't seem to be a reception line. With a sigh of relief, she nodded at several friendly smiles and went toward a chair beside a uniformed man wearing a sling. The orchestra swung into a cotillion as she sat down.

The soldier turned to her, a pleasant smile on his face, "Do you—" Without warning, cannonfire and explosions shook the room. "The Yanks," the soldier swore. "Ran the blockade after all."

The shelling continued, building in ferocity. As the concussions struck the hotel, lamps flickered and curtains swayed. In the dimness, Crystal pressed her hand against her mouth while she watched flashes of light through the windows of the hotel. Around her there was an uneasy rush of people. "Get out!" came the urgent cries. "They'll hit the hotel!"

"The Yankees—they've run the blockade! Get out!"

Officers blocked the rush to the door. "Be calm!" they shouted. "There's not a chance of their guns touching the hotel. The explosions you hear are our guns firing on the Union gunboats. It'll all be over in a few minutes. Go to your rooms and remain calm."

Crystal left the ballroom with the others. As she made her way through the dim corridor she made no attempt to hide her delighted smile.

But during the night she began to worry. "Father, all those shells. Please protect the Federal boats. And please, if you want freedom for the slaves—even for those like me—please help us win this war. No matter what happens to me, please don't let them back down now!"

Two days later Crystal faced the ticket agent at the railway station.

"Why is it impossible to take the train to New Orleans?"

"Ma'am, the Feds have the railway system torn up. They've ruined the lines coming and going. There's no travel at all. You can't travel to New Orleans, and you can't go back the way you came." He smiled wanly. "Be patient. Things won't continue like this. Soon the railway will be put in order. This problem with the blockade runners'll be solved. Then you'll see your mama."

That same night Crystal awakened to gunfire again. As she listened to the explosion of shells, she began to feel her loneliness and isolation return. In the morning, the newspaper beside her breakfast plate informed her that another Union transport had been sunk. *Two sunk*, she thought, *but they didn't say how many made it through the batteries. And they didn't mention troops; were the transports empty?*

That thought kept her musing over the situation for the remainder of the day. Finally, with a sigh, she murmured, "Crystal, you are in the middle of war; I think you'd better pull yourself up sharp, quit being a baby, and pray without ceasing."

April slipped into May, and Crystal remained in Vicksburg. The uneasy situation persisted as the Union gunboats continued their attempt to break through the river blockade. Life in the bluffs above the river continued much the same. Crystal tried to make friends with those around her as they all endured the restrictions that overtook them one by one.

By the middle of May, Crystal noticed that the newspapers now carried news about the enemy with a somber tone. There was speculation about Grant's maneuvers and the size of his force. But the biggest question seemed to be his whereabouts. Could he possibly be on the eastern bank of the Mississippi? If so, how had that happened? But always the news ended on an optimistic note. General Johnston would be in Vicksburg soon, and the minor difficulties would be over.

Crystal read more news about the mysterious leader of the Union raiders who were wreaking havoc with the Confederate railways. "No wonder the trains aren't running. This man has effectively blocked General Pemberton's supply route. But why must he tear up three railways and burn depots and freight cars?" As she stared down at the newspaper, the answer became obvious.

"I do believe the Union isn't going to stop until this war is won completely! General Pemberton is in Vicksburg. So am I. I wonder if General Grant expects to tear the whole South apart?" For a moment she closed her eyes and pressed her fingers against them. "Father, what do I do now?"

———

Matthew picked up the letter. It was from Sadie. He tore it open and read:

Dear Matthew,
     We've had a letter from Mike. It sounds like there's going to be a battle in the Mississippi River area. He says Grant has big plans and this time it looks as if he will make it or lose all. I'm wondering about Crystal. Have you heard from her?

There was more, but Matthew dropped the letter and sat down to count the days on his fingers.

"Surely Crystal is safe in New Orleans by now," he muttered as he paced the room. But the feeling of dread wouldn't go away. "She said she would be back in Pennsylvania by June." He snatched up the letter. Obviously Crystal wasn't there.

Then he tossed the letter aside. "It isn't June yet, you ninny," he muttered. Then a darker thought crossed his mind, a thought that had him pacing the room restlessly. *You deserve to lose her. After the way you have treated her, what can you expect?* He flung himself on his bunk. "Father, God, I'm sorry. I know you love both of us, and the past has been forgiven. Please, just tell me what to do now."

———

Matthew faced his commanding officer. "Sir, I know the offensive hasn't developed against Vicksburg, but I'm convinced it will. I am requesting you to transfer me to a division scheduled to support Grant in the west."

"It's not our policy to shift individuals around. Since it's such an unusual request, would you mind telling me what is behind it?"

"My wife left in March to visit her mother in New Orleans. Since I haven't heard from her, I realize she could be anywhere. I know little of the difficulties involved with travel. I'm guessing—maybe the Lord is telling me—that she could be in the Vicksburg area now."

"Thomas, I appreciate your concern for your wife, but we wouldn't have much of an army if we were to make such exceptions for everyone."

"Then I'm not the first?"

His commander grinned. "Caught me. You are the first. If you'll keep your mouth shut about this, I'll see what I can do. But I dislike the idea of you getting yourself shot up for nothing if she happens to be in New Orleans."

"Sir, I have a feeling I'll be shot up anyway. And thank you, sir."

"Matter of fact, I have sensitive material which needs to be transferred to Grant. It must be hand-carried. At the risk of your life, it must not fall into enemy hands."

"I know nothing about courier service, but I'm willing to try."

"Trying isn't good enough."

"I'll deliver it, or I won't get there myself."

CHAPTER 35

Beth paced up and down her bedroom. She glanced out the window, murmuring, "It's nearly dusk. Mr. Stollen should be here soon. Tomorrow is the third day of May." She shivered. Chewing her lip she thought of the journey beginning tomorrow. "For the hundredth time," she muttered, "I've studied my way through the train trip. Why should going into Virginia make such a baby out of me?"

Abruptly she stopped in the middle of the room. "What could possibly be more horrible than to meet someone I know?" She rushed to the mirror and studied her features. "Oh, dear, I look terribly familiar." She reached for the hairbrush and began to brush her flowing, flame-colored hair into a loose spiral of curls. Thrusting in hairpins, she studied the effect.

There was a tap at the door, and Cynthia's voice called. "Come in." When the door swung open, she faced Cynthia. "Does this make me look older?"

"You'll stick out like a sore thumb with hair piled that high. Twist it lower, and push those curls inside the roll. You're supposed to look respectable, not showy."

Cynthia sat on the edge of the bed. "You worried about meeting someone you know? Don't. It's not any of their business what you're doing. And besides, if they did know, they'd be green with envy. Now come sit down for a minute. You'll make yourself sick with this pacing back and forth."

"I've never done anything like this before."

"Is that so?" Cynthia asked. "I could ask questions. I'm still wondering about your clothes and the jewelry you wear. Sugar, I don't want an explanation; just don't underrate yourself."

Beth shook her head. "Cynthia, this takes better nerves than I have. Right now if someone says 'Boo!' I'll run."

Cynthia chuckled. "Remember, Beth, you're not doing this to please yourself; you are doing a brave, courageous act which will help win this war. Come on, let's go down to dinner!" She tugged at Beth's arm and smiled.

They had just finished dinner when Timothy Stollen arrived. He was alone and seemed even more remote and cold. After greeting Cynthia, he turned to Beth. "I have some bad news for you. Kathleen was injured in a carriage runaway this afternoon. You'll have to make the trip to Richmond alone."

Beth's throat tightened. "Is it serious?"

"No, just painful bruises. But it won't be possible for her to travel for a week or so."

Beth lifted her chin. "Wouldn't it be wise to delay the trip until she's recovered?"

His look was icy. "Impossible. Your contact will be expecting you. Furthermore, there will be a return message which must be delivered." He continued to look at her, then suddenly he smiled. "You'll make it. Just play the perfect lady, and our man will give you all the right signals. Here's the packet of messages. Of course they are coded, but don't take chances with them. You'll be able to hide them so there'll be no problems." Unexpectedly he bent over and kissed her cheek. "You'll do just fine. I'll see you back here next week."

With a grimace, Beth left the room rubbing her cheek. She was pulling pins from her hair when Cynthia came into the room.

"Beth, you don't have to like his kisses," she said, shaking her head. "Just remember he's the boss. Your obvious distaste was childish. Think of him as Uncle Timothy."

"Tim or Uncle Timothy, I don't like his kisses, and I feel ugly. It was worse than a pat on the head. He's done nothing except glare at me since we've first met."

"Beth, you're terribly young! That wooden smile is part of Tim. I don't think he's aware of how cold he is."

"Well, just the same, I don't like him a bit. Cynthia, please help me pack this party dress, and heaven help me if I have to wear it."

Beth dropped her hand and stared at the dress. *Heaven help me!* She shivered and went to the valise. Chewing at her lip, she thought of the things Olivia had said. *The Israelites were afraid of God? So am I.*

The train's wheels drummed a message against the rails, pounding out Timothy's last words to her: *We'll wear them down; the man who knows the plans of the other side will be the victor. We'll wear them down, slowly, steadily.* Beth felt the packet of papers crackle against her waistline.

The wheels were slowing, and she moved to lean against the window. The evening shadows left wedges of light and dark across the landscape. The dark was a depot, the light a barren meadow. The train stopped.

The conductor came through. "This junction is the main exchange point; from here you may travel south or west as well as north. The Richmond train is due here in two hours."

Beth watched the passengers gathering up their bags. Picking up her valise, she fell in behind the uniformed men and dumpy little ladies carrying their bundles.

A feeble light burned in the depot. As Beth hurried toward it, a man stepped quickly out of her path. "Oh, beg your pardon," she murmured.

He turned. "I thought you sounded familiar! You're Beth Peamble, aren't you? Remember me? I'm Matthew Thomas, Olivia's brother."

"Of course I remember!" she cried. "Matthew, how nice to see you again." She stopped, looked quickly around. Uneasily she shifted her bag while her mind filled with a list of all the things she shouldn't say.

"Did you just get off this train?" She nodded, and he continued, "I saw your red hair at the front of the coach, but didn't guess it was you. Are you are headed west?" he asked, taking her bag and leading the way to the depot.

"No," she said slowly. He put the bags on the floor and waved her to the bench. She sat, adding, "I'm actually going into Richmond. Just a brief trip."

"You're brave," he murmured. "Crystal started for New Orleans over a month ago. The few hours I've had on this train raise my concern." He examined her carefully and said, "I don't think the South's trains are in the best of condition. I've been listening to the rails clatter since we've left Alexandria, and I wonder about their safety."

"They've been moving a lot of troops on them," Beth said.

"I know. I've waited several days to get a train which wasn't filled with troops." A studied, thoughtful look took over his face.

Now isn't the time to begin asking questions, she reprimanded herself. She sighed and straightened.

"Do you have family in Richmond?" he asked. "I wouldn't caution you against visiting them, of course. With conditions the way they are, it's best to keep family ties when we can."

That thoughtful expression returned to his face. She hunted for words. "I've a very old aunt in Richmond. Yes, I agree, it is good to see family. I'd chosen this time to visit because it seems travel isn't too much of a problem."

Dropping his voice he said, "I'm heading west." He paused, glanced quickly around the room, and added, "Then you won't be staying long in Richmond?"

"No. I'll return to Washington in a week's time. Have you seen Olivia since she's come out East?"

"Yes, but not for several weeks." Surprisingly his face cleared. He smiled. "Just after Crystal left, Olivia contacted me." He moved close and dropped his voice. "Beth, I'm thinking of imposing on you. Is it possible to get you to carry some information for me? Just a verbal message," he added quickly. "I wouldn't want to jeopardize you."

"Jeopardize?" she whispered. "Oh, Matthew, what are you getting me into?"

Matthew leaned forward. "I think my train has arrived. This will have to be quick. When you get back to Washington, will you go to the Capitol and ask to be directed to the Department of the Army? It doesn't matter who you talk to, just be certain to give my name." His voice was low, and she took a step closer. "Tell them I've been listening to some talkative men; there are good indications that Lee is moving troops east. Also, tell them it appears our knowledge of the South is based on misinformation. Word has come to me that indicates they're without sufficient food, clothing, and even arms. Their morale is nearly gone. That's all. Goodbye, and God bless you."

He sprinted toward the train. Beth sat frowning down at her hands as the train left the depot. "Matthew Thomas, how can you possibly think that information is worth passing on? Why should I bother?" *Why, indeed?* she thought briefly. *Whose side are you on?*

She was still musing over the strange visit with Matthew when her train was announced. Gathering her shawl and valise, she joined the group of people pressing their way onto the train.

The man standing behind her smiled down at her; he pulled a heavy gold watch out of his vest pocket and scrutinized it. "Very late to begin this leg of the trip. It's unfortunate there are so few trains going into Richmond these days." He straightened his tie, adding, "Hopefully the matter at hand won't continue much longer. Meanwhile we must put up with inconveniences for the sake of the men fighting." He tilted his hat at Beth and she nodded as she passed to her seat.

Beth was settled into her seat when the conductor came into the car and faced the passengers. "Ladies and gentlemen, before we reach Richmond we must pass the large enemy camp just across the river from Fredericksburg. There is a chance they'll try to tear up the railroad tracks; therefore, we will proceed to within fifteen miles of the encampment and wait until daylight before continuing our trip. Travel by day enables our men to see the track ahead of them. I am deeply sorry for the inconvenience, but it is for your welfare. Good night."

Dawn colored the windows across the aisle from Beth when the train finally began to move again. Slowly they traveled down to the river and crept forward. Beth leaned against the window and stared curiously at the mass of dark huts and tents obscuring the view of the river.

The uniformed man across the aisle stood, stretched, and sat down beside her. "That's the Yankee camp." He shook his head sadly. "Sure having a time. Gone through three generals, and they're still bumbling. I'm of the opinion they'd do better without a general. Might be they'd all go fighting off in different directions, but at least they'd feel like something was done when it was all over."

He grinned down at her. "Guess I shouldn't complain; it's their men getting killed." Then he sobered. "But friend or enemy, it's a shame to see people getting killed like this. There ought to be a better way."

"Do you suppose if people followed God this wouldn't happen?" She nearly bit her lip when the surprising words slipped out.

His eyebrows slid up. "Ma'am, they are. At least in the South. In the North they've got the abolitionists telling them what to believe. But in the South, we take the Bible as our guide." He grinned as he said, "It tells us slavery is God's will for some people."

Beth frowned. "I thought the war was because the South wanted to be free, not because of slavery."

"Where do you come from?"

"Tennessee," she replied hesitantly. "Up in the mountains."

"Honey chile," he murmured, "I'm surprised to see you wearing shoes!" She flushed, and he chuckled. "That's all right. But you people up there don't get in on a good share of what's going on."

She noticed the buildings beyond his shoulder. With a nod toward the window she said, "This must be Richmond."

He chuckled again. "Now you tell me this is the first time you've been to Richmond." Beth gave him a curt nod and turned to look out the window.

The train slowed and puffed into the depot. In a cloud of flying ash and hissing steam it stopped. Beth stood up and found the soldier beside her. With a mocking smile, he reached for her valise. "I feel responsible for a baby sister."

She followed him out of the train and claimed her bag. "Thank you, sir," she murmured, turning smartly and walking quickly toward the street. A hack driver sprinted to her side and she surrendered the valise. "To the Claremont Hotel," she ordered.

As she signed the guest register, the clerk handed her an envelope. *It's all happening just as Mr. Stollen said it would.*

In her room upstairs, she closed the door and leaned against it. Her heart began a slow, heavy thump. Beth pressed her lips together and walked to the window to look out across the city. She could see stately trees on broad avenues lined with buildings of brick or sparkling white. "Quite different from Tennessee's hills," she murmured. "So feast your eyes, Beth. Hopefully it will all sink in. Maybe someday people will think you're a lady."

She turned to pace the room. Frowning over the memory of the brash soldier, she bit her quivering lip and finally dropped into a chair. *He sure didn't treat me like a lady. Baby sister!* She picked up the square vellum envelope the clerk had given her and pried it open.

It was an invitation to a reception for a name she didn't recognize. A carriage would call for her. Eight o'clock. "Two hours," she mused. "Then I'll meet this man, my 'contact,' and day after tomorrow I'll go home. Never, never again will I do this," she vowed.

Cynthia had said something about helping the South, of being honored. Beth contemplated the idea. She walked to the window and looked out at the graceful white mansions and the dignified brick. "I'd be respected, welcome in those places. Perhaps, if they see me often enough, when it's all over, I'll be invited there," she murmured, standing back in the curtains to examine the houses, the carriages, and the group of young ladies strolling down the street.

At the appointed hour, Beth was handed into a carriage as large as any she had ever seen. She quickly ran an admiring hand over the velvet and walnut appointments before she turned to look out the window. The carriage went down one of the broad avenues she had seen from her window.

Her destination turned out to be a white house situated at the end of a long curving lane. The inside was filled with music, flowers, and softly pitched voices. She was handed down the reception line, from one gloved hand to the other, murmured over, and pressed out into the large ballroom where clusters of people with subdued voices and dignified clothing drifted in and out of groups.

A tall, dark, stern-faced man came into the room and the crowd parted around him. "President Jefferson Davis," someone whispered.

Suddenly she felt a firm hand under her elbow, heard a voice close to her ear. "Miss Martha Matlock, I presume." Her heart pounded. This was the contact.

"Sir, I don't believe I have met you."

"Robert Swalling. May I bring you refreshments? There is a table tucked back in behind the potted palms."

"Most certainly. Just fruit punch, please."

When the evening was nearly at a close, Beth heard the new voices. Like exclamation marks the excited, strained voices were interjected in the midst of gentle laughter and low-voiced conversation. She turned to watch the crowd. President Davis left with several uniformed men following.

"It sounds as if there's been a prison break," Mr. Swalling said. "Libby Prison. That is the place where the prisoners of war are kept. Union soldiers."

Beth looked at Mr. Swalling. "I believe it would be best to give you this packet now."

"Yes, I see they are starting to order the carriages," he murmured. Turning to her, he held out his hand. "Thanks to the palm trees, we needn't worry about prying eyes." She handed him the slender packet. He tucked it in his pocket and said with a smile, "It's ridiculous to think there's danger in this room, but who knows? I have a small case for you to give our man." For a minute his hands clasped hers. She glimpsed a small case of delicate gold and slipped it discreetly into the front of her frock.

He escorted her to the carriage and kissed her hand. "My dear Miss Matlock, I look forward to seeing you again soon." His teasing eyes mocked her as he stepped back from the carriage.

CHAPTER 36

Beth started down the Capitol corridor, still struggling with her desire to run. At last she stopped at an imposing office door marked DEPARTMENT OF THE ARMY. She resisted the urge to turn back. *Official business. Beth, you promised.* With her hand on the doorknob, she pondered the heavy weight in her heart. *Why do I feel as if I must do this?* she wondered. *I haven't done anything wrong. Then why do I feel as if delivering Matthew's message will somehow make up for my deception?* She paused and shook her red curls into place. *I don't care about Matthew's silly message, but I'll do anything to get rid of this guilt.* Brushing aside her doubts, she faced the door resolutely.

The door opened, and a uniformed man nearly collided with Beth. "Oh, I'm sorry," he murmured. He looked at her more closely and said, grinning, "Didn't have my wits about me. If there's anyone inside who can introduce us, let me escort you in."

"No, but I need to see someone. It's urgent."

His smile disappeared. "Come in then. Are you certain it's the Department of the Army you want?"

"I was told to come here; it's about the war."

An older man came out of an office, hesitated, and came toward them. "Sir, this young lady wants to talk to you. Says it's urgent."

"Thank you, Henry. Come this way, Miss." He gestured toward a chair and sat down behind the desk. "I'm Colonel Samson. Whatever you have to say will be held in confidence, and you'll be protected if the matter warrants it."

"I'm Elizabeth Peamble," she started. "Colonel Samson, I don't think it's such a serious matter," she said slowly. "I've just been in Richmond. It was at the train junction north of there where I met Matthew Thomas, a Union soldier. He asked me to come here with a message."

Beth repeated Matthew's message, adding, "It seemed so silly to be concerned about this, but I promised."

"Do you know why he sent you here?"

She shook her head. "I'd guess it's because he's a soldier and someone here will recognize his name."

The colonel stared absently at his tented fingers, then said, "I'll see what we can do with the information. As you say, it's not extremely—sensitive. But the statement about the Confederate Army is encouraging. Thank you for coming."

At breakfast the next morning, Cynthia dropped a newspaper beside Beth's plate and pointed to an article. In a surprise attack against the Federal Army, the Confederates under Beauregard's leadership were able to separate marching divisions en route to the western battlefields and inflict severe damage on the unsuspecting army. Slowly she refolded the paper and contemplated the hard knot in her stomach.

"You don't look too happy," Cynthia said. "Don't you realize you've made a strike for the Confederates?"

"I don't think I'd like to be responsible for men being killed."

"Someone's going to be killed anyway; better them than us."

"Cynthia," Beth said slowly, "do you sometimes question whether slavery and the Southern cause are really right?"

Cynthia was silent a moment, then carefully she said, "I don't have any doubts. Beth, since you've come back from Richmond, you don't seem happy like you were before. What's the problem?"

Beth sighed. "Maybe I'm growing up, changing my mind about some things. To tell the truth, I feel guilty about what I did."

It was a long time before Cynthia asked, "You don't intend getting out of this, do you? Beth, don't even consider it. Stollen can't afford a leak. Remember, he's not the big boss; he'll be trying to save his neck, too. I suggest you forget your silly little-girl emotions."

Beth gave her a shaky smile. "I'll try." Inside she thought of Olivia and desperately willed her to come.

Two weeks passed, and then three, and still Olivia hadn't come.

Beth dressed for a walk and told Cynthia, "I'm going out. I need the fresh air, and I must check on my friend. I hope she isn't ill, but at least I need to know."

"How will you find her?"

"She said that the hospital where she works is close by. There are several hospitals in the area; I'll start with the nearest."

"You know Tim and Nat will be here this evening. Kathleen Cogall may accompany them."

"I'll be back," Beth promised as she left the house.

After a short walk in the direction Olivia had indicated previously, Beth found the long, drab building with its small sign. "Union Hospital," Beth murmured as she entered the barren hall. A steep flight of stairs wound upward, while double doors seemed to lead into the hospital itself.

She pushed at the doors and stepped through. The dim room was lined with cots, two deep. At the far end was a table. Several figures dressed in white were scattered through the room. One walked toward her, but Beth wasn't aware of her. She saw and heard only the men.

Some lay without movement, while others tossed restlessly; she saw some who would never rise, and others sitting up. She looked at the expressions on their pale faces. Most turned uncaring from her gaze. She saw blood-soaked sheets and bandages that hid swollen stumps.

Olivia touched her arm. There was sympathy in her face. "Come outside, Beth."

They went into the entrance hall, Beth shaking and breathing heavily. Olivia glanced up as Dr. Whitt came through the doors. "Mrs. Duncan, everything is under control. Why don't you take your friend out for some air and sunshine? I think you both need it."

Olivia nodded and looked at Beth. "I need to change my frock; come upstairs with me."

While Olivia removed her soiled uniform and washed her face and hands, Beth looked around the room. "This is your home? Olivia, it's terribly barren."

"I come here only to sleep. You were so pale; do you feel better now?"

Beth nodded. "How do you stand it?"

"If it weren't for the grace of God, I wouldn't be able to." Slowly she added, "Beth it's terrible to see these young men in such agony. At times I hurt for them so badly, I nearly find myself complaining to heaven about the whole war."

"If you think this has anything to do with God, how can you *not* complain?"

Olivia thought a moment before answering. "I do believe God cares deeply about what is happening, but there's absolutely no way I can think this tragedy is of His doing. He's given us the right to choose, even when our choices hurt Him deeply. I know in the end there is righteousness and justice, but now while we humans try to run our world—" she sighed and shook her head. "Apart from Jesus Christ, I couldn't face life," she concluded slowly as she sat down on the cot.

Astonishment filled Beth's face. "Olivia, why did you say that?"

"Because we are all sinners. There's no way possible for humans to please God without His help."

"Then how—"

"Beth, it's what Christ has done for us that counts. Accepting Him means we are clothed in the righteousness of God. I know you're not *willing* to accept this, but don't say you *can't*. If I can believe God's word, then anyone can. Believing means trusting God's message to us, and being willing to make Him the most important part of life."

Olivia got to her feet. "Beth, I'm sorry. I can see you're troubled. Want to talk?" She touched Beth's shoulder. "Forgive me; it's just the only way I know to deal with the difficulties we face. Only the dear Lord knows how much misery we've pulled in upon ourselves."

"Your nice doctor suggested we walk," Beth said with a shaky smile as she stood up.

"Fine. Let me brush my hair," Olivia said, going to the table. She picked up the brooch and pinned it to her dress.

Beth touched the brooch. "You're thin and you look tired. Why do you stay? You know Sadie would love to have you come back."

"Right now I can't," Olivia whispered. "The only thing that makes much sense to me is being useful."

Outside Olivia took a deep breath of air. "There's music in the park this afternoon. Shall we walk that way?"

"A band?"

Olivia nodded. "Army band. I understand there's a new piece of music they'll be playing. I haven't heard it, nor do I know the words, but I've been told President Lincoln is very fond of this song."

"It'll just be good to hear something lively," Beth said.

When they reached the park gate, the band was playing and the grounds were filled with people. "Let's stand up here on these steps," Beth said. "We'll have a better view."

"It's like looking down on a stage," Olivia whispered. "The audience has become part of the play. Look at the tiny flags the people are wearing pinned to their lapels."

Abruptly the drums began a heavy, rolling beat. The band stepped back. While the sun flashed from the horns, a troupe of uniformed men surged forward. Marching in position, they began to sing. Olivia felt the force of the words striking her, and she wiped away tears as she listened: "Mine eyes have seen the glory of the coming of the Lord. . . . I have seen Him in the watchfires of a hundred circling camps. . . . Glory, Glory, Hallelujah! . . . In the beauty of the lilies Christ was born across the sea. . . . As He died to make men holy, let us die to make men free. . . ."

The wind off the Potomac chilled the tears on Olivia's cheeks as she lifted her face. She whispered, "His truth *is* marching on!"

The setting sun drew a final flash of light from the brass. The wind swept the people, stirring them back to life. When the soldiers marched from the park, Olivia saw the new spring in their step. From the crowd a wavering voice rose as an elderly man waved his hat. "God bless you soldier boys; God bless."

Then Olivia saw Beth's face. "It's so scary," Beth whispered. "It's like being whirled, tossed with nothing to catch me. Oh, Olivia, there's nothing steady and certain anymore. It seems everything I grab slides away from me."

"God doesn't slide away." As Olivia spoke, Beth turned to listen. "He's the only thing that won't change or disappear. Beth, sometimes you remind me of a child chasing rainbows. You can't look at the sky forever; you aren't heeding your feet. Beth, my dear, I don't want to see you fall."

The girl was shivering, clasping her arms around herself. Olivia pulled open the bag she carried and took out a sheet of paper and a pencil. She wrote on the paper, stopped, wrote more. She nibbled at the pencil, brushed at her eyes, and wrote again. Finally she folded the paper into a tiny square and handed it to Beth. "Here, take this. It's scriptures; you'll have to find a Bible and look up the references. Someday, somewhere, these verses will be more valuable than gold. Please keep them until that day."

Olivia stood up. "It's nearly dark. We both need to go. Please come see me again. I've missed you."

Olivia watched Beth hurry down the street. She turned back toward the hospital with a deep sense of loneliness. The damp wind made her shiver and she hurried inside and entered the long corridor filled with beds.

She saw the nurses and Dr. Whitt rushing from one bed to another. Mattie ran up to her. "Help us, please! They've just brought more patients, and some of them are critical."

Olivia dropped her shawl and rolled up her sleeves as she hurried to the far end of the room. As she turned, Olivia saw the dark curly hair, the beard. She gasped and reached for a chair. *It can't be!*

"My husband, that's my husband!" Olivia gasped, running across the room, throwing herself to her knees beside the cot. The man's face was bloodied, raw with festering wounds. "Alex, *Alex!*" Then she saw the man's ear—smooth, unblemished, with no sign of a gold ring. Slowly she stood and turned, staggering as she walked toward Dr. Whitt.

"Olivia, we can get along without you."

She focused on his face and blinked. "No I'll stay. I can't go up to that room now. Don't you see? I'll be more alone than ever. It's better if I stay down here. My husband is dead, really dead, and now I think I'd better accept it."

———

Alex got to his feet and moved around the damp, filthy concrete prison. His foot touched flesh. "Watch where you're going," came the snarl.

"I'm sorry," he muttered. "My legs are cramping."

The man grumbled, "This hole will kill us all."

The close-packed group shifted, and the fetid odor of disease, human waste, and unwashed bodies assaulted Alex's nostrils. He heard, "How long does it take to die in a place like this?"

Alex peered at the man who had spoken. "Aw, Stenson! You've got to want to live. I don't think a one of us is beyond survival unless we give up." Thoughtfully he added, "I think the Lord still has things for me to do. I'm hoping to go home, to see my wife and our baby born last March. It's hard, but trusting God is the only thing that counts."

He paused, thinking, "I've learned plenty since I've been here. I thought life was tough back in camp; now that seems wonderful. Plenty to eat, freedom—"

"Why don't you fellows hush it up? It's getting close to midnight. I need my sleep. Got a field to plow tomorrow." Silence greeted the feeble joke. For a moment Alex listened to the snores, then carefully made his way to the barred window. The moon was waning, but there was enough light to see trees, buildings, lights glowing in windows, carriages, and the Confederate flag snapping in the breeze.

With his face close to the fresh air, he tried to figure out the days that had passed since the Rebel soldiers had crashed through his post that March night. It could be late May or early June by now.

Arnold joined him at the window. Alex glanced down at the slight man. The moonlight dug dark caverns on the man's face. "Mind if I join you?"

"Help yourself to some air, so far there's a decent supply."

"I could use some water. Alex, you said you've learned plenty. What do you mean?"

Alex turned back to the window. "Prison isn't all bad. Maybe it was good for what ailed me."

"I can't see any good in it."

"Arnold, I realize now I had a pretty childish idea about God. My want list was too long and my give list too short." He looked at the bony face and continued, "I'd been complaining to the Lord about a number of things back in camp. Now there's real peace in me, knowing God has all this under His control. In addition to His promises—"

"He's made promises for this?"

"Yes. He promises that no matter what our circumstances, He will provide a way of escape that will enable us to bear—" Alex stopped suddenly. "But on the other hand, that sounds pretty much as if that's happening right now. Arnold, I've been feeling good about the presence of God, almost content and at peace in this situation because of Him. Now it appears it's just the working out of those very words, a result we should expect. It's real, this encounter with God. Do you know that?"

"Yes, but I guess He's not as real to me as He is to you. I can't see a way of escape." His voice dropped dismally. "Earlier this evening, you sounded like you were planning something. Alex, you outta your mind? We're nigh on to rotting in this place; don't give us no bright talk now."

Alex's voice rose insistently over Arnold's. "For me it's confidence in His ability to work out the very best possible solution to all of this. But the peace came when I accepted God's unknown plan as being worthy of waiting for, with a good deal more serenity than I'm capable of all on my own."

Arnold moved away. "Guess I'd better lie down; I'm getting fuzzy in the head."

There was a crunch outside the window. Alex grasped the bars and pulled himself up, panting with the exertion. He saw dark forms, and a slash of white teeth. He grinned and dropped back down.

"What is it?" Arnold asked.

"Might be some slave trying to meet his sweetie under the trees. Might be the same fellow I saw a couple of days ago."

He heard the crunch again, but was too tired to pull himself up to the bars. Even the squeak of metal didn't call him back to the window.

Alex found a place to lie down and soon was able to sleep.

When he awakened, the moon had spread a path of bright stripes across the roomful of men. Turning on his side, Alex noticed the bands of dark seemed to weight the room with a double burden of bondage. He heard a whisper of feet in the corridor.

Now wide awake, he moved to the barred doorway, hoping for a breath of air. By pressing against the bars he could see down the hallway. At the end there was more light and shadow. A whisper. A darker shadow stopped before the bars, and Alex stepped away from the door. There was a the clink of metal, a grating noise followed by more clinks. The door swung open.

Excitement surged through Alex. A guard, and he doesn't know I'm here! He raised his fist, took a step, then stopped. Their guard wasn't a black man, but this man was. The figure slipped through the door.

The man turned and listened. Alex heard quick steps and a strangled exclamation, followed by a dull thud and a muffled plop. The new-comer grabbed Alex. "Ya'll soldiers? Wanna come out? Follow us."

For a moment Alex's hands hung limp. Behind him an incredulous gasp rippled through the room. "Quiet!" he whispered.

Now moving like floating shadows, the men flooded into the hall and out the door. Alex brought up the rear. By the dim light of the lantern, he saw the guard sagging against the door, his blood making a dark puddle around him.

Sucking his lungs full of fresh air, Alex stretched his legs, stepping carefully at first, then hurrying after the dark figure.

Their benefactor was as black as the night and moved as stealthily, leading them behind the line of warehouses along the river. "Go fast!"

They headed for the river. The black man pointed. "Barge," he breathed. Alex saw a line of dark figures holding the barge steady with poles. Lumber and empty sacks were piled in the center of the barge. The black man gestured, and one by one they slipped into the water, crawled up onto the barge, and crept under the sacks.

Their barge floated into the channel. Alex stretched out beneath a smelly gunny sack and watched the stars while he breathed the musty river air. They were moving eastward, toward the ocean. When the trees along the river thickened and the last barking dog had been left behind, their rescuer beached the barge. "Hurry! Let's get back into the trees!"

Alex heard the shouts, saw lanterns, and heard the baying of hounds. "Ya'll hurry straight ahead! There's more water; we'll kill the scent before the hounds git here. Move!"

"God!" Alex whispered, knowing only He could get the weakened men safely away.

They followed the shallow creek downstream until their leader climbed up the bank and beckoned them to follow.

When they were deep in the trees, the fellow said, "Union Army, suh; we been watching that prison for some time. Been down in the Carolinas on the islands. Now we're headed for the West. Before we go, we decided to see if we could pick the locks on that prison."

"Where do we go from here?"

A voice answered, "I don't care where you go. I've had enough fighting and prison. I'm going over the hill."

The grin disappeared and the black man said, "You's free men. If you wanna come with us, we'll try to get you to the Union men."

"I'll take my chances. Thanks for the help, buddy. I'm going home to see my wife and family. Anybody with me?"

Alex clenched his fists and watched shadowy figures move around the speaker. "If'n you're coming with me," the black man said, "head this way. We've got a goodly march ahead of us just to catch up with the rest of them. Here's some hardtack and cheese to keep you until breakfast."

Slowly Alex got to his feet and went to stand with the black man. "Hey, buddy," a voice called, "thought you said you have a baby you haven't seen. Come on; you can always come back and fight."

"Don't think I will," Alex said. "I'll just stick it out. If I go, sure enough, the war could be over before I get back."

CHAPTER 37

Olivia walked among the cots, stepping softly to avoid disturbing the sleeping men. Dawn was beginning to touch the eastern windows with pale light.

She turned to nod at Mrs. Thorner as she extinguished the last lamp. Olivia watched the woman walk down the long corridor, her feet dragging with weariness as she went up the stairs to bed. Dr. Whitt finished checking a fresh amputation. Nodding at Olivia, he left. She knew he would be sleeping in the attic of the hospital, ready to come if they needed him. Olivia turned back to her patients.

Billy was awake; she felt his eyes, sensed his restlessness and made her way through the corridor. She bent over him. "Am I going to make it?" he asked.

"If you try. Your fever is down, but you haven't been eating. How about some milk?" He started to shake his head, but closed his eyes and nodded.

Olivia carried a mug of milk to him and lifted his shoulders. She watched him struggle with the milk. Smiling down at him, she pushed the red curls off his forehead. He studied each detail of her face. "You're always here, except when that girl comes. Is she your sister?" Olivia shook her head and held the mug for him. "Do you have a loved one fighting?"

She hesitated. "My brother is in the army."

"That's all? I'd guessed you were married, maybe had children." She bit her lip and blinked back the tears. Billy raised himself on one arm. "I think I shouldn't have asked. I'm sorry. Is that why you wear that pretty brooch?"

"Yes," she whispered, "to remember—and strangely, to hope even when there's no hope. I've tried to accept. I just get to the place where it seems real, and then—"

"Why?"

"I don't know, Billy. Sometimes at night the Lord seems unusually close to me. Sometimes I dream—" She got to her feet and tried to smile. "That's enough for now. I need to bring hot water and wash-cloths. If you drink enough of that milk, perhaps by next week you'll be helping me."

He grinned. "When you talk like that, you remind me of my mother, and I wouldn't dare disobey her." He settled back, and she saw the faraway expression in his eyes.

Olivia carried the hot water and cloths to the first bed. "Good morning, Harold," she whispered to the older man. He would be leaving soon. "The tough ones always make it, don't they?" she murmured, handing him soap.

"Looks that way," he muttered. He jerked his head toward Billy. "Those stomach wounds are bad. Poor young'un hasn't even had a chance at life."

Blinking at the tears in her eyes, she glanced at the empty bed beside Harold. Roger had been there until last week; now it was waiting for another patient.

Lettie came into the room, picked up a container of hot water, and passed Olivia with a nod and smile.

When Olivia went after the porridge and coffee, Lettie was waiting to help. "What's the problem?" she asked, picking up the tray of mugs.

"It's just Billy; I worry about him so much. Lettie, I'm convinced he isn't trying."

"Don't say that." She stepped close and peered into Olivia's face. "You agonize over these men. It's too much. You can love them and care for them, but you must learn to forget them."

"But not Billy," Olivia whispered. "Not as long as he's here."

"You've forgotten how to laugh," Olivia said and turned away. Lettie added, "Remember, the joy of the Lord is your strength."

"Nurse! Olivia!" Hearing the shout, she ran. "Something's come loose," Harold cried. "Where the doctor amputated—it's bleeding."

Maggie rushed past. "The doctor is sleeping; get him!"

Olivia ran. Dr. Whitt met her on the stairs, looked at her face, and took the stairs in a leap.

It was late afternoon when Dr. Whitt leaned back and grinned. "Looks like he's going to make it. Thanks to you, Harold, we got that artery in time." He looked at Olivia. "Go take a walk."

Olivia changed clothes and started toward the park. Just as she rounded the corner, she saw bright red curls bobbing under a parasol coming her way. "Beth!" The girl's startled face appeared. "I thought you were going to run me through with that parasol."

"Sorry. I was coming to see you. Didn't realize it was a dangerous weapon." Soberly she stared at the tip of her parasol while Olivia watched her.

"Shall we walk in the park? It's cool under the trees."

"Yes." Beth nodded. She glanced at Olivia. "I have some questions to ask. I read those verses last night."

"Let's find a bench in the shade, and I'll answer the best I can," Olivia murmured. She sat down beside Beth and watched her pull the Bible out of her bag. In an instant, while Beth fumbled through the pages, Olivia remembered Alex's hands on her Bible, moving down the text with his finger. She could nearly hear his voice. She felt tears spring to her eyes. Olivia sank her teeth into her lip until the pain chased the tears away.

"What does *repentance* mean?"

Olivia caught her breath. She swallowed hard, and with her voice husky, said, "Alex told me it means to turn around and take the way you should go."

Beth looked puzzled, but she took out her paper and pencil. She muttered, "Go back the way you should go." She wrote the words carefully, then looked up at Olivia. "I still don't understand."

"God created man to be perfect and holy. When He tells us to repent, He's saying we should come back to Him, start over again, and learn to be His child."

"How can that be?"

"Remember, Jesus' atonement for our sins makes us sinless in God's sight. Now we only have to live in obedience to Him, just the way He wanted Adam and Eve to live." Olivia sighed heavily. "Oh, Beth, I'm struggling so hard to say it all. I wish Alex were here to say it better." She pushed her fingers against her eyes and whispered, "All day it's been like this. Suddenly it's difficult to believe he's gone. I thought I'd struggled to accept for the last time; now it's more difficult than ever."

"Would you rather I didn't ask?" Beth's voice was low. "I can wait."

Olivia dropped her hands. "No, you can't wait. Now, tell me what else is on your mind."

Beth fumbled with the pencil. "What does it mean to be *born again*?"

"Oh, from John chapter three. That happens when we accept Christ's atonement. All things become new in Jesus Christ." Olivia watched Beth write the phrase on her paper.

Beth lifted her face, frowned, and asked, "What does it mean when it says that if we don't believe we're condemned already."

"Beth, it's the difference between life and death. We're pronounced guilty if we don't believe." Beth hesitated, then slowly wrote more words on her paper.

"It isn't complete, but there's enough for me to recall what you've said."

"Beth, you're very troubled. Do you want to tell me about it?"

"No, there's nothing you can do about it. It's my problem. I've got myself into the mess, and now I'll have to find a way out."

Olivia wondered how far she dared probe. Gently she said, "It would be easier if you had God's help. A child of God needs only to ask."

"There's too much. I can't load you with my problems."

"Beth, you've changed so much in these past months. When you came to Pennsylvania, you were a lighthearted, carefree—"

"Child," Beth supplied with a bitter smile. "I found out I can't remain a child forever. I must grow up, or—"

"Or what?" Olivia saw the bleak expression in Beth's eyes. "Beth, you're totally miserable. Please, wouldn't talking help?"

Beth shielded her eyes with her hand. "It's terrible. I just can't bear to lose your friendship." She dropped her hand. "Do you know you're my only real friend?"

"I thought real friends were for times like this."

"You're so—holy."

Olivia shook her head. "I'm only letting God remake me into what He wants. Alex could tell you what a terrible person I was."

"How do you know what God wants you to be?"

"I don't, but He says that He's not going to stop until He's done or I'm done letting Him." She smiled briefly and added, "Today was a day I'd like to stop being a nurse. But I'll keep at it, trying to be what He wants."

"God *makes* you?"

"No, God makes me want to do it until I can't abide not doing it." Olivia looked at Beth. "We're trying to address your problem."

With her head down, Beth muttered, "I did a really terrible thing to a friend. She tried to help me become a better person, and I—Olivia, that isn't all. Now I'm getting involved in something that's very bad."

Olivia sighed. "And I'm supposed to help you with that little information? I say tell your friend you are sorry—if you are. If you are involved with people you shouldn't be, then get out. But Beth, this is all just my advice. What you really need is—"

"I need God. Right?" Beth's voice was bitter. "Olivia, I don't think I want God until I'm ready to die."

"And if you come to Him then, you'll realize He intended to help you live. Surely that's the worst part of dying for a Christian—not having given God a chance to do with us all that He planned from the very beginning of time."

There were tears in Beth's eyes. She got up, shook her head, and charged down the path to the street. When she disappeared from sight, Olivia slowly stood and began her walk back to the hospital. *Dear Lord, something is terribly wrong. Please help Beth. Don't let her destroy herself.*

The following day Billy died. At breakfast time, with a mug of milk in her hand, Olivia bent to lift his head. There was a trace of blood on his colorless lips. He smiled and tried to speak.

Trembling, she went to Dr. Whitt. "It's Billy," she whispered, blinking tears away. From a distance she watched the doctor bend over him, then shake his head. For a moment his hand lingered on Billy's shoulder.

Dr. Whitt came back to Olivia, took the mug, and drank the milk. "Better stay with him. It won't be long."

She knelt beside his cot. There was a scrap of paper in his hand. "Would you write—my mother?"

"Yes." She took the address and wiped the blood from his mouth. "Billy, are you trusting Jesus as your Savior?"

He nodded. There was a hint of a smile on his face. "Forever, since I was a little tyke."

She took his hand. "Would you like me to read the Bible to you?"

He shook his head. "Sing that new song, about His truth marching on."

Her voice was robust as she sang the words that had constantly flowed through her mind since she first heard them. "Mine eyes have seen the glory of the coming of the Lord . . . His truth is marching on! . . . In the beauty of the lilies Christ was born across the sea, With a glory in His bosom that transfigures you and me. . . ."

His eyes were closed, his hand limp. She stayed on her knees, tears dampening the flecks of blood on her apron.

When she stood and slowly walked down the corridor, the final line rang in her ears: *As he died to make men holy, let us die to make men free. While God is marching on.*

Dr. Whitt met her at the foot of the stairs. "After you've written that letter, I want you to pack your bags and go home. Mrs. Duncan, you are in no condition to continue this work."

She listened in dismay. "Dr. Whitt, please don't send me away. This is the only thing in my life that is important. Please don't deny me this task."

"I am afraid for your life."

Her head jerked up. She looked up at him, strangely. *So that's the meaning of the dream!* "Dr. Whitt, I beg you, don't send me away. If the time comes when I can't work, I'll leave."

He sighed. "Very well. But Mrs. Duncan, I've noticed you have lost weight. You must consider your health."

"I will; and thank you, sir."

She started up the stairs, smiling for the first time in weeks. *If Alex can't come to me*, she thought, *then perhaps I'll go to him.*

CHAPTER 38

Let's march," Colonel Woodrow ordered quietly. They moved out, Alex and the other white soldiers surrounded by the Negro regiment with their white commander. Within an hour the sound of baying hounds and shouting men was left behind. They reached the trees, formed columns, and pushed west.

The sun had risen when the black man who had led the rescue dropped back beside Alex. "Marching too fast?"

"Some of the fellows are in bad condition. They've been in prison most of the year," Alex said, "Food situation was bad."

They trudged silently through the trees. "Private Johnson, Colonel Woodrow wants us to keep in the trees along the James River; he figures that way we'll know we're headed west, and we'll always have cover."

"Johnson," Alex repeated, "I'm Alex Duncan, and I'm very glad to meet you fellows. I've heard about the Negro regiments, and have wanted to see you in action."

"I'm Louis," came a voice at Alex's elbow. "Tag along with us, and you'll see plenty. Johnson, the colonel wants us deeper in the woods; we'll eat and rest."

They followed him and found the first regiment hunkered around cold bacon, beans, and hardtack. "Sorry, no fires yet." The colonel's eyes lingered on Alex. His eyes crinkled. "We whites are outnumbered;

might need to find some charcoal so we'll look like the others. Most of your buddies took off," he added.

Alex grinned. "Can't blame them. I think most of them will check on the home fires before they look for a rifle."

"How about you?" The colonel's eyes were keen.

Alex shifted restlessly. "It's a temptation, but I'd feel guilty taking off without leave."

"Where's your unit?"

"I left them on the Rappahannock."

"Hooker's men. Were you at Chancellorsville? Those men were pretty well shot up."

"Our division wasn't," Alex admitted. "We spent most of the time waiting to be called up. We didn't seem too well organized."

"Can't understand the Confederates losing so many men and still winning the battle. Heard their losses were twenty-two percent. Also heard they were ready to pounce on the Feds the next morning."

Alex muttered, "Most of us came out of there sick at heart because we'd scarcely fired a shot and our buddies were dying without aid."

Woodrow shook his head. "It's a big responsibility, generaling an army that size. I wouldn't want it."

Alex looked around. "Tell me about this regiment. I didn't realize it was this big."

Woodrow pointed his fork at the trees. "You don't know the half of it. We've got two regiments spread through these trees. Been on the sea islands, mostly raising cotton. But the fellows want to fight. That's where I came in. Just after the Proclamation became official, I was assigned. Now we're headed for the Mississippi River."

"Mississippi!" Alex exclaimed. "You're a brave bunch. How the Confederates feel about Negro troops is no secret. They've given out proclamations of their own—a promise to do in any white man who's heading up such an outfit."

"I know. There's also reports of captured Negroes being sold as slaves."

"Colonel Woodrow," Alex said taking a deep breath, "I'd like to follow along with you. I suppose I should be looking for my unit, but it appears the chance of making it alone is pretty poor. I want to be with your men. I'll carry a gun."

"We'll put you in," Woodrow said. "And I hope when we get to Mississippi, we find someone who can give you a musket." He got to his feet. "Come on fella, let's get a little sleep. We'll march out of here at nightfall. By dark we can cut away from the river. I want to be in the mountains by morning."

"Mountain people are Union," came a soft voice. "We'll be safe, maybe get something to eat besides hardtack."

That evening Colonel Woodrow said, "Duncan, I want you to move up with the front regiment. Lieutenant Hansen will put you to work."

Alex was still looking for Lieutenant Hansen when he heard his name. He turned and saw the black man charging toward him. "Caleb!" Alex dropped his pack and grabbed him. Pounding him on the back he exclaimed, "Man, this is nearly like being home!"

"Alex!" Caleb choked and shook his head. "I didn't ever expect to see you this side of heaven. How's it all at home?"

"I don't know. I haven't had a letter since last December. Olivia was expecting our baby in March. It's hard to not be fearful," he added slowly.

"And you here instead of going home? Alex, I think Lincoln would let you go home and check on things."

"Burnside wouldn't, and neither would Hooker. I guess I won't waste my time pounding on President Lincoln's door. As soon as I get to Mississippi, I'll post a letter." He noticed Caleb's eyes no longer reflected the deep despair he had seen before.

With his arm across Caleb's shoulders, Alex asked, "You better now?" Caleb nodded and shrugged. "If we get separated," Alex said, "I want you to know you're welcome at the Coopers'. We want you."

Caleb's grin flashed. "What you going to do when this is over? There aren't any more slaves to run to Canada."

"Guess we'll have to take the *Golden Awl* downriver for a fishing trip." Alex was silent for a moment as he looked at Caleb. "I've been thinking about it, Caleb. There's much to be done for the people. We can't stop now."

"I know. Sometimes it scares me to think about it all. Me, I think I'd like to head west. There's sure to be a better feeling there."

Alex was conscious of the circle of dark faces around him. "One thing's certain; we'll all have the job of putting this nation back together again, no matter who wins."

"Suh—" the heavy voice at his elbow brought Alex around. The black man faced him. "If we don't win this war, we'll be worse off than before. Don't even think we won't win. If I gotta fight for twenty years, I'll fight until we're all free."

God, please give me this much conviction, Alex thought. He looked at the man. "I wish I could feel as you do. Fighting still seems wrong to me."

The man looked astonished. "Didn't say I like pulling the trigger. But worse is seeing what slavery does to my young'uns."

The regiments reached the mountains and followed them down to the Kentucky state line. Turning north, they tramped through rain to the Ohio River.

While they waited for transport down the river, Caleb said, "Alex, you're close to home; why don't you go?"

He shook his head. "Don't tempt me; it's hard enough to keep my feet pointed west. If I go now I'll miss out on the battle." He tried to grin as he added, "I'd never be able to live with myself if you were killed while I'm sleeping on a feather bed at home. The best I can do is a letter. I've talked to that bunch heading into Ohio. They'll mail a letter for me. And the Lord willing, we'll soon be home."

"That young'un will be knee high when you get there," Caleb said heavily as he clapped Alex on the shoulder.

Mike Clancy stood behind the wheel of the gunboat and watched the eastern Mississippi River shoreline. He trained his field glasses on the line of transports upriver. "Grant's men ought to be huddled on the Louisiana side of the Mississippi, just below Vicksburg, waiting for us. I think we're ready to go."

He dropped the glasses and nodded at Captain Frazier. "Sir, shall I lead the way? It'll be near ten o'clock before we pass Vicksburg. There won't be a moon tonight."

"A little anxious, aren't you?" Frazier said. "Give them another half hour. I've been told they're having a ball in Vicksburg, celebrating Grant's pulling out of the field. I didn't get an invitation." He chuckled. "Frankly, I've got a feeling it's a little premature to celebrate."

"Think we have it sewed up this time?"

Frazier glanced at him. "Might. Grant's using his head. With the troops being pulled in, I'm inclined to be optimistic."

Mike nodded. "After being in this gunboat for five months, I'll opt for a quick victory."

"I don't think Grant's put a time limit on it," Frazier murmured, peering through the binoculars. "Mike, looks to me like the lead boat is heading out. Get on his tail, and remember, try to shield the transports."

Mike nodded. "After February and the *Indianola* affair, we've enough nerve to try anything." Frazier chuckled and pointed his binoculars downstream.

They pulled out, found the channel, and started downriver. The paddles churned water as the sluggish ironclads drifted into the current.

The river was brown with spring runoff; the water moved swiftly. Frazier gave Mike a pleased grin. "It'll be a snap this time. There's current enough to shut the engines down and drift past Vicksburg." He poured coffee for them both and carried one mug to Mike.

"I hear they brought in two Negro regiments to supply our garrison at Milliken's Bend."

Mike nodded. "They offered me a job piloting one of the gunboats stationed there, but I decided I'd rather be in on some action this time."

Frazier turned. "For a newly married man, you're pretty reckless."

Mike took a gulp of coffee. "Didn't get married."

Frazier lowered his mug. "Might be wise. Sometimes we rush through life a little too fast. If she's serious, she'll wait."

Mike eased the gunboat into the channel and Frazier went down to the chart room. With his hand easy on the wheel, Mike's thoughts were full of memories: Beth with her laughing face tipped to his, her soft body in his arms. How often her teasing voice enticed while her eyes flashed recklessly.

Lord, I miss that girl something terrible. I can't understand. You don't want me to have her, yet I can't forget her. Please help me, Father; I'm confused. Giving her up didn't take her out of my heart.

As the lights of Vicksburg appeared, Mike sighed and muttered, "Father, one thing is certain. Without her, life is misery. Yet at the same time, I'm living closer to You. Do I understand You don't want me married?"

Mike tensed at the sight of Vicksburg. As he grasped the wheel more tightly, bonfires suddenly flared along the bluff above the shore.

The first big gun boomed into action. A miss; the water geyser spurted up in front of him. At that moment the second explosion came. Now the shells were flying, one after another; to his left was a splash and explosion. The guns fired continuously, but the flotilla held its course.

The lights of Vicksburg were behind them when Frazier came to the pilothouse. "We lost one transport. Fortunately, it carried only a skeleton crew and no soldiers. Mike, we made it!"

———

Beth turned from the mirror. "Come in, Cynthia."

"Beth, Tim is here. There's a message to be carried."

"Sounds important."

"I know you didn't expect him this evening, but please come down and talk to him." She hesitated. "Now."

Beth looked up. She saw the firm line of Cynthia's mouth. It said more than the one hard word. "Why don't you go?"

"I told you; I've been recognized. You've made only one trip. Come do this, and next week I'll talk to Timothy about finding a replacement." Her voice rose abruptly. "Can't you see, Beth? This isn't a game. I like you too much to pretend. These people will do anything before they'll risk being discovered."

"Cynthia, you got me into this!"

"You're a loyal Southerner," she soothed. "With your looks and spirit, you can pull it off without trouble. Some girls would be shaking in their shoes."

"I am. Spies go to prison."

"Don't be a baby. Come on." She left the room.

When Beth walked into the drawing room, Timothy Stollen turned from his pacing. The irritated frown was replaced with a smile. "Sorry to bother you, my dear, but problems are developing. General Hooker has begun to move his army this direction. We need to get a message into Richmond immediately."

"And I'm to walk right past his army?"

"No, you are a pretty little lady taking the train into Richmond to visit an ailing aunt. This message is important. You will be carrying a detailed list of interested parties who will be ready with material and information once General Lee moves his troops over the Potomac."

"It sounds as if there's something big going on."

He threw her a quick glance. "Certainly. Our whole network is built to support this ultimate campaign."

"Ultimate?"

He grinned. "This war can't last forever. This should finish it, and we'll all be free to go home." He handed her the silk belt. "The information is sewn inside. Fasten it around your waist. There will be a carriage at the door in half an hour. My man will take you on a round-about route to the junction outside of Richmond." He paused and leveled his cold gaze at her.

"You'll stay at the same hotel. Tomorrow evening you will meet Mr. Swalling at the Richmond Concert Hall. He has reserved a seat for you. During the performance he will pick up the information. Do you understand?"

"Of course." She lifted her chin. He smiled, nodded, and left the house.

Beth turned. "Cynthia, I'm frightened nearly to death. If the Union catches me, they'll hang me just as they did that other spy."

Cynthia chuckled. "You've mixed up your stories, it was the Confederates who hung the spy, and it wasn't a woman. Beth, you're working for them, so don't worry!"

Beth sighed. "All right, I'll go—just this one last time."

Cynthia's jaw tightened. "Better give it more thought; remember what I said."

All night long the train wheels clattered. Don't worry . . . don't worry . . . don't worry. Beth tried to ignore them, but they invaded her restless slumber. In the morning, still half asleep, Beth cried out, "Why will no one listen to me?"

"I beg your pardon, ma'am?" The portly gentleman across the aisle tilted his hat. "I'm getting very hard of hearing. Will you please repeat your question?"

"Oh—sir, will they stop for breakfast?"

"I don't believe so. Would you care for some dried apples?"

She shook her head and turned away. In the distance Beth could see the skyline of Richmond.

———

Upon reaching the hotel, Beth immediately unpacked her valise. Placing the Bible on the table, she ran her hand over the scuffed leather cover and thought about all the things Olivia had said.

"So I need God. Is this the way to get Him to pay attention to me? Condemned already. Sinner. I know all that. I am guilty—real guilty."

With a heavy sigh, Beth got to her feet. Slowly she removed her frock and chemise. Untying the silken pouch, she pulled out the papers. "Of course they're in code. A bunch of numbers. I can't understand any of it. But when I give them to Mr. Stalling, I will be passing along information which will help the South win the war." She threw the papers onto the table beside the Bible.

Beth selected a fresh dress and put it on. Taking up her hairbrush, she tried to tame her brilliant curls. She bent forward to look at her reflected image and muttered, "Louisa, you have terrible taste in clothes. Even I know they're too extreme. This gray looks as if it belonged to a nun."

She shuddered and spoke to the serious face in the mirror. "You are supposed to attend a concert, but you didn't bring a dress suitable for a concert. And why did you bring that Bible and Olivia's list of verses? They'll do you no good tonight. God isn't listening, remember?"

She flung the brush on the bed, hurried to the table, and opened up the Bible. The first verse was John 3:16. Slowly she read it aloud: " 'For God so loved the world, that he gave his only begotten Son, that whosoever believeth in him should not perish, but have everlasting life.' "

Glancing up, she mused, "Why am I doing this? It just makes me feel worse."

Beth thought about Olivia. "She said God wants to help us live. I thought that was going to happen with Mike, but he wouldn't marry me because of God. So God isn't interested in me."

Impatiently she jumped to her feet as the bitter memory of that day surged over her. "I was terribly angry at Mike," she whispered. "It was horrible to be left wearing a wedding gown with no groom." Her cheeks flushed hot with remembered shame.

Her thoughts ran on, and she spoke them aloud. "If I hadn't been in a rage over Mike, I'd never have listened to Cynthia—or would I? She made it sound fun and daring, and I didn't think it through. It was another lark, like marrying Mike."

With shaking hands she pressed her eyes closed and saw Mike's face, twisted in agony. Surprised, she whispered, "He really cared! I can't believe he could care that much and still not marry me. Why did he say he couldn't? I suppose I'm just not good enough."

Beth fingered the Bible as it lay open on the table and thought of home. "Dear Mama, this is the only thing of yours that I have. Did this Bible mean something special to you?"

She pulled Olivia's list from between the pages and flipped through the Bible until she found 1 Timothy 4:8, " 'But godliness is profitable unto all things, having promise of the life that now is, and of that which is to come.' " She peered at the list. "That sounds like something Olivia said, but I don't have it written here."

She took up her pencil and quickly wrote, "Profitable, promise of that which is to come." She leaned back and thought about the words, then glanced at the list. With a frown, she picked it up and studied it. Slowly she read:

Go back the way you should, J3, 16.
All things become new, when we get, R3, 23.
Difference between life and death, condemned, R6, 23.
Wages of death . . .

"Oh dear!" she gasped, "I've made a mess of this. It doesn't make sense. How will I ever understand?"

She threw down the papers just as she heard a knock on the door. With her heart hammering, she froze. The second knock was followed by an urgent voice. "I know you're in there; open the door."

Beth looked around. It was nearly dark. She stuffed papers into the Bible, then ran nervous hands over her hair, and went to the door.

Swalling glared at her, a tight line around his mouth. "You were to have been at the concert nearly an hour ago. What happened?"

"Oh, dear!" she moaned. "I didn't realize it was so late. Here, I'll light a lamp. I was just thinking, and lost track of the time."

"Forget the light." He looked from the silken belt to the papers on the table. "I see you have the belt here, and this is the information. Tim and his bumbling couriers! Miss, I hope this is your last trip."

He peered at the paper, glanced at the window, and stuffed it into in his pocket. "I'll have to decode it later. Here's a message for Stollen. Kindly deliver it to him on time," he snapped as he headed out the door.

Beth huddled on the bed, shivering and angry at first, then finally trembling with fear. "Cynthia, even if they don't hang women, I'll never do this again."

As the rising moon presented itself at her window, she pressed both hands to her empty stomach. Shaking her head, she muttered, "Right now I'd rather starve than risk seeing that man again."

During the night Beth awakened with a word on her lips. She sat up. "Condemned. That verse said I was condemned already. How can that be? I haven't done anything." But she knew better even as she said the words. The guilt she carried would not leave her alone.

"Louisa," she whispered, "I confess, I took all of your pretty things. I took your dresses, jewelry, even your shoes. I did it because you had so much and I didn't have anything."

But confession and repentance didn't seem to help. "I might have read that verse all wrong," she muttered. She groped for the Bible under the bed and went to light the lamp on the table.

Beth hunted for Olivia's list, but it wasn't there. After thumbing through the Bible again, she murmured, "Oh, I remember—it's in John."

She found it and read the words over and over. "If I believe, I'm not condemned, but I'm condemned if I don't. What is the significance of believing? Olivia said repentance meant to go back and do the right thing." Beth held the book tight and thought about Louisa's clothes, the beautiful things she had stolen, the deception she had put over on those around her.

As she started to close the Bible, she saw the next verse: " 'For God sent not his Son into the world to condemn the world; but that the world through him might be saved.' " Beth chewed her finger and tried to remember the other verses Olivia had written on the paper.

"I wonder what I've done with those papers," she murmured, thumbing through the pages of the Bible. Folded papers fell out. She spread them on the table and horror filled her. "I gave Mr. Swalling the wrong papers!" she breathed. "What shall I do? I've no idea how to contact him."

There was nothing to do but wait. After breakfast she paced the room and wrung her hands. "I can't go to you, Mr. Swalling. I don't know your real name, and I don't know where to find you. If you want these papers, you must come after them."

She picked up the Bible and thumbed listlessly through it. "This is terrible," she muttered. "It's like being in prison; I can't leave, and there's nothing to do."

She began to read. " 'If we confess our sins, he is faithful and just to forgive us our sins, and to cleanse us from all unrighteousness.' "

Beth looked at the ceiling and declared, "I did confess my sins, and You didn't hear me." There seemed to be nothing else to do except continue to read. She curled up in the chair pulled close to the window. "Olivia said John, but she also mentioned Romans and Timothy. I wish I had the list. Perhaps it doesn't matter where I read."

As the sun set, Beth discovered she wasn't hungry. She lit the lamp and returned to the chair. "All day long I've read Olivia's verses. I feel the words are piling up inside of me. God really does love us—me, but He's demanding. He sounds like my father. I suppose I need to follow the rules, just like at home."

When Beth crawled into bed, clear thoughts were taking shape in her mind. The first was that Mr. Swalling wasn't coming. The second was a strange new fact. She didn't *want* to deliver those papers to him. That thought was enough to bring her out of bed. She lit a candle, found the papers, and carefully tore them into tiny pieces. Amazed, she looked down at the pile of scraps and whispered, "I feel wonderful. Why?"

The final thought came after she returned to bed, staring into the darkness. "No I don't feel wonderful; I feel wretched." Olivia had talked about Jesus, about knowing God, being reconciled to Him, accepting salvation through Jesus Christ. Of not *doing*, but *being*. Beth tossed and punched her pillow.

Finally she sat up in bed and lifted her face toward the ceiling. "I did confess," she said again. "You didn't listen." Then the words she had been reading fell into place in her mind, like the critical pieces of a difficult puzzle. "I have to confess to Louisa and take the clothes back to her. That's repenting, which means I'll become different. I'll go the right way now. But what is the right way?" *Why is this important? Why am I afraid of God?* Suddenly exhausted, she fell back on her pillow and slept.

Early the next morning, she quickly packed her valise and carried it to the train station. "I want a ticket to Burton, Tennessee."

The ticket agent pushed his cap back on his head and grinned at her. "Come back in a couple of weeks, and we'll see what we can do. The tracks have been torn up that way."

She chewed her lip. "Is it possible to get back into Washington?"

"You can go to Alexandria. Will that do?" She nodded and pulled out her ticket.

———

Mike whistled tunelessly, repeating the same monotonous notes. Captain Frazier came into the pilothouse and glanced at Mike. "Can't be that bad, can it?"

"Guess it gets a little boring, running up and down the Mississippi, taking pot shots at these shaggy guerrillas."

"Someone has to do it," Frazier answered shortly. Then he grinned. "Aw, you're wanting real action with all the glory. I'll let you go talk to some of Grant's men; it won't be hard to change places with one of them."

Mike nodded. "I sure never expected to see Grant push as hard as this. When Briggs was on board last night he said that Grant's men jumped out of those transports and headed inland like they were going after apple pie. I guess it nearly scared the boots off Johnston's men. Grant was almost to Jackson before Johnston began to move toward the Mississippi."

Mike glanced at Frazier. "They told me this time Grant took his cue from the Confederates and lived off the land. His boys were doing well—ham and poultry, as well as all the vegetables and milk they needed." He chuckled. "They say a plantation owner rode his mule into camp to complain to Grant that the fellows were robbing him blind. Grant looked him in the eye and said they weren't his men, because if they were, they'd have taken his mule too."

Frazier sobered. "It's sad to see the state we're all being reduced to—plundering, wasting, fighting not with dignity, but with a desperate need to survive no matter what. And they're saying it'll get worse." He paused. "I came up to tell you we'll go as far as Milliken's Bend and then head back upstream."

Mike nodded. "I heard there was action on the bend."

"Yes. Kirby Smith was at it again. Fortunately two Negro regiments were sent to support the Iowa regiments; otherwise we'd have lost the post. The Rebels drove our men to the bank of the river. But with the new regiments and the aid of a gunboat, we managed to hold our position."

Captain Frazier paced the cabin. "You know, last August, just after Lincoln decided the Negroes could serve in the army as well as the navy, the Confederate Army headquarters issued a directive saying the officer of any black troop would be treated as a felon and executed. God help us if it happens here. I did hear there were a number of Negro soldiers killed and some captured."

As they passed Milliken's Bend, Frazier took his binoculars to the window. Mike gazed at the lonely post. The Union flag was flying from the pole.

Suddenly Frazier dropped the field glasses. Mike heard his sharp exclamation and followed the direction of his pointing finger. "Turn the boat! Those aren't our batteries, and they're pointed at us." He ran for the stairs.

As Mike leaned on the wheel, he saw a flash of fire and felt the shudder sweep the length of the boat. The steering was gone. He turned to shout at Frazier just as a shell crashed through the pilothouse. The boat swerved, and he fell.

Rudderless, the boat swept into the current and drifted toward the batteries. Vaguely Mike heard the guns below. They were still firing one blast after another as they approached the shore.

Still stunned by the blow, Mike pulled himself to the window and focused on the sight of gray coats flying over the sand hills as the gunboat drifted closer, her guns still booming.

There was a shout of alarm from below. The gunboat crashed against the abutments. Dazed, Mike tried to sit up. He looked down at his leg and saw the blood flowing.

"Mike!"

"Cap, I need a hand up here." He grasped the window casing and tried to pull himself up, then sagged and fell, hitting his face against the rough boards.

CHAPTER 39

The pastel blossoms of spring had disappeared, replaced by vivid color and heavy perfume. All Vicksburg, from tree-lined avenues to walled gardens and stately buildings, was lush with summer. But Crystal found it impossible to reconcile this beauty with the threat which had driven her into taking sanctuary in Vicksburg, making her an unwilling prisoner of all the beauty.

Each day she walked the streets of Vicksburg. In the beginning she was driven by frustration and her frantic desire to be gone. Gradually this impatience was replaced by curiosity and loneliness.

Crystal grew fond of the lovely city on the Mississippi River. Often she walked to the top of the hill overlooking the river. One evening she discovered that her favorite spot was occupied by an elderly couple.

They turned at her approach. "Good evening, ma'am." The gentleman bowed. "I'm Colonel Ethon, retired, and this is my wife, Mattie. We've seen you about the streets for the past month. Welcome to our fair city; are you enjoying your visit?"

"Yes," she responded with a rueful smile, "although it is an enforced stay. I'm Mrs. Matthew Thomas; please call me Crystal. We have been living in the North, and I was on my way to New Orleans to visit my parents. Since the railways are immobilized, I've been a prisoner in your lovely city."

"The North, huh?" he commented. "This must be very distressing to you. But I do believe General Pemberton is capable. Hopefully he will encourage this young scalawag Grant to retire gracefully."

"I doubt that he shall," Crystal murmured. "From what I hear, General Grant is a very determined man."

Colonel Ethon nodded soberly. "With General Sherman working alongside, we Southerners have cause to shiver."

"We want peace more than anything else." Mattie searched Crystal's face. "You're from New Orleans; are you Creole?"

Crystal hesitated, thinking again of all the secrets hidden for so long. "Yes, my parents' kin were some of the original settlers. French."

"Your skin is dark; I suppose it's to be expected that you'd prefer the North."

"Don't think that we hold color against anyone," Colonel Ethon said. "But I must admit, it's difficult to release our hold on the old life."

"I can't believe the North will be victor," Mattie interjected, "but I have sympathy for the Negroes. Slavery is wrong, however—"

"It takes more than a handful of us to effect change," Colonel Ethon finished. "I don't expect either Vicksburg or the Confederacy to fall into Union hands. And I expect life to go on as it always has."

Crystal turned toward the river. "It's such a beautiful, peaceful scene; it's nearly heart-wrenching to consider fighting here." She faced the couple and added, "I've been enjoying the serenity. But I shudder when I recall all that's going on just outside of Vicksburg. If only this could be solved without fighting."

"But someone must give in order to have peace. The South won't surrender their slaves, and as long as the abolitionists rule the North, slavery will continue to be a sore spot. Compromise is impossible."

Mattie shook her head. "I refuse to be frightened by a possibility which doesn't exist. I'll cross my bridges only when necessary."

"My dear," Colonel Ethon said slowly, "the handwriting is on the wall. The North no longer seems inclined to give us our heart's desires."

Each day Crystal followed the news, and nearly every day brought change. One morning she opened her paper in the dining room. "So now the Southern railroads are gone." She scanned the report. "General Sherman is moving like a scythe in a field of grain. He's leveled trains and their tracks. Warehouses and army supply depots are gone. And General Grant is moving on Jackson."

As she folded the paper, her throat tightened. The waiter standing beside her chair said, "The news isn't good, is it ma'am?"

She touched her throat and shook her head. "I wonder what will become of us all?"

As the days passed, food supplies became limited, and tension within Vicksburg grew. Crystal watched housewives leave the grocer with worried frowns. The daily newspaper continued to be optimistic, but it decreased in size each week.

One May day the newspaper carried the story of General Pemberton's defeat at Champion Hill, and later that day he entered the city with the remnant of his army. Crystal was on the street when they arrived.

Saddened by their shame and defeat, she turned away, nearly colliding with the woman at her side. Looking at Crystal, the woman dabbed at tears on her face and murmured, "Is this what war means? Never did I dream of seeing such men. Beaten into exhaustion, worn down to nothing. They are barefoot, gaunt, starved. How can they keep a foot under themselves?" Without answering, Crystal rushed to her hotel.

Later Crystal began to sense that the Union forces had launched an attack on Vicksburg which showed no signs of being abandoned. Sporadic gunfire had been replaced by constant bombardment. The newspaper admitted that Grant's army surrounded the city from the east, while Union gunboats and mortar-boats unceasingly attacked from the river.

The nights were quiet, but each day the gunfire was renewed at dawn. No longer was it safe to admire the sunset over the river from the highest bluff. The women and children had been ordered to stay off the streets during the day. While the dismal reports indicated neither army would yield, casualties were growing on each side.

As the worried people of Vicksburg huddled in their damaged homes, the unrelenting fighting continued. General Pemberton's army was firmly entrenched about the city. From the sound of crossfire, Crystal guessed the Union Army was just as firmly entrenched somewhere very close.

The newspaper, now produced on rolls of wallpaper, assured the people that General Johnston would come to the rescue. A statement by an army surgeon acknowledged that Vicksburg was in a difficult position, but certainly not critical. He ended by saying, "We need to take courage; President Davis has no intention of sacrificing us to the Yankees."

As Crystal discovered, the pressure of war reduced the barriers between people. Each day as the clock struck at noon, she went to the church to pray. Daily the noontime prayer meeting grew in size. Shoulder to shoulder, all differences forgotten, the people came. Men and women entered with pinched, fearful faces, and came out tear-stained, but serene.

One noon as she went to pray, the street in front of Crystal began to fill with slaves. One by one they slipped out of houses, massed together, and rushed down the street. She followed, puzzled by the nearly frantic pace of the black people. As she rounded a corner, she saw the group disappearing behind the feed store. Close on the heels of the black people, Crystal slipped through the door in the rear of the building, and found there a sanctuary. A storeroom, festooned with empty grain sacks and perfumed with sawdust, had been transformed with a crude altar.

The group of people knelt around the altar, and Crystal knelt with them just inside the door. Then the prayers began.

"Lawd, be merciful to us; we are Your chillen, too. God grant us deliverance. We want Pharaoh to let us go. We want to go to Canaan land. Freedom! Father, bless Massa Lincoln with wisdom and powah. Bless General Grant and give him sticky feet that he'll keep in the path of victory. Bless us, Lawd, with freedom!"

Forgetful of her own prayers, Crystal rocked back on her heels and watched the faces shining with tears and hope. With a lump in her throat and a new burden for the people, she rose and walked slowly back to the hotel.

———

The June sun blistered the people of Vicksburg. Food supplies, which had been severely rationed, continued to dwindle. The supply of beef was completely gone.

Crystal continued to live in the damaged hotel. Each day, before the shelling began, she walked the streets in the early morning coolness. One day she stepped outside the hotel to find people running through the streets. "Meat! Jacob's market has meat. Hurry, it won't last long!"

"What kind?"

"Most of it's mule, but they say it's good. I don't know about the rest; they're not saying. But when you're starving, a little boiled with some greens is better'n nothing."

As Crystal stood on the street, a woman stopped to talk. "You hear? A shell struck another house yesterday morning. They say someone was killed."

"I'm so sorry," Crystal said with dismay. "Maybe we'll need to abandon these houses."

"Go to the caves?" The woman asked, "Did you see the newspaper?

The mayor is ordering the women and children into the caves that the men have been tunneling back in the hill. They say it's the only place that's safe during the day. Better come. We'll play some games. Bring your knitting."

Caves! Crystal shuddered. For several weeks the hillsides surrounding the city had been under excavation. Now tunnels honeycombed the hills, planned for use as shelters for the residents of Vicksburg. The following day she joined the other women as they carried food and chairs to the caves.

Despite the heat in the city, the tunnels were cool inside. Loose soil drifted down Crystal's neck occasionally, but there didn't seem to be any spiders. The shelling sounded distant.

Crystal read to the children while the other women talked and shoved listless needles in and out of the dark yarn.

One day as Crystal finished reading, one of the young mothers said, "If this fighting isn't over soon, I'm going to sneak down the hill some dark night and pitch rocks through the windows of the Vicksburg Emporium."

"Why, Nettie, what's got into ya'll?"

She peered through the dimness. "You haven't heard? That shyster Martin and some of his slick friends have that big building chuck full of just about everything you can think of in the way of food stuffs— hams, canned goods, flour, you name it."

A chorus of outraged cries arose. "That's terrible!" "Why is he holding it back?" "The scoundrel; he deserves to be shot!"

"He's going to wait until he can get the price he wants." Nettie sneered. "Another week of this, and he thinks we'll be selling our souls to him."

From across the room came a weary answer. "I will; my babies cry with hunger pangs."

————

Matthew saluted. "General Ord, I have a sealed communication for you." The man looked surprised, accepted the paper, and slit it open. As he read, his face began to crinkle into a grin. "Well, Private Thomas, welcome to Grant's army. You've come hastily, perilously, with a paper stating that your commanding officer requests you be allowed to fight with General Grant since your wife appears to be confined within the walls of Vicksburg. Good luck, Private Thomas; and if you don't find her as soon as we enter Vicksburg, come to me and I'll help."

"That's all?" Matthew laughed. "Guess I'm glad I didn't have to defend that with my life! Thank you, sir, and I'm happy to hear that we'll win."

General Ord nodded toward the private standing in the doorway of the tent. "Private Webber, see that Thomas gets a uniform and a musket. Thomas, he'll escort you to your post."

————————

Alex got to his feet and leaned against the side of the boat. "I recognize the scenery. Caleb, we're getting close to Milliken's Bend."

"Remember that first trip we took?" Caleb asked. "It was right along here that we started having trouble with the monkey rudder again."

"How could I forget?" Alex chuckled. "A boatload of slaves and the river patrol nosing around. But we did make it farther upstream before we had to call it quits."

Colonel Woodrow came on deck. "Fellows, get your gear together. We've reached the end of our journey. A detail from the Iowa regiment will be here to escort you to the fort."

"How far is it to Vicksburg?"

"A good mile over, then down a piece. Maybe three, maybe five, I don't expect to see action from here."

One of the black men pointed. "My pappy and his folks were from right over there. Louisiana. Still can't hardly take it all in that we're none of us slaves anymore. We can settle where we want. We can visit kin and never have to wear a tag that has a number telling where we belong." He shook his head and went below.

Cecil's bright teeth flashed. "It's a good feeling. I might not ever live to enjoy it all, but my young'uns will. Freedom is worth dying for."

The June sun burned down on the clearing at the edge of the Mississippi. The fort was an oven and the river a haven. Each midday the regiments took turns standing guard while the others bathed in the tepid, muddy waters.

Alex was on guard the afternoon the picket rode in. The man slipped from his horse, saluted Colonel Woodrow and said, "Spotted dust coming from up river. Rumor has it that Kirby Smith is heading this way with his guerrillas."

The men in the water rushed out, dressed quickly, and headed for the fort. A fellow from the Iowa regiment fell in step with Alex. "Sure glad you lads brought us some more ammunition. And I'm sure glad we get to use it. Gets kinda boring with nothing to do but go swimming. See you later, bud." He loped toward the batteries overlooking the Mississippi.

Alex filled his pockets with shot, caps, and gunpowder, then followed Caleb to the long line of trenches circling the fort. His eyes met Caleb's. "Looks as if we'll have a little diversion."

"Alex, I'd rather toss stones in the river." He hesitated. "You get an answer to your letter yet?"

"No. I've been to every mail call. Can't believe that letter didn't get there."

"Here they come!" came the shout from the battlements. The dust nearly obscured the band of horsemen.

"Men, hold your fire until I give the order." As Alex waited, he looked at the black men around him. They were tense and determined.

The cloud of dust divided, and the Rebel yell came from all directions at once. Alex felt the hair on his neck stiffen as he lifted his gun and sighted along the barrel. "Fire!"

The volley was returned and the Union line wavered. Men dropped around Alex, but Caleb was still there.

Abruptly the entrenched soldiers in the next section jumped to their feet and ran scared toward the river. For a moment Alex's musket dipped as he watched the rout. Horsemen bore down on the men. He saw the line of fleeing soldiers fall. The gunboats opened fire.

"Down!" Woodrow yelled. An explosion left a cloud of dust and smoke. Alex lifted his head and saw the gap in the Southern cavalry as Woodrow yelled, "Fire." In another surge of cavalry, more men ran.

"Retreat!" Woodrow shouted. The men wavered, looking at each other and then at the horses charging.

"Run!" Alex yelled, shoving Caleb. He grabbed at Cecil, but the horsemen were on top of them. He lifted his rifle and dropped it.

Gray uniforms surrounded them, pressed closer. "No quarter," called a sergeant as he took aim at the circle of black men.

"Stop!" Alex yelled, rushing at the man. "You have us; don't shoot these men."

"Men? Stand aside nigger lover." The soldier raised his musket and pointed at Caleb. Alex threw himself at the horse and fell to the ground as the misdirected shot tore through him.

Caleb dropped to the ground beside him. "Alex are you hurt?" Alex turned, saw another gun pointed, and shouted, "No!" But his warning came too late.

Alex heard the gunfire and felt Caleb move. He tried to raise himself as Caleb's blood spurted over them both. "Bertie!" Caleb called.

"Oh, God, help!" Caleb's hands groped through the blood. A boot kicked him; he rose and then sank to his knees as he heard another shot. It was all over.

———————

Moving numbly, as if in a fog, Alex responded to the jeers and the prodding gun as he walked into a nightmare of wounded men. Black, white, red. Over and over he looked at the men around him, hoping for a familiar face. Clutching the rag bound to his side, he staggered behind the horsemen.

Later, inside a nameless prison in a nameless place, he discovered that the black men were gone. He questioned the guard and received an answer. "Sold, of course; that's where they belong, hoeing cotton."

Sold? Caleb, thank God you're out of this forever.

He examined his wound. A clean gunshot, a deep graze on his side. It would heal, but it was stiff and sore. Gradually the numbness began to clear from Alex's mind. He thought about Caleb. "I guess I'm glad for your sake," he murmured. "But, friend, I'm going to miss you."

CHAPTER 40

Whe she reached Alexandria, Beth hired a hack to take her into Washington. At the outskirts of the city, she gave the driver directions to Cynthia's house. Exhausted, she leaned against the side of the carriage and watched the soothing summer scenes of green pastures and serene flower gardens.

As she rested, she realized it was impossible to ignore the strange agony of the past two days. "One thing is certain," she mumbled with a tired smile. "I'm a failure as a spy."

"Ma'am, is it that house up ahead, the one with the fancy carriage?"

She looked, and her heart sank. Timothy Stollen was at Cynthia's house. "On second thought," she said quickly, "take me back to the Union hospital. I need to stop there first."

He sighed, flicked the reins, and turned the corner. "Want I should wait?"

"No, it could be some time."

He carried the valise inside, peered through the door at the line of beds, shuddered, and left. Beth waited until he clattered down the steps, then she faced the door into the hospital ward. A man dressed in white came through the door. He looked at her curiously. "Are you wanting to visit someone?"

"I'm looking for Olivia Duncan."

"I'll tell her. Please be seated." She sat. Nervously twisting her hands, she tried to plan out her next step. *I can't see Timothy Stollen; he mustn't know what I've done, that I've torn up his message. And now I have a new one to deliver.*

Olivia came through the doors. "Beth! You look simply terrible! What has happened?"

"Olivia, I can't go back. I've done something horrible. At least I think I have. I need to talk."

Olivia hesitated a moment. "In about half an hour, I'll be through for the day. Would you like to go to my room and wait?"

"Please."

Forty minutes later Olivia entered her room to find Beth curled on the cot asleep. Slowly she sat down in the one chair. She looked at the tired lines on Beth's face, waited, and finally dozed herself.

It was late afternoon when Beth stirred and opened her eyes. "Oh, I've been asleep for hours. I'm sorry. But I've scarcely slept for the past two nights."

"Why?"

Beth hesitated. "I've got to tell you everything, it's—I need help. Olivia, what shall I do?"

Olivia sighed and got to her feet. "I suggest that first we go down to the kitchen and find something to eat. Then I think we'd better have them move a cot in here. The rooms are all taken, but there are extra beds."

A very subdued Beth said, "Thank you, Olivia."

After they had eaten and the cot had been moved, Olivia met Beth's eyes. "Want to talk or sleep?" They were facing each other across the cot as they spread sheets and a blanket.

"Talk." Beth sat on the cot and tucked her feet under her. "I've really got myself in a fix now, and I don't have any idea what I should do. Shall I start with what just happened, or tell you all about the past?"

"Maybe you'd better begin with the present trouble."

"Have you guessed what I've been doing?"

"I didn't try to guess; there's too much to think about around here."

"That one time I went into the hospital was terrible. I don't know how you stand it. I wanted to run."

"Sometimes I do, too." Olivia looked into Beth's eyes. "Beth, about all I can offer you is a listening ear."

"And a bed and a place to hide."

"Hide? I think you'd better explain."

Picking at the lint on the blanket, she admitted, "I'd like to blame it all on Mike, but that's only part of it. Cynthia is a spy, Olivia, or she was until she got too familiar."

"What do you mean, familiar?"

"Tim said people were recognizing her. See, Tim says there are people in Richmond who are for the Union. Some of them watch Southerners when they think they're passing information."

"Beth," Olivia cried, "are you telling me you've been passing information to the South?"

"Just twice. At first it sounded exciting, and I didn't think of it as bad. Until two nights ago, that is."

"And this Cynthia is responsible?"

"I suppose you'd say so. I should have refused in the beginning, but—" She winced. "By the time I had to pass a message, I began to realize it was serious." Beth leaned toward Olivia. "Honest, after one time I didn't want to go again, but I had to. Cynthia seemed to think she could get me out of it, but that Mr. Stollen has the most frightening eyes." She paused, adding, "And he kissed me. That was terrible."

"You're very young," Olivia murmured.

"I'm not; I'm old enough to know better. Olivia, I'm almost nineteen."

"So what happened?"

"I had to go again. They said the message was important. It was a list of people who would be helping the Confederates after they cross the Potomac."

Olivia sat up. "Potomac? Oh, dear, I think we'd better go see someone about this."

"It isn't necessary; Matthew has sent a message."

Olivia crossed her arms and frowned. "What do you know about Matthew?"

"I met him at the junction—you know, just outside of Richmond where all the trains meet. That's where people switch trains when they go from one line to another. He was traveling, but I can't remember that he told me where."

"What about a message?"

"He gave me a message to pass on to the War Department. Which I did, and they seemed interested, although I thought it was a strange message."

"And you delivered the message Mr. Stollen gave you to carry?"

She shook her head. "Do you remember the pieces of paper with the Bible verses you wrote out for me?" Olivia raised her eyebrows, and Beth said, "I had it with me. I took my Bible along. That afternoon while I had nothing to do, I started looking up verses. Would you believe, I forgot to keep my appointment with the man who was to get the message?"

"Oh, Beth, I'm afraid you aren't much of a spy."

"I figured that out for myself." She smiled briefly. "Well, I was reading when he came. When I heard the knock, I just took the papers— the wrong papers—and shoved them into my Bible. When Mr. Swalling came, he was angry. He didn't say much, just grabbed up your list and left."

"The wrong paper," Olivia said slowly. "I'm surprised he didn't come back after the right one."

"I am, too. I've tried to figure out why. Do you suppose he could have passed it on without looking at it more closely? But no," Beth quickly corrected herself, "that couldn't be, because when I got back, I took a hack to Cynthia's house. I saw Mr. Stollen's carriage in front; that's why I had the driver bring me here. I have a strange feeling that Mr. Swalling has telegraphed for the real message."

"Where is it?"

"I tore it up. But Mr. Swalling left a message for me to take back to Mr. Stollen."

"What are you going to do with it?"

"Olivia, I don't know. But suddenly all this seems wrong. That's why I came here. I don't want him to know I'm in the city. See, I wouldn't be, if my first plans had worked out."

"Where were you going?"

"To take the clothes back to Louisa." Olivia looked confused, but Beth hastened on. "That's part of the problem. Remember you talked about repentance and being condemned? I read the verses and started feeling so terrible that I decided I must give them back to Louisa. But the train tracks are destroyed and I couldn't go into Tennessee."

"What clothes are you talking about, and why?"

Beth's face began to crumple. "Everything I have. Olivia, this is terribly hard to tell you. See, I've lied to every one of you since the beginning." She dropped her face in her hands. "I'm not the daughter of a rich man. My dad is a poor farmer. I didn't go to school. I never had a decent pair of shoes until Louisa gave me some of hers."

"Who is Louisa?"

"My father is a tenant farmer. Her father owns the land where we lived. Louisa is rich; I am poor. She was good to me. I don't know why she paid attention to me. She gave me some of her dresses—ones she didn't want. She taught me how to read, even to talk and act like a lady."

Olivia sighed and her face cleared. "So in reality, you were running away from Louisa when Mike found you. Did you tell him all this?"

"No," she whispered, shaking her head violently. "I couldn't admit that to him. Olivia, even my wedding dress was stolen from Louisa. I didn't dare tell Mike. See, this part of my life was something I wanted to forget."

"If you felt that way, why did you decide against marrying him?"

"I—" Beth looked shocked. "I supposed you had guessed by now; Mike wouldn't marry me. He wouldn't say why, only that he couldn't because God didn't want him to. Oh, Olivia, don't look at me like that! From his expression that day, I thought he really wanted to. I can only guess he'd discovered I wasn't good enough for him."

"Beth, Mike isn't like that. If you'd told him all this, I think he'd have married you anyway."

Olivia waited. Beth's face was brooding and shadowed; finally she whispered, "I hated Mike after that. I was so ashamed of being humiliated. It's been horrible. But that's no reason to betray my country. Olivia—" She pressed her hands against her face. "I'm continuing to pile up so much wrong in my life. God will never forgive me."

"You want Him to?"

"Of course. Olivia, since you said those things and wrote the verses out, I've nearly gone crazy. I read through the Bible, just pages and pages of it. I've been trying to see if you were wrong about repentance and condemnation and obeying God. I thought just going to church and living a good life would be enough. But it isn't. God doesn't forget what I've done, and now He won't let me forget, either."

"But Beth, you've missed the important part," Olivia whispered. "We've all sinned. God doesn't measure sin by what we've done, but instead by what we've done about it. Do you believe those things you read in the Bible?"

"Yes. I couldn't help believing. The words felt like they were jabbing inside of me."

"Then believe the rest. God says that if you ask for forgiveness, He'll give it to you. That's all you need to do. Ask and believe." She hesitated, "Do you want to ask Him—"

"What about the clothes and jewelry?"

Slowly Olivia said, "I don't think it's possible to do anything now. Beth, confess it to God and ask His forgiveness. If he wants you to see Louisa, He'll help you do it. Right now, with this war going on, it seems impossible." Olivia stood up. She hesitated before asking, "Beth, are you going to—"

"Olivia, I can't ask God now. Mike—I don't want to even think about him." Slowly she added, "I don't know what to do now. I don't have a home, and I'm afraid to go to Cynthia's."

"I know you don't like nursing, but if you want a job here, I'm certain they'll take you."

"Oh, I can't!" Suddenly she looked up. "Kinda like penance, you mean?"

"No. That's not the way God's love operates. It would only be because you want to help," Olivia paused. "Beth, you need not do this."

Beth thought for a moment before looking up at Olivia. Hesitantly she said, "Olivia, you've been married; but how can I care for these men? I know what nursing is like; I've never even seen a naked man."

Olivia touched her face. "Beth, you needn't worry. These hospitals have male nurses to do the heavy lifting and all the intimate care. Can you imagine me lifting a man? For us women, nursing means bathing their faces, feeding them, even writing letters. I've had to help change bandages on some of the wounds. Believe me, you won't be offended, and these soldiers will be very appreciative of your care."

"Then I'll do it," Beth whispered. "And Olivia, I think I need to take that message to someone. It might be important."

The next afternoon, Beth and Olivia carried the message to the War Department. The uniformed man looked at it, questioned Beth, and said, "The message tells us nothing we didn't guess previously. Lee is coming. His destination appears to be Pennsylvania. The most important information will be the names and descriptions of the people you have aided." His voice was serious. "You realize you could be in danger?"

Beth swallowed hard and said earnestly, "I'll be glad to tell you all I know. About the danger—I guess I can blame no one except myself."

Beth was quiet and Olivia worried when they returned to the hospital. Olivia said, "I'll not let you out of my sight. Promise me you won't leave the building alone."

"I won't," she whispered. "I'm frightened nearly to death."

———————

By the first of June news began to trickle into Washington. The Confederates had left the Fredericksburg area. Lee was marching westward. Later in the month, rumors indicated that General Lee was in the Shenandoah Valley, shielded from Hooker's army by the Blue Ridge Mountains as he pressed north.

Dr. Whitt and his staff began preparing for more patients. Many men were furloughed to return home for the rest of their convalescence.

Just as Olivia finished her shift one afternoon, Beth came into the hospital, looking worried. "Beth, is something troubling you?"

Beth looked up and forced a smile. "Oh, I suppose I'm just being a baby."

"Perhaps you'd better tell me about it."

"I think I've seen Timothy Stollen on the street in front of the hospital. Yesterday Lettie told me a man has been asking about me. Do you suppose he's going to cause problems?"

"What did she tell him?"

"Just that I work here. Cynthia knew I had a friend working at a hospital, and that was probably information enough for Mr. Stollen. Olivia, you don't think he'd do something to me, do you?"

"I really can't believe you're in danger," Olivia answered, "but I don't think I'm willing to risk something happening. Go to work; I'll talk to Mrs. Thorner." She patted Beth's arm and left the room.

Maggie Thorner and Dr. Whitt were in the reception hall when Olivia pushed the door open. They turned, and Dr. Whitt said, "Olivia, Maggie tells me there have been several people asking about Beth Peamble."

She nodded. "I was coming to talk to you about it. Beth could be in danger. I don't like to think such things, but I'm convinced she should return to Pennsylvania."

"Has it something to do with spying for the Confederacy?"

"Yes," Olivia said reluctantly, "but she's not involved now."

Dr. Whitt thought for a moment, then said, "Perhaps that is why this man is looking for her. It's not a comfortable position for a young girl to be in," he added.

"I think Olivia should send her back to Pennsylvania," Maggie offered.

"If she were my daughter," he said slowly, "I'd *take* her to Pennsylvania. I'm not convinced the trains around Washington are totally safe right now."

"You think she would be followed?"

"If they are trying to find her now, do you think they'll stop? It's possible she's being watched. I can't imagine what their intentions are, but all this certainly seems very strange."

"I feel responsible for her welfare," Olivia said. "Perhaps it would be wise for me to ride with her to Pennsylvania. Maggie, can you spare me for a couple of weeks?"

"Certainly. I wish you'd stay there for a rest."

———

Rumors of Lee's advance northward continued to appear in the Washington newspapers. But until Beth and Olivia were at the train station, preparing to leave Washington, the news hadn't alarmed them.

Settled in their seats, waiting for the train to leave, Olivia opened the newspaper. "Beth," she said, "it appears the Confederate army has moved into Pennsylvania. According to this article, they destroyed iron works near Chambersburg. Railroad property has also been destroyed. It seems the Confederate soldiers have seized shoes, clothing, horses, cattle, and food, leaving behind Confederate IOU's."

"I've heard about those IOU's," Beth drawled. "I don't think people will find them too valuable."

"One town was raided for supplies for the army, and shops were broken open." Olivia trembled with anger. "It says Southern soldiers seized scores of black people living in Pennsylvania and sent them South into slavery."

"Olivia," Beth said, "right here on the front of the paper it says General Lee has a hundred thousand men with him. It's reported his army stretched from Culpepper, Virginia, a hundred miles to the Potomac. We're surrounded." Beth looked at Olivia over the top of the paper. With a nervous giggle, she said, "I'm glad we didn't know about this, or we would never have left Washington. Now will you stay in Pennsylvania?"

Olivia looked out the window. As the train jerked and began to move, she touched the brooch pinned to her frock and said, "No, Beth. I suppose this sounds strange to you, but I just can't forget about Alex. I dream about him. As long as this war goes on, I must care for every soldier as dearly as if he were Alex. Just perhaps—" Hastily she added, "It will be important to some wife or mother." She leaned against the window as the train gathered speed.

Beth buried her nose in the newspaper. "Oh dear, the Union has waited too long. General Lee captured twenty-three hundred men. Why doesn't General Hooker do something?" She lifted her head. "It seems if there was any possibility Alex is alive, he would have written to you."

Olivia was silent.

———

Vicksburg's humid heat penetrated even the cool depth of the caves. Crystal wiped the perspiration from her brow and smiled at the child leaning against her knee. "Annie, I've read this book twice today. Shall we see if we can find another?"

Crystal heard another burst of gunfire and a distant boom. "That was a hit," a woman said bitterly. "I wonder every time if it's my house."

"I don't like playing in caves; the dirt comes down," Annie interjected. "Besides, it's crowded and we have to be still."

"Annie, don't stand in the entrance, you could be killed by those guns." Annie looked at her mother and pouted. "Please darling, come here."

A young matron watched and smiled at Annie. "Soon it will all be over and you'll be out in the park again."

"If there's still a park."

"No matter what," Crystal said slowly, "we must keep our spirits up. I know it's hard when this has been going on for over a month."

"And we don't have enough to eat and our homes are in rubble. Crystal, you can talk glibly; your home isn't being shelled. New Orleans is beyond the fighting now."

"But not beyond all that follows the fighting," Crystal added. "We'll all be a part of the rebuilding—North and South. I believe God expects us to mend the fences in our brother's pasture."

"If the North is so caring, why don't they just go home and leave us alone? We are ruined; must they take a final measure?"

A shell whistled overhead, and all conversation stopped. They looked at the ceiling of the cave, then brushed dirt from their faces. An explosion seemed to rock the earth. Annie's mother whispered, "If this doesn't stop soon, I shall go mad."

The gray-haired Mattie put down her knitting and glared at the woman. "Don't you say such a thing. Just get hold of yourself, pray for strength, and start planning new curtains for your house."

Ignoring Mattie, the woman continued, "Rats and mule meat. Last week's newspaper was printed on wallpaper. Two weeks ago it said, 'General Johnston is coming.' This week it asked, 'Where is Johnston?' " She stopped, listened. They all looked toward town.

"That's a different explosion—it's muffled, far away."

"My man says the Union is trying to break into our defenses by tunneling in close to the trenches and setting off explosives," Mattie said. She paused, took two stitches, and added, "He says from the sound of things it's within their power to blow holes right into Vicksburg—like the enemy tunneling under Jerusalem back in the Old Testament."

"I hear the soldiers sent a letter to General Pemberton saying that if he couldn't feed them, he'd better surrender. Personally, I think he'll surrender."

"Tomorrow's Independence Day," came a bitter voice back in the shadows. "All we wanted was independence. I guess we don't have much to celebrate."

The following morning, while there was still a touch of freshness in the air, Crystal left her hotel room and started down the hall. She stopped when she reached the window overlooking the city. From her top floor viewpoint she could see east. Today the familiar Confederate trenches blossomed with white flags waving in the morning air. She blinked and looked again.

Turning she ran down the stairs. "Flags!" she gasped to those clustered in the lobby. "There are white flags in the trenches!"

A gentleman turned. "Ma'am, General Pemberton has surrendered to the Union. If you hurry, you will see these poor, half-starved men stacking their arms." His voice was bitter.

Crystal turned away, saying, "I don't want to be a spectator. I want only to have the affair finished."

"As we all do, ma'am."

But nevertheless the town came to watch. High on the hill where Crystal had admired the Mississippi sunset, the townspeople huddled together and watched the Union boats move in. Until three in the afternoon the gunboats and transports continued to arrive. When the final boat docked, General Grant and his men walked into the city. Strangely the somber air seemed to lift in expectancy.

Crystal hurried down the hill and turned toward the wharf. She had gone only a block when she stopped. Astonished at the spectacle before her, she stepped back in the shade of a store front and watched. Below her, the streets were filled with Negroes. They lined the sidewalks, waiting in respectful silence, wearing big smiles. *This is it! Vicksburg has surrendered.*

At the first triumphant note from the bugles, Crystal lifted her head and saw the flag come slowly down the street. With tears in her eyes, she eagerly watched the colors moving with each step of the men. The band played; Crystal recognized *The Battle Cry of Freedom*. As tears streamed down her face, she heard a masculine voice behind her softly singing the last lines: "*For we know while freedom lives, Not a man must be a slave! Shouting the battle cry of freedom.*"

Crystal wiped her eyes and watched the Federal troops. Stalwart, smiling, they marched swiftly down the street. "My, don't they look nice! Different from our poor men, starved and ragged." Crystal nodded to the woman. Suddenly she turned and ran down to the street, searching the faces eagerly, wishing, yet not daring to wish that Matthew would be among those men.

Ahead troops marched into the park, breaking rank as they filled every available space. Suddenly Crystal stopped. That distant profile—could it be? Crystal ran, gasping, "Matthew, Matthew!" He turned, broke rank, and caught her in his arms. "Oh, thank You, Father, thank You! How I prayed you'd come, Matthew!"

"My dear, you are so thin!" he murmured, looking into her face, touching her cheek.

"It doesn't matter. Nothing matters except that you are here."

Now townspeople and soldiers mingled. The news swept through the streets. "General Grant has paroled the prisoners. Our men are going home!"

As they linked arms and walked toward the square, Crystal noticed the cheerful faces of the Federal soldiers were changing as they looked around at the people. Small clusters of blue uniforms formed. They seemed to be talking. With determined and stern faces, the soldiers turned as a woman ran to them.

Crystal saw her as she pointed toward a large building.

"Oh, I recognize her," she murmured. "She's telling the soldiers about the merchants holding back food." Crystal began to smile as the soldiers ran down the street.

She nodded toward the woman. "She'll get her ham yet!" Crystal tugged Matthew's hand. "Hurry, I want to see this."

They could hear glass breaking. By the time they reached the warehouse, Grant's men were hauling merchandise into the streets. Sacks of flour, canned goods, hams—even tins of imported English biscuits. As the barrels and boxes were forced open the soldiers yelled, "Here, Rebs, come and get it. Take it all! You're starving; you need it now!"

Crystal trembled against Matthew's arm. "Are you hungry?" he asked.

"Not as hungry as those women and children are. I've stayed at the hotel and have been fairly well fed. There's been little variety, but that's not important now."

Matthew turned and held her shoulders firmly. "I'm staying here with you until my commander releases me, then I'm taking you home."

CHAPTER 41

The train carrying Olivia and Beth passed through Philadelphia and continued north before turning west. Since leaving the city, Beth had been sitting with her nose nearly against the window. "How can the countryside seem so peaceful if the Confederates are actually in the state doing all those things the newspaper said?"

"It's a big state," Olivia replied. "It disturbs me because we aren't seeing Federal troops. I wonder what has happened to all those young men who took their training in our neighbor's pasture? But we've avoided the Chambersburg area where the Confederates entered; perhaps our army is there now. Surely we'll see the state militia." She smiled at Beth and added, "It's a relief to know we bypass places the Confederates are most likely to be."

The train slowed and chugged into a small city. "Where are we?" Beth asked.

"I don't know," Olivia said. "It's too dark to see."

A small boy came through the car. "Want a newspaper? There's news about President Lincoln getting a new general."

Beth reached for the paper and handed the youth coins. "And now it's too dark to read."

The conductor came in. "We will be staying here overnight. A bridge west of here is out. Across the street is a nice little hotel, just behind the depot. The train will leave at eight o'clock in the morning."

Olivia smiled and stood up. "Beth, you're fortunate! You'll have all evening to read that paper under a bright lamp. Let's go!"

After a quick meal in the hotel dining room, Olivia and Beth returned to their room. With the one lamp in the middle of the table, they bent over the newspaper.

Beth said, "It says here that President Lincoln replaced General Hooker with General Meade. That happened yesterday. Oh, dear!" she murmured. "I wonder if this had anything to do with General Hooker being replaced: the fifteenth of June a Union General named Milroy was attacked, and twenty-three hundred of his men were captured."

Olivia winced. "How terrible for those men!"

"It says the rest retreated into Pennsylvania, and it sounds as if the Confederates are right behind them." Beth looked thoughtfully at Olivia. "Don't you think you'd better stay with the Coopers too?"

Olivia shook her head. "Beth, please don't even suggest it. I have a feeling I'll be needed more than ever. And I have agreed to return; they'll be counting on me."

In the morning, Olivia awakened to find Beth already dressed. Quickly tossing back the sheet, she said, "I'm sorry I overslept. I'll be with you in a moment."

"Oh, there's no hurry. Olivia, I've been thinking. I'm nearly home, and surely the threat of meeting Mr. Stollen is gone. Why don't you just return to Washington today, and I'll continue on. Last night's paper talked about both armies coming into Pennsylvania. If you go back the way we came, there should be no problem, but if you wait—"

Olivia finished, "I may not get through. I believe you're right, Beth. But I don't like leaving you."

"And I don't like the possibility of your being stranded," Beth countered.

"If there's a battle close to Washington, the hospitals will need all the help they can get," Olivia added thoughtfully. "I'll go with you to the depot and check on a train going east."

At the depot, the man behind the counter looked at Beth and said, "Sorry, Miss. The bridge is still out. It seems they are uncertain when it will be repaired. I'd advise you to return to Washington if the travel isn't critical. We've had communications indicating the Confederates are moving deeper into Pennsylvania. Could be all the lines will have problems soon."

"I'm of the opinion we should return to Washington," Olivia said. "At least we'll be together."

The station master nodded in agreement. "Of course we'll be safe in the capital," Beth replied.

The station master looked at the clock. "There's a train returning to Washington by way of Gettysburg. It will leave in fifteen minutes. They've switched it, and it's nearly ready to go. Frankly, we've advised travelers to return, but most will wait for repairs to the bridge. Can't understand what the problem is. Some of the telegraph lines are down around Harrisburg, so our communication isn't the best."

Olivia looked at Beth and saw her nod. Olivia said, "I'd just as soon return to Washington. Let's go."

The coach in which they rode was nearly empty. Gratefully Olivia tucked her shawl over the back of the seat and settled down beside Beth, who was almost asleep. It was nearly ten o'clock when Olivia felt the train slow. She sat up and opened her eyes. Beth yawned and pointed to the small depot. "We stopped here yesterday. I wonder where the people are?" She settled herself against the hard seat and tried to retreat into sleep.

Olivia pushed her face against the soft shawl. Again she had dreamed of Alex. Desperately she tried to avoid the reality of loss. But the hard facts measured against the nebulous dream brought tears to her eyes. She touched the brooch, trailing her finger over the delicate roses.

A door slammed. As the conductor grasped the back of a seat, the train jerked forward and gathered speed as it left the station. "Ladies and gentlemen, the station master has informed me of a telegraph message, just received, indicating the Confederates are in Harrisburg."

A passenger leaned forward. "So that's the problem! Did they tear out the bridge?"

The conductor nodded at the man. "Also, the line below Gettysburg has been disrupted. We will proceed to Gettysburg and remain there until the problem has been corrected."

He started to turn and the same gentleman asked, "Just what type of problem is this?"

"The Confederate army appears to have damaged the line. Also, it is rumored that they have marched east from Chambersburg toward Gettysburg. If this is the case, we will likely be caught between the Federal Army and the Confederates unless we reach Gettysburg first. The train will move at full throttle; please stay in your seats."

The coach was silent except for an occasional subdued murmur. Olivia stayed close to the window and tried to see down the track. As they approached Gettysburg, she leaned against the window to catch a glimpse of the rolling, grassy hills around the town. In the distance she could see dark, rocky outcroppings. The train was still traveling fast.

Periodically the whistle shrilled as they crossed bridges and bisected roadways.

Startled faces appeared beside the tracks. Just as Olivia began to wonder if the engineer would slow for Gettysburg, she heard three piercing blasts from the whistle. The train slowed with brakes grinding metal. Olivia shivered and rubbed her arms.

The conductor appeared, his face troubled. "Sorry, folks, but the Confederates have cut us off. I'm certain you'll be safe, but we must stay in Gettysburg until the lines are checked."

The train pulled into the depot. Olivia started for the door, glancing at the platform. It appeared deserted.

The conductor held out his hand. "Ma'am, we're placing everyone in homes. Please go with that young lady over there by the cart. Hurry."

Olivia and Beth rushed toward the cart as the girl ran to meet them. Without a word she took Beth's valise and pointed to the cart. Olivia climbed aboard.

The girl jumped onto the seat, snapped the whip and yelled, "The Rebs are coming. We have a cellar, and that's where we're going." Olivia looked at Beth's startled face. She grasped the wagon seat as the girl used the whip again.

The root cellar was behind a sturdy white house. "I'm Sue," the girl said briefly. My parents are the Northrups, and they're in the cellar. Go on down."

Mrs. Northrup, with two younger children, met them. Olivia looked around. Baskets of potatoes and dried corn supported lamps, while bags of wheat and beans served as chairs.

"Mrs. Northrup, Rhonda, and Mark," Olivia murmured, smiling at the shy-eyed children. "Thank you for giving us a place to stay."

"Sorry I can't offer you my parlor," Mrs. Northrup said, "but they told us to take cover. They are saying there'll be fighting in the streets of Gettysburg. Too bad. They say General Lee has about seventy-five thousand men with him. I suppose things will be trampled."

"Mama, I heard at the depot this morning that General Buford took his men down toward Chambersburg this morning," Sue said. "There was a skirmish with the Confederates. But I couldn't see or hear anything, so we may be safe."

"Don't count on that, daughter," Mr. Northrup said, getting to his feet. "Mabel, I'm going to sit this out in the barn. I have my musket and plenty of ammunition, so don't worry."

"Pa, can I come?" Mr. Northrup tousled the boy's hair.

"Better stay; if you go, there won't be a man here. I'll come back at supper time."

Sue lifted her hand and listened. "They're moving this way. I hear horses." She looked at her mother and frowned.

"Now, don't you worry," Mabel Northrup said. "Your pa knows how to keep his head down."

As they waited, the sound of cannon and rifle fire drew nearer. Conversation ceased. Olivia strained to hear until it seemed the explosions were nearly on the Northrups' steps. There was a high-pitched yell. "Rebel yell," Mabel said. "It's the first I've heard." The sounds retreated. "I'm of a mind to go out. Seems all the activity must have moved up the hills."

"I'll go with you." Olivia jumped to her feet. "I've done nursing in Washington. Perhaps I can volunteer to help." Beth followed them up the steps.

Mabel pointed south. "That's Culp's Hill. There's action up yonder. You can see the soldiers from here."

"Oh, look," Beth murmured, pointing. "I believe they're coming with wounded soldiers. Where will they take them?"

With dismay in her voice, Mabel said, "To every house and building in town. I think we're all going to be nurses today. Dear Lord, help us!"

"There's a woman in that wagon," Beth whispered, just as the wagon wheeled through the Northrups' gate. Olivia saw the woman's agonized face and ran toward the wagon.

"Oh, please, please help us," she cried. "My husband is hurt terribly."

Olivia grasped the wagon and stared up at her. "You were with him in battle?"

"No, I was in camp. A kind man, a Confederate general named Gordon, found Francis. After General Gordon gave Francis water, he sent a man for me."

"Have the men carry him into the house," Mabel said. "Is there a doctor?"

"At one of the other houses, ma'am," said the bloodied man lifting the injured one from the wagon. "He'll be making his way this direction, so there's nothing to do except wait. There'll be more doctors coming up in the morning to help with the rest of the wounded. You ladies know how to use tourniquets? Give them plenty of water; some have been in the sun all day."

"Tourniquets? I do," Olivia answered as she followed the stretcher into the house. Mabel washed wounds while Beth and Olivia followed with bandages. Sue came with water. The wounded continued to arrive throughout the hot afternoon.

Sunset brought relief from the July heat, and with the darkness, the gunfire ceased. Olivia was slicing bread when she heard the lowing cattle and realized it was the only sound in the evening air.

Mr. Northrup appeared in the doorway. "Lots of milk for the lads. You ladies crumble some of Mabel's good bread in it, and that's about all these fellows could dream of tonight. I heard the roads are filled with Federal troops moving in. Guess we'll have a repeat of this tomorrow." Olivia looked up at him. Despite his cheerful words, she saw the shadows in his eyes.

"Going to get the neighbor lad to help me throw hay down," he said. "I think we'll need it to bed down some of the wounded tomorrow."

An officer came into the kitchen. "Our men were chased up Cemetery Hill. There are casualties up there. We'll be able to move them down later. Have any more space?"

"The barn," Mr. Northrup said. "Come and have something to eat."

The colonel shook his head. "Thanks, but no time."

———

Early the following day, as Olivia and Beth moved among the soldiers on their pallets, they listened for sounds of battle. Beth said, "I hear the creaking of wagon wheels and the snorting of horses," she added. "Do you suppose they're finished with the fighting?"

Olivia shook her head and picked up more of Mrs. Northrup's white sheets to tear into strips. "Strange that it is quiet."

During the late afternoon, the first gun was fired. Mr. Northrup came into the house with another bucket of water. "They're fighting in the peach orchard and through the wheat fields," he said. "Right now the Union lads are holding Little Round Top, but they came close to losing it for a time. I think our men will be able to hang on to Cemetery Hill."

At dark the Colonel came again. His face was haggard. "The doctor here? We need him up there. The fields are full of wounded." He looked at Beth and Olivia. "Will you come too?" Olivia nodded and followed him out the door.

Throughout the night they worked with water and bandages, compressing torn arteries, splinting broken bones with every scrap of wood they could find. When the stretcher bearers were outlined against the dawn, the fighting resumed.

Swaying with fatigue, Beth said, "How is it humanly possible to continue? Olivia, these poor men are exhausted; how can we hope to win?"

"The Confederates are exhausted, too. Beth, we must help."

Just after noon, as Olivia walked among the men with her bucket of cool water, the cannonading began. She stopped to listen. One of the wounded raised himself to his elbow. "Dear God," he groaned, "that's thundering hell. Nobody can live through that kind of fire."

"This is the third day of fighting," Olivia whispered. "How long can these men endure the agony?"

That night the barn was filled with soldiers lying on the hay. Nearly exhausted herself, Olivia moved among them with dippers of cool water. The doctor came, his face lined with fatigue. Olivia gave the bucket to Beth and returned to help him.

Together they treated the dirty wounds matted with soil and grass, flesh riddled by bullets. They probed, washed, and covered the torn flesh. After helping splint a broken arm, Olivia lifted a youth into a comfortable position against the hay.

He was nearly delirious. "That charge!" he said. "Did you hear the guns? Covered the whole valley with smoke."

Olivia nodded. "We saw it here. Could scarcely breathe."

"About the time the smoke lifted, the Rebels moved out," he muttered. "Some say there were fifteen thousand of them. I think they carried fifteen thousand flags. Marched right out from Seminary Ridge and charged our center. Man, we cut them down as fast as we could load and fire. They kept coming. Cool under fire. They stepped right over their fallen buddies, closed ranks, and kept coming. Ma'am," he whispered, "we watched whole brigades fall apart. Finally they leaped the wall on top, screaming that banshee yell. By then there was only about a hundred or so of them that came over." He choked, recovered, and said, "Why did they keep it up? Senseless. Those still on their feet were captured. The rest are wounded or dead. Why?" She could only shake her head.

Evening quiet settled over the valley. The last gun had been fired, and now silence and darkness claimed the town. In every house, building, and barn, limbs trembled with fatigue as men and women moved among the wounded with water and comfort.

On the following day, as the sun rose overhead, Olivia dragged herself out of a troubled sleep and listened. "I don't hear guns. Could it be General Lee has retreated?"

"I don't know; please God, let it stop."

Later Beth said, "Olivia, I'll go back to Washington with you. I've no heart to leave you and the others right now."

As if peering through a smoky haze of fatigue and frustration, Olivia began to see the changes in Beth. She hugged her, murmuring, "Bless you, Beth. We'll need you."

Mr. Northrup came into the kitchen. "There's a meeting going on outside; you'd better come."

Olivia and Beth followed him. They found a group of townspeople, some standing in the yard, others spilling over into the street. The colonel faced them. "General Lee has retreated from Gettysburg. We will need help. Although he carried all his ambulances filled with wounded, we are left with seven thousand seriously injured Confederate soldiers in need of care. In addition, the Confederate dead are still on the battlefields."

He hesitated, paced the dusty street, and said, "We'll need homes in which to house these men. We also plan to use every large building in town which can be converted into a hospital facilities. Please let me know what you can do. It is urgent we begin making provision for these men immediately."

Olivia closed her weary eyes. Her mind was filled with Alex's face. "I'll stay to nurse them," she whispered.

The school, two churches, and a large warehouse became hospitals. Most of the volunteers were townspeople. The dead were buried, and life settled into a routine. Beth and Olivia were given quarters at the Northrups' home, and through the autumn and winter months they stayed to nurse the wounded.

At last the snow came. The drafty buildings were equipped with additional stoves, and donations of warm blankets arrived, accompanied by warm woolen socks and tins of home-baked cookies.

Olivia looked at the gifts. "Beth, I can nearly hear Sadie saying, 'If they were our boys, we'd want someone to do something for them.' "

She glanced at Beth. "How lonesome I am for the Coopers and for the life there!"

Beth nodded. "I keep thinking I need to write a letter to them."

"I doubt it would get through. Perhaps when these men are sent home, we can go to see Sadie and Amos."

———

Sadie looked over the peaceful scene. Cattle grazed and haystacks towered against a brilliant sky while the last of the brown leaves dropped gently from the trees.

With a sigh, she went into the house and slowly unwound her shawl. Amos dozed beside the fire. "So peaceful," she murmured as he opened his eyes. She perused the newspaper. "This has President Lincoln's address. He was at Gettysburg to dedicate a cemetery for all the men who died there. It starts out nice, but they say it was awful short: *Four score and seven years ago, our fathers brought forth on this continent a new nation . . . dedicated to the proposition that all men are created equal.* She handed him the newspaper.

"Another letter came from Alex. My, 'tis strange. Gives me a queer feeling, like he is reaching down from heaven to her, my poor sweet girl. I'll put it away with the others to save for Olivia when she comes. They'll be a comfort. How I wish for her letters, but I know she's busy nursing our men back to life; that is more important than writing to an old lady."

Amos looked over the newspaper. "Don't you think they'd comfort her now? Seems you could just send them to that hospital in Washington."

"As long as it's taken them to come to us? I dare not trust them to the mail again."

CHAPTER 42

Matthew quickly climbed the stairs of the Vicksburg hotel, came into the room, and closed the door. He grinned at Crystal. "I explained the situation to the commander. He's given me a furlough, with permission to visit home before returning you to Pennsylvania. It'll be a quick trip, but as I told him, it's more than a casual visit."

Matthew sat down, and Crystal came to perch on the arm of his chair. "Matthew, I know you feel this burden to talk to your parents is from the Lord. I agree that it needs to be done as soon as possible. But are we wise to go now? I wonder if the trains have been restored."

"Commodore Porter is sending gunboats down the river. He'll give us passage to Natchez."

She pressed her face against his. "I must confess," she murmured in his ear, "I have a lot of qualms about meeting your parents."

"It could be unpleasant," he admitted. "Mother is particularly sensitive about my marrying someone she has not approved. And you can be assured she's set her mind to disapprove of you. Crystal, even now I'll not press you to go. Would you rather go on to New Orleans? It will be only a matter of weeks before steamers will be moving freely on the Mississippi."

"No." She nuzzled his ear. "Don't mention being separated again." She shuddered, adding, "I'll endure anything—even facing your mother—to be with you."

The following week the Union gunboat steamed into harbor at Natchez. Because of the muggy heat, Matthew and Crystal had spent most of the morning on deck, searching for a cool breeze. Just before they docked, Crystal said, "Matthew, for the past ten minutes you've had the strangest expression on your face. What is troubling you?"

"I'm not certain you'd call it trouble," he said slowly. "Mostly I'm recalling the last time I was in the city. Remember? It was the day those very exuberant Confederates insisted I would preserve my health by enlisting in the army. Recalling it made me do some thinking. Crystal, I want you to carry all the money—even our identification papers and passports.

"Fortunately I have civilian clothing. I don't anticipate problems, but I'd rather not take any chances." He kissed her and whispered, "Don't look frightened; just be prepared to scream if necessary."

She smiled. "I'm not frightened. Matthew, with our accents, they'll know we're Southern. We'll be safe."

"Of course, my dear." He glanced toward the harbor. "We're here; I'll go after our bags."

As they walked away from the wharf, Crystal asked, "Do you want to visit your uncle before we leave town?"

He shook his head. "We'll need to leave for home immediately, or we'll be traveling in the dark." Waving his hand, he shouted, "Laddie, we need a hack."

The young man strolled toward them. He shoved his hat back and reached for the bags. "Where to, sir?"

Matthew turned to look at the youth. "Herm!" he said slowly, "Well, do surprises ever cease?"

Crystal watched the young man's loose mouth tighten into a straight line. "Hey, it's my buddy, Matthew Thomas," he said slowly. "I haven't seen you since New Mexico. What happened to you? Didn't slip over the hill, did you?"

"Something like that," Matthew said slowly. Crystal felt the tension mounting in her husband. His hand momentarily touched hers. "Matter of fact, I was wounded. The people who picked me up were Union, and more than glad to help me on my way."

Herm grinned, shook his head slowly, and said, "Well, I'll be an army mule if I don't catch that. Hop in. Put the little lady in the back seat."

Crystal watched as Matthew reached for her. His mouth was open to speak her name. Abruptly he closed it, and his face tightened. He helped her into the carriage, gave her hand a squeeze, and got into the front seat with Herm.

"Where to, buddy?"

"Up the hill to the hotel."

Herm glanced at Crystal. "I'd expect you to want a hotel *under the hill*," he leered.

Matthew was silent. Herm snapped the whip, and the horse started up the hill. Matthew asked, "This your hack?"

"Naw, don't have that much money." He glanced at Matthew and grinned. "Not that I wouldn't want to."

The cab stopped in front of the hotel. "You know there's a bounty for deserters?"

"That so?" Matthew took Crystal's arm. "Come, dear."

Herm came around the hack. "Send the little lady inside, I want to have a word with you."

Crystal lifted her chin. "I prefer staying. I don't want to be dumped again."

Herm chuckled a deep mirthless sound. "Go on, sugar."

Matthew said, "It's all right. Go inside, Crystal."

Quickly she hurried inside, rushed to the desk. "That man out there, we need help!"

She whirled to point out Herm, just as an elderly man rushed through the door. "Call the police. I saw that cabbie knock a man over the head. He shoved him into the carriage and left in a hurry."

"That's my husband! Please do something quickly."

The clerk eyed her curiously, glanced at the old gentleman, and asked, "Was he a darky too?"

"Oh, I don't know." He glanced at Crystal and murmured, "Perhaps that would explain the matter."

Crystal dropped her hand and stared at the men. From their expressions, she saw how futile it was to say more. Dazed, she looked around. *The boat! the gunboat is still here!* "Please, I need a ride down the hill."

"I'd guess you could walk faster than I could get a hack up here," the clerk said with a smile.

Crystal picked up her valise and ran out the door. She hurried down the curving street toward the gunboat. As she rushed across the wharf, she could see the captain on deck. "Captain! Captain Adams!"

He came over the railing and dropped to the wharf. Panting and sobbing, she gasped, "A man named Herm hit Matthew over the head and left with him in the carriage."

"Get on the boat and stay out of sight," he said as he turned and ran across the wharf.

———

Crystal paced the captain's quarters, knowing deep inside that it was useless to hope. It was dark when Captain Adams returned. With a weary sigh he stood in front of her and said, "Ma'am, I've done everything I can think of, including going to the police."

Choking on her tears, she turned away. "That man said there was a bounty on deserters."

"Deserters!"

She nodded. "Two years ago when Matthew was here, he was forced to join the Confederate Army."

Slowly Captain Adams shook his head. "Ma'am, I'm sorry, but I don't think there's a thing that can be done. We're heading upriver in the morning. Want us to take you back to the transport? We'll get you home and let the commander start negotiations for his release." As he turned away, he muttered, "I just hope he can escape, because that'll be a great deal less complicated."

Matthew sat up and touched the tender lump on the back of his head. The concrete floor of his cell was damp and smelly. He looked down at the rough prison garb he wore and thought about Crystal. *Dear Father, please take care of her. And thank You for helping me see the possibility of this very thing happening.*

He tried to get to his feet, but when the walls began to whirl, he relaxed against the floor.

Slowly the days passed. Matthew's only contact with humanity consisted of the guard's brusque greeting and the plate of food shoved into his waiting hand. He lost count of the days as time passed in a haze of pain and troubled wondering.

One day the guard came with an empty hand. "The warden wants to see you. This way."

The man wore a friendly smile. "We've finally found your records. Matthew Thomas of Natchez, Mississippi. Enlistment date of February 1861. Reported missing in March of 1862, New Mexico. You're lucky. According to the procedure, you have a choice. Because of the war you don't get shot first thing. You can stay with the army and have an opportunity to honorably discharge your duties, or you can choose court martial. I must warn you. You could be charged with treasonable conduct. These trials don't last long." He stopped to take a breath before adding, "You're a smart fella; you know how badly the army needs men. If you prefer prison, fine, but if you don't we'll get you back into the army. Naturally, it will be an assignment where there's no chance of your slipping out on us again. You'll have constant supervision, and a shot in the back if you don't cooperate."

Matthew sighed, "Not much choice. I'll stick with the army."

The gray uniform was a size too large. Fortunately, Matthew thought with relief, the Confederate Army allowed him to keep his own shoes. The following day, after a night in the barracks and a meal of hardtack and beans, Matthew was called up for assignment.

"Private Thomas. You will be sent to Georgia. A new prison facility is being established there. They'll be able to put you to work as a laborer. After the facility is in use, you will become a guard at the prison." The man hesitated, grinning. "Might say that right off, the army isn't going to trust you too close to Federal lines."

———

Alex heard the footstep and turned. His jailer swung open the barred door, and Alex's heart leaped with hope. The man grinned. "Don't ya'll go celebrating yet. Yer all being put in a safer spot. Come along; we got no time to waste. There's a bunch more to round up fer the trip."

Alex and the group of shabby Union prisoners were herded together. Three of the prisoners were Negroes. Alex looked at the men and nodded. When their guard moved away, he said, "Seen action?" The expression in their eyes was dismal as they nodded. Alex started, "I would—"

The guard nudged Alex with the butt of his gun. "Don't open your mouth again. We don't cotton to this kind of friendship. We're moving out shortly. Learn to keep your mouth shut and your feet moving." With their guards prodding them on, they faced east.

The Alabama prison was a crude stockade built on the edge of the forest. Alex looked around at the prisoners, noting the infected wounds and sunken eyes, and his heart sank.

———

The second day after their arrival at another stockade, Alex discovered that all the Negroes had disappeared.

"What happened to the black men?" he asked one of the other prisoners.

The man beside him laughed and shook his head. "Didn't you expect it? Beyond a doubt, they were sold down the river."

"So that's all the good the Emancipation Proclamation has done," Alex said bitterly.

"Did you think them Rebs would take kindly to it?"

"I suppose it's just a shock to be back in the middle of it all."

The man looked at him. "You're Southern, aren't you? How did you get mixed up with the Yanks?"

"Because I believe human bondage is wrong."

"Said with a passion," the fellow snorted. "Even us born-in-the-north Yanks don't feel that strongly. Might say we're wary about them coming up and taking our jobs."

"I've a feeling there's jobs for everyone who wants to work," Alex replied shortly. "Don't forget the emancipation makes the black man a consumer, too. He'll be right in there beside you spending money."

The oak leaves changed color and fell. Alex paced the narrow strip of soil which was slowly turning to a muddy slough under the onslaught of autumn rain. He flexed his arms and carefully tightened the muscles that had been torn by the Confederate slug. Rod Ames, a fellow prisoner, watched with a sardonic smile. "Wouldn't hurt you to move around a little," Alex muttered. "You'd keep your blood moving."

Rod jerked his head toward their shelter. "I'm trying to toughen up. There's little chance of gaining anything around here except endurance." Alex looked at the shelter. The prisoners had constructed crude huts from the branches of trees, which did little to stop either sun or rain. Their beds were of shredded bark laid on the ground.

Alex stooped and made his way to the rear of the shelter. "Sleeping on the job?" Rod asked.

"Thinking about this winter, wondering if there's a dry spot in here. I keep remembering a nice piece of canvas I had. I suppose some Confederate is enjoying it."

"Well, I just about decided I'd rather take my chances over the hill than to sit here and rot in the rain," Rod muttered. "With wormy meal and moldy bread, I don't think I'll hold out all winter."

Alex sighed and admitted, "I've had the same thoughts. But right now I don't see much chance of moving out."

"Pence, over yonder, is working on a tunnel. It starts back in his shelter and will come out over in the bushes beyond the fence."

Another prisoner, Doug, strolled over and squatted beside them. "I hear rumors of being moved out of here. Some say Georgia. That'll be warmer in the winter." Alex studied the man. In the brief time Alex had been in the stockade, he had watched Doug's face change from healthy tan to a waxy yellow. The man's hands were like claws.

Doug lingered. Alex glanced up at him. "Something on your mind?"

"I was thinking about what you said a week or so ago. About the comfort God gives even in situations like this. I've always been a church-going fella, but don't know that my religion's gone very deep."

Studying the intent eyes, Alex said slowly, "Jesus Christ invited us to come to Him. The words are, 'Come unto me . . . and I will give you rest . . . my yoke is easy, and my burden is light.' " He looked up at the man. "Doug, I guess I haven't thought too much about creeds, but I do believe the Bible is God's word to us. It says Jesus Christ is God, and that He came to this earth for the purpose of reconciling us to God through dying on the Cross. I didn't know what it was to live at ease with myself until I asked Christ to be my Savior. It works here, too. Every day I'm conscious of God close to me. If you'd like to know Him in the same way, all you need do is ask Him."

"A fellow would be a fool to not ask, especially in a place like this."

"In any place. But Doug, Christian faith isn't just a religion for those who are dying; it's for the free and living too. Knowing God makes all of life worthwhile."

All too soon the cold rains came. Mornings revealed an edging of ice in the water buckets. Food rations decreased to a handful of beans and another of hardtack. Occasionally there was coffee and bacon, but the supply of cooking wood dwindled sharply.

As the weather turned cold, Doug's cough worsened. Watching his fragile frame tremble with the effort of coughing, Alex realized the man wouldn't live much longer.

On the morning after Doug died, Alex joined the group of planners. He listened to the talk and said, "If you're serious, we'd better all help with the digging."

"We gotta get out soon. We won't last the winter here."

The rains had turned to sleet, and moisture penetrated everything. Alex's boots stiffened with cold and he pitied those with bare feet.

Rod saw his glance and said, "Just don't take them off, they'll be gone in a second. Seems the ones who die are those without shoes or blankets."

"I had all my gear taken away from me," Alex admitted. "At the time, I hurt so bad I didn't care. Now I'd like to have that rubber sheet and my blankets."

"Same thing happened to the rest of us," Rod muttered. "If something doesn't happen around here soon, we're all going to be like that fellow over there." He pointed to a prisoner tossing with fever.

"I'm ready any time you fellows are," Alex murmured. "When do we start digging?"

Using a slab of wood for a shovel, one of the men would disappear into the hole in Pence's shelter while the group huddled outside, making enough noise to cover every hint of sound coming from the shelter.

The rains continued, helping to wash away the dirt from the excavation, and the cold wind blew. Occasionally there was snow. Alex developed a cough. Rod Ames watched him with a furrowed brow. Gruffly he said, "We can't afford to lose a digger. Drink this coffee."

That night Pence said, "I figure we're nearly through. We need to take advantage of dry weather. Don't want to leave footprints out there. Let's speed up the digging, I'd like to be home for Christmas."

"According to my calculations," Rod drawled, "it's closer to Easter."

At last the rains stopped, and Pence said, "I'm going to start digging toward daylight. I've eye-balled that stretch of tunnel until I'm positive we're in the right position." He turned to look beyond the fence. "I just wish those guards weren't so fond of cutting through the underbrush."

One evening Pence came out of the tunnel with his eyes shining. "Grass roots," he muttered. "Tonight is the night."

The sliver of moon disappeared behind the clouds. Rod touched his shoulder and Alex followed him to the tunnel. Alex counted the men in the shelter. He signaled Pence, and they began to drop into the tunnel, moving quickly, pushing against the person in front.

When Alex crawled out of the hole, the cloud across the moon had disappeared. He saw the glint of metal just as he stood up.

The guard muttered, "Pence, Ames, Stoddard, and Duncan. When are the others coming?"

Pence sighed wearily. "This is all."

"Well, start marching. There's a long walk ahead of you. Clear to Georgia. Too bad, fellows, but you might say you brought it on yourselves. They need help over in Georgia; they're building a better prison. Need prisoners to fill it."

CHAPTER 43

Olivia looked at the cherry-red stoves glowing at each end of the long room. Rubbing her hands together she said, "The warmth in this warehouse is simply an illusion." She tugged at the heavy shawl draped across her shoulders and tucked it into her apron.

As she started for the center of the room, she noticed a young Rebel lieutenant watching her. "I can see you're cold." He grinned at her. "After listening to your speech, I think you like cold weather as little as I do, and you come by those feelings naturally."

She stopped beside his bed, smiled at him and felt his forehead. "Your temperature is down, Paul. I love the snow; it's beautiful. But I agree, it's astonishingly cold." He chuckled and she started to move on.

"Stay. With all these empty beds, you can't be very busy."

She smiled at him. "I need to check on Tony." She glanced at the line of empty beds. "There are only a few more days left in the year. How nice it would be if you all were headed home by the new year."

He nodded. "My wife is coming any time. She's bringing our son, and we'll travel home together."

"Oh, that's nice. How old is he?"

"Nine months. I haven't seen him yet."

"That's young to be out in this cold."

"I know. I hope she doesn't regret coming."

Olivia moved on to the next bed. *Nine months. Our baby girl would have been that age.* She smiled at the youth. "Tony, have you tried the wooden legs again?"

He shook his head. "Scared I'll fall."

"Beth is coming in a few minutes. Why don't you fasten them on and the two of you can go for a nice stroll."

He grinned. "In the park? Where's the music?"

"You can't go home until you can walk. And you know why; the doctor is afraid you'll need more surgery." She watched his face pale. "Come on, I'll help."

Beth dashed into the room, her cheeks burnished as brightly as polished apples. "Oh, it's cold out!"

Tony grinned. "Let's go make snowballs."

She blew him a kiss. "Only if you'll race me to the garden across the street."

"I would if you'd really kiss me."

"Ha! I'd be the loser." She laughed and backed away. "Get dressed, and I'll return with your dinner in a minute."

The door at the end of the room opened, and a woman carrying a baby entered. With wide eyes, she looked slowly around the room.

Paul sat up. "Betsy!" Olivia watched the woman run to Paul. With her heart heavy, Olivia turned away as the woman dropped the baby into Paul's arms and fell to her knees beside the bed.

Bruce waved his bandaged arm. "Olivia, it's my turn."

"Bruce, I think you're going to be the next one to go home. Your forehead feels cool, and this arm looks good. You were right to refuse amputation, but last July none of us believed that." She patted his shoulder and moved on to Cap.

"Wanna talk?" he asked. She blinked the tears back. "I saw you were nearly ready to cry. All this war business getting you down?"

"Doesn't it hurt everyone? No, Cap, I don't need to talk. Some problems have no solutions. How about you? Is your wife coming after you?"

"No, I didn't want her to make the trip. She's in Georgia, and travel isn't that safe right now." He touched her hand. "We soldiers don't say much, but I want you to know all of us appreciate what you've done for us—treating us like family, not like strangers or enemies."

She smiled slowly, folding the bandage. "When we face the enemy, we find he's a brother. Cap, I'll be so happy when this is all over. Do you suppose we'll ever live normal lives again?"

"I think it will be hard," he said slowly. "At times I wonder if any of us will be able to go back to what we left. Olivia, there's one thing that bothers me. Why, with all the agony and suffering, do we all feel close to each other? You've seen me at my worse moments, and I've seen your miseries, too. Will we go home and let friends and neighbors know us this way? I think not."

"For some of us the hurts are too deep."

"Don't let them turn on you and eat clear through your soul," he said intently.

"Only God can keep that from happening. And Cap, I sense that's possible when we're able to accept these hurts as part of God's better plan. I'm still trying to accept that." Olivia gathered up the scissors and ointment and turned to go.

Dr. Thompson came into the hospital. He stopped in the middle of the room and watched Tony's hesitant steps. "Does it still hurt?"

"Not bad," Tony gasped. "Mostly I'm afraid of falling. Do you send nurses home with patients? I think it would help." He grinned at Beth.

Dr. Thompson chuckled. "Walk around as long as you can; then come back here and let me check the stumps."

He headed for Olivia. "Nurse, I think you ladies have about worked yourselves out of a job. The majority of the men are ready to be released. I'd say by next week you can go home."

"Home?" Olivia echoed. "I'm going back to the hospital in Washington."

He stared at her incredulously. "Why are you pushing yourself this way? Go home and rest before you take on another assignment."

He continued down the line of patients, and Olivia fingered the brooch. "He's right," Cap said.

Olivia looked at him and lifted her chin. "Cap, you wondered about me. I'm a widow who can't accept her husband's death. Am I crazy?"

"I've never met a more level-headed woman," Cap answered. "Let's just say that in this war there's much we can't accept. In time—the Lord's good time—you'll be able to."

She touched his hand. "Thank you, Cap."

———

By the end of the following week, the last of the patients had been moved or released. As Beth and Olivia helped remove the hospital equipment, Olivia asked, "Beth, are you ready for that trip to see Sadie and Amos?"

Beth looked at Olivia with a troubled expression. "I don't like leaving you. Olivia, I can see how tired you are, and it makes me feel guilty."

"Is that why you've looked so troubled lately?"

Beth caught her breath, glanced at Olivia, and blushed. "I guess I've had a few things on my mind."

Thrusting the pile of blankets into Beth's arms, Olivia said, "Well, take these into the doctor's office and let's go back to the Northrups'. I need to get my things in order and begin packing."

When Olivia and Beth walked out of the warehouse, the wind caught them, swirling snow in their faces. "Oh, let's hurry!" Olivia gasped.

"Mr. Northrup said he knew we were going to have a blizzard," Beth said. "He said the horses and cows were restless this morning."

They rushed into the Northrups' kitchen and unwound their snowy shawls. Mabel turned from the stove. "My, I'm going to miss you two. Sure you don't want to stay until spring? I've an idea they'd find work for you."

Olivia accepted a cup of coffee and sat down close to the stove. "If this snow keeps up, the trains won't be running tomorrow. And I really need to get back to Washington. I know they've needed me desperately."

Mabel turned to Beth. "How about you? Are you going to Washington, too?"

Beth hesitated. "Before all this started, I was on my way to the Coopers'. They live in a little town on the Ohio River, just inside the Pennsylvania line."

After the supper dishes were washed and back in place, Beth and Olivia went to their room. The wind howled around the eaves of the house, throwing snow against the windowpane. For a moment before she pulled the curtain across the window, Olivia watched snowflakes stick to the glass and slowly slide down.

"I have a feeling we'll all be snowbound tomorrow."

Beth shrugged. "I don't mind. I'm still not convinced I should go to the Coopers'."

"Why?"

Quickly Beth pulled the nightgown over her head, and with a shiver jumped into bed. Thoughtfully she said, "I wonder if I'll be welcome there. Looking back, it seems I've been more trouble than I should have been."

Olivia crawled in beside Beth. "I don't feel that way. I know Sadie was concerned about you and Mike, but I know she honestly likes you. Right now, I'd guess she would welcome company, so don't let those feelings keep you away."

The girl was silent so long that Olivia reached to put out the lamp. Finally Beth spoke. "I might as well say this; maybe you can give me some advice. Olivia, I think I'm starting to care for Mike very much.

What if he's there? I just don't think I could stand it."

Olivia turned and frowned. "Care for him? I thought you loved him enough to marry him."

"Back then I don't think I knew what love meant." She turned to look at Olivia. "Maybe I was just—I don't know, fascinated with him. An older man, a riverboat pilot. And besides, he seemed to like me so much. That was exciting."

"And now you don't want to see him? Beth, why?"

"I honestly don't know. Maybe it's because I still feel as if I must tell him all these terrible things about myself."

"You might as well get it said, Beth. If you want to be honest about this whole thing, I'd think Mike deserves your explanation more than anyone else." Beth didn't answer. Olivia extinguished the lamp and lay wide-eyed in the dark. *We'd never love if we knew the final pain of it— or would we?* With a gentle smile she turned to sleep.

In the morning Olivia looked out at the frozen world and said, "I think it's just as well that I didn't pack my valise last night."

Mr. Northrup carried the pail of milk into the kitchen. "Milk nearly froze on the way to the house. But we didn't so much as lose a chick. I doubt you ladies will be going far on the train today. From what I could see, I'd guess it won't leave the station."

"Pa told me the smoke froze in the chimney of the train," Mark said.

Olivia laughed. "Mark, I wondered how cold it gets before smoke freezes; now I know. Too cold!"

———

The following week, Olivia took the train to Washington and Beth left to visit the Coopers.

When Beth walked through the Coopers' back door, Crystal was in the kitchen. Carefully putting her valise down, Beth looked from Crystal to Sadie and whispered, "Crystal, what has happened?"

"Matthew hath been taken prisoner," Sadie answered. "Crystal has been in Washington these past months trying to get the army to intervene."

Wearily Crystal said, "They've told me that legally nothing can be done, since there is no proof he was forced into the Confederate Army two years ago. They told me to go home and wait."

Crystal pressed her fingers against her eyes. "Sadie told me Olivia lost her baby, and that Alex is dead. Where is she?"

"Working at an army hospital in Washington." Beth glanced at Sadie. "We started to come here last July, but we were trapped at Gettysburg during the battle. Both of us stayed on to nurse the Confederate soldiers Lee left behind when he retreated."

"Is she all right?"

"I think she is working too hard," Beth said slowly. "But it seems to make her happy. Mostly I believe she keeps herself too tired to think about her problems." She looked at Crystal. "What will you do?"

Crystal shook her head, and Sadie said, "She's been helping us pack kits for the Sanitary Commission. Guess we'll put thee to work too."

Beth heard the sounds of footsteps in the hall. Apprehensively she turned. It was Mike. He leaned on a crutch and looked at her. One trouser leg had been carefully folded where his foot should have been. Beth groped for the door frame. As the room turned black, someone called her name.

A few minutes later, Beth opened her eyes and felt a pillow under her head. Crystal knelt beside her. "Beth, would some tea help?"

Beth pressed her cold hands against her face. "No, I'll be up in a moment. I suppose I'm tired. I've been working with men like—" She fought for breath. "It shouldn't bother me now."

That evening Mike came late to the table. His eyes were remote as he looked at Beth and said, "Sorry, I didn't mean to upset you."

"I was simply tired," she said, turning away. Amos looked from Beth to Mike. The question in his eyes brought a lump to Beth's throat.

After the dishes were washed, Beth lingered in the kitchen. "Beth, thou wilt get used to it," Sadie said. " 'Tis no worse than thou hast had back there."

"I know," she murmured. "I suppose it's just the shock. If you'll excuse me, I'll go up to bed. It's been a hard two days on the train."

The following week the snow melted and the sun shone. While Beth mixed cookie dough, Sadie came into the kitchen wearing her bonnet. "If thou art baking cookies today, I'll go into town with Amos. Here are some hazelnuts. Mike could shell them for thee."

Beth looked at Sadie. "How long will he be staying?"

Sadie's eyes held Beth's in a long questioning look. "Long enough for that leg to heal completely." Sadie headed for the door.

Beth bit her lip and watched Sadie's skirt swish as she left the house. The clock ticked loudly. With a sigh Beth began shaping cookies. "You and your mouth—particularly since you are the intruder," she muttered to herself. Her heart sank as she realized she must talk to Sadie.

As she shoved the first pan of dough into the oven, Beth heard the irregular step on the stairs. Mike limped into the kitchen. She noticed he wasn't using his crutch. While she wondered if she dared mention the fact, he nodded. "Good morning." He sat down at table and watched her roll dough.

"Would you care for breakfast? Sadie fried ham for you."

"No thank you." He watched her hands cutting and lifting the dough. He looked up. "Is there coffee? Those cookies smell wonderful."

She nodded and reached for a mug. "The cookies will be done in a few minutes."

"I could smell them upstairs." He avoided her eyes as she poured coffee and set it in front of him. Lifting the pan of cookies out of the oven, she placed some on a plate and brought it to him.

"If you don't mind," Beth said, rolling dough, "there are hazelnuts to be shelled. It isn't terribly important; Sadie just mentioned them."

He nodded. "The cookies are good." He stood up and went to the stove for coffee.

"I'm sorry," she murmured. "I forgot that—"

"It's all right." His voice was rough. "I don't expect you to wait on me. I need the exercise."

Carefully she cut and lifted the dough. "Does your leg bother you a great deal?"

"No. I suppose I could go back. I won't be the only man with a wooden leg. It's just that it's a little tricky to regain balance and speed."

"I know," Beth said softly, "especially for a man whose job takes him up and down stairs all day. Mike, I hear they've nearly perfected artificial feet. They flex."

"How do you know?"

"I've been working with amputees." He leaned back, a curious expression on his face. In a rush of words she said, "Olivia and I were at Gettysburg during the battle. We stayed to nurse Confederate soldiers."

She finished filling the pan and brought the freshly baked batch to the table. He shook his head, "No thank you." He paused and took a deep breath. "Beth, I think we need to do some serious talking." She glanced at him, and hastily he added, "I realized too late I bungled everything I tried to say. Now I need to attempt an explanation. Will you hear me out?"

Still holding the pan of cookies, Beth turned away and carefully placed it on the cupboard shelf. She gulped, wondering if she dared trust her voice.

They both heard the pounding on the door. "I'll go," Mike muttered. Beth watched him limp out of the room. With a sigh of relief, she took the last pan out of the oven and lifted the cookies onto the cooling rack. From the parlor she could hear two voices, heavy and loud. *Did he say Roald?* She removed her apron and rushed to the parlor.

She stopped in the doorway as the two turned. It *was* Roald, thin and pale, but smiling. Slowly she went to him. Holding out her hand, she whispered, "I can't believe what I'm seeing. Did you know they listed you as dead?"

"Yes. That was the information my mother received. I thought I'd better come rather than write."

"Please come sit down." She led him to the chairs beside the fire, and Mike quietly left the room. "Roald, would you like coffee or tea?"

He hesitated. "Neither. I know this is an inconvenient time to call. But I saw Sadie and Amos in town and couldn't bear for you to have the news in another manner."

She sat down in the rocking chair. "Roald, this is a shock. I hardly know what to say. Please, what happened?"

"I was captured. Had a minor wound. It seemed to heal without problems, but after I was exchanged I had to enter the hospital. It was one thing after another. It started with pneumonia, then I had the measles." His face twisted in a sheepish grin.

"I know," she said hastily. "I've been working in a hospital and I know how serious these diseases can be for a person who is in poor health."

"By then I didn't have the strength to contact you. The hospital nurse wrote to my mother. Last summer she came after me, and I've been all this time regaining my health. Beth, it's good to see you. Will you forgive me for not getting word to you?"

"Certainly, Roald." They were still watching each other, cautiously looking for some point of recognition. *Was it possible to be strangers after being sweethearts?*

Hesitantly he said, "I'll be going back to duty in two weeks. Beth, I feel like we no longer know each other. I can't expect you to pick up right where we left off, but I need to know. Do you want to see me again?"

Honesty, she thought. *I have to be honest.* She caught her breath. "Roald, I can't encourage you. I think I've grown up enough to know what real love is. I still think very fondly of you and our good times together, but I suppose—"

He got to his feet. "I sensed that as soon as I saw you, but I thought it would be only fair to ask. Beth, thank you for being kind to a lonesome soldier boy." He took her hand, adding, "I wish you happiness. I'm not surprised; I've always been afraid of losing out to Mike."

With her hand pressed against her aching throat, she watched him walk down the snowy path. Slowly she went back to the kitchen. Mike was gone, and the nuts hadn't been shelled.

Upstairs, Mike leaned against his closed door. "Thank you, Lord. I've been trying to understand that fiasco between Beth and me, and now I see. This day would have been unbearable for her if we had married."

He sat down on his bed and picked up the Bible lying there. Cradling it in his big hands, he ruefully said, "Lord, much as I . . . well, like her, I'd never have wanted such a thing to happen. I guess it's better to love and lose than to rush into something against Your will. I believe I can accept it now."

He waited. He looked down at the wooden peg extending beyond his pant leg. With a cheerless grin he muttered, "A fine prize you are, anyway."

Mike limped to the window. *Might as well get it out, he thought. It doesn't work to hold back on the Lord and pretend all's well.*

He went to sit on the edge of his bed, dropping his face in his hands. "Lord, I've struggled with this problem until I'm ashamed," he said. "I'd like to give it to You again. It's Beth. I love her, can't get her out of my mind even now when I know she's downstairs talking to the fella she loves. I know I got myself into this mess when I forgot about how much she needs you and started thinking how much I need her. Father, what do I do now?"

CHAPTER 44

Matthew looked down over Andersonville prison. It had been ripped out of the forest, denuded of vegetation, and sealed off from the world. The men who lived there were as deprived and tortured as the land. Both were a wilderness of anguish.

He slammed his fist into his hand and said, "I'm sick of this! No self-respecting farmer would keep his pigs in such squalor."

"Matthew Thomas," growled the sergeant, "you complaining about the way we treat prisoners? You're asking to be reported to Henry Wirz. With your record maybe you'll join 'em." Matthew continued to pace the soggy ground in front of the guards' tents.

He turned as the sergeant hunkered down beside the fire. "We're not supposed to have a conscience about such situations? I wouldn't even feed wormy hardtack to an animal. We're not supposed to help them? This is January; the men don't have blankets."

"This is war. We've hardly decent rations for ourselves. We're doing the best we can. Northern prisons aren't a bit better than Andersonville."

The sergeant walked away from the fire and Cody Daniels poked Matthew. "Flapping your mouth will get you nowhere. Most of us don't like what's going on. You make changes by keeping your mouth shut and watching to see what can be remedied."

Matthew looked into the fellow's sympathetic eyes and said, "I'm going to come out of this feeling like a beast."

"So are the rest of us."

A guard named Tom spoke from the other side of the fire. "Belle Isle isn't the only place prisoners are coming from. Last night they marched in some men from over Alabama way. Couldn't handle them. I guess we get the job of whipping them into line. God, I would like this to be finished so's we could go home and act like humans again."

"Might do us all more good if we'd get down on our knees and repeat that sentence over about a dozen times," Matthew muttered.

"I hear the troops down Virginia way got revival. Heard General Lee's been preaching. Seems like a kindly fellow. If I get reassigned, I'd like to be with him."

"You and everyone else," Cody snorted. "The way things are going, we may end up fighting for Grant."

"He's purt' near as good as Lee. Didn't think the North would ever come up with a man worth saluting. But he's a fighter."

"That Sherman worries me. He's tough."

"Wish they'd get both those fellows out of Tennessee. Things are getting tight with them hanging on to Chattanooga."

Cody nodded. "That railroad line there tying us to Atlanta and on into Tennessee is all we've got. We can't afford to have them mess with it."

"I've got news for you." They turned when they heard the heavy voice. The fellow was built like a boxer. His huge hands didn't seem to go with shrewd eyes. "I'm Tinker Dixon. I was up that way on a skirmish the end of November. The Yanks are working up to something big. They were building bridges across the Tennessee River. As fast as they'd get the timbers up, the trains started shooting over, hauling in men, munitions, food—about anything you can name. I say, it liked to have scared me silly. You watch. We're going to be in trouble soon as warm weather hits."

The sergeant strode back to the fire. "Hanson, Thomas, Dennis, and Jennings; you're on guard duty tonight. First watch. Better get your grub and step lively."

Matthew picked up his battered musket and looked at it thought-fully. He shook his head and sighed. "Pretty sad gun. At least it shoots."

A light rain was beginning to fall as he walked toward his guard post. Hanson passed him. "Sure a shame they stripped all the trees and bush outta here. Those poor fellers sitting out in the mud can't be too comfortable." Matthew followed his pointing finger.

"Is that the new bunch? I don't see a scrap of cover for them."

"Came over from Alabama. They'll be lucky to survive the month unless somebody dies and bequeaths them all their earthy possessions."

Matthew hunched his shoulders against the rain as he made his way to his post. Already he could feel the wetness seeping through his uniform. Slinging his gun into position, he began to march his picket.

With each turn he surveyed the scene before him. The only thing of substance in the prison was the wall. Just over the wall, the miserable prisoners huddled in makeshift tents or under scraps of wood. Some, like the new bunch of prisoners, tried to creep close enough to the tents to be afforded shelter from the wind-driven rain.

As daylight faded, the rain stopped and clouds drifted away. As Matthew paced out his picket, he prayed. *Holy Lord, if my heart aches, Yours must break over this sight. Oh God, please deliver these men from their agony. If there's something I can do, show me and give me the wisdom necessary.*

Feeling the burden of his inadequate prayer, he marched on. The night air carried the sound of coughing and ragged breathing. Moonlight revealed men restlessly pacing, slapping their hands together to stir circulation.

Watching them, Matthew realized that seeing life reduced to these levels was exacting its toll on him. No longer did he wince as he watched the harvest of the cold night being carried to the burying ground. The sharp outrage, the pain of it all had been blunted into a nearly bearable hurt. As he shivered in his own inadequate clothing, with a stomach complaining against the grease and wormy food, he began to realize what had happened.

Father, do You care that Your creation is dying in this meanness? God, strike me dead lest I turn against Your mercy and grace. Or give me an opportunity to strike back at the ugliness around me.

In the silence, waiting with desperation, he accepted the fact that being killed for one act of honor was better than living with subhuman callousness. *Lord, please let me go out doing one decent act to help someone reach above despair.*

In the rotation of duty, it became Matthew's task to pass the rations to the prisoners. On that first day, carrying his box of hardtack to his station inside the walls, Matthew shook his head and groaned. "This isn't enough to feed those men more'n a mouthful."

Inside the fence, close to the sea of faces reduced to yellow wax, limp with apathy, Matthew took his place beside the hardtack, praying desperately that the food would last as long as there was a face in front of him.

The supply was nearly gone when he lifted a chunk and saw the curly dark hair, the gold ring in the prisoner's ear. Carefully he bent forward. Grasping the hardtack more firmly, he waited. The man reached, lifted his head. Matthew saw the eyes blaze with recognition. Joy flared in the haunted eyes while Matthew blinked tears from his own. He released the hardtack. The man moved away.

With his throat bursting, Matthew stepped back and shouted, "God bless you, one and all. May He multiply the bread in your mouth." He saw the man's shoulders twitch.

As Matthew turned away, an officer turned a contorted face down at him. "One more trick like that, and you'll face court martial."

Matthew scarcely heard; he was watching the man with the earring. When he had noted the shelter he entered, Matthew smiled with satisfaction. It was close to the prison wall.

That night, flat on his face, Matthew prayed, *Father, thank You. Alex is alive. Thank You for giving me a reason for living—to deliver my brother Alex. Grant me the wisdom and power, surround us with Your grace.*

That week Matthew discovered that the slightest infraction of the sergeant's rules rated late-night guard duty. He also discovered that a small flat rock served well as a message carrier. On that first late night guard duty, Matthew penciled the word HOPE on the rock. Standing in the trees beyond the picket's line, he pitched the rock against Alex's crude shelter. Alex's head appeared in the cave-like opening; he saw Matthew and began to search. After Alex read the message he tossed the rock back.

Later that week Matthew lingered beside the fire listening to the guard's conversation. He hunkered down to watch Cody clean his rifle. Matthew said, "You give a lot of attention to that old gun."

Cody grinned. "If I get a better one, I'll give it twice as much. I mean to have this in top condition, ready to fire."

He pulled the plug out of the end of the powder cartridge, poured in the powder, and rammed the ball firmly into place. "Now, if I see a rat, I'll bag us some dinner." He got to his feet and dusted his britches over the fire. There was a pop and a flare, Cody stepped back. "Guess I had a flake or two of gun powder on me. See ya later, fellas, I have picket number eight tonight."

Matthew watched him stride off into the darkness while he mused, *Gunpowder . . .* He got to his feet. "Guess I'll see if I can get to sleep while my feet are still warm."

Gunpowder isn't hard to get, but fuses are. He grinned in the darkness. Matthew began to collect extra cartridges, begging them one at a time from the other guards; he was cautious, careful to ration out his requests to avoid arousing suspicion.

But his casual collecting could not go on. While on guard duty one day, he became uneasy about Alex. The day had passed without his appearance. *All of them are getting weaker by the day. I must act soon,* he thought. He scrutinized the growing pile of cartridges and went for a walk behind Wirz's comfortable cabin looking for provisions. There didn't seem to be a trash dump. Boldly he approached the back door.

A black woman answered his knock. "Please, I'd like an empty tin can. You know, like peaches come in."

With wondering eyes, she nodded. "I's got one on the shelf, but it has peaches in it. Want I should feed him peaches tonight?"

Matthew grinned. "That would be just fine. Could you put the peaches in something else and give me the can now? And would you happen to have some string? I'd sure like a couple of lengths. Just plain old string is fine. I appreciate your help."

With a puzzled glance at him, she said, "String's precious. But I guess so; de boss don't mind giving out a little." She grinned and disappeared.

Matthew eyed the kerosene jug leaning against the cabin. Shifting nervously from foot to foot, he waited. She came back to the door and handed Matthew the empty can and a handful of string. When she closed the door he stopped, let the last drops of peach juice trickle into his mouth, then he dropped the string into the bottom of the can and poured kerosene over the pile.

Inside he could hear the banging of pans, and the black woman singing, "Swing low, sweet chariot, coming for to carry me home—"

Matthew approached Cody. "Let me have a couple of cartridges."

"Sure. Any reason why you can't just walk up to the quartermaster and ask for a new bag?"

Without answering, Matthew returned the grin. After that bold move, Matthew approached a different soldier each day. *How much gunpowder does it take to blow up a wall?* he wondered.

One evening as he and Cody sat beside the fire, Matthew realized Cody was watching him. His jaw was a hard line as he leaned forward saying, "You know, you gotta pack that in real tight. Pressure, else it won't work. Rocks'll help ya out. There's a piece of oilcloth under my bedroll."

"Obliged," Matthew muttered.

By the end of the week he realized there was nearly enough gunpowder to fill the peach can. He waited until he drew guard duty for the third watch.

Early that evening he wrote three words on the small stone: MOVE AWAY WATCH. At sunset he circled the wall and threw the rock.

Alex came out of his hut, found the rock, and slowly limped back.

Matthew chewed his lip. "Lord," he murmured, "give him strength."

During the second watch, Matthew shouldered his rifle and stuffed his pockets with bits of hardtack he had saved over the past week. Carefully he concealed the heavy can inside his coat and headed for the point nearest Alex's hut.

With his ears straining to hear the crunch of the picket's feet, he hid the can in the bushes and began to dig out the loose soil at the base of the wall. Several times he retreated hastily into the woods. He took the kerosene-soaked string out of Cody's oilcloth and inserted it deep into the gunpowder.

Finally he settled the can in the hole, tightly packing in loose soil and rocks. He left one small opening for the fuse. Carefully he strung the fuse he had constructed from the kerosene-soaked string, dabbed on bacon grease at the place it entered the can, and placed rocks to support the end of the fuse.

Then he strolled back to his tent and waited for the sentry's call.

The night was calm with scattered clouds. Grinning with satisfaction, Matthew took a deep breath and lifted his musket. He had been at his post for nearly an hour when he slipped down to inspect his handiwork. Carefully he felt around the contraption. It was just as he had left it. Visualizing the touch of the match and the explosion, cold sweat poured off his face and down his back. He rubbed his sleeve over his face. Finally, knowing he could no longer delay, he got to his feet. *Lord, this is it, please help!*

Grasping his musket firmly in his left hand, he steadied his other, struck the match, and held it to the fuse. For a moment it smoked, then flamed to life. He backed away, turned, and ran through the trees.

Panting, straining to hear over the pounding of his heart, he waited. It seemed forever. Deciding the fuse had gone out, he got to his feet to check it. As he hesitated, the gunpowder exploded. Matthew held his breath. Time seemed to stand still. There was a brief flash of fire just before the wall separated and crumbled, quenching the flame. A figure came flying through the opening. Matthew ran toward the wall. There were others coming. Spotting Alex, he fell in beside him.

"Keep going, man, keep going," Matthew panted when Alex seemed to slow. They were into the trees now and the ground sloped away in gentle swells. Matthew heard the sharp rasping breath beside him and cut his speed. "Take it easy, Alex; we've got a long way to go."

———

The sky overhead was bright with dawn when they finally collapsed under the trees. Alex lay flat, his arms outstretched and his chest heaving. Matthew watched for a moment, then followed the sound of water to a brook splashing down hill. He drank and returned to Alex. "There's water down aways, but I've got no way to carry it."

Alex sat up, nodded, and shoved himself to his feet. After they drank, Alex washed his face. "You can't imagine—clean water for bathing," he murmured.

He dropped flat again and Matthew warned, "Better not, Alex. It's a good way to come down with lung problems after being this hot and tired. I have some hardtack. Let's eat and move on."

Throughout the day they walked, rested, and walked again. Alex's color began to improve. At one of their intervals of rest, he turned to Matthew. "Tell me, what's happened?"

Matthew stared at him for a moment, then the facts began to sink in. "Happened?" he echoed. "Alex, we had word that you were dead over a year ago."

Alex's head jerked. "Dead? How could such a mistake happen?"

"Your name was posted as killed in action. At first Olivia wouldn't believe it, but when they get a guy's name and hometown right, you can't suspect it's a mistake."

Alex's head sagged against his chest. "My poor darling Olivia." He lifted his head. "The baby?"

"She lost it. Born too early."

"Because of me?" Matthew nodded. "How is she taking all this now?"

"Better. Finally got herself under control. She's in Washington, working as a nurse at an army hospital."

Alex sat up. "Tell me, what's the idea of all this?" He gestured toward Matthew's uniform.

"Crystal and I were in Natchez, going to visit my parents. I ran into a fellow who knew me when I was in the Confederate Army."

"Come on, Matt. You?"

"That happened in sixty-one." His grin twisted. "Might say the Confederacy makes enlistment a difficult proposition to turn down. At least it is when the recruiter is passionately Southern and carries a gun.

"I took the first opportunity to separate myself from the army. That happened in New Mexico Territory. But before it happened, unfortunately for me, I rubbed elbows with a fellow also from the Natchez area. We'd grown up together. Crystal and I met him again just after reaching Natchez, and it seemed he was anxious to turn me in as a deserter."

"Where is Crystal?"

Matthew sighed. "I hope she's gone back to Pennsylvania." He glanced at Alex. "Strange how I felt the Lord was warning me to be careful. I gave her all the money I had and told her to head for home if something happened."

Alex straightened, coughed, and said, "It might be a good idea to get ourselves out of this area as soon as possible. Have any ideas?"

He nodded. "At Andersonville I heard around the campfire that the Federal Army holds Chattanooga, Tennessee. If we can get to Atlanta safely, it might be possible to make contact with Grant's men. If we're really lucky, maybe we can take the train from Atlanta into Chattanooga."

"I hope you have funds."

"I have a little hardtack. We're going to have to find something to eat and then start walking."

"Which army do we represent? You have a Confederate uniform on and I have Yankee blues."

Matthew chuckled. "Under the circumstances, I think we should take turns holding each other captive. There's no other way to explain the situation."

A short time later, Matthew said, "Looks like I have the first turn." They were out of the forest. The countryside was dotted with farms. "Let's head for the nearest place. We should reach it about sundown. If it looks harmless enough, let's ask to sleep in the barn."

The wide-eyed woman who answered the door looked from Alex to Matthew holding the musket. "I'd be glad to feed you, sir, but it isn't much. Have only potatoes and cornbread."

"Ma'am, that sounds wonderful. I can't pay; don't even have script with me, but I'll write you a note."

"No." Hesitantly she opened the door and allowed them to enter.

An elbow-high lad standing behind her said, "Soldier, aren't you afraid of that Yank getting loose from you? I could find a piece of rope to tie his hands."

"I don't reckon he's too anxious to get away from me," Matthew drawled. "Matter of fact, I'm of a mind to think he considers me his meal ticket. Bet your mama wouldn't have let a Yank into the house."

After they shared a potato and some cornbread, Alex and Matthew headed for the barn. Matthew patted the cow's head. "Nice bossy. You just keep giving good milk like that for these folks." He eyed the swaybacked mule and shook his head. "Alex, on both sides of the line, folks are going to be suffering for years to come."

At daylight they headed out of the barn. Their benefactor met them with two eggs in her hand. "I kin give you breakfast."

Matthew shook his head, and Alex said, "Ma'am, we appreciate it, but you feed those eggs to your young'un. A couple more eggs in him, and he'll be pushing that plow come spring. Thank you again for your kindness. God bless you."

As they strode down the road, Matthew looked up at Alex. "Did you ever think you'd be begging food from such as these?"

"No, and it goes against the grain. Matt, it's a humbling experience, this war. We're all equal now; there's not the same aristocracy in the South. I wonder if these people will treat us more kindly than we have treated them in the past?"

Matthew glanced at Alex. "If the line no longer exists, how will we know one from the other? It might be asked instead, 'Who will take the initiative to be Christlike regardless of the circumstances?' "

Alex stared curiously at Matthew. "I think you've learned much about the Lord in these past two years."

Matthew dropped his head, smiling gently at the memory. "There are interesting people in Colorado Territory. One who helped me a great deal is Amelia Randolph."

Alex stopped in the middle of the trail. "Matthew, that's unbelievable."

"I won't start talking about her now, but one of these days, when we're all together—Sadie, Amos, Olivia—then Crystal and I will tell you all about it. Unbelievable? Alex, I've discovered that God seems to enjoy the toughest of the unbelievable. Don't we shortchange Him by not giving Him a chance to work in the worst of situations?"

"Unbelief," Alex said as he nodded.

———

It had taken over a week to walk the hundred miles to Atlanta. Looking down over the city, Alex said, "They don't appear to be concerned with the happenings in Tennessee."

"Maybe the Union victories have been reversed," Matthew muttered. "I suppose the easiest way to find out is by going to the train depot."

"Wait," Alex said. "Aren't they going to question your taking a Federal soldier into Tennessee? Matthew, I don't think it's worth the risk. If we start walking toward Tennessee, we'll know soon enough."

"I suppose you're right. The fewer questions we raise, the longer we both will live. Come on, Yank, let's stretch it."

Another week passed. The easy walking was behind them, and the Blue Ridge Mountains lay before them. As they paused to rest, Matthew surveyed Alex and said, "You're doing fine. When we started this,

I wondered if you'd make it. With food and clean water, distance between you and disease, you're starting to get a decent color. When I first saw you, I wouldn't have recognized you without that earring."

"The congestion in my chest is clearing, Matt." Alex added abruptly, "I think it's time for me to start carrying the musket."

"What makes you think so?"

"That canyon ahead of us. Doesn't it look like an encampment? If so, it's either our troops or Rebel."

"Maybe we'd better look for a house and ask a few questions," Matthew said. Alex nodded and got to his feet.

A barking dog announced them. As they approached the house a woman came outside. She looked at the gun in Matthew's hand and said, "You heading into the mountains? The Yanks are over in the gap."

"Thanks for warning me," Matthew said. "Is there any way to avoid their camp?"

"Stay south, but keep away from the train tracks. They're guarding them right sharp." She turned worried eyes their direction. "It can't be long before they push in on us. I figure the lot of us stand to lose everything."

As they walked down the road, Matthew said, "Well, we know it's Union and that they've got control of the tracks."

They stopped on the next ridge and Alex said, "Sure looks like the Stars and Stripes to me. Let's go. But give me that musket first."

CHAPTER 45

Sadie came into the kitchen. She looked from Beth to the pile of dirty dishes. Beth's hands were submerged in the dishpan, but her thoughts seemed miles away. "Would thou like me to help?" she said gently.

"Oh, please! Sadie, I've wanted to talk to you for so long, and now it's—terrible." Sadie watched the tears roll down Beth's cheeks.

"I had in mind to help with the dishes, but thou dost seem troubled. Sit down here at the table; I'll make us some tea."

Beth shook her head. "I don't want tea. Sadie, since I've come back it's getting worse, and I simply can't endure it any longer."

Sadie sat down at the table. "If it is Mike, I won't stand in the way. I don't want to interfere—"

"It's me." Beth's head nearly touched the table. "I've been a fake and a cheat. I must have your forgiveness and help."

"Child!" She lifted Beth's chin and said, "No matter what, thou art loved and wanted here. There's nothing thou needs to agonize over in regards to me."

Beth flung herself at Sadie's knee. "There is. Sadie, I'm not a rich girl. I'm from the scum of the earth. I stole all those pretty clothes, and the jewelry, too. I am a liar and a fraud." She burrowed her face into Sadie's lap.

"Why art thou telling me these things?"

"Because—" Beth paused and looked up, brushing at the tears. "It's God. Olivia helped me see that I need God." For a moment there was a strange, wondering expression on her face. "I always thought I was a Christian. Oh, Sadie, I don't know how to say this, but I prayed for forgiveness. Olivia said that was the thing that made the difference, asking and being willing to obey God."

She trembled against Sadie's knee. "Olivia said God would forgive me because of Jesus dying for my sins. Atonement. Is that right? Am I really a child of God now?" She paused, sobbing. "It's strange; being close to Him has made me see how terrible I am, and I thought I was doing just fine." Again she pressed her face against Sadie's knees. "I've been so miserable. I thought I would feel better if I could tell you I'm sorry for being such a terrible person."

Sadie hugged her. "Oh, Beth, thou art a child of God! How I rejoice! Certainly thou art forgiven by me, but I never thought thee other than just a high-spirited girl. A child of God, oh, that is wonderful!" She hugged her again and said, "Shall we tell the others?"

Beth pulled back and looked at Sadie. Slowly she said, "Do you mind waiting? I feel I must say these things to Mike, and right now I don't have the courage to do it."

"Yes, we will wait." Sadie hesitated and gently said, "But thou must not delay; the Enemy will torment thee over it."

———

The aroma of breakfast sausage and eggs still hung in the air. Mike sniffed as he came into the keeping room. He looked at the women wound in shawls. "You're all leaving?"

"We're going into town," Crystal answered. "We have over a hundred bundles to pack for shipping. Want to come along? Amos will be helping."

"Well, yes," Mike said. "I'd be glad to help out, but I had this figured as an all-ladies group."

Crystal smiled at him. "You won't feel out of place. Some of the village youths are helping, too."

Sadie removed her shawl. "But thou art not going without some breakfast first. Beth, tell Amos to come in for another cup of coffee."

"It's late. Guess I deserve to go hungry," Mike said. "Didn't sleep too well last night."

"That's reason enough for us to feed thee." Sadie patted his shoulder and he followed her into the kitchen.

Getting coffee for himself, he sat down at Sadie's table. She cracked eggs into the sizzling fat and asked, "Thy leg is bothering thee?"

"Oh, not much. I suppose I'm getting restless. I might go into Pittsburgh and talk to the doctor about one of those new-fangled artificial legs. I need to get on with life."

She looked at him. "Where did thee hear about such?"

"Beth told me. Heard about them at the hospital in Washington."

Sadie carried the eggs and sausage to the table. As she continued to hold the plate, Mike looked up and saw the worried frown on her face.

"Do I get my eggs hot or cold?" he teased.

"Mike, I worry about thee."

"I'm doing fine. In another month I'll take your worry back to the navy." He glanced up as Amos and Beth came into the kitchen. "Sadie, did I take all the coffee?"

"Thou didst not. Amos, would thou like a tart to keep thee until dinner? Beth," she turned to the girl standing in the doorway, "how about thee?"

"What? Oh, coffee, I suppose." She carried her mug to the table and sat down. "Mike, you're going back to the boats?"

"What else should a river man do?"

"I thought perhaps you'd stay at home now."

"Beth, there's a war. There's also a shortage of pilots. I'm healthy again; I don't have much excuse for hanging around here."

Crystal poured coffee and came to the table. "You make me ashamed, Mike. I could be doing something besides baking cookies and packing boxes."

"Thou aren't much of a knitter," Sadie laughed, shaking her head. "Art thou thinking of doing what Olivia is doing?"

"I don't like the idea, but certainly there's a need."

"Well, thou had better keep contact with us; Matthew will want to know where thou art." Crystal smiled as Sadie spoke, and patted her hand.

"It's getting late," Beth said. "Have you had enough, Mike?" She watched Sadie and Crystal take up their shawls and walk down the hall.

"I suppose so; you've just taken my plate." He grinned up at her. She blushed. He chuckled as he stood. "Beth, I don't think you've changed much after all."

"Flighty, huh?" Her skirt swished as she turned to the stove. Quickly she washed the plate and mugs.

He came to her side and picked up the towel. Studying the scarlet spots on her cheeks he asked, "How's Roald doing?"

"I wouldn't know," she snapped irritably. "I'm not writing to him. You might inquire around. I think the Phillips girl may be in contact with him."

"Are you disappointed?"

"Mike, you are being—nosy." He grinned as she hurried out of the kitchen. *So they aren't writing to each other.*

Sadie called, "Coming, Mike?"

Mike followed Sadie. Beth slammed the door behind herself. "What's wrong with Beth?"

"Why nothing, Mike. Art thou being too sensitive?"

He caught her eyes. "Maybe not sensitive enough, huh?" He paused. "Did Roald and Beth have a falling out?"

Sadie tilted her head; her eyes were twinkling. "Ask thy questions of the right person."

————

That evening when they returned from the meeting house, Mike recalled Sadie's statement. He watched Beth moving about the kitchen and keeping room. She swept the floor, spread a fresh tablecloth, and began carrying dishes to the table. He measured his statement against his earlier picture of Beth. A year ago Beth couldn't find a task without being told. He recalled the picture of that Beth, with her pretty pouting lips and roguish air, she teased with her eyes and tossed her beautiful hair. *A princess without a kingdom. And I loved her then.* Painfully aware of his loss, he heaved himself to his feet and crossed the room.

"I'll help you."

She looked surprised. "Mike, I'm going to set the table. Sadie has supper nearly ready. Why don't you rest your leg?"

"Beth, you keep fussing about my leg. I realize I'm just a cripple now, but even the cripples are fighting in this war. I don't need rest; I'm working on getting myself back in condition," he snapped. "I want to be out of here as soon as I get one of those new contraptions you talked about."

Slowly she put the stack of plates on the table. He saw the hurt in her eyes and stood numb with regret. She lifted her chin and said, her voice icy cold, "Mike, you're not the first man to lose a leg. Neither are you the first one I've babied along when he's been overdoing it. It is nothing personal."

"I'm not doing too much." He turned away.

"Mike, let's at least be friends. I do care what happens to you."

"Because a cripple needs pity? Forget the nursing, Beth. If I wanted pity, I'd have stayed in the hospital for another month."

She rattled the plates. Stiffly she said, "Since I'm familiar with the situation, would you like me to go with you to see about the leg?"

"No." He gentled his voice and added, "It isn't necessary. I've contacted the doctor, and I'll leave next week. Thank you." She looked up, and he added, "I appreciate your helping me find a better arrangement than this peg."

In the three weeks Mike was gone the weather changed. The February snows didn't linger as long, and the sunny days brought warmth to the Pennsylvania countryside.

"Sadie, I'm starting to feel very guilty about not being in Washington," Beth said. "I've been with Olivia, and I know how much they could use my services. I ought to be going back just as soon as Mike returns and I know he's okay."

Crystal had been listening to their conversation. "Why should that delay you?" she asked. "Sadie will be here if Mike needs help." Without waiting for an answer, Crystal said, "Beth, I want to go with you. This waiting to hear from Matthew is terrible. If I'm of use somewhere in this war, I think I'll be more content with waiting."

"Then I suppose we should leave as soon as possible," Beth said.

That evening Mike returned. Beth heard the hack and went to the parlor window. She watched Mike walk up the lane with his bag slung over his shoulder. His stride seemed stronger, more certain. She firmly stifled her desire to rush to him. Slowly she went to open the door.

"Hello, Mike; welcome back."

He hesitated while she tilted her chin at him. "I—it works fine, Beth," he said awkwardly.

"That's wonderful. I'll tell Sadie you're here." She went to the keeping room.

Supper was late that evening. As they sat around the table with the aroma of Sadie's good pot roast and vegetables competing with the fragrance of fresh, warm bread, Amos addressed Mike. "Did Beth tell you that she and Crystal are going to Washington to nurse at the hospital there?"

Even by lamplight Beth could see the questions in Mike's eyes. *It's tonight or never. I must no longer delay talking to him.* She looked at him. "We're leaving tomorrow afternoon."

Soon after the kitchen had been tidied, Crystal excused herself. "I have packing to do. With the prospect of at least two days on the train, I need to get extra sleep. Good night, all." She patted Mike's shoulder as she left the room. "Mike, you're doing just fine."

Amos said, "I'm coming down with a cold or something. I'm for bed, too."

Sadie headed for the kitchen. "I'm going to start my bread tonight.

Need to take some to meeting tomorrow."

From the doorway Beth addressed the back of Mike's head. "Do you mind coming into the parlor, Mike? I must say something to you."

He followed her, stirred up the parlor fire, and sat down in the rocking chair across from her. He waited.

She stared at her hands. *There's no easy way,* she thought as she began. "Mike, I need to ask your forgiveness. For many things. I'm ashamed of the way I handled that—last day."

"Beth," he broke in roughly, "it's my fault it went badly. I realized later I'd bungled it all and left you with a terrible impression. I must—"

"No, no, Mike. That isn't what I want to talk about. Please, let me say it."

He settled back in his chair. "Go to it."

She gulped and tried unsuccessfully to meet his eyes. "Do you remember that day you picked me up—all frills, toting my huge valise? Mike, from that moment I've lived a terrible life of lies, before you and everyone else. I must beg your forgiveness. I've been nothing I represented myself to be. I'm a cheat: a thief. I wasn't a rich girl driven out by a terrible father. I ran away. I ran from all I'd ever known."

Her voice dulled as she continued, "I'm from a dirt-poor, but honest, family. Mother died young, and Father did remarry. I suppose I didn't get the attention I needed, but it was more than that. They were hard pressed to keep me fed."

He started to speak, and she lifted her hand. "Mike, don't. I stole my clothes, money, jewelry—even the valise I used to carry it all. A woman named Louisa, the daughter of the man who owned our farm, befriended me. We lived up in the hills and didn't have anything, not even a schoolteacher most of the time. Louisa taught me to read and act like a lady. In the end," Beth gulped, "I took everything of hers I had wanted for so long.

"That's when you came along," she continued. "I was toting off her belongings when I saw the sheriff at the train depot and ran for the river.

"For a time you nearly made me forget my plans. But I wanted the big things—going to Washington, finding a rich man, learning to live like a princess.

"Then something happened." She caught her breath. "I nearly came to disaster. Mike, I was frightened into seeing what I was doing, as if God was standing there, just looking at me. I realized how horrible I had been. Mike, please, please forgive me for being deceitful. Everything we had was built on a lie, and there's nothing left except to ask you to forgive me."

He lifted his head and looked at her. *Everything built on a lie. Nothing left.* "Well, certainly I forgive you, Beth. I didn't realize how little we knew each other." Getting to his feet he said, "Even about God." His grin twisted. "Sorry if I act like the wind's been knocked out of me. All this time I'd thought you knew God like I did. It's more like— instead of pulling us together, God is pushing us apart."

He turned to look down into the fire. Resting his arm against the mantle, he struggled through the words she had said. At last he murmured, "Beth, I forgive you; certainly I won't hold the past against you."

He heard her step and turned as she dashed up the stairs.

In her room, Beth leaned against the door. She repeated Mike's words. "So, God is pushing us apart. Very well, my dear Mike. I'll accept that as God's answer to all my questions, too."

She contemplated the future stretching on without Mike. Blinking at the tears brimming over, she whispered, "Olivia is living without Alex. Hard as it seems, I guess God wants me to live without Mike."

CHAPTER 46

Once again Alex looked at the Stars and Stripes and the line of blue uniforms. "Colonel Brady, if there's anything that makes a fellow appreciate army life and hardtack, it's being in prison on the other side."

He answered Brady's question. "I was with the Army of the Potomac, under General Hooker. We were positioned just north of the Rappahannock. Just after the Chancellorsville battle last May, I was captured by the Confederates while on guard duty."

Colonel Brady said, "Duncan, you've been in prison twice and were at the battle of Milliken's Bend? That won't be hard to check. Thomas, your story is strange, but being with Grant at Vicksburg gets you a clean record, as soon as we check it out. I'll telegraph Washington tonight.

"We have supply wagons going in to Chattanooga tomorrow. I'll write a pass for you to travel by train to Louisville and then take a steamer to Wheeling. From there you can travel by train to Washington. Without a doubt, both of you rate a furlough. I suppose your wives will be able to put up with you for a couple of weeks." He got to his feet. "Thomas, let's find a decent uniform for you. My men might use you for target practice before we had a chance to explain."

As they left Colonel Brady's tent, a sergeant fell in step with them. "Come over to that tent; we'll get Thomas a uniform and issue a tent and blankets. Also your rations." He paused and gave Alex a quick glance. "You don't look too much in the best of health. Better take it easy with the grub for a day or so. Could be hard on your innards.

"We know all about that," he added. "Last October the Confederates cut off General Rosecrans' supply route. Plenty was coming our way, but the Rebs were beating us to it. Our horses were starving to death and we nearly didn't make it. But it ended up fine; President Lincoln shuffled things about, sent in troops and supplies."

"Matthew filled me in on the battles at Vicksburg and Gettysburg. Looks like the Federal forces are doing well," Alex said. "I hear Meade replaced General Hooker. What's the Army of the Potomac doing now?"

"Not much. Kinda been stirring around, just keeping the fires lit under the South."

When Alex and Matthew reached Chattanooga late the following day, General Brady's confirmation was there, and they received orders to report to headquarters in Washington upon their arrival.

Alex read General Brady's paper over again and rubbed his hand across his eyes. "Matt, this is nearly as nice as going to heaven."

"Shall we ask them to notify Olivia?"

Alex hesitated. "It sounds like the kind thing to do. But, after all this time, I've a feeling it will be easier on her if we just walk in."

Alex nearly regretted his decision when they reached Washington. After they got out of the hack, Alex and Matthew stood in the street and looked up at the long, stark building. "So this is a soldier's hospital now," Alex murmured. "Washington's changed. Has a drawn look to it, like I felt after leaving Andersonville. Starved."

"Well, let's go in," Matthew prodded him. "She should be working right now."

Alex saw her as they walked through the doors. Her dark hair was coiled close to her head and she wore a white apron, but the curve of her face was very familiar. Blinking tears out of his eyes, he watched the tilt of her head, the graceful gesture of her hand as she bent over a cot. When she started down the corridor of beds, he stepped past Matthew and called, "Olivia!"

She looked up, pressed her trembling hand against the brooch on her collar, then ran to him.

As he reached her, she began to smile through the tears. "Olivia, my dear!" With one quick look, he caught her close.

From the beds around the room, their audience gasped and began to cheer.

Olivia touched his face, his shoulders. Kissing away the tears, he held her close. *Father, it wasn't worse for me, was it?*

"Alex, tell me, am I dreaming again?" She leaned back to look at him, and he saw her wince.

"It's real, and everything's going to be just fine."

They heard a door bang and saw Crystal running. "Matthew! Oh, Matthew!"

Matthew met her halfway. "Crystal! I'd no idea you were here too!"

The door opened again. A concerted exclamation rose from the beds. "Teacher's here. You're in trouble!"

Olivia turned, "Mrs. Thorner, I—"

The woman came forward, smiling as she held out her hand. Trying to be prim, she said, "Since you don't usually behave this way, I believe you must know this man."

Alex heard the thread of tension in Olivia's voice as she said, "I can't quite believe it, but this is my husband! I thought—" She turned to touch Alex, to stare into his face.

Gently Mrs. Thorner said, "And since Crystal seems disinclined to let go of this man, he must be your brother. Run along, youngsters. I suppose the army was generous enough to give you furlough?"

"Three weeks," Alex and Matthew chorused.

Feeling slightly silly, but unable to keep the grin off his face, Alex stroked Olivia's hand and said, "If the army doesn't change its mind and ship us out right away, we'll send them back in three weeks."

Mrs. Thorner was still smiling. "I understand. We have enough standby nurses to handle an emergency. This is an emergency."

Again the audience cheered.

Alex followed Olivia upstairs. He held her, wiped her tears, and touched her face. "Olivia, this is my dearest dream! How good God is to bring us together again."

"Oh, Alex, I'm so ashamed."

He studied her face, "What do you mean?"

"The dream—I kept having it, seeing us together, but I didn't dare hope. Alex, surely God was trying to keep me from being—this broken. Oh, Alex, please don't say another word."

"You are exhausted," he breathed. "You'll need this rest as much as I. And now—" He held her away to smile into her eyes. "We're going to our hotel to try to forget for at least three weeks."

She winced and wrapped her arms around him. "Please don't mention leaving again."

"I'll try. Now, let's get your things packed." He removed her apron and wrapped her in the cloak. "You're very thin," he murmured.

"I must leave a note for Beth. She'd never understand my leaving without telling her."

When they reached their hotel room, Alex closed the door behind the old man who had carried their bags. He looked at Olivia and smiled. "It seems a hundred years ago that we stayed in this very room. My dear, we must make up for the terrible days we've endured."

Her face was rigid as she asked, "Matthew told you all about it?" When he nodded, she replied, "I knew nothing about you."

"Matthew told me about—everything, losing the baby." He held her hands against his face as he carefully added. "I sent letters to Pennsylvania, and I'd been distressed because of not hearing from you, but if I'd guessed the reason behind it, I would have come immediately."

"In wartime? But never mind, my dear, you are here now, and only that is important."

She leaned against him, touched his earring, and ran her fingers over his face and shoulders. "You're thin too, and you don't look well. Alex, you must go to bed now and rest. I shall order something for you to eat."

He tugged at her hand. "Stay; I want to talk some more. Olivia, since Matthew told me all that happened—about my name getting on the list—I've wondered how such a mistake could be made. A terrible thought has come to me.

"During the time just before the Fredericksburg campaign, I became pretty good friends with a fellow. We exchanged names and hometowns, intending to get together after the war. I'm wondering if something has happened to him. Since he possibly carried my name on him, that could explain—"

Olivia winced. "Oh, that poor woman." She studied Alex's eyes and shuddered. Leaning against his shoulder she whispered, "Alex, I can't begin to tell you of the horror, but now I see it has been this way for you, too. My dear, for you it was a different kind, wasn't it? I see it has sunk deeply into you. I want to pull you back to me, to make you the wonderful, joyful friend and lover you were before."

He touched the lines on her face before he took her hand, kissed the palm, and pressed it against his face. "If anyone can do a miracle in my life, it will be you," he murmured. "I suppose we'll need to do that for each other. Now come rest with me and tell me about it all."

During the night Olivia awakened. With her heart pounding, she sat upright and groped. Touching his warm body, she began to cry. He pulled her down into his arms and cuddled her. "It's just that I believed, and then I didn't," she tried to explain. "I thought it was all a dream. Oh, Alex, at the moment all of this is too much."

Holding her close, he murmured, "Then you know how it has been for me."

She was nearly asleep when he stirred and said, "Olivia, we'll likely be separated again."

Moving her head against his arm, she whispered, "Not to love would spare the pain, but I made the decision to follow love a long time ago. Alex, I didn't dream it would hurt like this. But in those dark days when both you and the baby were gone, I found myself thinking back to the good times. When I knew how rich my life had been because of you, I started to recover from the sickness of it all. Also I realized that in some form I must continue to love. Even with the pain it will bring, there must be love in my life. It's as if there is a life-spring inside that fuels love, and somehow love doesn't die—even after the worst of it all."

Again she turned to him. "Love seems to be worth everything, even pain."

"That is so," Alex whispered. "Olivia, Matthew risked his life to save mine. It's a miracle that we're here. But beyond all miracles is God's will. Is there anything that can escape the final reckoning? His will must be done. If we fight against His will and are bloodied, ruined, how can we blame God?"

———

The next afternoon Olivia entered their hotel room, stopping just inside the door. Alex was sprawled on the bed, surrounded by newspapers.

He looked up with a grin. "I'm not asleep."

"I know. I just can't fill my eyes with enough of you." She placed her parcel on the table and came to kiss him. "What is it?" she whispered. "You look troubled."

"I was thinking about us. Olivia, we'll have such a brief time together, and it bothers me to leave you here, working yourself like this."

Slowly she said, "After all you've been through, must you go back to more fighting? You've been in prison; you have a wound which still doesn't seem healed. Must you return to battle?"

"I'm still in the army. The war isn't won. Grant still expresses his determination to finish things up this summer, while the whole North seems doubtful, ready to give up." Impulsively he said, "Olivia, it's still possible I'll die. Have you dealt with that?"

"Alex! How is it possible to be reconciled to something that shouldn't happen? My dear husband, I can scarcely stand to be out of your sight! Just now, when I returned from the shop, my hand trembled until I could hardly get the key in the lock. I'm still trying to comprehend your being here when I thought you were dead. Now you want me to think of what your leaving will mean?"

Alex sat beside her. "I've had plenty of time to think. I guess life boils down to one word. *Commitment.* We measure a man by his commitment. In the army, a man's honor depends on him keeping his word. Strange, I hadn't thought of it this way before, but there's not many of us honest fellows who'd go over the hill, even in order to gain life rather than death. We may be tempted, but it's honor above life.

"When I said commitment, I thought of God. Now I wonder if we're committed enough to God's purposes that we're willing to die for them."

Slowly Olivia said, "Alex, are you saying we put honor of country above honoring God's will?"

"Why else do we have to fight to make our fellow man free, when God ordains freedom for all men?"

Thoughtfully she added, "And the responsibility for my fellow man's welfare rests heavily on my shoulders. Alex, you're forcing me to recognize something very painful. This is my commitment just as much as yours.

"You cannot go over the hill when you are tired of war. I cannot go over the hill when I am tired of my commitment to God." She took a shaky breath. "Alex, I won't back down in my commitment to Him. Neither will I cling to you—go when you must go. There's only one thing I ask. Please, I want your child."

"Even that, Olivia, is asking for something only God can give. In God's time, remember?"

"And if God doesn't have a time?" He pulled her close and wiped the tears from her eyes.

CHAPTER 47

Mike had just taken his gunboat out of the Cairo harbor when Lieutenant Parker came into the pilothouse. "Head for Paducah. We want to check out Fort Anderson. Just had contact with Bradford from Fort Pillow. Reconnaissance indicates Confederate forces from General Forrest's guerrilla band are moving around the Mississippi states. It worries me. Forrest appears aware that only token forces hold the forts down the Mississippi. Guess everyone knows General Grant is gearing up for the campaign in the East."

Mike nodded. "It's kinda lonesome with him gone and General Sherman stuck on the far edge of Tennessee. I suppose he's still there."

"I believe so," Parker said. "Haven't heard news from Chattanooga for some time. Sherman's about taken out all the rail lines across Tennessee, as well as the lines north of Memphis. He may have ripped up the tracks going into Atlanta by now."

He went to the window and picked up the field glasses. "We're to patrol these forts. Haven't enough gunboats on the river to stay in any one location very long."

Turning to Mike, he said, "How you doing on that leg?"

"Still a little sore. But it's easier to get around now that I have this fancy peg with a foot on the end."

Parker glanced out the window. "I have a feeling things are going to be rough up and down the river this spring and summer. The whole war is changing character. I've a hunch the South is getting desperate."

"How so?"

"Guerilla activity has stepped up. That tells me Grant's activities in the East have the Confederates concerned."

"Why's that, sir?"

"Lack of food—not only for the people but for the army. The Confederate Army relied on Tennessee for pork. With the tracks torn up and Sherman plugging the roads, they're suffering for supplies."

"I heard Sherman's hit Jackson, Mississippi again, for the third time."

"That's so. I suppose you've also learned that he's ruined it this time. One of the fellows told me Sherman sacked the city. They're calling the place *Chimneyville*. All the furniture—even baby beds—clothing, and books were stacked and burned in the streets. Sherman's men lined the street to control the people while their homes and belongings were torched. It's a shame."

"Makes a person sick," Mike muttered. "War is ugly, but I think it's getting worse all the time."

"I just hope General Brayman has enough men to hold all these places down the Mississippi."

"What's his force?"

"Not even twenty-four hundred men. Three fourths of them are Negro, which makes me uneasy." He shot a quick glance at Mike. "Not because they aren't good fighters, but because of the way the South has handled Negro prisoners."

"He doesn't have many men there."

"General Hulbut has furloughed his veteran soldiers by order of the War Department. Mighty thoughtful move, but the general has let us know he can't send us a man from Memphis. He has a skeleton crew. Meanwhile, General Brayman is keeping busy shuffling his men from one hot spot to another, trying to pin Forrest down."

"Paducah coming up, sir."

"Let's take it in. I see there's another one of our gunboats in port. That surprises me." Abruptly Parker lifted his glasses. "Looks like there might be a problem," he said. "Let's keep our distance until we see what's going on."

Mike hit the gong twice.

"There's an officer on deck, can you hear him?"

"Yes," Mike said slowly. "He's calling for the women and children to come down to the boats."

"I'm going below." Parker dashed for the stairs.

Mike moved to the window and watched the crowd of townspeople walking toward the wharf. Mike had just spotted the gray uniforms among the people when the Confederates opened fire. Unable to believe his eyes, he murmured, "It's got to be Forrest."

Herding the people ahead of them, with guns directed toward the two gunboats, the Rebel guerrillas shoved the women around like shields as they blazed their way toward the gunboat. A movement inland caught Mike's attention. A flag of truce was raised at the fort.

While he studied the scene, a bullet shattered the side window and Mike dropped. When he came up he saw the gunboat retreating from the harbor. He jumped to hit the gong and the bell, muttering, "Reverse it!" Rushing to the window he watched. "Parker, why don't you fire?"

One look gave his answer. "People. There's not a shot we can take without hitting some of those people."

A detachment of soldiers, both Negro and white, broke away from the fort and streamed toward the water. The air was filled with the shout, "*No quarter, no quarter!*"

Feeling totally helpless, Mike clenched his fists and watched soldiers being chased down to the river. Again came the volley of musket fire. One after another the soldiers fell into the water as they were shot. Beyond the line of trees, Mike could see flames spreading, mounting high.

Parker came into the pilothouse, his face ashen. "They're holding us off. We dare not fire; they're using the women and children as shields. God help us! This is butchery."

The following day Parker came into the pilothouse. "We've been given permission to land for the purpose of burying the dead and rescuing the wounded. It appears that Forrest has done his evil and run. Take us in."

The sailor who met them stated flatly, "The streets look like a battlefield, only this time the slain are children and women."

On April 12th, Mike took the gunboat into the harbor at Fort Pillow, a small fort sixty-five miles above Memphis. From the harbor Mike could see the fort situated on a bluff overlooking the river.

Bringing the boat in, Mike decided the scene was as peaceful as a medieval castle. He noticed the fall of thick brush down the side of the hill, and the small village tucked in a ravine at the foot of the bluff.

Parker stood beside Mike, holding his glasses on the fort. As they approached the harbor Mike saw him stiffen. Parker ran for the stairs, yelling, "It's Forrest again. Man the guns."

Until nearly mid-afternoon the gunboat fired on the Rebel guerrillas with little effect. Mike watched from the wheel as he stood ready to move the boat into a new position.

At last Parker came to the pilothouse. "Forrest just sent in a flag of truce. We'll have to wait and see what develops."

Mike pointed to the trees. "It might a flag of truce, but it seems to me the Rebs are continuing to push the line to their advantage. Look at them moving up there."

As he spoke, unarmed men leaped over the enclosure and streamed down the hill toward the gunboat. Mike groaned as he watched. "White soldiers and Negroes," he muttered. "They don't stand a chance!"

Helplessly they watched the guerrillas' pursuit. Mike turned away. "They're violating their own flag."

"I've heard Forrest is as slippery as an eel, a hit-and-run raider," Parker groaned. "There's not a thing we can do for them."

"Why aren't the Rebs honoring their own truce!"

Parker rounded on him, "So we should be lawbreakers, too?" His voice gentled. "I'd tempted, but we don't have arms or men to fight."

During the weeks that followed, Mike found himself unable to keep his thoughts away from the scenes of slaughter. The thunder of artillery and cries of agony echoed through his mind. He saw Paducah, its women and children slain in the streets, and defenseless men streaming down the hillside with the raiders gaining ground.

Numb with the memories, he continued to handle the gunboat as Parker ordered them downriver. At Vicksburg, the Stars and Stripes flew above the harbor. Natchez was peaceful. The late spring was pleasant on the river, and finally the horror released its grip and he began to relax.

Parker came in one morning, looked at Mike and grinned, "You're starting to act as if you like life. We should be in Cairo in another two weeks, Mike. Sounds like the whole crew will be given furlough. Think that'll work into your schedule?"

Mike chuckled. "You mean sleeping all night without expecting that gong in my ear? I suppose I can find something to do."

After Parker left the pilothouse, Mike thought of the Coopers and their serene Pennsylvania home . . . and Beth. It was the new Beth who held his attention. *Why is there this constant, unrelenting need to see her?* Just in time he saw a snag in the river and jerked the wheel.

Surrender, Mike. Pray for guidance. The Lord knows the direction your thoughts are going.

"Here I go again, Lord. It's Beth. I need to surrender her again, huh? It's not Your will that—" He stopped and begin to think. Slowly he began to put the clamoring thoughts into words. "Lord, I've been fearful to even think about her. It's like a sore tooth I shy away from. Now I wonder—dare I think You are trying to tell me something more? Have I failed to be open to the possibility of something good? If You want to talk to me about Beth, please don't let me make a mistake."

Mike began to grin and to whistle as he thought about Beth. Finally he chuckled aloud. "Mike, are you getting the message? You asked the Lord to wash Beth right out of your mind, since He didn't want you to marry her. How come the desire is growing?" Hastily he added, "Lord, is it possible I'm starting to go a direction You don't want me to go?"

The grin faded away and Mike lined up the facts. *Beth didn't seem to mind having you around, in fact she wanted to go help you find a wooden leg. Maybe she won't mind if you have a wooden leg.*

"Might be a good idea to talk to Sadie," he muttered.

Mike took the gunboat into Cairo. Shouldering his pack, he signed out on a thirty-day furlough.

As the train wound through Ohio, Mike discovered that the air was sweet with spring. Along the river, the Pennsylvania farm country was fragrant with meadow grass and apple blossoms. The water still gurgled through Amos Cooper's pasture, and Sadie's kitchen was still scented with fresh bread.

Slowly he walked up the steps and stood in the farmhouse doorway. The clock on the parlor mantle struck deep mellow notes and the peace of the whole countryside seemed to slip through the house. He looked at the pine-and-white plaster walls, the hand-braided rugs mellowed into pastels, the old rocking chair, Sadie's knitting lying forgotten on the hearth.

The pain in his chest reminded him it was all a scene from a moment past, a never-to-be-forgotten time, but also a stepping stone into a future that must be shaped—perhaps for a son of his own. The thought gave him courage and he called, "Sadie!"

She came out of the kitchen her arms opened. "Lad, thou art as fine-honed as it's possible to be and still have flesh on thee. Come have some fresh buttermilk and a slice of warm bread."

He sat at the kitchen table and asked, "Are any of the others here?"

"No. I've had a good letter from Olivia since thee hast been gone. Alex is home. He's alive; 'twas but a tragic mix-up. My, we are grateful and happy.

"Alex will be going back into the army soon. Crystal and Matthew are together in Washington."

"And Beth?"

Sadie looked into his eyes and began to smile. "Thou always hast her name on thy lips. Why?"

In that place, surrounded with sunshine, it was easy to say, "Because I love her."

Sadie was still smiling. "Did she tell thee she hath accepted Jesus as Lord? I do believe she is growing up, and will soon become a girl worthy of thee."

He bent over and kissed Sadie's apple cheek. "Worthy of *me*? And thou, my dear lady, hast been kissing the blarney stone!"

For the first time he noticed the lines on her face, the touch of weariness in her smile. "Is Amos here?"

"Yes, we are the same. But life passes on, Mike. We will not be forever." She sighed, "This war is hard on us; we weary ourselves in prayer, but it must be."

He nodded. "Not be forever? Neither shall we, Beth and I." He was silent as he thought back over the weeks just past. He looked at her and knew he couldn't bring that horror into this home.

"War is wearying, isn't it?" she said. "The spirit of us all is heavy with the sadness. But even with broken hearts and missing legs, we must go on. Mike, I do think the Lord expects us to spread beauty instead of ashes. It takes work to do so. Beauty comes from God; it is a gift. But like a beautiful jewel hidden away in a chest, it doth no one good unless it is brought out for all to see." She stood up.

"Take thy bag to thy room. Amos will be here shortly."

Mike spoke carefully. "Sadie, I hope I will not disappoint you, but I think I will stay only one day. I must see Beth."

She smiled. "It is a long trip for just a few days, but I think it will do thee good." She started for the kitchen and turned. "Thee might tell Beth that I mended the dress; she may wish to wear it."

"What dress?

"The wedding dress. She nearly destroyed it, tearing it off after thou left her at the church."

He hung his head. "Sadie, I didn't say those things lightly. It was because of the Lord Jesus that I felt we couldn't marry. I still do not know why He impressed that upon me. And I'm not certain it should be any different now."

"Might it be that the Lord wanted your dear girl to grow up first? She was such a child."

"Is she still?"

"No. She will make thee a lovely wife, Mike Clancy."

CHAPTER 48

Alex awakened with the first light of dawn. Turning, he saw Olivia standing in front of the open window. A breeze lifted her hair and gently pressed her white nightgown against her body.

He went to stand beside her. Wide-eyed wonder filled her face. Tiny wrens lined the window ledge; they chirped a gentle conversation and pecked with sleepy contentment. He smiled, glancing beyond them to the city park, the Potomac, and the hazy stretches of Virginia.

She was watching him now, wonder still in her eyes. Pressing her hands across his shoulders, she touched the red scar on his side, murmuring, "Jesus said not a bird falls apart from the Father's knowledge." He waited, seeing the sparkle of tears on her face.

"I didn't realize how much God had to do in me. Now that the tension is gone, I do trust Him. God really does love us." She lifted her face. "Do you understand that? In this worst of times, is it real to you?"

He nodded. "I'm deeply aware of His love. I see Matthew's capture in Natchez as an example of God's intervention in my life. Olivia, all these things don't just happen. God is there tenderly caring for us. I know He has given us the freedom to choose our way, but I also know if we surrender our choosing to Him, He guides us and helps us make the right choice."

"Alex, I'm going with you, as a camp nurse." He moved uneasily. Quickly she pressed her fingers across his lips. "I've prayed about it. It must be my decision, and I know I can handle it well with God's help. It isn't even a pleading prayer that God will spare you; instead it's another opportunity for me to allow God to work as He wishes. I'll be stronger for having trusted Him in something completely beyond my little human ability.

"Alex, that happened at Gettysburg. God didn't stop us from making that hasty, even foolish trip. But when the battle stopped us, Beth and I had to depend upon God in a way much more significant than we had done before.

"We lived through that horrible time, not just surviving, but doing all the terrible, difficult tasks with quietness and strength. And Alex, we both grew. Beth became a woman. I was tried to my limit, and God was always there."

As he wrapped his arms around her and rested her head against his shoulder, she said, "I had read all those Bible verses about the power of Jesus Christ being in us, but I only marveled and yearned. Now I have proved that He will do this for me. I will continue to allow Him to make me strong."

"Olivia, my precious one, you have become such a source of quiet and strength to me. Yes, God is that for us—power and endurance. We also help each other. I need you. While I live, I can't risk your life. Even nurses aren't safe on the battlefield."

She leaned back to look at him. "Alex, I have learned to live with loss. It was very painful, but it taught me that God will bring me through disaster stronger, not weaker. We don't have control over our lives. That's in God's hands. Why struggle with living or dying, when instead we can put our energies into doing and being?"

He circled her with his arms and turned her to the window. "The day is beautiful. Let's walk through the city and talk about the future. I don't mean tomorrow, but when the war is over. If it is best to be doing and being, then let's plan."

She turned her head to look up at him. "Alex, I've sensed a restlessness in you. It's there when you talk with Matthew, when you read the war news. I sense you're ready to go."

"Yes. I've seen too many men die to be content sitting idle at home."

"I thought that was the case." She took a deep breath. "After breakfast let's find Matthew and Crystal. If you want, we can invite them to go with us."

Matthew and Crystal were in the dining room when they found them. Crystal looked up. "Good morning," she said. "We're going for a walk this morning, want to come?"

"Thank you," Alex said. "We'd mentioned walking too." He looked at Matthew. "Are you catching up on the news? Sounds like Sherman is still lying low in Tennessee."

Matthew nodded, chuckled. "It's to our advantage that Generals Bragg and Johnston seem to be at odds."

"A comfort," Alex muttered. "But right now I wish Sherman would do something. About Bragg, I'd begun to think the Army of the Potomac was the only outfit having leadership troubles.

Matthew nodded soberly. "Doesn't make for high spirited troops when their leaders can't agree on a line of action. I do think Generals Grant and Sherman are strong-minded enough to stick to their plans."

Mike walked down the Washington street reading the signs on the buildings. A woman stopped beside him. "Sailor, are you looking for a particular building?"

"Yes, ma'am, the new Union hospital for soldiers."

"It's that building just across the street." She smiled and hurried down the street.

Mike took a deep breath and muttered, "Well, Lord, here it is. I can't back down now. Please help us to know Your will. Don't let her be willing if you don't want this to happen."

He entered the hall and saw the rows of beds through the windows in the swinging doors.

"Are you looking for someone?"

He turned to face a smiling older woman and asked, "Is Beth Peamble a nurse here?"

"Yes. Come in, she's just finishing her shift." Mike followed. The afternoon sun drew patches of light on the white sheets on the beds. He looked at the men and cringed with the memory of the horror and pain during his time in the hospital.

A woman walked toward him, nearly hidden by a large white apron, her hair was bound away from her face. She recognized him, and he watched the emotion flicker across her face. For a moment he thought he detected a smile, then uncertainty followed by fear. "Mike, what is it?"

"I—nothing; I just wanted to see you."

"Oh. I'll be through here in a half hour. Are you in a hurry?"

He grinned. "Since I've come from Pennsylvania just to see you, I think I'll wait."

She blushed. Turning away she said, "I need to change. There are chairs in the hallway, or you could come back."

He settled down in the entry hall and thumbed through an old newspaper. Beth's face, shy and uncertain, claimed his attention. He moved his shoulders and grinned self-consciously.

When she came downstairs she wore a dark blue dress with a white lace collar. Her hair was loose and curly around her face, a torch against the dark cotton. She held a soft shawl.

He swallowed hard and smiled, then reached for the shawl. "Do you want this around your shoulders?"

"Is it cold?" He couldn't remember. Tucking it around her he reached for the door.

Her eyes were wide, still startled. Watching him she said, "There's a city park just down the street. Lots of trees, and a place to sit and talk."

"Sounds nice." Feeling awkward, careful not to touch her, he followed her. They walked down the street with Beth chattering.

She stopped. "Oh, Alex and Olivia and Crystal and Matthew are still here. Perhaps you'd rather see them."

"Not now. Sadie told me they were here." He took her arm as they crossed the street. She glanced uneasily toward a house opposite the park and he wondered about the sober expression as she led the way into the grove.

"There's a lake down through the trees. Ducks and some swans live there. Poor things; even they look scrawny."

She took a deep breath. "You know, it's a real miracle to see Alex come back." He nodded, and she rushed on. "And Matthew was the one who found him."

"Beth, let's sit over here on this bench. Will the sun be too much for you?"

"No, after being in that place all day, I love the sun." They sat, and she turned to face him. He saw her eyes darken, and she whispered, "Mike, what is it?"

"That I've come to see you?"

"No. I have never seen you like this. Was it terrible, Mike?" Caught off guard, he could only look at her. Her eyes seemed nearly dark lavender.

"I've been reading the newspaper, thinking about you. Mike, they've said there's been merciless guerrilla forces in Tennessee and Mississippi. I wondered about you."

He dropped his head, the pictures flooding his mind. "We ran into the results of their work; it was pretty bad."

"I can see you don't want to talk about it. Mike, why have you come so far to see me?"

"Isn't that what friends are expected to do?"

She shook her head. "Not the kind who fight with you most of the time. Mike, we just don't get along now, I don't think we have— anything in common. When I saw you, I was afraid. All I could think was that something terrible had happened to Sadie or Amos."

"But not that something terrible had happened to me?"

"I can see you are alive and well—at least I thought so. But I think you're terribly troubled."

"I am; you won't be still long enough for me to ask you a question."

Flustered, she suddenly fell silent. "I'm sorry, Mike. What is it?"

"Beth, will you marry me?"

"Now?" her voice trembled.

"Just any time. Now, or ten years from now. I just want to marry you."

"Mike, then why—back then?"

"I knew you'd ask. Beth, I don't know why. All I know is that God burdened me with the feeling that we shouldn't marry then. I supposed he was asking me to give you up forever. Just the past two months I got the feeling that it isn't our marriage He didn't want, it was simply the time we had chosen. After I had my leg shot off, I decided that was a reason. No girl wants to be married to a man with one leg when there are plenty around with two."

"Mike, if you're asking me now, that implies I can't attract a man with two legs. It also implies I'm—" She stopped, and slowly said, "But I am not very level-headed."

"Beth, I don't care what you are. I love you and want to marry you. In fact, I want to marry you right now."

"Mike," she whispered, staring wide-eyed into his face, "I didn't tell you all. I didn't tell you about—"

"Beth, I don't care. Just marry me." There were tears in her eyes. She sniffed and nodded. "Would you let me kiss you, right here?"

She laughed. Wiping her eyes, she lifted her face. "Yes, Mike." There was no teasing in her eyes, no coy games. She loved him, and he knew it.

"Beth, my darling Beth." He kissed her, then kissed her again, holding her close.

Suddenly voices came from the walk. "They are supposed to be looking at the ducks."

"Shall we throw them in the lake?"

Mike and Beth turned. "Alex! Matthew!" Mike stood up and held out his hands.

Olivia smiled down at Beth. "You're blushing!"

Crystal folded her arms and shook her head. "Beth! I want to know how long this has been going on? I thought you couldn't stand to be around that man."

Mike turned. "I found out she likes men with one leg, so I asked her—"

"Asked her to marry you! Oh, Mike, Beth!" Olivia turned to the others. "Quick, let's find someone to marry them right now, before they change their minds again."

"We won't," the reply came from both.

While Beth and Mike looked at each other, Olivia said, "But we don't trust you. Crystal, I think we'd better go plan this wedding now."

Thoughtfully, Beth said, "That might be a good idea." Mike blinked, and she added, "Do you want to risk losing me to someone else?"

———

The following day Crystal looked through Beth's clothes. "Not dark blue. How about this one with the tiny rose blossom print?" She turned. "Beth, you aren't listening."

"I'm afraid to rush into something as serious as marriage."

"Rush? You've known him forever."

"I don't think you're rushing," Olivia said, "and neither will Sadie. Don't you want to be married today?"

"Oh yes!"

"Let's go! The fellows are waiting at the church."

———

The organ music was thin and reedy; one note was flat. Beth clutched the roses Olivia had given her and looked at Mike. He didn't seem sorry.

The thin gray-haired pastor was very sober. He looked from one to the other. "Dearly beloved, we are gathered here before God, for the purpose of uniting this couple in holy matrimony."

Olivia looked at Alex and whispered, "I do." Crystal squeezed Matthew's hand while he looked down at her and smiled. Mike kissed Beth.

As they left the church, Alex said, "And now, Beth and Mike, we've arranged dinner for all of us at the hotel. Also, they are holding a room for a Mr. and Mrs. Mike Clancy."

"Mrs. Mike Clancy," Beth blushed and looked at Mike.

Mike raised a skeptical eyebrow at Alex.

"Honest, no horse play. But come on, I'm hungry."

CHAPTER 49

Alex, we could lose this war; things aren't going well," Olivia watched him. He continued packing his kit without answering. "In addition to the war, President Lincoln is fearful of losing the election. Those men are trying to get him out—Fremont with his campaign, and General McClellan, who's running against him on the Democratic ticket."

Alex nodded. "I've heard McClellan has been accused of holding back his army because of his pro-slavery feelings." He smiled down at her. "The South's interest in the Federal election is interesting for two reasons. First, their avowed reason for war is freedom from the North. Second, if the South expects to win the war, there is no reason they should concern themselves with this election."

She nodded. "But if Lincoln fails to win, we could lose the war and freedom for the slaves."

"That's right." He packed his new Bible. "But to say things aren't going well is to overlook the obvious. The North has been flopping around for three years, needing a strong general. Without a doubt, Grant is the man. We know Sherman will clean out his end of the South—perhaps not in the manner the South would care to have this done."

"What do you mean?"

"*Total war* is Sherman's pet phrase. The North came into this war reluctantly, as if they couldn't believe the South was serious. Given the outcome, both at this minute and at the final battle, I doubt there's a man on either side of the Union who doesn't wish he'd done his best to prevent this war."

Slowly Olivia said, "If we hadn't become involved in the Underground Railroad, some of the bad feelings would have been avoided."

"Freedom for the slaves, for all people, isn't an option; it's an absolute necessity."

"But the South's way of life—Alex, you and I know what a wrenching situation it has been to give up slavery. These people are losing millions of dollars in slave labor. It is worse than burning plantations and fields, factories and stores. To them it is as if their very heart has been pulled out."

"My dear, they'll have to hire laborers at a decent wage and with acceptable living conditions," Alex stated. "Is the South's problem any different than the upheaval these black people suffered when they were torn from their homeland and from their people? In their culture, some of these people were as influential, wealthy, and content with life as our parents and grandparents have been. Can we say there is a difference?"

"You know I agree. Alex, what are we going to do with our lives after this is over?"

"I'm not certain, Olivia. I've prayed for wisdom, mostly because there is one thing catching my attention now. I'm not certain how the Lord will guide. Olivia, when this is over, I'd like to pass my bar exams and use my law education as a means of seeing change in this country. Emancipation is only on paper; it needs to be stamped on the hearts of every American."

She smiled and touched his face. "Oh, Alex, it's just exactly what I would expect of you." Patting his cheek, she said, "Crystal and Matthew want to be part of the educational system. Crystal told me that for years she's been haunted by the illiteracy of these people."

Alex nodded. "But right now we have a war to fight. Have you packed all you'll need?"

"Yes, and I've made arrangements with the Sanitary Commission to nurse in their facilities." She crossed the room to kiss him. Gently tugging his face around, she said, "I'm telling you this now, there may not be opportunity later. Alex, you are more precious to me than anything or anyone. Without you I'm incomplete, but I've lived with loss and if necessary I can do it again. Please, don't worry about me, either about my being hurt or about your—" she caught her breath and finished, "leaving me behind."

"Yes, Madam General," he said tenderly, touching one of the gold blossoms on the brooch. "I have a feeling you'll do just fine. Furthermore, I expect to see you ordering around the Army of the Potomac within two weeks."

Ignoring the twinkle in his eyes, she said, "I'm glad Beth is going to Ohio with Mike. She's surprisingly level-headed in a crisis. The hospital will find a place for her."

"I'm praying you and Crystal will be in the same nursing group," he said tenderly as he pressed her palm to his lips.

Later that day Alex and Matthew were placed in regiments assigned to the Army of the Potomac. Just before they left, Alex squeezed Olivia's hand and said, "This is ironic, but we're heading for the Rappahannock. We'll be encamped nearly in the same spot we were a year ago after the battle of Chancellorsville." He kissed her and said, "I'll see you next week when the supplies and ambulances are sent in."

The following week when Olivia and Crystal boarded the Union supply train going south, Crystal asked, "Why the stack of newspapers?"

"Because Alex asked me to bring them."

"The news will only discourage him. General Grant has sent three of his generals out, and all of them have failed to accomplish his assignment. General Banks botched his Louisiana job; the Rebels are entrenched firmly across the Mississippi. General Butler was so slow that his campaign on the James River became a plum in Beauregard's hand. Shall I go on?"

"No, it sounds worse when *you* say it!" Olivia looked up with a smile. "But there's West Virginia! Crystal, it's been nearly a year since that slice of Virginia became a state. And now she has emancipation written into her constitution."

"I understand Arkansas did the same thing," Crystal murmured, picking up a newspaper.

The following day, medical personnel and supplies were unloaded on the banks of the Rappahannock. They were told the troops had begun their march across the Rapidan River in their first move against General Lee.

The surgeon in charge, Dr. Jason, briefed the group of male and female nurses. "You have fifteen minutes to get your tents and supplies, and be here waiting for the ambulances. We will cross the rivers on pontoon bridges. When the battlesite is abandoned, we'll move in, establish our camp, and treat the wounded."

Crystal began shivering. Glancing apologetically at Olivia, she muttered, "Sorry; give me a day to grow accustomed to this."

During the day a courier came with news for the team positioned north of the Rapidan River. "The battle is taking place in the wilderness. The men are fighting in thick woods, and it appears the woods have been set afire by all the shelling. We'll have to attempt rescue of the wounded before they are burned to death."

Olivia turned to the southeast and saw the heavy columns of smoke. One of the male nurses stopped beside her. "I hear the soldiers have started rescue efforts. Dr. Jason has ordered the women to remain here while we go in." As he turned away he said, "I wonder if he'll keep his promise to Lincoln."

"What promise?"

"Grant told Lincoln that no matter what, there'll be no turning back. They've regrouped, but they're holding their position."

The next morning Grant's army moved, not in retreat across the river as everyone expected, but south. From the tents where Olivia and Crystal dressed wounds, they could hear the men singing as they headed toward Richmond.

"There's no skedaddle here," chortled one of the wounded. He added, "Lady, I was here the last time, and I tell you it feels good to push on. For the first time in a Virginia campaign, the army has stayed on the offensive."

General Grant continued to press the offensive. Day after day the Federal Army pursued the Confederate Army, and just as doggedly the Rebels fought back. Casualties mounted.

At Spotsylvania the Confederates built strong fieldworks, and slowly the Union troops gave way under the continued pressure.

Briefly Olivia saw Alex when he came into camp. His face was coated with black from biting off the ends of cartridges.

"This is a difficult battle," he murmured, taking a mug of coffee from her. She wiped his face with a wet towel as he continued, "We're no longer fighting an organized battle. This has become a clawing, digging fight for survival. I heard that Grant wired Lincoln that his intention is to fight it out on this line, even if it takes all summer."

Olivia said, "One of the men on burial detail said they found a trench with a hundred and fifty dead Confederate soldiers sprawled on top of each other. He said the team just pushed the dirt in upon them."

A week later, Crystal looked around the tents filled with wounded. "And these are the ones who can't be taken to camp. How much longer is this going on?"

"They are talking about moving the hospital tents nearer Petersburg. I don't know when it will happen."

"Just don't talk retreat." A wounded soldier lifted his head, "Ma'am, I ain't seen nothing like it. Last time we were here, we rested before doing battle again. This General Grant keeps nipping at our heels. The men are bloody tired."

"If our heels get nipped," his comrade said, "think what's happening to Lee's. Grant might know something about fighting we don't."

During the following weeks the relentless General Grant kept his men hard on the trail of Lee's army. Alex reported to Olivia, "We move, they move; it's like some elaborate ballroom dance. It's been four weeks now," he recounted, "and we've never lost sight of each other."

The next encounter took place at Cold Harbor. Grant was backed into a corner and forced to retreat. For a few days the men were in camp while Grant sent General Hunter up the Shenandoah to destroy railroads and the Confederate supply depot at Lynchburg.

Alex had lost weight. Even his voice was hoarse with fatigue. "Our losses have been the worst of the war," he said.

He and Olivia were in their tent, shuttered away from the others. Exhausted by the heat, they lay on cots, hoping for a cool breeze. Restlessly Olivia sat up to listen to the cries of the wounded. "Alex, the men are dying, being wounded at a rate I didn't believe possible. This can't continue; General Grant won't have an army in another week."

Alex turned his head. "My dear, if you think Grant will be without an army, don't worry. More men are being brought in. Artillery is coming in from Washington."

"This seems desperate."

"Not so," he insisted. "For the first time, I'm seeing these men fight as if there's no back door. They are exhausted, but strangely committed. It's more spiritual than physical. I think we've all accepted an unstated fact. It's now or never. We are fighting for our collective life." He reached out to touch her shoulder. "And Olivia, I think if you were out there, you wouldn't be this discouraged. We're close to Richmond; when all is quiet, we can hear the church bells."

She began to smile and he came to kiss her, whispering, "Don't give up now. Your attitude will affect the wounded. Livie, it's going to be over soon, and we'll go home, back to Pennsylvania."

"But the country will be—"

"No, not destroyed. It will recover, and we'll be around to help." He touched the brooch she wore and kissed her again.

During the following days, General Lee entrenched at Petersburg and General Grant followed, moving his men in to face the Confederates as they dug their own trenches. Siege was inevitable.

"Just like Vicksburg," Crystal murmured. Her eyes were dark and troubled as she turned away.

As September waned, the intense heat lessened. The medical personnel as well as the soldiers began to recover their strength and spirit.

General Grant sent General Sheridan up the Shenandoah Valley to rout General Early. When they heard the news, Olivia said, "Dare we say we're on the winning side?"

"At least we're on the side doing the most damage right now," Crystal commented wryly. "Sheridan's goal is to sweep the Shenandoah Valley bare of all the produce, grain, and cattle, since it supplies the Confederate Army and all the guerrillas in the area. He's ruined everything."

"Oh!" Olivia looked up. "Finally, the Republican Party is getting their act together. They are no longer talking about replacing Lincoln. General Fremont has dropped his bid for the presidency, and some of the other radicals are declaring their intentions to support the President."

Again the hospital tents were moved nearer the Richmond-Petersburg area.

October passed, then came Election Day. As Olivia adjusted a bandage and reached for the mug of water, her patient drank gratefully and said, "I'll be glad when I can use my hand again. Be glad, too, when we hear President Lincoln has won. Sure would be a shame to change horses in midstream."

"I don't expect that to happen, do you?" She moved on.

The following morning General Grant was advised by telegraph of Lincoln's victory. News quickly spread through the entrenchments and the hospital tents. Olivia watched the excited men discussing the election. "Too bad we can't have election every day," she declared. "Not a one of you has complained about his wounds."

A curly-haired youth with mischievous eyes said, "They're still there." She tousled his hair.

When the next supply train arrived, the newspapers stated that General Sherman had left Atlanta and was sweeping toward Savannah. "He's spreading a broad path of destruction as he goes," Crystal commented. "Everything is being destroyed—homes, railroads, food supplies."

Alex came into camp the following day. Olivia handed him the newspapers she had saved.

After the men were fed and settled for the evening, Alex followed Olivia to their tent. She looked at him and said, "My tired, dirty husband. I'm going to beg the cook for some hot water, and then you can scrub."

When she returned, Alex was asleep. By the light of the lantern, she studied his thin, care-worn face and sighed. He sat up. "That sigh was like a rifle shot."

"Sorry. I was looking at your face."

"Is it that bad?"

"You need to rest away from battle." She found a towel for him. "Alex, is Grant going to stay holed up all winter?"

"I wouldn't be surprised. Certainly we can't breach the fortifications Lee's thrown up. We're not too uncomfortable. Considering the circumstances, it beats running all over the country. I wish you could see the trenches. We learned much from observing Lee."

"Isn't a trench just a groove cut in the ground?"

"No. We tunnel around like moles, only our burrow doesn't have a top on it. It makes a nice way to get around the territory without having your head shot off."

"Is Petersburg important to the Confederates?"

"Very. Fortunately for us, Richmond doesn't have food to feed their soldiers during a siege; their stores are at Petersburg. But they only have enough for about thirteen days; they need access to the trains. Unfortunately for us Yankee newcomers, Richmond has had two years to build works around the city, and they are deeply dug in.

"Richmond is the hub of the railway coming in from the agricultural areas in the other states. Since Virginia doesn't produce much food, that's very important. If—*when* we cut the three rail lines, they'll have to surrender."

"Destroying railroads doesn't sound too difficult. You've destroyed train track in the past."

"Not like this. Richmond and Petersburg are surrounded with the same dense forest they have in the wilderness. We can't get close to Richmond, so we'll concentrate on the lines south. The Confederates have the easy job. It's easier to guard the rails than to tear them up."

He nuzzled her neck and murmured, "But I think we're about to call it quits for the winter. That means we'll be free to come behind lines more often. It'd be nice if we could close up shop, just lock the door on the whole business for the winter." Alex reached for her. "Now, no more war talk. Do you have the Bible here? Will you read to me?"

"Only if you promise to stay awake." She sat beside him and opened the Bible. " 'He that dwelleth in the secret place of the most High shall abide under the shadow of the Almighty. I will say of the Lord, *He is* my refuge . . .' " She saw he was asleep.

"Duncan, Warren is taking his men out to tear up some track. They can use a few extra men. Round up a detachment from your regiment, draw your rations, and report to Warren."

When Alex and his men reached the road, Warren was briefing his men. "The Weldon Railroad has been destroyed only for a short way. The Confederates are still making use of it. They obtain supplies from the blockade runners at Wilmington, and carry them by train to within a few miles of Richmond. From there freight wagons pack the goods on in. We'll line the track in battle formation. Each man will be responsible for tearing up the track in front of him. When that section is destroyed, the division will move to the left and continue. Let's go."

After arriving at the tracks, Warren walked the line, watching the men rip up the rails, heat them in bonfires, and twist them around tree trunks. "Fellas, you're doing fine. We'll have destroyed twenty miles of track by day's end. I—" The general wheeled around as he heard a rifle.

"Men, give it to them!"

Around the curve of tracks Alex saw the Confederate battle flag, the gray uniforms. He lifted his musket and charged. Within minutes they were into the trees, and both armies became obscure shadows in the darkness. Alex faltered, fearful of hitting his own men.

A shot seemed to explode in his ear. Tree branches lashed his face. When he moved and opened his eyes only the quietness of the forest surrounded him. His leg was beginning to throb. Slowly he sat up. From the thigh down, his uniform was soaked with blood. A dark pool of it spread in the spongy soil.

Fighting the blackness that seemed to be moving across his vision, he began shredding his coat into strips. *Father, help me! I can't manage.* With shaking hands he tied the strips around his leg above the gushing red. He hesitated, pulled the fragments of his trousers over the wound and tied the final piece over it all. Slowly he moved backward to a level spot and lay flat on the mossy ground. Above him the trees moved and dipped. He closed his eyes.

"Help, somebody, help me!" Alex turned his head and listened. The cry came again, faint now. He sat up and looked at his leg. The bleeding was a slow seepage. "Help!"

Taking a deep breath, Alex began to ease himself over the ground toward the voice still calling feebly. At last he saw a figure on the ground. Perspiring and trembling, he stopped. The man's torso was covered with blood; his shoulder, encased in shredded gray, seemed shattered. "Hey, buddy, I'm here. Guess we're both in about the same condition."

"Water?"

"I don't know of any around here. I could use some, too. Maybe I can look around."

"Don't leave me. I—I'm dying. Please Yank, don't leave me here by myself. It's too late for help. Seems dark, but don't leave me to die by myself."

Cautiously Alex stretched out beside the man. The ground began to seem warm and comforting, and he wondered if he were dying, too.

The man spoke. Alex turned his head; he could see the man's eyes were wide and dark. "Charles Temps, from Macon." He licked his lips. "Could be we die before we learn to live, huh?"

"Seems that way. I'm Alex Duncan."

"Do you mind dying now?"

"I don't think I'm that badly hurt. I tied part of my coat around the wound." He sat up and loosened the rags. The bleeding increased, and he replaced the primitive tourniquet.

Alex glanced at his companion, silent now, pale. The lad swallowed, licked his lips. "Took a shot right through the middle. Makes you wonder if war's worth dying for. Ever hear that song about the Bonnie Blue Flag? It's funny, they come around singing, and it makes fighting sound like the thing to do."

The lad's eyes closed. Suddenly he looked around. "Are you here?"

"I'm here."

"Back then I didn't think about dying. Did I die for the right cause?"

"Seems now's not the time to ask. Back then what did you think?"

"It's easy to enlist, then we're caught. Now that I must die for the cause, it's too late to back out. If I had it to do over again, I'd—"

"Boy, we all make mistakes. Do you hear?" The lad closed his eyes and then opened them. Alex said, "Now's not the time to chew them over. But dying isn't the end of it all."

"How d'you know?"

"God's Word, the Bible. His Son, Jesus Christ, died for your sins because He loved you."

"I know. I heard General Lee saying all that to us soldiers. About how knowing God was most important, even more than loyalty to country. But that comes second."

"Do you believe Jesus died for your sins?"

"Yes. Sometimes I don't spend much time thinking about it, but now I guess it's the time to think. Soldier, do you think I'm going to heaven?"

"If you've asked Jesus to forgive your sins, and you believe He has, well then you're part of the kingdom of God." The lad's face relaxed.

In a few minutes his breathing stopped. For a time Alex watched, aware of the quietness around him, the creeping dampness of the forest chilling him.

When the evening mists moved through the trees, Alex sat up. He measured the strength of his good leg and saw the dry branch just beyond his hand. "Better get at it, man."

Using the stick as a crutch, he moved slowly through the forest toward the spot of light. Occasionally he stopped to check the bleeding, to ease the tightness of the crude bandage. The moon was rising like a milky splash of light behind the fog. He followed the road, wondering how long he could walk without breaking the wound open, and how long he could lie on the ground without freezing. He was still pondering when he heard the jingle of harness, the creak of wheels. Looking up, he was relieved to see an ambulance.

"Well, soldier, come along. Are there others in there?"

"I don't know. I heard only one, and he died while I was there." There was a firm hand under his arm, hay in the bottom of the ambulance, and a warm blanket to cover him.

CHAPTER 50

Olivia was in front of the hospital tent when the ambulance arrived. "A battle? I didn't know anything was happening."

"Naw. A detachment out doing damage to the Rebels' railroad. We need a stretcher for this one; he's lost a lot of blood, leg injury."

As they lifted the soldier out, she gasped and threw herself at the stretcher. "Alex!" He opened his eyes. "Oh, thank God, he's alive. Please hurry. What is it?"

"My leg. Olivia, my dear—" he murmured. She took the hand he tried to lift. Running to keep up with the stretcher, she helped lift him onto the surgery table and hung over Dr. Jason. As he cut away the cloth, he said, "Looks to be just a flesh wound. Ugly, but the bleeding has stopped. We'll get him into bed and keep him flat."

"Are you certain there isn't shattered bone?"

He smiled. "I'm certain. My dear Mrs. Duncan, I do believe you'll be more trouble than your husband."

Alex turned his head, smiled weakly and asked, "What, dear Olivia, have you done?"

"I'm pregnant." He struggled to sit up. "Lie down," she murmured. "I can handle this, and I do believe it will be nice to have you where I can keep my eyes on you."

The male nurses lifted Alex to a cot on the sunny side of the tent. They removed the tatters of his uniform and Olivia came with a basin of hot water. "I'll bathe him; he's my husband."

Crooning over the abrasion on his face, she pressed her cheek against his. One of the nurses returned with a hospital gown. With a wry smile he said, "Better watch it, or we'll have to import all these fellows' wives."

Olivia looked up. "Oh, I had forgotten; were there more patients?"

"Yes, but they've been taken in to Dr. Jason and he said we shouldn't bother you. I think he's spoiling you. Call us if he needs to be lifted."

Alex appeared to be asleep. Working quickly, she finished bathing him and covered him. He opened his eyes and grinned. "I'll expect this treatment all the time."

"Want some soup?" He nodded. When she sat down with the bowl and picked up the spoon, she saw his puzzled frown. "What is it?"

"Things are pretty fuzzy. Did I hear you say something special?"

"You did. Alex, I'm certain we're going to have a baby. But don't worry," she whispered. "Even Dr. Jason thinks that we'll do just fine." When she brought the spoon to his mouth, he swallowed the soup, took her hand, and kissed it.

"Want to hear something else? Crystal is also going to have a baby. When I told her about ours, she confessed being fearful of telling her good news because of how I would feel."

"So now I'll be a father *and* an uncle." He chuckled weakly while his eyes warmed her. "Wish I could congratulate Matthew; I haven't seen him for over a month."

"He was in camp just a week ago. He was concerned about you, because it had been so long since he'd seen you. I'd think since you're neighbors in those trenches, you'd be waving to each other occasionally," she said. "He told us they are continuing to hold the Confederates in Petersburg and Richmond with artillery fire, but material and supplies are still coming in to them."

"I know; we were out tearing up railroad line when skirmishers got us." He rubbed her hand gently. "Nearly as rough as it was from washing dishes on the *Golden Awl*."

"Oh, Alex," she whispered, "I'm so sorry you were hurt, but it's such a relief to have you here."

Crystal came rushing through the tent, "Olivia—Alex! They told me you were here. What happened? You look a little pale."

He grinned. "Is this the way mommies always act?"

She glanced at Olivia. "I think he'll recover."

———

Later that week, Olivia began to see the symptoms she had dreaded.

The jagged furrow cutting into the muscles on Alex's leg had begun festering and his temperature climbed.

Dr. Jason looked grave. "There's not much to be done, except to encourage the drainage and keep him resting."

"And pray," she added soberly. With a nod, he moved on to the next bed.

By the end of the week, when Matthew came, Olivia was beginning to see improvement. Matthew frowned as he looked toward the cot. "Infection?" She nodded, watching Alex's face brighten as Matthew stepped up to the bed. "Am I going to have to rescue you from this place?"

"Matt, am I glad to see you!" Alex clasped his hand, adding, "It won't be necessary; I'm better, and I expect to be back in the trenches in a couple of weeks."

"Better hurry, or you'll miss the war." Matthew settled back and crossed his legs. "Things are starting to look good. Sherman took Savannah in December. The nervy guy broke all lines of communication and cut himself off from both supply and help. I hear General Grant's been pretty concerned about him."

"How did he feed his army?"

"Lived off the land. There's no doubt about it—people are scattering like leaves in the wind. They said the mayor of Atlanta protested when Sherman shooed all the residents out of the city before he leveled it. Sherman told the mayor war was hell and there wasn't any way to refine it. And the sooner the people accepted it, the better it would be for them."

"I'm sorry for the people," Alex muttered, "but I admire the general's grit. The Army of the Potomac would probably have done much better if we hadn't let the South intimidate us. From the way we've reacted most of the time, you'd think we were the ones in the wrong."

Matthew nodded. "Is it lack of confidence or lack of conviction? There's been enough opposition in the North to sway us either direction."

In a moment Alex asked, "You in just for the day?"

"No. The commanders have been good about letting us break out of the trenches on a regular basis. I guess it's about the only way we'll hold up under this." He paused. "Those poor fellows in Petersburg and Richmond. I heard a report that Richmond's been out of meat for some time. The last of it was issued to Lee's army. The Southern economy is ruined. Most of their rail lines have been destroyed. Some supplies are coming through the blockade. I suppose that'll be Grant's next target."

"I've been reading all the old newspapers," Alex said, rubbing his forehead wearily. He looked at Matthew. "At least I believe I've learned why the South's been so doggedly determined to win the war. In an address just before the '64 campaign began, General Lee stated that if the South was victorious in this war, they would have everything to hope for in the future, but if they were defeated, there would be nothing left to live for."

Matthew shook his head sadly. "I've heard they fight like madmen. Maybe that's the reason."

"I wish they'd quit stalling and get this over," Matthew added. "I'd like to get home before this baby comes."

"Olivia told me," Alex said. "We're happy for you. By home, do you mean Pennsylvania?"

Matthew nodded. "Where else? I don't expect to be welcome in the South. This war has changed us all forever. I'm concerned for our parents, but—" Alex was asleep, so Matthew left.

Olivia and Crystal were working together in the next tent. Matthew approached them. "I have a gift for each of you ladies. Hold out your hands." He dropped a coin in each hand.

Olivia turned the bronze coin. "A bright, shiny two-cent piece!"

"Read the inscription," he urged. "It's the first coin to bear it."

Crystal read, "United States of America, In God We Trust."

Olivia clenched her coin. "In God We Trust," she repeated slowly. "This is just what I need. Thank you, Matt."

It was dark when she started back to the tent where Alex lay. Shivering in the January wind, she hurried inside. He was awake, and his forehead seemed cool. "Are you hungry?"

"Starving. Had a good chat with Matt."

"He gave me a gift; I'll share it with you." She dropped the coin in his hand and went to the kitchen. After she distributed the meals to the other patients, she carried Alex's food to him.

He still held the coin and was smiling. "Olivia, I'm going to save this coin for our grandchildren. I'll tell them how it became a bright promise in the final days of the Civil War, just before the Union victory."

She brushed the tears from her eyes and bent over to kiss him. "Alex, I love you. May you have many children and grandchildren to share the story of the coin with."

Within a few days Alex was out of bed, testing his wounded leg gingerly as he hobbled around the tent on crutches.

Matthew came in, dropped several newspapers on Alex's bed and said, "I'm returning to the trenches, but I thought you'd like these papers. The December one has lines from Lincoln's address to Congress. Read it all;

he says the resolve of the people to maintain the integrity of the Union has never been more firm. He goes on to talk about how we're doing. He says production is up in every area, and that we're better off financially than before the war. Encouraging, isn't it?"

"What else do you have?"

"The story of Fort Fisher being taken. Butler tried to bomb the place with a boat loaded with explosives. Quite a fiasco."

"I think you should volunteer your services as a bomb expert," laughed Alex.

"Sorry, I haven't seen a peach can since," Matthew murmured.

Alex shook the paper. "This is encouraging, Matt. There's only one more port which the blockade runners can enter. After that—"

"Lee'll have to surrender."

"Here's the proposed Thirteenth Amendment to the Constitution!" Alex exclaimed. "Short and to the point: 'Neither slavery nor involuntary servitude, except as punishment for crime whereof the party shall have been duly convicted, shall exist within the United States, or any place subject to their jurisdiction.' Man, am I glad to see this."

Matthew got to his feet. "See you in a couple of weeks, unless you decide you want to join us before."

"I'll wait until I have two good legs. Right now, I know just how Mike Clancy felt."

———

Spring came in late February. Grass began to show green, and the dogwoods began to bloom. Union casualties had decreased markedly, and Alex was starting to use his leg. He had been discharged from the hospital, and had moved into the tent with Olivia.

One day Crystal came to visit while he was admiring Olivia's thickening waistline. He eyed Crystal's expanding figure and said, "Crystal, I think you'd better retire from nursing. I'll find a rocking chair for you." She protested, and he teased, "You'll have to give up feeding soldiers unless you grow longer arms."

"A rocking chair sounds wonderful," she admitted. "I may even learn to knit."

Before long Alex took Crystal's place at the hospital. When Olivia protested, he said, "I can't outrun the Confederates, but I can push a washcloth and change bandages just as well as you."

When Matthew returned, he chuckled and said, "Alex, I'm going to find one of those head dresses for you. And I think you ought to borrow Crystal's apron."

Matthew managed to fit a rocking chair into their tent. "It's a good thing this baby will come in the summer," he said. "Otherwise I'd be shipping you home."

He turned to look at Alex. "The Confederate soldiers are deserting," Matthew continued, "and coming into our camp. I hear they're leaving North Carolina at the rate of around a hundred a night. We've been getting a large number."

Olivia sat up. "Why would they come to you?"

"Mostly for food. They know we'll feed them. I think one of the main reasons they're heading home is to plant crops for their families. They certainly can't be blamed for that, but it's a big drain on Lee. I don't know where he's going to find food for his men. Wilmington has finally been closed; that's the last of the blockade runners' ports. Most of the North Carolina coast is in Federal hands." He paced restlessly around the tent. "It's exciting, but frustrating. The end is right here, but Lee doesn't see it that way."

"I have a newspaper you haven't read."

"What makes you think so?"

"Because you'd be talking about it. Since General Sherman left Atlanta, he's had thousands of Negroes following him. Naturally he's not doing anything for them—he can't fight a war at the same time.

"News of the situation hit Washington and Secretary of War Stanton went to Savannah to talk to him and to contact the black leaders. He wanted to see what could be done to help them.

"The slaves asked to be given land, so Sherman took military action under war powers, designating the sea islands and the rich plantation land along rivers in South Carolina for settlement by former slaves. Each family will receive forty acres."

"That's wonderful news!" Matthew reached for the paper.

"Yes," Olivia said, "they certainly deserve the help. Many of the freed slaves are fighting in the army. I read that Southerners put strong pressure on the Confederate government to use the slaves as soldiers."

"My guess is," Matthew said slowly, "Lincoln's refusal to talk peace with the South apart from unconditional surrender will produce a move toward enlisting Negroes as soldiers."

———

By the middle of March, the spring rains appeared to be over. Puddles disappeared, and the fresh scent of spring nearly made it possible to forget the horror lying just beyond their camp. The sound of artillery still came from the entrenchments, but except for small skirmishes, war no longer seemed a constant threat.

News drifted out of Richmond, giving them a picture of life there.

The first informant was a peddler. The old man seemed to relish having an audience. "Naw, nobody's worried about the war. President Davis seems as happy as the rest. Them people are celebrating the Confederate victory every Saturday night. Guess it's all right, since they're all in church come Sunday morning. But life goes on as usual. Sure, food's hard to come by. No different than other places.

"Without a doubt, them people have confidence that General Lee will win this war. Nearly every day the newspapers carry news that's encouraging them on."

Olivia watched the peddler walk out of camp and said, "Do you suppose he'll go back into Richmond and tell some outrageous tales about us?"

"Might be outrageous, but it might be the truth," Alex said thoughtfully. "But given the evidence, I wonder why Richmond is so happy?"

"What evidence?"

"All winter General Lee has advanced his troops only two miles. He is hurting for men to cover his lines. Perhaps this winter hasn't been a waste."

"The injuries and deaths indicate General Lee is still active."

"Proportionately, Lee has lost more. With spring upon us, we can expect action to increase."

She looked at his worried frown and said, "You're thinking about Crystal?"

"And you. I wish you would both take the supply train back to Washington."

"Since spring is upon us," she said lightly, "I think we might be safer right here." He kissed her cheek and headed for the surgeon's tent.

When Olivia went to the supply tent the next day, she looked around at the opened packets of bandages. "Dr. Jason cleaning house?" she asked Sergeant Howe.

"No. We're gearing up to meet any need."

"And that means I'd better be ready too," she said. "What shall I do here?"

"We need bandages separated by size. Supplies must be packed to go in the ambulances, and surgery needs help. Dr. Jason has a theory that if instruments are handled differently, there won't be as much infection among the men." He shrugged, grinned, and said, "I don't have any patience with the idea, seems a waste of time. However, if you're inclined to pamper him, go in there and see what you can do." He shook his head. "Never heard of boiling stuff like that."

CHAPTER 51

Matthew had picket duty at Camp Stedman the night the final offensive began. The little moth-eaten fortification was tucked down between Fort Haskell and Fort McGilvery. It blocked the way to General Grant's headquarters at City Point and shielded access to the heights guarding Grant's supply rail line. Because of its location, the fort had received countless shellings, which had nearly reduced its logs to kindling.

Just before dawn, shortly after the officer on duty checked the picket lines, Matthew heard the crunch of gravel. "Halt!" He ordered. He saw the man, another deserter. He sighed with relief. "Hands up and state your intentions."

"Going over the hill. Have a bite to spare? I've got my gun."

"We don't need any guns. Save it for squirrel hunting," Matthew lowered his musket. Suddenly the Rebel yell erupted from all points on the picket line. As Matthew whirled around, men in gray surged into Camp Stedman, surrounding the surprised Yanks before they could rush to arms.

"Gotcha!" The musket nudged Matthew; he hesitated, unable to believe the deception as he stared into the face of the ragged, gaunt Rebel. "Look behind ya!" chortled his captor. Matthew looked. The first light of dawn revealed the crowd in gray swarming into the Federal fortification.

"We've lost it if they've covered the other two forts," muttered the guard at Matthew's elbow.

The gray clad sergeant grinned at them. "It's been a long time since I've seen this many Yanks together. Pack in close, men; we don't want to waste ammunition." He nosed them toward the log shack.

The rest of the garrison was prodded in behind them. From the fort they watched the sun rise, spreading light across the field in front of their window.

The fellow beside Matthew tensed. "Maybe all's not lost; look out the window." Matthew looked one moment before the blue troops surged into the clearing with muskets blazing. In every direction the Confederates fled for cover.

Matthew reacted, yelling, "Down, or our men will get us!"

"What did they do with our muskets?"

"I'll look around." Before their scout returned, the prisoners saw the battle had reversed. Waiting for a break, they dashed out of the fort, nearly colliding with the Ninth Corps.

"Fall to it men; up to the batteries," snapped General Parke. They ran, but it seemed to Matthew that he had barely reloaded when the battle was over. Pale smoke drifted away, revealing the encircled gray army.

"We've taken two thousand prisoners," he heard Parke say. "Lee can't afford to lose that many men."

"Has the final bell rung?"

"No, but this is a good start."

———————

Olivia dressed quickly and went to Crystal's tent. "You've heard the gunfire?"

"Yes, I suppose this is what we've all been waiting for." Olivia saw the shadows in Crystal's eyes. She nodded as Crystal said, "I'll come help."

"I'm not certain it's necessary. I just came to check on you. Listen, all seems quiet now. Go back to bed; I'll call you if necessary."

Olivia hurried to her post at the hospital tents. Later in the day Alex joined her with news. "The first attack was a Confederate offensive, the second ours. We have losses, and the wounded are coming in now. The first indications are that Lee has lost heavily."

"Be prepared to receive a great many wounded," he added. "This was just the first show of force. General Grant is moving out now. It appears that Lee's days of staying entrenched have come to an end." He paused. "I'd say this is the turn of events we've been hoping for."

Crystal added in a low voice, "And dreading." Olivia hugged her.

The following day they walked out of their tents into heavy rain. "What dismal weather!" Crystal shivered and rubbed her arms. "All I can do is wonder about Matthew. Occasionally I've heard a gunshot this morning, but it's nearly too quiet."

Silently they walked to the hospital tents. As Olivia began to distribute the breakfast bowls, she said, "The rain is a blessing; it keeps them from fighting."

One of the soldiers raised himself on his elbow. She said, "Sam, lie down. You're putting pressure on that wound."

"Ma'am, don't pray that we stop fighting. We gotta hang in there— get it finished up once for all; otherwise the problems will never be settled."

She nodded her head slowly. "I know, but all the bleeding and dying is gnawing at me until I can scarcely stand it."

"Jest your condition. Now you go sit down and drink some tea. My wife was the same."

Olivia turned away. Blinking tears from her eyes, she said, "You are sweet, Sam; now lie down."

"They're pushing for Five Forks," the orderly reported. "Know what that means?"

The answer came from one of the beds. "Victory at last." Olivia looked at the grinning man. "They'll cut Lee's supply route. Can't fight without food."

"Those poor, poor men," Olivia murmured as she carried the dishes back to the kitchen.

The cook was a Negro who had freed himself by walking into camp. "Ma'am," he said respectfully, "de rebels started dis. For us dis fightin' is like takin' a slivah outta a young'un's fingah. Hurts, but it gotta be done."

Soon the rain stopped and cautious gunfire was heard. Rumors floated about the hospital compound. They heard that supply wagons and cavalry alike had been bogged motionless in the mud.

On the next day, shortly after noon on April 1st, the campaign was resumed. "Five Forks," Olivia stated. "That soldier said if the Confederates lose it, they'll surrender. Dear Father, please."

When the first ambulance pulled into the field in front of the hospital, a wounded soldier sat up. His head was swathed in bandage. "Ma'am, nurse," he demanded, "wrap this head up so's the blood doesn't get in my eyes. I want to get back in there. Grant's got them. He's capturing men right and left."

Olivia smiled as a motherly gray-haired nurse shook her finger at him. "You just lie there until the doctor has time. You have to take your turn. I've got a feeling this war's going to get won without any more outta you. Now, do you want a drink of water?"

On April second, with dawn lighting the sky in a glorious display of color, Olivia followed Alex to the hospital tents. He stopped outside a tent and turned to look toward Petersburg. "I hear gunfire. Guess we'd better get ready for them." He glanced down at Olivia, "Do you know what day this is?"

"Palm Sunday, the day we commemorate our Lord Jesus entering Jerusalem," she mused thoughtfully. "This morning I recalled His words as He wept over the city. 'O Jerusalem, Jerusalem . . . how often would I have gathered thy children together, even as a hen gathereth her chickens under her wings, and ye would not! Behold your house is left unto you desolate.'

"Alex, how frightening those words are! Desolate! It's a picture of cold wind sweeping through barren rooms, banging shutters." She shivered, and whispered, "Is that a picture of America? Have we so displeased the Lord?"

"I don't know how this war could be pleasing to Him, but Olivia, we still have His promise. If we return to Him with our whole heart, He will hear and forgive."

"We can only try to right the wrongs which have been done," she agreed. "Alex, I have a feeling that all will suffer, the innocent as well as the guilty."

That day, when the first of the injured came in, they were grinning despite their pain. "We did it! Broke through Lee's lines. It's an open door to Petersburg. His railway lines are not worth patching up."

As darkness fell, information coming into the hospital compound indicated that Lee was at Petersburg, with pickets posted. "That means he hasn't surrendered," Sam said. "I can't believe he's holding out so long."

––––––––––

During the night, Olivia and Alex were awakened by excited voices. The two dressed hastily and joined the group outside. Crystal appeared just as the explosions began. "It's Petersburg; the Rebels are destroying their stores!" One after another the blasts came, diminishing in ear-shattering sound as they moved north toward Richmond. Alex said, "It's the batteries along the river."

"Look!" The group turned to the north. Flames were rising above the trees.

"I've an idea that's the bridge."

"Look at Petersburg. They must have burned all the warehouses. What flames! Are the townspeople in danger?"

"I don't know about Petersburg, but I heard Richmond's grand folk left yesterday afternoon."

"Seems to me those flames are over Richmond way," came a careful voice.

Olivia and Crystal turned away, while Crystal murmured, "Those poor people. All the fighting, with loved ones lost forever, and now they are beaten down to nothing. How will they live?"

"I don't know," Olivia whispered. "Crystal, we both have loved ones in the South. I wonder how they've fared."

Crystal shivered. "We have a responsibility to help them, but right now I want only Matthew. I can live with poverty, but I want Matthew."

He returned two days later. Crystal clung to him, whispering, "I can't believe that after these terrible days you manage to smile as well as look healthy and happy."

He hugged her and then held her away to look into her eyes. "My precious Crystal. It's over; it's time to rejoice. It's also time to go home and settle into being a family."

As Alex and Olivia crossed the hospital compound, Matthew saw the relief on Alex's face. He slipped his arm across Alex's shoulders. "Tell me, brother, do you think we can get permission to pack up our wives and head for Pennsylvania? Crystal's showing every symptom of needing her own little nest."

Olivia smiled. "I've a feeling Dr. Jason will gladly recommend that. I don't think he's very comfortable with females in this condition."

She went to kiss Matthew. For a moment her eyes darkened. "We've come a long way, haven't we, Matthew—all of us."

"A very long way, dear sister," he said gently.

Olivia blinked at the tears in her eyes as she watched Matthew and Crystal walk toward their tent. "Alex, I want to go home, too. Is it possible?"

He nodded. "As soon as we can pack and get to the train."

"You won't feel badly about leaving now?"

"No. Olivia, it's over; the fighting is finished. Would you believe it, my conscience is at rest?" An expression of pain crossed his face, and she pressed her head against his arm.

"Alex, you needn't pretend with me. I know—possibly more than we'll ever be able to put into words—I know. But even scars heal."

"And lives?" he asked. She nodded, and he put his arm around her shoulders. "Olivia, who would have dreamed all this would happen to us."

"God knew." She touched the brooch and saw the flash of recognition in his eyes. "Perhaps we knew; inside, we knew something would be demanded of us—"

"Something that would call for the deep resources of God. Life has demanded a sureness, a trust in God much deeper than I would have thought possible. It's been a necessity for facing all of this."

"His Holy Spirit. I tremble to think of running into this blindly. But even now, Alex, I doubt you'll assure me that life from this point on will be just golden roses without a touch of darkness."

"Is that what you want me to say?"

"No. I stand by the commitment I made then. Alex, back then, before I dreamed life would treat us in such a manner, I struggled with the big step of trust. If I had it to do over again, I'd still tremble and wonder, but I wouldn't hesitate. Alex, my lover, my friend, I—" She gasped and reached for his hand. "Quick! Feel there. That is your child, feel how strong he kicks!"

She saw the tears on his face as he held her and quoted softly, " 'Be glad then, ye children of Zion, and rejoice in the Lord your God: for he hath given you the former rain. . . . And I will restore to you the years that the locust hath eaten. . . . And ye shall know that I am in the midst of Israel.' "

She looked at him. "And God blesses and blesses again."

Tenderly he tucked her arm through his. "Let's go home, my dear, and get ready for that little one."